continued . . .

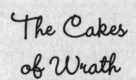

The Cakes of Wrath

Jacklyn Brady

BERKLEY PRIME CRIME, NEW YORK

THE BERKLEY PUBLISHING GROUP
Published by the Penguin Group
Penguin Group (USA)
375 Hudson Street, New York, New York 10014, USA

USA I Canada I UK I Ireland I Australia I New Zealand I India I South Africa I China

Penguin Books Ltd., Registered Offices: 80 Strand, London WC2R 0RL, England
For more information about the Penguin Group, visit penguin.com.

THE CAKES OF WRATH

A Berkley Prime Crime Book / published by arrangement with the author

For information, address: The Berkley Publishing Group,
a division of Penguin Group (USA).
375 Hudson Street, New York, New York 10014.

ISBN: 978-0-425-25826-2

PUBLISHING HISTORY
Berkley Prime Crime mass-market edition / September 2013

PRINTED IN THE UNITED STATES OF AMERICA

10 9 8 7 6 5 4 3 2 1

Cover illustration by Chris Lyons.
Cover design by Diana Kolsky.
Interior text design by Laura K. Corless.

ALWAYS LEARNING   **PEARSON**

To the women of Navarre First Assembly of God.
Y'all have prayed me through some mighty tough stuff.
I am constantly blessed by your friendships.
Love you all!

One

One of these days I am going to learn how to say no. And
mean it. And stick to my guns once I've said it. Especially
when it comes to my former mother-in-law and current
business partner, Miss Frankie Renier. I made a solemn
vow to myself, right then and there, in the middle of a
stuffy upstairs room in a renovated house on the edge of
New Orleans's Garden District. One of these days.

My name is Rita Lucero. I'm a trained pastry chef, and
for the past year, I've handled the daily operations at
Zydeco Cakes, a high-end bakery known for its
one-of-a-kind cake creations. I took over at the shop after
Philippe Renier, my almost-ex-husband, died and his
mother inherited the business. She had offered me a part-
nership, and since being my own boss (almost) was a dream
come true for me, I'd jumped at the chance.

Miss Frankie is not a trained chef, but she is determined
to carry on her only son's legacy. She's a mostly silent
partner. . . except when she's not. Like when she decides
to volunteer my services without asking me.

Which was how I ended up sitting in that overcrowded
room on a hot August evening, listening to a bunch of

people shouting at each other when I would much rather have been at home watching the latest episode of *Castle* and spending quality time with Ben & Jerry.

The circus going on in front of me was actually a meeting of the Magnolia Square Business Alliance, a fancy name for a collection of small business owners who had decided it was time to improve the neighborhood. The square, which covers eight square blocks and borders the Garden District, is made up of an eclectic mix of shops, restaurants and other businesses. I was here because while Miss Frankie felt strongly that Zydeco should have a seat at the table, she had no interest in occupying that seat herself. She thought getting involved would help me connect with the neighboring business owners and help me become part of the community. As she so often did, she'd committed me to the venture without bothering to discuss it with me.

The venue for tonight's meeting was Second Chances, a thrift store two blocks north of Zydeco. Aquanettia Fisher, owner of Second Chances, was also the acting chair of our group—a position that would likely become official if the elections scheduled for next month went as anticipated.

Aquanettia, a fifty-something black woman with short hair, a sturdy frame, and a no-nonsense face, banged her gavel on the table. "People! People!" she shouted, and glared around the room. Not that it did any good. Only a handful of us had stayed out of the argument. The others weren't paying attention to anything except what they wanted to say next.

I drained the last drop from the water bottle in front of me and wondered if anyone would notice if I slipped out. Earlier, a wave of hot moist air had moved in from the Gulf of Mexico, leaving everyone in its path cranky. I was no exception. Even though the sun had slipped low on the western horizon, there was no relief from the heat and humidity, and that gleaming ball of brilliant orange turned everything it touched the color of rust. Two small fans at one end of the room whirred softly in an effort to stir the heavy air. I couldn't tell if they succeeded. I was too far away to reap the benefit.

Aquanettia had passed out a two-page agenda full of important issues to discuss, such as whether to require all member businesses to install identical Dumpster-disguising fencing and whether to start a neighborhood watch program. I was still on the fence (no pun intended) on both votes. While she tried to regain control of the meeting, I folded my agenda in half and waved it back and forth in front of my face. It didn't do much to lower the temperature, but at least the air in my personal space was moving.

In the seat beside mine, Edie Bryce, Zydeco's office manager and second alliance member, watched the fracas with a mixture of irritation and concern. Edie is mid-thirties, around five-four, and a definite force to be reckoned with. She sat with one hand resting on the baby bump that had only recently become noticeable. Her dark chin-length hair seemed shinier since she'd become pregnant, and despite her unsettled expression, her almond-shaped eyes and her porcelain complexion were luminous. I don't think her Chinese-American heritage had ever been more evident in the years I'd known her.

"Do something," she said, leaning over to me. At least that's what I think she said. I couldn't actually hear her over Felix Blackwater's bellowing.

Felix owns the neighborhood market down the block from Zydeco. They advertise the best muffaletta sandwiches in town, and I'm inclined to agree. Normally, Felix is an easygoing guy. Mind-mannered and almost shy. In his mid-fifties and paunchy, he has a ring of graying hair circling his freckled head, a bulbous nose, and small nubby teeth that were currently bared in an uncharacteristic snarl.

I knew what Edie wanted me to do. She wanted me to speak up and side with Felix on the question at hand, but I was still undecided. Under the circumstances, I figured there was no time like the present to begin my "Just Say No" campaign.

I shook my head firmly and mouthed back, "I'm not getting involved."

"But you *have* to," Edie insisted. "Aquanettia is clearly in over her head."

Luckily, Aquanettia chose that moment to assert her authority again. *Bang! Bang! Bang!* "If you can't settle down and be quiet right now, I'll have every last one of you removed from this meeting."

I wondered how she planned to manage that, but decided she'd probably call on her two sons to carry out the protesters. Both Isaiah and Keon were in their early twenties and strong enough to manage most of us if it became necessary.

On my left, Gabriel Broussard, six feet of Cajun sexy, watched the ruckus with a secretive smile. I couldn't tell if he was annoyed or amused, but knowing Gabriel and his appreciation of the absurd, I'd put my money on the latter. That meant he would probably vote against Felix, and knowing that put me in an uncomfortable position.

Gabriel and I have gone on a few dates since I moved to New Orleans last year, but we're nowhere near an item. That's exactly how I want it, for several reasons. None of which had any bearing on this disastrous meeting.

Gabriel was here because he tends bar at a local watering hole known as the Dizzy Duke. In the "That's News to Me" department, I'd recently learned that he was also one of the bar's owners. Which probably shouldn't have surprised me, but it did. Finding out he was more than just a bartender had changed something between us, and I was still trying to sort out how I felt. I liked knowing he was more ambitious—and more stable—than I'd first thought, but I was still a little miffed at him for withholding what I considered vital information.

Gabriel caught the exchange between Edie and me, and his smile grew a little wider. "Edie's right. It looks like Aquanettia could use some backup."

They were ganging up on me? That was *so* not fair. But two could play that game. I grinned at him and shrugged casually. "In that case, maybe *you* should do something."

He gave me a heavy-lidded look. "I would, *chérie*, but I'm not a board member."

"Technically, I'm not one either," I reminded him. "My position is only temporary."

"But you're going to be elected," Edie predicted.

That was no doubt true, since nobody was running against me. The entire slate of candidates was running unopposed, mostly on a candidate-by-default basis. If Edie hadn't been due to give birth in another three months, I would have nominated her for the board seat. Policy, procedure, and rules were the kinds of things she loved.

Clearly growing more aggravated by the moment, Aquanettia gave up on the gavel and began shouting along with the rest of the group. The more frustrated she became, the more I felt my resistance weakening. I held back for two reasons. One, I didn't want to be here in the first place; and two, if I stepped in without an invitation, I risked either alienating Aquanettia or (infinitely worse, in my opinion) giving the others the idea that I was leadership material. I wanted to avoid that at any cost.

I waved my makeshift fan a little faster and did my best not to make further eye contact with either Edie or Gabriel. After a moment, I realized that there was at least one person other than me in the room who wasn't trying to shout louder than the rest.

I didn't know Moose Hazen well, but I wasn't sure I wanted to. He was probably in his forties, a big man dressed in black biker leather, which by itself didn't intimidate me, but his shaved head and the tattoos covering almost every visible inch of skin gave him a menacing look. The deep scowl on his big square face didn't help either. I gave him points for maintaining his cool in the middle of the craziness, but the fact that this shouting match had all started because of his wife pretty much canceled them out.

I knew even less about Destiny Hazen than I did about her husband, which wasn't saying much. They own the Chopper Shop (quality motorcycle repairs and refurbishing), a three-person operation consisting of Moose, Destiny, and Destiny's father, Scotty Justus. To be honest, I wouldn't want to meet any one of them in a dark alley. Moose could snap me in half with his bare hands, Destiny would probably shank me before I could get a word out, and Scotty would hide my body.

This was the alliance's fourth monthly meeting, and the fourth meeting in a row that Destiny had missed. And that was why Felix had made a motion to remove her as one of the Chopper Shop's two allowed representatives under the alliance's temporary rules. The fact that Felix had made the motion at all had caused an uproar. That he'd made it without first being recognized by Aquanettia had only stirred up more emotion.

Edgar Zappa, owner of EZ Shipping, got right in Felix's face and shouted, "Why don't you sit down and shut up?" He's thirtyish, tallish, a Nordic blond with an "I pay a lot for this spray" tan.

"Why don't *you* back off?" Felix shouted back. "Destiny doesn't even care about this organization. It's hard enough to start a new group like this one. How are we supposed to accomplish anything if half the members don't care?"

Edgar rolled his pale blue eyes. "We're talking about one person, Felix. *One*. And it just so happens that the woman has been sick. Now you want to kick her out. What kind of way is that to repay her?"

Felix's mouth fell open in shock. "Repay her for *what*? She hasn't done a damn thing. She hasn't even been to a single meeting."

I wondered why Edgar was rallying to Destiny's defense while her husband looked on in silence, but I told myself that was none of my business. Both Edgar and Felix had valid points, assuming that Destiny really had been ill for the past three months. Which might have been true. Although she'd looked robustly healthy when I saw her last week.

I waffled, one minute thinking we should remove Destiny from her seat, and the next agreeing that we shouldn't be too hasty. The decision in front of me wasn't as easy as it might seem. If we voted Destiny out, Scotty would be the only possible replacement. Frankly, I wasn't sure he'd be much of an improvement. With his long salt-and-pepper hair tied back in a ponytail and his trademark Hawaiian shirts and khaki shorts, Scotty had a laid-back Caribbean island look going on that seemed to appeal to women his own age. But he was also a retired commercial shrimper who spent most of his time sitting outside in a lawn chair, nursing a beer, and collecting cans for the recycling bin.

One of those women who seemed to find Scotty charming was Zora Rappaport. She's sixty and plump with mousy brown hair cut chin-length, an unflattering look on a face so round. She owns the Feathered Peacock Yoga Salon, though she hasn't actually practiced yoga since injuring her neck in an accident several years ago.

She shook a finger in Edgar's face. "That's the trouble with your generation," she said in a voice surprisingly husky and deep. "You think that keeping a promise is optional. Destiny accepted the position in this group. She ought to be here." She tossed an apologetic smile at the big man in leather. "I'm sorry, Moose. You know I think the world of you, but everyone knows you let that wife of yours get away with murder."

Moose's lips twitched, but he didn't look amused. "With all due respect, Miss Zora, that's not something you need to worry about."

"It's not just you she takes advantage of," Zora said. "You know better than anyone how she treats poor Scotty. All he wants is to get to know her. Make up for lost time."

"Which is neither here nor there," Aquanettia interjected before Moose could speak. "We're not here to discuss anyone's family issues."

Moose leaned forward, resting his massive and colorful forearms on the table. "Destiny said she'd be here tonight. That's all I know. Can't we wait a few minutes? She probably got caught on the phone or something."

Felix snorted. He was at least ten years older than Moose and half Moose's size, which made him either remarkably brave or ridiculously foolish. "I know she's your wife," he said. "I know you feel like you have to stick up for her. But think about the rest of us, man. She's been wasting our time from the very beginning."

"She said she'd be here," Moose said again. He didn't speak loudly, but he didn't have to. His deep voice carried easily. "You've gotta understand my wife. She's—"

"A flake," said Lorena Babcock, a short, round woman with short blond hair who works at the market with Felix. "The rules say we can kick her out if she misses four meetings in a year. This is number four."

Sebastian Walker, the pharmacist at Magnolia Street Drug, jumped into the conversation. "I saw her outside right before the meeting," he said to Felix, "with that cop who was in the market the other day."

"Good Lord," Lorena moaned. "Was she being arrested again?"

Sebastian answered but I couldn't hear what he said over the new wave of shouting that erupted.

Felix slapped the table and shouted over the others. "She is not here. The reasons don't matter. I say let's vote. Right now."

Two dozen voices rose in response. I tried to measure the reaction, but as far as I could tell, the group was evenly split.

It looked like Ben & Jerry would have to wait for me awhile longer.

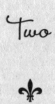

Chaos reigned for a few minutes, with people aligning on both sides of the argument and Aquanettia whacking the table repeatedly. "Quiet!" she shouted. "Quiet! You're all out of order, and you're going about this all wrong. We shouldn't be talking about one of our members by name unless we're in executive session. Stop now. I mean it!"

One by one, the others fell silent and most of them resumed their seats. Only Felix and Lorena remained standing. "Then put us in a whatchamacallit if that's what it takes," Felix demanded. "This alliance is only as strong as its weakest member, and I think we all know who that is."

"We'll move on with official business if and when you *sit down*," Aquanettia said sharply. She looked around the room, ready to kick some small business butt. "The first matter on the agenda is the election, followed by the neighborhood cleanup effort, and so on, as presented in the agenda. We'll stick to the order as presented. New business comes at the end, and that includes your motion, Felix."

Lorena snatched up a piece of paper from the table in front of her and cried, "Then I call the question. Is that the right term?" Her round cheeks were pink with excitement.

"Whatever I'm supposed to say to get this matter settled, I'm saying it. Let's vote right now."

Aquanettia wagged the gavel at her. "There's nothing to vote on, no question to call. And there won't be unless Felix makes his motion in the right way and at the right time. Now sit down." Lorena looked as if she might argue further, but Aquanettia kept right on talking. "We all agreed to follow the rules of order, and that's exactly what we're going to do. Is that clear?"

Obviously disappointed, Lorena looked around for backup, but when she saw Felix sitting in his seat, eyes straight ahead and a murderous look on his face, she dropped into her own chair with a grudging sigh. "Fine, but you all know what you need to do when the time comes. No offense, Moose."

He lifted one beefy hand and treated us all to a sad-looking smile. "None taken," he said in a tone that made me think he'd been down similar roads because of his wife before.

With a prim smile, Aquanettia sat and folded her hands on the table. "All right then. The matter up for discussion is the upcoming elections. As you know, we do not have a full slate for the executive committee—that's president, vice president, and secretary-treasurer. The deadline for declaring is midnight tonight. We need someone to step up for the secretary-treasurer spot."

She paused and glanced around, waiting for one of us to leap up and volunteer. I could feel Edie shifting in her seat next to me, itching to be that person. I shot her a warning look. We'd already discussed the idea of her becoming more involved and we'd agreed that she should wait until she'd had the baby and adjusted to life as a single mother.

I caught Gabriel's eye and nodded toward Aquanettia, silently urging him to step up. I knew he'd be horrified, and I was right. He shot me a look and mumbled, "Not on your life," under his breath.

After the silence dragged on for a while, Aquanettia cleared her throat and continued. "Of course, if you want any of the five general seats on the board, you need to put your name forward. We presently have candidates for all five seats, but it would make a better election if members had choices. And remember that only one person from each member business can be on the board at a time."

She looked around again, waited a breath or two, and then said, "The same holds true for anyone who wants to run for vice president against Felix or for president against me." By now, it seemed that even she was ready to admit that was unlikely. "Get your names on the ballot by midnight tonight, or you'll lose your chance."

To no one's surprise, nobody jumped at the chance. Silence reigned until, just as Aquanettia opened her mouth to go on, we all heard rapid footsteps climbing the stairs. Every head turned toward the door as Destiny Hazen blew into the room, wide-eyed and panting from exertion.

She's roughly my age, which puts her in her late thirties. She's roughly my height, which makes her around five-six. She's roughly my coloring, although my curly brown hair is all natural, and hers has chemical origins. That's where our similarities end.

I gravitate toward jeans and T-shirts; Destiny prefers lace, leather, and lots of skin. Tonight's selection was a pair of jeans so tight I wondered how she could breathe at all and a skimpy tank top cut so low that her ginormous silicone breasts threatened to spill out of it with every step she took.

She teetered into the room on a pair of four-inch patent-leather stilettos and treated us all to a broad, toothy smile and the overpowering punch of cheap perfume. I think only half of the room's occupants saw her smile. Every male eye in the room was glued to her breasts and their battle for freedom.

As she passed Edgar's chair, she ran a couple of glossy red and lethal-looking talons across his shoulders. She treated her husband to a sloppy wet kiss, and sat in the empty seat beside his with an R-rated jiggle. "Am I late?"

Aquanettia's mouth pursed so tightly it looked like she'd been sucking on a lemon. "Yes, you're late. The meeting started half an hour ago. Really, Destiny, if you can't get here on time—"

"I'm sorry," Destiny interrupted. "I got caught in a conversation I couldn't get away from." She gave another bounce and smiled. "It won't happen again, I promise. Tonight's the deadline, right? There's still time to get my name on the ballot?"

Felix catapulted out of his seat. "You? You want a seat on the board? You've never even been to a meeting."

Destiny waved her red talons at him. "So? I'm here now. And I don't just want a seat on the board. I'm running for president. Or whatever you call it. Against Aquanettia."

Aquanettia let out a strangled sound that might have been the lemon lodging in her throat.

"That's impossible," Felix said as a deep red stain crept up his face. "You have a criminal record."

My ears perked up at that. Not that I could see what difference it made for a figurehead position on a community alliance, but still, this was juicy stuff.

"Why am I not surprised?" Edie mumbled.

Destiny tossed a lock of overprocessed hair over her shoulder. "I do not have a record."

"She was only charged, not convicted," Moose put in. "We're still waiting for her court date. Isn't she supposed to be innocent until proven guilty?"

Well, sure. Technically. But I could see doubt on a few more faces around the table.

"And what about after court?" Felix demanded. "What are we supposed to do if the president of the alliance is sitting in a jail cell?"

"That won't happen," Destiny assured us all. "The charges are all bogus anyway."

"That's what they all say," Lorena argued. "You can't know what's going to happen in court until you get there."

"Oh, yes I can," Destiny said, spreading a pleased look around the room. "In fact, if I play my cards right, the whole thing could just disappear. I might not even have to go to court at all. So put my name down there, Aquanettia. And may the best woman win."

Lorena shared an appalled look with Felix. "I knew we should have voted on your motion," she grumbled.

Edgar winked at Destiny and smiled up at Aquanettia. Edie's mouth fell open in shock, and Gabriel chuckled. "Oh, this is going to be fun," he said in a voice so low only I could hear him.

Fun? I wasn't sure I agreed with him, but I did think the election had suddenly become a lot more interesting.

It was after ten when Aquanettia finally banged her gavel for the last time and the promise of escape danced in front of me. With Ben & Jerry whispering to me, I groped my way toward the door but Sebastian Walker stopped me before I could get away. He's a tall man with a Will Ferrell look. Curly brown hair, a wide-open face, and a friendly smile that sets customers at ease when they visit the pharmacy. "Don't go anywhere yet," he said. "We need to have a quick meeting of the cleanup committee. It won't take long. Twenty minutes at the most."

I groaned aloud, stuck out my tongue at Gabriel as he slipped past me to freedom, and grudgingly resumed my seat. I watched Destiny sashay out the door with Edgar and pretended not to notice the look on Moose's face as his wife tottered off with another man.

Thanks to her, we'd accomplished next to nothing during the past three hours. First, we'd had to discuss her eligibility to challenge Aquanettia since she'd never been to a meeting. She'd won that round because we hadn't anticipated the problem and so hadn't addressed it in the temporary rules. Then we'd spent far too long explaining for her benefit why we couldn't just hire an outside firm to handle the neighborhood cleanup, followed by a lengthy discussion about the brand of whitewash we'd chosen for the storm shutters. Destiny had wanted to vote again on the theme we'd chosen for the spring sidewalk sale at our last meeting, but she'd been on the losing end of that vote. All of that had made Felix fume, and sputter, and shift around in his seat just waiting for the moment when he could make his motion to remove her on the record. Which, of course, had resulted in another hour of shouting and ranting (mostly Felix and Lorena) and crying and jiggling for the benefit of the voters (Destiny and . . . well, just Destiny) and multiple excuses (also Destiny).

In the end, Moose's short but impassioned plea to give his wife another chance had decided the vote. By a narrow margin, we'd given Destiny a reprieve, along with a firm warning that one more absence would result in automatic removal from the alliance membership. She'd reacted with tearful accusations that half of us were trying to skew the elections by making her appear ineligible to run. Discussing that accusation seemed like a colossal waste of time to me since I didn't think she stood a chance of actually winning the election but we discussed it to death anyway.

Swallowing a yawn, I settled in for a rundown of the plans the committee had put together for our first neighborhood-wide cleanup effort scheduled for the coming weekend. I'd been put in charge of collecting donations of food, water, garbage bags, and tools in one spot to make distribution easier on Saturday morning. I got that assignment mostly because Zydeco is located in a lovely renovated antebellum home with plenty of storage space. The collection was supposed to take place the following afternoon.

Sebastian took his role as committee chair seriously, so I accepted the checklist he handed out and resigned myself to sticking around. But by the time the cleanup committee had gone over the game plan three times in a row, I was bone tired and my sunny disposition had given way to gray clouds. Once Sebastian finally ended the meeting, I shot to my feet and told Edie I'd meet her outside as I headed out the door.

Halfway down the stairs, I heard someone call my name, but I pretended not to hear it. Whatever it was could wait until tomorrow.

"Rita?" the man called again. "Hold up. I need to talk to you."

I wasn't interested in talking about trash collection or tire disposal, but I paused at the foot of the stairs and turned around to see who was calling me. Amid displays of jewelry, outdated electronics, used shoes, vinyl records, a couple of boxy TV sets, some teacups and coffee mugs, and an old cigar box filled with key chains, I found myself looking up into Moose's earnest gaze. He towered over me by at least a foot and was probably twice my size around so I turned on a friendly smile in the interest of self-preservation. "What can I do for you?"

He jerked his head toward the front door. "Let's go outside. This is kind of private, and I don't want Destiny to overhear us."

I wasn't sure where he was going with that, but since I wanted to get out of the building almost more than anything at that moment, I went along. He held the door and I stepped out into the night. Streetlamps cast a dim light over the sidewalk near the street, but together with the massive trees in the front yard, they created deep shadows that made it hard to see the uneven walk across the yard.

I was curious about what Moose wanted. Our businesses were close in proximity, but he doesn't fit Zydeco's client demographic, and I have never felt the need for a Harley. I could have counted on two fingers the number of conversations we'd actually had, and neither of them had gone much beyond saying hello and discussing the weather.

Maybe he wanted to court my vote for Destiny in the election, but if so, he was going about it all wrong. I didn't want to align Zydeco publicly with either candidate and risk alienating neighbors from either camp. I planned to cast our vote in secret and do my best to appear neutral during the campaign.

While I followed Moose through the gate and along the sidewalk in the direction of the Chopper Shop, I practiced saying "no" in what I hoped would be a friendly, "please don't hurt me" manner. I noticed Lorena talking to a couple of people across the street in front of the pet store and heard bits of conversation as people left Second Chances behind us. When we were about halfway between the two stores, Moose stopped walking and looked around to make sure we were alone. I presented my most impartial expression and channeled my inner Switzerland.

He shoved his beefy hands into the pockets of his jeans and hunched his shoulders. "I hope this isn't overstepping, but since you're coordinating donations for the cleanup, I was hoping you'd let Destiny help out. She wants to get involved. You saw that for yourself upstairs at the meeting, but some people keep trying to block her."

That wasn't exactly what I was expecting, but I didn't let the element of surprise throw me. "Of course, she's welcome to donate supplies like everyone else," I said. "In addition to the cleaning stuff, we're going to need lots of water to keep volunteers hydrated, and snacks to keep their energy up."

Moose ran a hand along the back of his neck. "No, I meant *help*. Be part of the team. Or the committee. You know . . . work with you. It would go a long way to making the others take her seriously."

Personally, I thought a change of wardrobe might gain more ground, but I didn't say so aloud. In fact, I couldn't make myself say anything. I think it was the way Moose was looking at me—like a hopeful little boy peeking out of that huge man-sized body. All I could think was, why did he have to ask me? Why couldn't he have found someone else to ask? I didn't have the heart to say no to him, but Edie would blow a gasket if I said yes.

"Things have been pretty rough the past few years," Moose confided. "And the thing is, Destiny and I really need a new start, what with the arrest and all."

I just nodded and said, "Everyone deserves a second chance." I didn't know what else to say.

Moose's eyes lit up and a smile tugged on one corner of his mouth. "Yeah. That's right. It wasn't as bad as it sounds, you know. Possession with the intent to distribute. She just had a few prescription drugs she got from a friend. But they make it sound like she's some kind of drug dealer or something."

I was still at a loss for words, but I managed, "So it was a drug charge?"

Moose nodded and scratched idly at a tattoo of a rose dripping blood on his shoulder. "Yeah, but like I said, it was really all a misunderstanding."

I wasn't sure I believed that, but once again Moose's plea on his wife's behalf won me over. Who knew I had such a soft spot for men who could crush me with one hand?

"So anyway, is it okay? Can she help out tomorrow?"

"No." That's what I should have said. What I actually said was, "Yeah. Sure. We're going to meet at Zydeco after lunch, so tell her to be there around one."

That would give me time to explain my decision to Edie and maybe bribe her to cooperate. I saw a flash of gratitude in Moose's eyes. At least, I thought I did. It was dark, so I couldn't see his expression that well. Plus, at that precise moment a panel van roared around the corner, temporarily blinding me with its headlights.

What happened next is a blur. I must have turned to look at the van because I realized those headlights were coming directly toward us. Time seemed to move in slow motion, but my brain and my body were moving even slower. "Watch out!" I shouted. "I think he's dr—*urrff*!"

Something huge and hard slammed into me with enough force to knock the air out of my lungs. I flew through the air for an instant and then hit the sidewalk. My bare arms and legs scraped across the pavement, setting half of my body on fire. The other half had lost all feeling from the impact.

My head throbbed and I tried to catch my breath, but my lungs refused to cooperate. Other than some dim light on the edge of my peripheral vision, I couldn't see a thing. Sluggish and dazed, I tried to figure out what had happened, my ears seemed to be the only part of my body still in perfect working condition. I heard a chorus of voices shouting, some running footsteps, and the roar of an engine as the van sped off.

And then I died. Or maybe I just wished I had.

Three

All the warnings Aunt Yolanda had given me when I was growing up raced through my aching head. She'd tried to instill the tenets of her Catholic faith in me, but I'd been an angry kid after my parents died and I'd wanted nothing to do with God. As I now floated gently up to heaven, I realized I should have been a better person. I should have been kinder. I should have . . .

A deep groan interrupted my thoughts, and my vision slowly cleared as Moose moved off me. "You okay, Miss Rita?"

I would have breathed a sigh of relief, but my lungs still weren't working properly. "I'm not sure," I croaked. "What happened?"

"We nearly got hit by that sonofabitch in the van." Moose leveraged himself up with one hand and looked me over carefully. "Sorry I tackled you so hard. I just didn't want you hurt."

Um . . . too late. Not that I wasn't grateful. As bad as I felt, I knew it could have been a whole lot worse. I moved slowly, gingerly, testing each part of my body as I tried to sit up. There wasn't a single inch of me that wasn't numb or throbbing with pain.

"Felix is calling 911," Moose said as he got to his feet. With his two-hundred-fifty-plus pounds off my chest, I could finally breathe a little better. I held out a hand, thinking he would help me up. He motioned for me to stay put. "The cops and paramedics should be here soon. I hit you pretty hard. It might be a good idea to get checked out before you try to walk around."

"I'm fine," I assured him. But we both knew I was lying. I struggled to sit up straighter, but an electric current zapped up my neck and dizziness swamped me. With a groan, I sank back onto the pavement. "Where's the van?"

"Gone."

I closed my eyes and sighed. That hurt, too. "Seriously? The driver didn't even stop?"

"The jerk didn't even slow down."

"Probably drunk," I said, finally getting out what I'd been trying to say when Moose hit me. A fresh wave of pain rolled through my neck and back, and tears of frustration burned my eyes. I wanted to get home, take a hot bath, and let TV and ice cream provide me with the comfort I so desperately needed. But Moose was probably right. It would be a mistake to try walking back to Zydeco, and an even bigger mistake to attempt driving home. I felt horrible now, but I suspected I'd feel a whole lot worse tomorrow.

The paramedics agreed and insisted on transporting me to the hospital. Hearing that, Edie appeared out of nowhere and offered to go with me. I didn't want to rob her and the baby of their sleep, so I sent them both home. Destiny and Edgar had vanished after the meeting, leaving Moose some free time, I guess. He followed me to the ER and hung around the waiting room, helping me answer questions for the police. They'd made a few notes and some noises about doing their best to find the van and its driver, but they didn't instill a lot of hope. Finally, the doctor announced that I would live. Moose drove me home, and offered to come inside to make sure I got settled in, but I turned him down for two reasons: First, I was way too tired and sore to want anybody hovering over me. And second, he was married. To Destiny. Who might have been busy elsewhere but could still take me out if I crossed her. I didn't want her thinking there was something funny going on, so I took my aching body inside alone, stripped out of my shorts and T-shirt (which now looked like roadkill), and fell into bed.

I woke the next morning to sun shining in my eyes and a body that felt as if I'd been hit by a moose. Which I guess I sort of had. Unlike in my hometown of Albuquerque, where the sun rises slowly behind the mountains, in New Orleans it pops up over the eastern horizon like a jack-in-the-box. After a year in the city, I'm still trying to adjust my body clock to brilliant sunlight before seven in the morning.

I might have gone back to sleep, but I had a meeting with Miss Frankie at ten, and I didn't want her to get to Zydeco before me. I knew I couldn't keep her from finding out about my brush with that rogue van last night, and since losing Philippe, she worries about me a lot. I wanted her to see me at the same time she heard about the accident, so she'd know I wasn't seriously hurt.

Doing my best to ignore the pounding in my head, I stumbled down the hall to the bathroom and checked out my reflection for the first time. Big mistake. A massive purple bruise colored one side of my jaw and another spread across the opposite cheek. It would take more makeup than I owned to completely hide the bruises, and I couldn't do a thing about the swelling. But I could wear long pants and sleeves to cover the ugly red scratches on my arms and legs. Maybe that would keep Miss Frankie from freaking out too much.

I stood under the hot spray of the shower for a few minutes, then dragged myself out and blotted myself dry with a towel. I was still sore, but I thought the shower had loosened my tight muscles a little. Or maybe it was just wishful thinking.

After plastering foundation over the bruises, hoping to at least dull the lovely black-and-blue effect, I added blush and mascara. Since my car was still at Zydeco, I called a cab. The emergency room physician had given me a couple of prescriptions before I left the hospital. Last night I'd been convinced I wouldn't need to fill them. But whatever they'd given me at the hospital had long since worn off, so I asked the cabbie to drop me off at Magnolia Street Drug. I hate the feeling of being drugged, but I figured I'd have a better chance of convincing Miss Frankie that I was okay if I didn't groan or grimace every time I moved.

I paid the cab driver and hobbled inside, heading straight for the pharmacy at the back of the store, where Sebastian Walker was on duty. He took one look at my face and gasped. "Good Lord!"

I touched the bruise on my jaw with the tip of my finger and tried to laugh. "And here I thought I'd done such a good job with my makeup."

Sebastian leaned in for a better look, his gaze tight with worry. "Is this what happened last night?"

I had expected the news to travel through the neighborhood quickly, but I'm always surprised by how fast information actually makes it from one end of the block to the other. "You heard about that, huh?"

"I was there. You don't remember?"

I shook my head and winced. "Sorry. It's kind of a blur."

"Moose was really worried about you. We all were. He hit you pretty hard. But I had no idea it was this bad."

"Yeah. Well. As you can see . . ." I held out my arms, felt a little dizzy, and lowered them slowly. "Thank God for Moose. If he hadn't been there to knock me out of the way, I think the van probably would have hit me."

"Probably?" Sebastian said with a disbelieving laugh. "The police might think it was an accident, but I swear that van was heading straight for you. If Moose hadn't been there, we'd be planning your funeral right now."

That odd electrical impulse zinged up my neck again. "I don't think it was quite that close."

"You'll forgive me for arguing, but I know what I saw. I'm sure Lorena will back me up. I saw her right before the van came around the corner."

"He was probably drunk," I said. "He shouldn't have been driving at all. I don't suppose you actually saw the driver?"

Sebastian shook his head. "Sorry. It happened so fast. I saw that van heading for you and freaked out a little. The best I can tell you is I think the driver was alone. I'm pretty sure there was only one shadow inside."

"Are you sure he didn't swerve to avoid us? Not even at the last minute?"

Sebastian pulled a clipboard from a hook on the wall and frowned down at it. "He didn't swerve. In fact, I'd swear he was trying to hit you. You must have an enemy out there somewhere."

I tried to laugh, but managed only a choked sound. He was wrong. What he suggested was impossible. Wasn't it?

"No enemies," I said firmly. "If it wasn't a drunk driver, it was probably someone texting a friend so he didn't see us there."

"Yeah," Sebastian said, but he sounded uncertain. "I'm sure you're right. What else could it have been?"

What else indeed?

The conversation was making me uneasy, so I changed the subject. "Luckily everything turned out all right. But I have a couple of prescriptions here. Some kind of pain medication and an antibiotic, I think. Should I wait, or come back later?"

Sebastian looked over the prescriptions. "You can wait if you want. It shouldn't take more than fifteen or twenty minutes. Just make yourself comfortable. I'll let you know when it's ready." He nodded toward a small strip of plastic chairs joined by dented pieces of metal. A handful of magazines lay on a chipped table, offering reading material that was probably several months out of date. On a corkboard behind the chairs, flyers and bulletins hung lopsidedly from multicolored pushpins.

The waiting area held no appeal so I picked up a small basket from a stack against the wall and strolled away slowly. Aunt Yolanda's birthday was in two weeks, and I still hadn't picked up a card or a gift. Maybe I could find something here.

I checked out a display of inexpensive perfumes and decided to pass, looked over some cheap costume jewelry, and sniffed several varieties of shower gel. Okay, so maybe this wasn't gift central. Instead, I picked up a bottle of ibuprofen, added deodorant and Febreze, and then moved into the greeting card aisle.

Someone else was standing at the far end of the aisle, and it took only a second to recognize Destiny Hazen. She wore short leather shorts, a lacy pink tank top, and matching pink stilettos. A real class act.

Until that moment, I'd forgotten all about my conversation with Moose and my promise to let Destiny work with me this afternoon. My feet stopped moving and I stared like a deer in the headlights while I tried to decide whether to duck and run or to act like a grown-up and go over to say hello.

Before I could make a decision, she glanced up, spotted me, and jiggled in my direction. "Ohmigod, Rita! Look at you!" She held out her arms as if she intended to hug me.

I flinched inwardly and shifted to avoid a direct hit. I didn't want to seem rude, but ouch!

Since I'd avoided the embrace, she settled for a thoughtful scowl and took my chin in her hand. Thankfully, her touch was gentle and the pain minimal. "Moose told me what happened. I just couldn't believe it. Are you all right?"

"I'm fine," I assured her. "I look worse than I feel."

"Well, that's a blessing isn't it? Moose said the driver just took off!"

"That's what they tell me. I don't know for sure. I couldn't see much."

"Hmmm-hmmm-hmmm. Can you believe it? What is this world coming to? That's what I want to know." She peered into my basket and nodded toward the ibuprofen. "I'll bet you're all kinds of sore today."

"That's an understatement."

"You think that's going to be enough? I've got some Lortabs at home left over from when my back was so bad a few months ago. I could give you a few if you want."

I shook my head and tried not to look surprised by the offer. Maybe she really had been sick. Who would have guessed? "I'm sure I'll be fine. Sebastian is filling a prescription for me right now."

"Oh?" She pursed her glossy pink lips and tilted her head like a curious bird. "What did they give you?"

"I don't remember. Something for pain and an antibiotic. That's all I know."

"Well. Good for you. And I hope they catch the guy who did this soon. You should make him pay for everything. I have a cousin who's an attorney if you need one."

"Thanks, but I don't think that will be necessary. I doubt we'll ever find out who was driving the van. And besides, technically Moose was the one who knocked me down."

Destiny's eyes widened in surprise. "He wouldn't have knocked you down if the van hadn't been trying to get you. And I'm sure you'll find out who was driving. Edgar recognized the van—at least that's what he told me."

"I didn't realize Edgar was there at the time. Didn't the two of you leave after the alliance meeting?"

Destiny nodded. "Yeah, but we were talking on the corner by the dollar store. I just heard the van. It was gone before I turned around, but Edgar saw it."

"Did Edgar say whether he saw the driver?"

"No, but he's almost positive it was the Second Chances van."

I'm pretty sure my mouth fell open at that. "But that's impossible. Why would Aquanettia drive around like a maniac? How could she have done it? She was still upstairs when I left."

"I didn't say it was her," Destiny said with a smirk. "Although I wouldn't put it past her. But it was probably one of her boys. Keon most likely. Isaiah's all right, but Keon's practically always in some kind of trouble."

I knew Aquanettia's sons only by sight and reputation. Isaiah, the older at twenty-three, was tall, thin, and serious about his studies at a local tech school. Keon, two years younger, was shorter and stockier, tougher, and more rebellious. And if neighborhood gossip was right, a high school dropout.

Not that I listen to gossip.

"Well, then," I said with a thin laugh. "That proves it was an accident, doesn't it? Neither Keon nor Isaiah has any reason to run me down. I barely know them."

Destiny rolled her eyes and gave her attention to a fingernail. "You never know with kids, do you?"

"I guess not," I said agreeably.

Destiny turned her hand over and inspected the backs of her long nails. "I don't know. Maybe you're right. Maybe we'll never know who was driving last night. But if I were you, I'd keep one eye on my back, just in case."

I said that I would and hurried back to pick up my prescriptions. I tried to laugh off her warning, but her words had chilled me. What if she and Sebastian were right? What if someone had been trying to hit me? And what if he—or she—was out there, just waiting for a chance to strike again?

Four

The sun was high in the sky and beating down on the city with a vengeance when I left the drugstore. Humidity hung so heavy in the air I could see it in front of me like a sheer curtain. I'd lived in New Orleans for a year and I was slowly adjusting to the weather, but my lungs still preferred a nice, dry day with humidity in the single digits.

Sebastian's assertion that the van had actually been *trying* to hit me, and Destiny's warning to watch my back, nagged at me all the way to Zydeco. Most of last night's events were a blur, but I knew the questions would bug me until I got some answers. I should check with the police and ask if they'd found the van or its driver. I wanted to forget about Destiny's suggestion that it might have been Isaiah or Keon, but what if she was right about that, too? Maybe I should talk to Aquanettia. If one of her sons had some unknown issue with me, would she admit it? There was only one way to find out.

Before I talked to her, I should talk with the other alliance members who'd been around during the accident: Edgar, Lorena, and Edie. Maybe one of them had seen something that would cross the Fisher brothers off my list.

It might be good to find out before I talked to their mother. No sense getting her riled up if her sons were innocent. Which I really hoped they were.

I was hot, sweaty, and seriously regretting my decision to walk by the time I let myself in through Zydeco's ornately carved front door, but a blast of cold air from inside gave me a second wind. Thanks to a healthy bank account full of old family money, Philippe had installed an industrial-sized air-conditioning unit when he'd renovated the beautiful antebellum house into a cake shop. His decision hadn't been frivolous. We needed the cool air to keep cakes and decorations from melting in "feels like" temperatures that could soar to well over a hundred degrees for days at a time. Though it provided an extra benefit for those of us who worked there, granting relief from the brutal summer heat.

Breathing in the delicious aromas of cinnamon, nutmeg, and clove emanating from the kitchen and design area, I shut the door behind me and turned to say hello to Edie, who runs the front of the house from behind a large U-shaped desk and a massive computer screen.

She took one look at my face and came out of her chair. "Rita? What in heaven's name are you doing here? You should be at the hospital—or at least home in bed."

"I'm fine," I assured her, feeling like a parrot. I wondered how many times I'd have to say those words before the bruises faded and the swelling went down. "I look worse than I feel."

She sat slowly. "Well, that's good, because you look like death warmed over."

I laughed and headed toward my office so I could stash my things. "You sure know how to make a girl feel attractive."

"Sorry," she called after me. "I should have asked you to call me when you left the hospital last night. I barely slept."

She'd been worried about me? I tossed the bag from the drugstore onto my desk and shoved my purse into a desk drawer. I still had a few minutes before my meeting with Miss Frankie, so I wandered back into the reception area. Edie's concern was actually kind of sweet. We'd known each other since pastry school and hadn't always gotten along, but we'd become friendly since we started working together last year.

"I thought about calling," I said as I slipped into a chair in front of her desk. "I didn't want to wake you."

She ran her gaze over my face, more slowly this time. "You look rough, but I'm glad you're up and walking around. When I saw that van heading for you, I was sure you were dead."

"I thought I was dead when Moose was lying on top of me." Now that she was eating for two, Edie kept a bowl of M&M's beside her computer. I have a firm policy that nobody eats chocolate alone in my presence, so I helped myself to a handful. "I didn't get a chance to ask you last night. Did you see what happened?"

Edie nodded. "I saw the whole thing. I was just coming out the front door of Second Chances when the van came around the corner." She closed her eyes briefly and shuddered. "It was horrible."

"It was pretty rough from my end, too," I said, wanting to lighten the moment for her. "Did you recognize the van or see the driver?"

Edie shook her head. "Not really. I think he was wearing a ball cap, but that's about all I saw—and I'm not even sure about that. It was so dark and it happened so fast. Do the police have any leads?"

"Not that I'm aware of," I said, munching on a couple of candies. "I haven't heard from them since they took my statement at the ER, but I'll call later and find out if they've made progress on the case." I hesitated to ask my next question. I didn't want to upset Edie needlessly, but she had been an eyewitness and I needed to know if Sebastian and Destiny were right. "Do you think it was an accident?"

Edie's almond-shaped eyes widened in shock. "Well, of course it was! What else could it have been?"

I could have hugged her. That was exactly what I wanted to hear. I shrugged and popped another candy into my mouth. "I don't know. I was sure it was an accident, too, but I just came from the drugstore and Sebastian seems convinced that the driver was trying to hit me. And then I ran into Destiny Hazen and she said the same thing. In fact, she thinks the driver was one of the Fisher boys."

Edie's eyes flickered. "I'm sure they're both wrong."

Another perfect answer. We were two for two. "Yeah," I said. "I'm sure they are. But they both seemed so certain. I thought I should make sure I'm not delusional. But, I mean, who would want to hurt me? It's crazy . . . right?"

"Right." Edie looked away, but not before I saw that flicker in her eyes for the second time.

I leaned into her line of vision, "Edie? What aren't you saying?"

"Nothing! It *was* an accident. I'm sure of it." She tried to look outraged, but she didn't quite meet my eyes, and I guessed that she was hiding something.

"Let's start over from the beginning," I said. "What exactly did you see?"

Edie rubbed her forehead and thought for a moment. "I don't know. It's hard to tell. I mean, he could have been drunk or something. But he never did swerve, so either he didn't see you at all or he did see you and——" She broke off, clearly distressed.

My heart dropped like a rock. I'd felt bad enough thinking that my near miss had been an accident, Now, after hearing three people say the van had been aiming for me, I was starting to wonder if someone really had tried to hurt me.

I stared at Edie for a minute. Or maybe it was an hour. I'm not sure. "But why?" I said when I thought my voice might work again. "And who?"

She shoveled up a handful of M&M's for herself. "An unhappy client?"

Zydeco has a great reputation around town, and even though we'd lost some business after Philippe died, and

again when the economy tanked, we'd been slowly rebuild-
ing our client list all year. We'd had a few clients with
issues of one kind or another, but we'd resolved every problem. Even if we hadn't, no one had been angry enough to
come after me with a loaded van. And besides, who would
kill somebody over a cake? A beautifully crafted and very
expensive cake, but still . . . cake.

But if a cake order gone bad wasn't the motive, what
could it be? I'd lived a fairly tame life. I don't have a long
list of psychotic ex-boyfriends, and I'd never knowingly
stolen another woman's husband or boyfriend. I'd never
cheated anyone in a business deal or run over a neighbor's
dog. My list of potential homicidal enemies was a short
one, consisting of exactly nobody.

Edie looked as confused as I felt. "Maybe we should
look through the client files for the past year. That might
jog our memories."

"Good idea," I said, grateful that there was something
I could actually do.

"What about relatives?" Edie asked. "Are there any who
might be angry with you?"

"Not that I know of. And besides, none of my family
lives around here."

"But Philippe's does," Edie said, looking up from the
notes she was making. "He had a couple of aunts, didn't
he? Cousins? Maybe one of them is angry that you made
out so well when he died. Or maybe it was someone else
from Philippe's past."

I shivered involuntarily. My almost-ex-husband had
been murdered last year, which was why I lived and worked
in New Orleans now. The idea that some relative of his
might be angry with me for inheriting (since I'd technically
been his widow) or the notion that he might have more
enemies lurking out there made me ill at ease. "Do you
know something I don't?" I asked Edie. "Are you thinking
of anyone in particular?"

She shook her head quickly. "No. I didn't mean it like

that. I barely even know Philippe's cousins. And besides, everybody loved Philippe."

"Almost everybody."

Her eyes clouded with memory, and when she spoke again, her voice was subdued. "Almost. But that's over and done with. I was just tossing out ideas. And anyway, how would any of them have known where to find you last night?" She took a deep breath and made a visible effort to lighten the mood. "I'm sure there's nothing to worry about. There are a dozen reasons that van might have appeared to be aiming straight for you, but that doesn't necessarily mean anything. I'm sure when the police catch the guy, they'll find out he was just distracted."

"Or drunk," I said. "Or high." I scooped up another handful of M&M's for the road. "How well do you know Aquanettia and her sons?"

Edie frowned at me. "Don't tell me you're taking what Destiny said seriously."

"I can't just ignore it," I said with a shrug. "What if she's right?"

"Is that a real question? You honestly think Destiny knows what she's talking about?"

"It could happen. Do you think either of the boys is capable of something like that?"

Irritation tightened Edie's mouth but she answered me anyway. "Isaiah? No. He's a good kid, and he's serious about his schooling. Keon? Maybe. He's always been a wild card. I know that Aquanettia has had trouble with him for several years. But he wouldn't just randomly try to run someone over, and there's no reason at all for him to come after you. It might be different if he'd been after Moose. Those two have clashed a few times." She stopped talking abruptly and we stared at each other while her last few words echoed between us.

I don't know why the idea that Moose might have been the real target hadn't occurred to me before. I was probably in shock. Not that I wanted Moose to be in danger, but if the driver wasn't interested in killing me, I could relax and think about work. I was on the schedule to pipe three dozen buttercream petunias for a baptism cake due on Friday. Those petunias weren't going to make themselves.

"Maybe you should talk to Sullivan," Edie suggested. Liam Sullivan, a detective in NOPD's Homicide Squad, is a friend. A very good friend, and one of the reasons my relationship with Gabriel hasn't developed into something more. Which was only fair, since Gabriel was a major roadblock in my relationship with Sullivan. And let me just state for the record that both men are well aware of each other. I'm not playing anybody.

"I'd love to, but he's on vacation. Deep-sea fishing with friends. He'll be gone for a couple of weeks."

"So you're not going to tell him?"

"What's to tell?" I asked with an oh-so-casual shrug. "Even if he were in town, there's nothing he could do about it. Either the case will be solved by the time he comes back, or it will be nothing but a memory."

Edie gave me an "Are you kidding?" look.

I made a mental note to mention the idea of Moose as target when I called the police. Later. Right now, I needed to get ready for my meeting with Miss Frankie. Not that I had much I could do to prepare. I had no idea why she'd called this meeting or why she wanted to see me. I'd been trying not to think about it. If she'd volunteered me for some new project, I'd just say no. And this time I'd mean it.

I stood and turned to go back into my office, adding a mental note to ask Miss Frankie if any of Philippe's relatives were harboring resentments toward me, just in case. "I'm going to touch up my makeup," I said to Edie. "Will you let me know when Miss Frankie gets here?"

With a gasp of horror, Edie glanced at the stairs. "Oh my gosh! I can't believe it slipped my mind. You walked in and I saw your face, and everything else flew out of my head." Her voice dropped to a near-whisper. "She's already up there, waiting for you."

"Miss Frankie has been here the whole time?"

Edie nodded. "Sorry."

I waved off her apology. It wasn't the idea of keeping my mother-in-law waiting for a few minutes that had me worried. "You didn't mention anything about the accident, did you?"

The guilt on Edie's face sharpened. "I wasn't supposed to?"

I thought she knew Miss Frankie well enough to answer that herself, but I didn't waste time saying so. Miss Frankie had been bound to find out about what happened last night. I just hoped she hadn't been sitting up there and fretting over me this whole time.

I climbed the stairs quickly, groaning softly as my sore muscles screamed in protest. It wasn't until I heard the phone ring and Edie answering questions about that afternoon's supply drive that I realized I'd also completely forgotten to warn her about Destiny. But maybe that was for the best. She was bound to react badly to the news, and right now I had to focus on showing Miss Frankie that I wasn't at death's door. I'd have plenty of time to warn Edie later.

Five

I made it all the way to the second-floor landing before I was interrupted by the sound of heavy footsteps and equally heavy breathing on the stairs behind me. I glanced over my shoulder and found Estelle Jergens laboring to catch up with me. Her ample chest heaved and her face matched the color of her curly red hair. Estelle is the oldest member of the Zydeco staff. I don't know her actual age, but I put her somewhere around fifty, though I could be off by a few years in either direction.

"Hold on a minute, Rita," she wheezed. "I need to talk to you."

I didn't want to keep Miss Frankie waiting much longer, but I felt bad about turning Estelle away when chasing me had clearly required such an effort. "Okay," I said, "but I only have a minute. I'm late for a meeting with Miss Frankie."

Estelle climbed the last three stairs and paused to catch her breath. "Oh." *Huff-puff.* "Sorry." *Puff.* "I . . ." *Huff.* ". . . didn't realize you were busy." *Huff-puff.* "I can wait until after. It shouldn't take long." She finally managed a deep breath and wiped a trickle of perspiration from her cheek. "It's about Edie."

We've all been walking on eggshells since learning that Edie's doctor had warned her that her pregnancy was high-risk and I didn't want to ignore a potential problem, especially since the crew at Zydeco was Edie's only support system. I knew Miss Frankie would understand the delay. "What is it?"

Estelle looked over the banister at Edie's desk and tugged me away from the landing. "We need to talk about Edie's baby shower," she said in a near-whisper.

I laughed, relieved that we weren't facing some actual emergency. "What baby shower?"

Estelle looked confused for a moment, then chuckled and slapped my arm lightly. "For a minute there, I thought you were serious! We are going to give Edie a shower, aren't we?"

I was a little embarrassed that the idea of a baby shower hadn't even crossed my mind. In my defense, Edie was only five months along, which seemed early to be talking about a shower. But since Estelle had brought it up . . . "Sure. Go right ahead. I'm sure she'd appreciate it."

"Me?" Estelle rocked back on her heels. "No. I didn't mean me. I'm not . . ." She waved a hand to encompass her gray sweatpants, stained red shirt, and the bright green kerchief covering her hair. "I didn't mean me. I'm not good at that kind of thing. All of my artistic ability goes into decorating cakes. I thought you would want to plan it. You know. Considering how close you and Edie are."

Close? That was a stretch. Like I said, Edie and I had become friendlier in the past year but I wouldn't have ever said we were "close." "It's fine with me if you do it," I said. "Maybe you could get Isabeau and Sparkle to help you."

Estelle's mouth fell open. "Sparkle? Queen of the Dark?" She snorted a laugh and shook her head. "She's a sweet girl under all that goth makeup and all, but I shudder to think what kind of baby shower we'd have if she helped plan it. And I can't ask Isabeau. You know how bad she feels about the whole baby thing."

I did not, in fact, have a clue what Estelle was talking about, but for the sake of keeping the conversation brief, I pretended I did. "Oh. Yeah. I wasn't thinking."

Estelle gave me a maternal pat on the shoulder. "So you see, you're the one who should do it. I'm just here to offer my help if you need it."

I never talk about it, but I have baby issues of my own. I have no children. I've never been pregnant. Never came close, not even before Philippe and I separated. Philippe and I agreed to wait to start a family so we could focus on our careers. But after a while, the waiting had become less voluntary and more obligatory. I'd gone through a time of grieving every month for a couple of years and then eventually made peace with myself.

So while I don't dislike babies, baby showers just aren't my thing. I'm not into playing games and raving over diapers, burp rags, and other assorted baby paraphernalia. Apparently, Isabeau felt the same way.

"You're so clever," Estelle chirped, her ability to breathe now fully restored. "I can't wait to see what you come up with."

That made two of us.

"It's just that I haven't heard a peep about the plans, and you really shouldn't put it off much longer. You know Edie's not even close to being ready for the baby. She doesn't have a crib or receiving blankets. All she has is a couple of sleepers. We don't want the baby to get here before we can fill out the layette at the party."

Right. Estelle gave me a quick hug and a pat on the cheek. "I'm so glad that's settled. You'll let me know if you need any help at all?" And then she turned and hurried down the stairs without waiting for a response.

Considering how often Miss Frankie volunteered me for projects without consulting me, you'd think I'd be used to it by now, but I was feeling a bit shell-shocked as I continued down the hall toward the conference room. "No,"

I muttered under my breath. "No!" It was such an easy word. Why couldn't I say it when I needed to?

I found Miss Frankie (aka Frances Mae Renier) sitting at the conference table sipping a cup of coffee and looking through the contents of a black leather folder. I'd been married to her son, but I'd kept my own surname. Most people think it was a professional choice, but it was actually homage to my parents, whom I'd lost when I was twelve. I didn't want to lose their name, too.

I'd been expecting to find Miss Frankie pacing, but she looked cool as a cucumber in a pale green pantsuit and low-heeled sandals. Her auburn hair had been teased and sprayed to within an inch of its life, and her nails and lipstick were the same shade of dark plum.

She beamed when I walked through the door, but her smile faded abruptly when she saw the bruises on my face. "Lord have mercy," she said as she stood to hug me. "Edie told me what happened, but I had no idea it was this bad. Are you feeling all right?"

I'd managed not to groan when she wrapped her arms around me, but I couldn't stifle the sigh of relief when she let me go again. "I'm fine," I assured her. "Just a little stiff and sore." I motioned her back into her seat, poured a cup of coffee, and joined her at the table. "So what did you want to see me about?"

Miss Frankie laced her fingers together. "I need your help, Rita. My cousin Pearl Lee has gotten herself into a mess."

"Oh?" I might have met Pearl Lee at Philippe's funeral, but if so, I couldn't remember her. I was almost afraid to ask, "What kind of mess?"

"It's a man," Miss Frankie said with a solemn shake of the head. "With Pearl Lee, it's always a man. At her age, too."

"What age would that be?"

Miss Frankie gave me a stern look. When it comes to age, she has a firm "don't ask, don't tell" policy. "She's a bit younger than me. Not that her age matters. I wish I knew what she was thinking. Or maybe I don't. Some things are better left alone, don't you think?"

I said that I did and Miss Frankie fell silent, no doubt pondering the question anyway. I used the time to wonder what Pearl Lee's man troubles had to do with me.

"Anyway," Miss Frankie went on with a sigh. "I told her she could come and stay with me. She certainly can't stay in Pensacola after what happened. But Rita, I just can't have her sitting in my house all day long. She'll drive me crazy in two days flat."

My eyes narrowed. "You're not asking if she can stay with me, are you? Because the answer is no." There! I got it out, and I thought I'd sounded firm saying it.

Miss Frankie looked startled. "Good heavens, no! I wouldn't do that to you, sugar. Pearl Lee can be a real handful, bless her heart, but she's family so she's my handful. What I need is for you to give her a job."

I almost dropped my cup. "A job? Here?"

Miss Frankie nodded. "She's always been bad with money, but she's finally run through her share of Pawpaw's estate and she's in a fix. She'll tell you she invested it, but the truth is she spent it all on designer clothes and the wrong sort of man. We all agree that it's time she learned how to appreciate how to maintain a healthy bank balance."

I wondered who was involved in making this decision, but I didn't dare ask. The less I knew, the better. "But I—"

Miss Frankie cut me off. "Now, sugar, don't you worry. You just put Pearl Lee to work doing any old thing. I'll pay her salary. But don't tell her it's coming from me. It has to look as if the money is coming from Zydeco."

"May I ask why?"

"Because all her life, Pearl Lee's had things handed to her. She lived off Pawpaw and Meemaw until the day they died. It's not her fault, really. Uncle Skeeter spoiled her rotten, and Aunt Bitty just let him do it. But now everyone agrees that she needs to learn how to make a contribution to society. And don't look at me like we're being mean to her. We're actually doing her a favor."

I thought about old dogs and new tricks, but I didn't express my doubts aloud. I just wondered if Pearl Lee would see their interference as a favor. "And you want me to teach her how to make this contribution?" I shook my head. Firmly. "Not a chance."

Miss Frankie flapped a hand at me. "You don't have to teach her anything. Just put her to work. I've already made it clear that if she wants my help, she'll have to help with the household expenses, and that she'll have to go to work to do that."

I kept on shaking my head. "No."

"Just give her something to do. Anything. Keep her busy eight hours a day. You'll hardly even notice she's here. Now . . . she's arriving from Florida tomorrow night. I'll bring her by on Thursday morning."

"You're not listening," I said. "It's a bad idea. I'm not doing it."

"Oh, but you have to. It's all decided."

"You can't decide something like this without talking to me first," I said, my voice sharper than I intended. I softened it and said, "It's not that I don't want to help, but I've already got too much on my plate. I don't have time to make up busywork for somebody who doesn't even know their way around a kitchen."

"There are plenty of jobs around here that don't require special training."

"True, but we have two very complicated cakes on the schedule this week and I'm going to be out a lot. The neighborhood cleanup is this weekend, and Edie and I are in charge of collecting water, food, and tools for the volunteers, which is going to eat up most of today, and Estelle just this second nominated me to plan Edie's baby shower. If you want to teach Pearl Lee a lesson, you'll have to do it yourself."

Miss Frankie arched her eyebrows. "Really, Rita. I don't understand why you're being so hardheaded about this. But I'm willing to offer a compromise I think we can both live with. You take Pearl Lee off my hands for a few hours every day, and I'll handle the baby shower for you."

I had a "no" all ready for her, but when I heard the last part of her offer, I swallowed my automatic response and gave some more thought to my options. Keeping spoiled cousin Pearl Lee busy might not be fun, but it might be less awful than spending hours and hours planning a baby shower.

"You'll take the whole shebang?" I clarified, to make sure we were on the same page. "I won't have to do anything?"

A pleased smile curved Miss Frankie's lips. She could see victory on the horizon. "I'll take over the entire affair."

"It doesn't need to be lavish," I cautioned. "Just something small, but nice."

"Of course. A few friends. Some family—"

"Yeah. Only without the family part. Edie's parents haven't spoken to her since she told them about the baby. Even if she was okay with inviting them, I don't think they'd come to her shower."

Miss Frankie looked shocked. "But she's their child. And this is their grandbaby!"

"I know. It's a touchy subject. Edie doesn't talk about it much, and she tries to act like their reactions don't bother her, but I know their disapproval hurts."

So far, Edie had refused to name the baby's father, and her mother was livid. She was determined to see Edie married and respectably settled. Edie was determined to remain single and raise the baby on her own. Their disagreement had created such a huge rift in her family that everyone had been forced to take sides out of self-preservation. Unfortunately, the side they'd chosen left Edie with only her Zydeco family to see her through.

I couldn't imagine a relationship like that. Aunt Yolanda was from the "work it out" school of family relationships. If any of my cousins or I had stopped speaking for any extended period of time, she would have locked us in a room together until we'd talked it through.

"Surely there's other family," Miss Frankie said.

I shook my head. "None that would accept an invitation.

Her sister isn't speaking to her either. I'm afraid that unless and until Edie works things out with her mother, nobody's going to cross the line those two have drawn in the sand."

"Really? Hmmm. Well. We'll see about that."

I knew the look on Miss Frankie's face and it made me nervous. "Don't even think about trying to patch things up between them," I warned. "Their family issues are none of our business."

Miss Frankie waved off my concerns with the flick of a wrist. "I'm sure that her mother will come around once she realizes how much Edie needs her."

I was equally sure that Edie was going to kill me for telling Miss Frankie about her family issues. "No," I said firmly. "You're not getting involved. It's a bad idea. Very bad."

Miss Frankie stood and gathered her things. "Now don't you worry about any of this, Rita. I know what I'm doing. You said yourself that you wanted me to take over everything. Don't try to go back on our agreement now."

I picked up my cup and trailed her from the room. "I mean it, Miss Frankie. Let them work it out themselves." And then, in case she wasn't taking me seriously, I pulled out my secret weapon. "If you even try to get involved, I'll fire Pearl Lee so fast it'll make your head spin."

But Miss Frankie just kept walking. She'd already stopped listening to me.

Six

After Miss Frankie left, I joined the rest of the Zydeco crew in the design room, a spacious area with huge windows overlooking the employee parking lot and garden. It's easily my favorite room in the building, with its vaulted ceilings, brightly colored walls, and ample sunlight.

The first time I'd walked into the room, I'd wondered if I was dreaming. I'd sketched this area so many times in the early years of my career I could have drawn it with my eyes closed. Philippe had, of course, seen my designs when we were together. And he'd re-created my vision here at Zydeco. After we separated. Without me.

Through a strange trick of fate, I'd ended up with my dream shop and my dream staff. Half of them were quirky and creative friends from pastry school, the other half quirky and creative locals Philippe had hired when he opened Zydeco three years earlier.

One of my oldest friends was Wyndham Oxford III or, as we call him, "Ox." He'd been Philippe's closest friend in pastry school, so I hadn't really been surprised to find him working at Zydeco last year. He's a tall man in his late thirties with creamy coffee skin and a smooth shaved head that reminds me of Mr. Clean. I'd given Ox creative control over our largest project that week, a massive cake sculpted to represent the eighteenth hole at a new golf course opening in Houma this weekend. He'd drawn and redrawn the plans until the clients were happy with the results, and he'd spent hours dividing up the work and charting a schedule for the staff to ensure delivery of a cake that would knock the clients' socks off.

That morning I found him at his workstation, hands planted on the stainless steel table in front of him, boring holes with his eyes into the sketches and notes scattered all over it. He looked worried—and that worried me.

I stopped in front of his table and waited for him to notice me. He glanced up after a moment and gave me a chin-jerk greeting. "You look like hell."

I made a face and settled on a stool to relieve the ache in my back and legs. "Yeah? Well, you look concerned. Is everything okay?"

Ox nodded and swept the papers to one side. "Yeah. Fine. Just going over the schedule again to make sure I haven't missed anything." He ran a look over me and said again, "Seriously, Rita. You look like hell. Shouldn't you be home? You know . . . healing or something?"

"I wish everyone would stop asking me that," I said sullenly and then immediately felt like a jerk. Ox had only asked once, as had everyone else. I'd have done the same thing if any of them had turned up looking like I did. I flashed an apologetic smile. "I'm fine. A little sore, but otherwise ready, willing, and able to do my job. Did you and Dwight get that space on the dock cleared? People are supposed to start bringing donations this afternoon."

Ox jerked his head toward the metal door that led outside. "You want to double-check what we did? Make sure it looks the way you want?"

Normally, I would have but the ache in my neck was getting worse and spreading into the base of my skull.

"What's to double-check? I'm sure it's fine." I glanced around the room, taking in the activity buzzing in every corner, pleased to see that everyone was working.

Near the kitchen, Dwight Sonntag—another friend from pastry school—bent low to study the massive stacked cake. Twelve tiers of spicy Italian plum sheetcake held together with layers of chocolate mocha buttercream, all just waiting for Dwight's artistic endeavors with a serrated knife to turn it into rolling hills, water hazards, and sand traps. He scratched at the beard guard covering his scraggly brown whiskers and shaved a fraction of an inch from one corner of the top tier. Dwight is unkempt and his wardrobe leaves a lot to be desired, but his attention to detail when he's decorating is unmatched. He has undeniable talent.

Kitty-corner from him, Estelle crumb-coated a four-tier round cake that would eventually pass itself off as a tuxedo, an opening night cake for a local actor who'd landed the biggest role of his career. Estelle's red curls spilled out from beneath her bright green kerchief, and she laughed occasionally at the nonstop monologue coming from "perkier than anyone ought to be" Isabeau.

On the short side of twenty, Isabeau bounced around the workroom in a pair of blindingly white Keds and a red skirt so short it looked like it belonged in a cheerleading catalog. She'd paired the skirt with a white twin set. The only thing missing from her high school football game look were the bobby socks.

In the far corner—the only part of the room that the sunlight never reached—Sparkle Starr chewed one black-painted lip as she sculpted off-white gum paste into a cover for a tiny golf cart she'd molded earlier out of Rice Krispies treats and then covered with fondant.

Everyone seemed happy and productive, which was a good thing. "Do you still want me to work on those petunias?" I asked. "Or would you rather have my help on the golf course?"

Before Ox could answer, the door to the reception area flew open with a bang and Edie appeared. She gripped both sides of the door frame and glared around the room. "Rita?"

I could tell she hadn't seen me yet, and I had a sinking feeling I knew what had put that look on her face. I had the childish urge to duck behind Ox's table but I managed to ignore it. I was trying to earn the staff's respect, and hiding from a confrontation didn't seem like the right way to go about it. I gave Edie a little wave and sang out, "I'm over here, Edie. Is there a problem?"

She strode across the room. "You're damn right there's a problem. Guess who just showed up to help with the collections for the neighborhood cleanup? Guess who says you invited her to help out?"

Yep. Trouble. I glanced toward the door to make sure Destiny hadn't followed Edie. "I can explain—"

"Is that true? Did you *ask* her to help?"

"Of course not! Moose asked me to let her help. That's what we were talking about when that van came around the corner. I tried to say no, but it wasn't that easy. And then, after he saved my life, what was I supposed to do?"

"Oh, I don't know. Maybe bake him a cake to say thank you?" Edie put a hand to her forehead and sighed. "You can't seriously expect me to work with that woman all afternoon—and I use the word *work* loosely. She won't do anything except take up space and get in the way."

"You don't know that," I said. "She might actually be helpful."

Edie lowered her hand so she could shoot me a death ray. "She's wearing a pair of shorts that will expose everything she has if she moves an inch. Those boobs of hers will come tumbling out if she bends over. And I'm pretty sure she's high on something."

That surprised me. I glanced at the door again. "What makes you say that?"

Edie shot me an evil grin. "Why don't you come and see for yourself?"

Putting the petunias on hold for the time being, I followed Edie back into the front of the house. It was empty.

No sign of breasts or other jiggling body parts anywhere and only a faint whiff of Destiny's perfume. I almost sighed with relief but then I heard a noise coming from my office and Edie's evil grin morphed into a furious scowl.

She pushed past me and hurried through the door. "Destiny! What do you think you're doing?"

I could hear Destiny's voice, but I couldn't make out her reply.

"I told you to wait out here," Edie snapped. "This is Rita's private office. You have no business being in here." She turned back to me and muttered, "Some people. Can't trust them to do anything. I hope you're happy."

"Don't worry about her," I said quickly. "I'll have her work with me. You won't even know she's here."

Edie laughed through her nose. "Unbe*liev*able." She glanced at Destiny again and went back to her desk mumbling, "Have fun with that."

After a few seconds, Destiny strolled out of my office and into the reception area, blinking in the sudden glare of sunlight. Her hair was even more tousled than usual and her eyes were heavy. She made a sluggish effort to look excited, a far cry from how she'd looked only a few hours earlier. "Rita! I was just looking for you," she said in a voice so slurred and thick it sounded like she had marbles in her mouth. She dragged the strap of her purse onto her shoulder, but it slipped down again and she didn't seem to notice.

For the first time all morning, I got to ask the question of the day. "Are you all right?"

She laughed and took a couple of uneven steps toward Edie's desk. "I'm fine. Better than fine. I'm so glad you're letting me do this. I wanna make Moose proud of me."

"I'm sure he's proud already," I assured her, although I was almost positive that if I'd put "worn out by crazy wife" and "proud of wife's accomplishments" on a scale, the weary Moose would have won easily. "It's a little early," I said. "I wasn't expecting you until one o'clock. We're not quite ready for volunteers yet."

Destiny put a hand over her mouth and giggled. "Oops! Am I in trouble?"

Edie snorted again and turned away.

Which just made me want to show her how wrong she was. "Trouble?" I said with a friendly smile for Destiny. "No. It's just that I have some work to do before we can get started."

Destiny pulled the hand away from her mouth and flapped it around. "Oh, that's okay," she slurred. "I can wait right here. Edie and I can catch up."

"Over her dead body," Edie muttered.

I'm not sure Destiny heard her, but I got the message loud and clear. "Edie's really busy," I said. "Why don't you help me with some of the plans for this afternoon?"

I took Destiny by the arm and started walking her slowly toward the employee break room. She staggered a little and nearly ran into the wall. Okay, so maybe Edie was right. I wasn't sure what to do with someone who was so obviously under the influence. I didn't have time to babysit her, but I couldn't just let her wander around Zydeco on her own and I wouldn't feel right sending her out onto the street. She might be used to trolling the neighborhood in this condition, but I could almost hear Aunt Yolanda paraphrasing from the Bible in my ear, "Shut your ears to someone in need and God won't hear you when you're asking for help."

That wasn't a risk I was willing to take. I just hoped God wouldn't notice how much I resented having to devote attention to the woman in obvious need when I had so many other things I should be doing. I couldn't smell alcohol over her flowery cologne, so I had to assume she'd taken some kind of narcotic. In that case, would coffee help or just make things worse? Would it sober her up, or just wind her up?

I steered her toward a chair in the break room and put on a pot of coffee just in case.

She propped her chin in her hand and watched me. "You're nice, Rita."

I turned, surprised, and rummaged up a smile. "Thanks."

"I'm real sorry about what happened to you last night."

"Thanks. Me, too. I haven't had a chance to check on Moose. He didn't get hurt, did he?"

Destiny shook her head. "Naw. He's like a rock." She laughed softly and repeated, "Like a rock. Dumb as one, too, sometimes."

I blinked a couple of times as I tried to convince myself I'd heard wrong. "I'm sorry? I missed that."

Destiny grinned up at me. "Hey, I love the man. He's got a heart as big as . . . something really big. But sometimes he's one beer short of a six-pack, if you know what I mean."

Yeah? I'll bet I knew where the other five had gone. Moose had been nothing but nice to me, and my hackles rose in his defense. "That's a horrible thing to say," I told her. "He seems like a great guy."

Her arm wobbled and dropped to the table. Her head landed beside it, and she grinned up at me from behind a curtain of hair. "You want him? Go ahead."

"That's not what I meant!" I sat beside her and decided to stop dancing around the big pink elephant in the room. "What are you on, Destiny?"

She lifted her head and stared at me. "What do you mean?"

"I mean it's pretty obvious you're either drunk or high. Your words are slurred, you can barely sit up, and you're talking crazy. What did you take?"

Very slowly and carefully, she rose to her feet and glared down at me with as much dignity as she could muster. Which wasn't much. "You don't know what you're talking about. I took something for a headache, that's all."

"Yeah. Okay." Some headache. I stood to face her. "I know you were excited about helping with the collection this afternoon, but you can't do the work in this condition. I'm going to take you back to the Chopper Shop now. Maybe you can help out on another project."

I reached for her arm, but she jerked away from me so

fast she almost lost her balance again. "I'm fine. You just don't want me here."

There might have been some truth in that, but not the way she meant it. "I'd be happy to have you be part of the team, but clearly you're not feeling well today." Okay, so I fudged a little on the "happy to have you" part. But the rest was entirely truthful.

"I knew you wouldn't let me do this," she wailed. "I told Moose you were just like the others." She stumbled toward the door, ran into a table, and clutched a chair for support. "Remember when I said you were nice? Well, you're not. You're like all the rest of the assholes around here."

"Destiny, listen—"

"No, *you* listen." She squinted to focus on my face and jabbed a finger at me. "I've got something on my side for once. Something that's going to make a few people very sorry. And you'll be one of 'em." And then she squared up, found some balance, and ran from the room. I stood there for a second, arguing with myself about whether to follow her and make sure she was all right, or thank my lucky stars that I didn't have to sit here with her for the next two hours.

Guilt is a powerful master. I ought to know. I was raised on it. I couldn't just let Destiny wander off like that. Anything could happen to her.

But I want it on record that, so far, the day had been shaping up as one of my worst in recent memory. I couldn't have known then how much worse it would get before it was over.

Seven

Unfortunately, despite my best intentions to follow her, Destiny had disappeared by the time I made it to the front door, and Edie was no help at all in locating her. Eventually I went back to work in the design area and channeled all my guilt and frustration into the petunias. Bad idea. I overworked the buttercream and ended up with droopy petals on several of the flowers. The more mistakes I made, the worse I felt. Everyone has bad days in our industry. Things don't always work out perfectly. Fondant cracks, buttercream melts, cakes fall. But it's always maddening when it happens.

By noon, I had twenty-four usable petunias, ready for the finishing touches. In a perfect world, that would be enough, but it's always smart to make extras, just in case. I'd have to do that later, though. It was time to channel what little energy I had left into gathering supplies for the neighborhood cleanup.

I moved the flowers carefully out of the way where they wouldn't get bumped, limped into the break room for a Diet Coke, and then carried it back to my office. The muscles in my back and neck were screaming, and the scrapes on my arms and legs had started to burn. I'd have a quick lunch of pain pills and self-pity before shifting gears.

The past sixteen hours had been rough. People kept reminding me that I looked like death warmed over, and as the day dragged on, I was beginning to feel like it. And it was only half-over. I still had work to do prepping for the alliance cleanup. I didn't want to take Ox or Dwight off their jobs on the golf course cake, and I'd crossed Edie off the list of people I could put to work doing manual labor weeks ago. If she was even still speaking to me, she'd be coordinating our efforts from the comfort of a chair in the shade. I could only hope that I could enlist help from some of the other alliance members as they dropped by.

Sitting in my office chair, I looked around for the bags I'd picked up at the drugstore that morning. I thought I'd left them both on my desk, but only one—the one holding the Febreze and ibuprofen—was there now. I found my purse in its usual drawer, but the white prescription bag wasn't with it.

The bruises on my face throbbed and the headache I'd been trying to ignore for the past couple of hours took hold. I checked my desk, inside, out, and under. I pulled out my chair, pawed through a stack of files on the corner, and even looked inside the file cabinets, but I couldn't find the prescription anywhere. Terrific. Had the fall last night affected my memory?

After all that searching, I was too sore to walk all the way into the next room, so I speed-dialed Edie and said, "You didn't happen to see where I put the small bag from the drugstore, did you? I could have sworn I left it on my desk, but it's not here."

"You can't find it?" she asked. "Are you serious?"

"Unfortunately. Did you happen to see what I did with it?"

Edie disconnected with a click and came to the door so she could talk to me in person. "You didn't take it upstairs for your meeting with Miss Frankie, did you?"

"I'm almost positive I didn't," I said, trying to retrace my steps in my memory. "I thought I put it here in my office. My purse is here and so is the bag with the non-prescription things I bought, but the prescriptions are gone. I've looked everywhere. How could they just vanish into thin air?"

Edie leaned one hip against the door frame. "Maybe you did leave that bag here. Maybe somebody took it."

I looked up in surprise. "Nobody here would do something like that."

"I'm not saying it was one of *us*." The last word was heavy with meaning, but I was so tired and sore it took me a minute to grasp what she was saying.

"You think Destiny took it?"

Edie shrugged. "I found her sneaking around in your office. You tell me."

I thought about her dazed, unfocused eyes and slurred speech. I thought about her admission that she'd taken something for a "headache" and wondered if one of my pain pills could take effect that fast. I'd been raised to look for the best in people and always give the benefit of the doubt, and usually I tried. But under the circumstances, it was difficult to think the best of Destiny. "I think she has a serious problem," I said. "But Moose said she was changed."

Edie glanced over the top of my desk, probably to see if she could see the pills. I could tell she didn't expect to. "I have one word for you about that," she said when she'd satisfied her curiosity. "Relapse."

I felt a buzz of curiosity. I try not to gossip, but this was different. Two whole bottles of my prescription pills had disappeared. *And* the woman probably responsible for taking them was running for a position of responsibility, one that could affect the livelihoods of everyone in the neighborhood. I felt a duty to find out what Edie meant. "I guess that means that Destiny's had trouble with drugs before? I mean besides the arrest?"

"Duh! Why do you think she missed the first three alliance meetings?"

I took a guess. "Because she was high?" I couldn't say that I was surprised after what I'd witnessed in the break room, but I *was* surprised that no one had said anything about her problem last night. If Edie knew, then surely other people did. "Is that what Edgar meant when he said she'd been ill?"

"I'm sure it was. As far as I know, she doesn't have any other health issues—except the ones she makes up to get the drugs she wants." Edie lifted her chin and gave me a smug look. "Aquanettia told me a couple of months ago that Destiny was in rehab. Obviously, it didn't work."

I thought about Moose and felt a pang of sympathy. "Do you think her husband knows that she's using again?"

Edie shook her head. "Maybe. Maybe not. From what I've heard, he's been dealing with this for a while now. It's hard to imagine that he doesn't recognize the signs."

But he'd still asked me to let Destiny work here? That didn't seem very neighborly.

"I'm telling you, Rita, she's bad news. And if she actually wins the election next month, we're all in trouble."

"I don't think that will happen," I said. Inside I was arguing with myself about jumping to conclusions. I couldn't deny that Destiny had seemed to be under the influence of something, but maybe there was another, more innocent explanation.

We didn't get a chance to discuss it further. The front door opened and someone sang out, "Yoohoo! Anyone here?"

"Sounds like Aquanettia," Edie said, standing. "Are you ready for this, or do you want to sit it out?"

"And leave you to do it alone? You must be joking." I opened the bottle of ibuprofen. Swallowed two. Okay, three. And hoped they'd do the trick.

For the next hour, Edie directed traffic from a lawn chair on the loading dock and I stood by and gave her moral support. Aquanettia had taken one look at me and ordered

her son Isaiah to stay and do the heavy lifting. I was grateful for the help, but felt a little guilty at the same time.
None of the work would have been challenging under normal circumstances. I should have been able to stack a few
cases of water. But Isaiah seemed to be in front of me every
time I tried to help.

He was a good-looking young man, tall, with dark
mocha-colored skin and a broad, friendly smile. "Let me,
Miss Rita," he said for the hundredth time. "You shouldn't
be doing that heavy work, especially after what happened
last night."

I laughed and stepped away from the pallet. "I feel
useless just standing here. The water's not that heavy, and
there's not that else to do."

After spending the past half hour with Isaiah, I couldn't
seriously consider him a suspect in the almost-hit-and-run.
His brother Keon, now, was a different story. He'd come
with Aquanettia and Isaiah to deliver several cases of water,
a bag filled with boxed pastries from the dollar store, and
some rusty garden tools. While Isaiah had gone to work
with high spirits, his younger brother had grumbled louder
with every step. I wasn't sorry when Keon disappeared with
his mother. I just hoped Isaiah could tell me if I had anything to worry about where his brother was concerned.

Isaiah moved past me with a grin. "You aren't useless,
Miss Rita, but I do think you're trying to get my ass
whupped. That's what Mama'll do to me if you don't sit
down and let me move all this stuff where it goes."

I laughed softly. "Far be it from me to get you in trouble
with your mother. But are you sure you shouldn't be at
work? I hate to take you away from the store if your mom
needs you."

He shrugged and picked up two cases of water at the
same time. "It's not that busy today. I was supposed to pick
up a load of stuff from an estate sale, but I won't be able
to get over there until we get the van back anyway. Might
as well do something productive, right? You just sit down
and rest. I got this."

He disappeared into the storeroom, no doubt thinking the conversation was over, but he couldn't say something like that about the van and expect me to just sit there. I trailed after him and stood in the doorway while he stacked the water. "Something happened to your van?"

He stacked the water and turned back toward me with a slight frown. "Nobody told you?"

It felt like we were playing a game of twenty questions. I could have straight up asked him whether his van had been the one that almost hit me, but I really wanted to hear what he had to say on his own. So I took my turn at the game. "Told me what?"

Isaiah rubbed his face with one hand and his shoulders sagged. "Somebody stole the company van last night—right out of the parking lot."

Which meant that Edgar was right about what he saw. "Is it a plain white van?"

"Yeah. Just like the one that tried to hit you."

Had it really been stolen? Or was Isaiah trying to cover for someone else, like his brother? I tried to recall if Keon had been there at the time of the accident, but I couldn't remember seeing either of the brothers.

Isaiah didn't look like a crazed killer who'd offered to stack water so he could kill me on the loading dock, but crazy isn't as easy to spot as some people would like to believe.

"Did you report the van stolen?"

"Yes ma'am. Mama did that this morning, just as soon as we realized it was gone."

"You didn't realize it was missing last night? Didn't any of you recognize it as the van that almost hit Moose and me?"

Isaiah stuffed his hands into his pockets, but his shoulders tensed and he began to look uneasy. "We didn't have any reason to look. We weren't using it, and it's just plain white like a million others. Nothing special."

I didn't want to make him uncomfortable, but I wanted to eliminate the whole family as suspected killer van drivers if I could. "Do you have any idea who took it?"

Isaiah shook his head. "It could have been just about anybody. We always keep the van locked and the key behind the cash register, but Mama also keeps an extra key in a magnet box behind the tag. She started doing that a couple of months ago after Keon locked the keys inside. I told her to find a better hiding place. I said that's the first place somebody looking to steal a vehicle would look, but . . ." He gave an elaborate shrug and let me fill in the blanks for myself.

Obviously his mother had ignored his advice. "Did anyone else know the key was behind the license plate?"

"I don't know. Whoever Mama told, or whoever could've figured it out, I guess."

I assumed that included Keon, but I still couldn't imagine his reason for trying to run me down. He was little more than a kid. I don't think I'd ever had a conversation with him. The most we ever did was nod to acknowledge the other's presence. Okay, so I'm a lousy neighbor. Surely that wasn't a reason to try to kill me.

"Were you there last night?" I asked Isaiah.

"Yes ma'am. I was watching the store during y'all's meeting."

"So then you were inside when the van came around the corner? You didn't see what happened?"

"I didn't see anything but the taillights, and then you and Moose on the ground. *You* got any idea who did it?"

I shook my head. "It's a complete mystery." I wanted to believe him about the stolen van. A random act of violence by a complete stranger was more comforting than wondering if a neighbor had tried to kill me. A stranger might not feel compelled to come back and finish the job. "I'm sure it was an accident," I said, wishing I believed it. "Maybe somebody was in the process of stealing your van and panicked when he saw us all coming outside."

Isaiah nodded eagerly. "Yeah. I'll bet that's just what happened. Mama's fit to be tied about it, that's for sure. She says we're gonna make sure we get that neighborhood watch going just as soon as the election's over. If she wins, that is."

I didn't like thinking we needed to take that step, but maybe Aquanettia was right.

Isaiah jerked his chin toward the cases of water behind me. "It's getting late. I should finish moving those for you."

He hadn't completely set my concerns to rest, but I didn't want to push too hard and make him nervous, so I left him to work.

He disappeared into the storage shed with the last two cases of water and reappeared a minute later, empty-handed. Glancing my way, he sketched a salute and ambled off down the driveway.

I wanted to believe the stolen van theory, but I had a gut feeling there was more to last night's incident. I just hoped that my gut wasn't sending me on a wild-goose chase.

Eight

The rest of the day passed by quickly, interrupted only by a call from the police telling me that the van had been found in a park near the Mississippi River but that they hadn't recovered any evidence that would identify the driver. I drove home after work, soaked my aching body in a hot bath, and climbed into bed before the late news came on. Next morning, I felt even worse than I had the day before. I seriously considered calling in sick, but two things stopped me. One, we had way too much work to do (for which I was extremely grateful); and two, if I stayed home, I wouldn't be able to ask more people what they'd seen the night of the accident. The more I thought about that van almost hitting Moose and me, the more I wanted to know who was behind the wheel and why we'd been turned into a couple of bull's-eyes.

I pulled into the parking lot behind Zydeco a little after eight and climbed out into the already-steaming morning. It had taken me a few minutes to ease into the car, and it took just as long to get out again. I was just straightening my back when I heard rapid footsteps and spotted Zora Rappaport from the Feathered Peacock coming down the driveway toward me. She wore a pair of brilliant blue leggings beneath an oversized tie-dyed shirt and a matching headband holding back her thin blond hair. She waved one hand over her head to get my attention, and called out, "Rita? You got a minute?"

I leaned against the car and waited for her to close the distance. "This is a surprise," I said. "Your studio doesn't open until later, right?"

Zora looked pleased that I'd paid that much attention. "Doors open at ten on the dot. First class at eleven. I have to pick up a few things from the market before the workday starts. Since I'm here, I thought I'd stop by to see how you're doing. I tried all day yesterday to get over here but one thing and another kept getting in my way." She took me by the shoulders and looked me over thoroughly. "Unbelievable, that's what it is. Absolutely unbelievable."

"I'm having a little trouble processing it myself," I said with a grimace.

"What do the police say? Have they found the driver?"

I shook my head. "They don't know much, I'm afraid. I've been trying to find witnesses who might help identify the driver, but so far nobody has seen anything. Were you there? Did you see the guy who was driving?"

Zora's big open face clouded. She glanced around, spotted the chair Edie had used the previous afternoon, and tugged me toward it. "Come over here. I need to sit a spell." When she was comfortably situated, she said, "I wasn't there, unfortunately. I mean, not unfortunately in that I didn't get to see you almost hit by that van, but unfortunately because I can't help you. I didn't see anything. I only heard about it yesterday morning. Everybody was talking about it. So you don't know who was driving?"

It seemed to me I'd answered that question already, but Zora has always seemed a little flighty so I wasn't surprised I had to answer it again. I hitched myself onto a couple of boxes stacked in the corner. "I didn't see anything, really. Everything I know I've heard from someone else."

Zora tsked and wagged her head slowly. "Well, it's just

awful. I couldn't believe it when I heard. Scotty said—you know Scotty, don't you? From the Chopper Shop?"

"Destiny's father? Of course. I didn't realize he was there. Maybe I should add him to my list of possible witnesses."

Frowning slightly, Zora leaned forward to touch my hand. "Maybe you should leave this to the police. After all, if somebody was trying to hit you, looking into it could be dangerous."

"I'm not convinced that I was the intended target," I said.

Zora gasped and drew her hand away. "Whatever do you mean?"

"There were two of us standing there. What if somebody was trying to hurt Moose?"

"Moose?" Zora said with a laugh. "Why would anyone want to hurt him?"

"I don't know yet," I admitted. "And maybe I'm completely wrong about that, but I don't know anyone who would want to hurt me either!"

Zora put one hand on her tie-dyed chest and leaned back in her chair. "Well, for the record, Moose is a wonderful young man who deserves much better than he's got."

She'd said something similar at the alliance meeting, and after yesterday's encounter with the strung-out Mrs. Hazen, I had to admit, I was curious about their marriage. Again, a little tug of guilt over gossiping almost stopped me, but again I excused it away as my civic duty. If Destiny wanted my vote, then I needed to know more about her before I could decide whether or not to give it to her. "Are you talking about his wife?"

Zora slid a look at me. I could see disapproval in her eyes, but I wasn't sure if it was directed at Destiny or at me. "I don't like speaking ill of people," she said after a moment. "But that woman is nothing but trouble."

"Trouble for Moose?"

"Trouble for everyone she comes in contact with." Zora caught herself, smiled, and changed her tone. "She means well, bless her heart. And I think she does try. But she's made life a living hell for poor Moose. And Scotty . . . well, she's broken his heart more than once. All he wants is to make up for the past, but she . . ." She shook her head sadly. "But I'm not one to talk behind someone's back. You won't catch me telling tales."

No, of course not. I swallowed a grin and said, "Moose seems to love her."

"Oh, he does. The poor thing is smitten, though only the good Lord knows what he sees in her."

Like the cartoon of the devil on one shoulder and an angel on the other, my two sides went to war. Destiny's family issues were none of my business. Aunt Yolanda would have sent me to my room for asking about them. But the woman had stolen my pain pills. I was convinced of it. Didn't I deserve to understand why? Didn't I need to know what kind of person she was so I could decide what to do about it?

I fought the urge to gossip, holding out as long as I could (roughly two seconds), but finally I blurted out, "Someone told me that Destiny was in rehab. Is that true?"

Zora looked surprised, but she nodded and sighed softly and studied her hands in her lap. "It nearly killed Scotty to see his little girl go through that, but she was sinking fast. Drinking and running around and using Lord knows what. He and Moose staged the intervention, you know. They could see the writing on the wall." She flicked a glance at me and changed the subject. "But that's neither here nor there. I came to see how *you're* doing."

"Sore and bruised," I said, masking my disappointment, "but otherwise okay."

"I'm just as glad as I can be to hear it. I could hardly sleep last night, thinking you might be seriously hurt."

"Well, now you know. It's nothing to lose sleep over." I wanted to steer the conversation back to Destiny or the accident, but Zora stood up before I could find a way to do it.

"I made some oatmeal raisin cookies last night. I meant

to bring you a plate, but I ran out the door without them. I'm taking some to Scotty so I'll stop by later if you plan to be here."

I smiled at the offer. "Thanks, but you don't need to do that."

"I insist," she said as she headed for the loading dock steps. "Sometimes these things just take a little TLC."

Was she talking about my scrapes and bruises? Or about Scotty? She certainly seemed interested in him, which I found kind of cute. But I wondered how he'd feel about her discussing his personal family problems with me. On the other hand, I also wondered what it was that he wanted to make up for from the past. And whatever Destiny's daddy issues might be, whether they'd led to her drug abuse. I could almost hear Aunt Yolanda telling me to get my nose out of their business, but I paid no attention. Destiny's relationship with Scotty and the state of her marriage had nothing to do with the Magnolia Square Business Alliance or the upcoming elections, but they might have everything to do with why she'd stolen from me.

I should have known better. Ignoring Aunt Yolanda is never a good idea.

After Zora left, I tried to focus on making more petunias. Really, I did. I worked slowly, holding the flower nail just so and concentrating on the wrist action as I worked loops with the piping bag. But my conversation with Zora kept nagging at me, and the more I thought about Destiny and the missing prescription, the angrier I got.

I don't have a lot of experience with drug addicts, but I'd had a couple of school friends who'd had drug problems. The one thing I knew for sure was that most addicts think they're smarter than everyone around them. Destiny thought she'd gotten away with taking my pain pills. She probably thought I hadn't even connected her with the theft; or that if I had, I was too afraid or too polite to say anything about it.

Ha! I had news for her!

The angrier I got, the jerkier my movements became until I ended up scraping more lopsided petunias back into the buttercream bowl than I set aside to use on the cake. I swore under my breath and scraped yet another flower off its foil-lined nail. It fell into the bowl with a plop. I tossed the used square of foil into the trash and reached for a fresh piece.

"Maybe you ought to take a break," Ox said.

I glanced up, surprised to find him standing beside my workstation wearing a worried frown. Ox is one of my closest friends in New Orleans, but we've also hit a few rough patches in the past year. He'd come to Louisiana to help Philippe open Zydeco, so after Philippe died, Ox had expected to take over running the operation. Instead, Miss Frankie had given me the job and made me her partner. Sometimes Ox still tries to show us all that he would have been the better choice, which makes me a little touchy.

"I'm fine," I said. "Just having a bad day."

"So maybe you should take a break. Get some fresh air. Cool down for fifteen minutes and come back to it."

He was right, but I bristled at him telling me what to do. "I can do this," I snapped. "Just back off."

"It's not a question of whether or not you can," Ox said gently. "You're good at what you do, Rita, and everybody knows it. But it's clear to me that you need a break. Nobody here will think less of you if you take a minute and get some air."

The stubborn twelve-year-old inside, the orphan girl who worried about being good enough, wanted to argue with him, but he was being so nice I warned her to be quiet and answered with my adult side. "Maybe you're right," I said, stripping off my chef jacket and tossing it onto a stool. "I'll be back in a minute."

I hit the street five minutes later, with no clear idea where I was going. Or maybe I knew exactly where I was going. I just hadn't acknowledged it to myself. What I definitely didn't know was what a big mistake I was about to make.

Nine

Bright lights burned at the Chopper Shop, which seemed odd since the sun was up. I had expected to find Moose working, but in spite of the fact that every light inside the place was on and stadium-type lighting flooded the parking lot, the shop appeared deserted. Even Scotty's lawn chair sat empty in the parking lot with only a trash bag of empty beer cans to show that he'd ever been there at all. I fought down an uneasy feeling and told myself to get a grip, that I was just edgy from the almost-hit-and-run and the possibility that someone might have done it on purpose.

I looked into the three open bays—empty—then stepped into a small, greasy-smelling office. Half a dozen clipboards crammed full of invoices hung from hooks on a wall, and an open package of snack cakes and two half-empty cups of coffee in take-out cups acted as paperweights for another stack of paper. A cell phone lay half-buried under junk mail, and a pair of pale blue stilettos had been kicked off under the desk.

"Hello? Moose? Destiny? Is anyone here?" The echo of my voice bounced back at me, and the only other sound I could hear was the scuff of my own feet on the concrete floor. Strange. I figured that Moose was probably working in the back, and I moved through the office toward a door I assumed led outside. Instead, I found myself in a dim storage warehouse. Somewhere in the distance, I could hear soft music playing. It seemed to be coming from the far side of the space, so I walked slowly past several rows of shelves stacked high with motorcycle parts, a pile of greasy rags, and a gas can. Poking around on my own made me a little uncomfortable, but I was determined to let Destiny know that I was onto her. I might not get my prescription back, but maybe I could convince her not to take advantage of other neighbors in the future.

I followed the music to a small closet. The door was partially open and a sliver of light fell across the floor. The music was louder back here, but I still couldn't see anyone so I called out again. "Destiny? Moose? Is anybody here?"

Not a peep.

Where had everyone gone? I couldn't imagine Moose leaving the store unlocked, doors open, and lights on, but why wasn't anyone here?

I started to turn away, but something stopped me in my tracks. It took a minute for me to realize that I'd caught a whiff of a faint odor. Perfume. Destiny must be around somewhere, but why didn't she answer me?

I took a couple of steps into the closet and spotted a shadow edging out from behind a tall stack of boxes. Three more steps and I realized it was a foot. A bare foot. The bare foot of a woman who lay on her back, unmoving, her face turned to one side, eyes wide open as if she were looking at me. But I knew at once that she couldn't see anything at all. Her vacant stare told me that Destiny Hazen was dead.

I froze in place for what felt like forever while my mind took in details I knew I'd be asked to recount. She was wearing almost the same thing she'd been wearing yesterday—black leather shorts and a pale blue tank top. Her legs were bent at the knee. One hand lay on her stomach, the other stretched away from her body.

Shaking like a leaf, I told myself she might still be alive, but her complexion looked gray and waxy, and when I worked up enough courage to check for a pulse, her skin felt cold to the touch. I pulled out my cell phone and punched in 911, but just before I touched the "send" button, I realized that Destiny was clutching something in the hand on her stomach. An amber-colored vial with a white lid.

I stopped myself from pushing the button and tried to convince myself she wasn't holding a prescription bottle—or at least that it wasn't one of the bottles that had mysteriously disappeared from Zydeco. If she'd stolen drugs from me, she'd probably taken pills from other people. Right? But what if that *was* my bottle in her hand? Had my pills killed her?

My heart raced and my mind stuttered while I tried to figure out what to do. I knew her death wasn't my fault. I didn't even know yet how she'd died, but I battled guilt anyway. I didn't think the empty pill bottle in her hand was a coincidence. Maybe, if I'd been more careful with the prescriptions, she'd still be alive.

Tears welled in my eyes as I dialed 911 again and this time I pressed the green "send" button. I wanted to call Sullivan. If ever I needed his six feet of Southern charm, I needed it now. But he was out in the middle of the Gulf of Mexico, fishing.

The dispatcher asked me to wait outside, a request I complied with happily. I called Ox to let him know that I'd be delayed and sat in Scotty's chair to wait for the police. A cruiser arrived about twenty minutes later and two uniformed officers took my initial statement. They took down my contact information and asked me to stick around while they went inside. I was tired, achy, and sad, and I just wanted to get back to Zydeco. But I settled down in Scotty's chair again. Destiny and I hadn't been friends, but I hated thinking of her last moments on earth. Had she taken an overdose on purpose, or had she accidentally taken too many pills? Maybe she'd unknowingly swallowed a lethal combination. I felt bad about sending her away yesterday, and I kept hearing her telling me that I wasn't a nice person after all.

A long time later, a dark-colored Crown Vic pulled up to the curb and a heavyset man climbed out. He had a prominent nose and a ring of black hair circling his massive head. He wore a sloppy tan suit, a wrinkled white shirt, and scuffed brown shoes. Columbo for the new millennium.

He stood on the sidewalk, taking stock of the scene and hitching up his ill-fitting pants every few minutes. I'm just going to say that the man was no Sullivan. Not even close.

After a quick briefing from the uniforms, he disappeared into the building. He reemerged a while later and talked to Moose, who apparently had arrived at some point. The poor man looked shocked. Drained. As if losing his wife had sapped the life out of him.

When the Columbo clone finished with Moose, he lumbered across the parking lot to me. "Miss Lucero? Detective Aaron Winslow, Narcotics Division. Could I have a word?"

I nodded and shook his hand. He took a long hard look at the bruises on my cheek and jaw. "Looks like you got on the wrong side of somebody," he said. "You okay?"

"Yeah," I said. "Fine."

"You want to tell me about how it happened?"

Now? With a dead woman lying just a few feet away? I shrugged. "Somebody in a van tried to take me out Monday night. I was outside talking to Moose, the guy who owns this shop, and he pushed me out of the way. Moose saved my life, but I got a little banged up in the process. How is he taking the news about his wife?"

Detective Winslow gave me a sharp look. "Rough." He hooked his thumbs in his waistband, nudging his pants a couple inches down in the process. "Is there any special reason you ask?"

"About Moose? His wife just died. I just wondered how he's holding up."

"He'll be fine. Is that why you're here this morning? To see him?"

I shook my head. "I came to talk to Destiny."

Winslow glanced up from his notes. "Again, I wonder— was there some special reason you wanted to see her?"

I hesitated to admit the truth, but Destiny was dead. There was no reason to protect her reputation now. "She was at my bakery yesterday. After she left, I realized that my pain pills and my antibiotics were missing. She's the only one who could have taken them. I just wanted her to know that I knew what she'd done."

"I see. So what happened then? The two of you have an argument?"

"No! She was dead when I got here. I called 911 and came outside to wait."

Winslow arched an eyebrow. "That's all?"

"That's all."

"What were you doing inside the building?"

"Looking for Destiny, or Moose—or anybody, really. I heard music coming from the storage room and that's how I found her."

His eyebrow arched another fraction of an inch. "So Mr. Hazen saved your life night before last while the two of you just happened to be having a private conversation. Late at night. His wife came to see you yesterday and left with a couple of bottles of your pills. You came here this morning to see her and now she's dead. Do I have that right?"

I blinked a couple of times and shook my head. "No. I mean, yes. But *no*! It wasn't like that at all."

"Mr. Hazen didn't save your life?"

"Yes. I just told you he did."

"But you didn't come here to talk to him alone. Before the shop opened."

"No. And the shop *was* open when I got here. And I told you, I didn't come to see him. I wanted to talk to Destiny."

"I see," Winslow said with a smirk that told me he didn't believe a word I'd said. Maybe honesty wasn't such a great policy after all. "Did Mrs. Hazen happen to tell you about a conversation she had with me Monday evening?"

I started to shake my head, then remembered someone at the meeting saying that Destiny had been talking to a police officer. "She didn't say anything to me," I said, trying to recall just what she had said. "But she told everyone at the meeting that she might not have to go to court if she played her cards right."

His gaze locked on mine. He didn't look happy. "Did she now?"

"Yes, but that's all she said." And then I remembered what she'd said to me at Zydeco and added, "Except she did tell me yesterday that she had something in the works that would make a few people sorry, but I have no idea what she meant by that."

"She didn't tell you that the district attorney offered her a lesser charge if she'd give us the name of her dealer?"

That was big. I got an uneasy feeling as I remembered the two half-empty coffee cups on the desk. "Do you think she told her dealer about the offer?"

"That's what I'd like to know." He stared at me without blinking for so long I started getting nervous.

"I don't know what she told anyone else," I said. "I can only tell you what she said to me."

"Mmm-hmmm. Tell me, how long have you and Mr. Hazen been seeing each other?"

"What?"

"You and Moose," he said with a nod at the big man across the parking lot.

My head began to buzz and my heart thumped around in my chest. "We are not, and never have been, an item. We're barely even friendly. We just happen to be members of the same business alliance and were at the same meeting on Monday night."

Winslow's eyebrows beetled up onto his forehead again. "Oh? And where was that?"

I nodded toward Second Chances. "At the thrift shop next door. We left the meeting at the same time. While we were talking, the van came around the corner and he shoved me out of the way."

Winslow pulled a notebook from his wrinkled shirt pocket and made a note. "So tell me about what happened here this morning. What time did you get here?"

I wasn't sure he believed me, but at least he'd moved to a different line of questioning. "About an hour ago. You can check the time of the 911 call. I was here for maybe ten minutes before I placed the call."

"Mrs. Hazen was holding a prescription bottle when she died," Winslow said. "Any idea whose prescription it was?"

I laughed nervously. "I already told you that she came by Zydeco yesterday and that my prescriptions disappeared from my office. I have to assume the bottle was one of mine?"

He gave me a thin-lipped smile that practically screamed, *Liar!* "How many pills were in the bottle the last time you saw it?"

I had to think about that. I hadn't really paid attention. "I don't know. Twenty? Thirty? I just had it filled that morning. I hadn't taken any of them, so whatever the prescription called for, that's how many there were. How many are there now?"

"The bottle in her hand—one of yours—is empty. And you say you know nothing about that?"

"Of course not. I told you, she was dead when I found her and I didn't touch anything except her wrist to check for a pulse. I thought maybe I could help her." His questions and his attitude were making me nervous. "Can I leave now? I need to get back to work."

His eyebrows jumped again. "Oh, I'm sorry. Is my little investigation inconveniencing you?" He slipped the notebook into his pocket and took a step backward. "By all means, Ms. Lucero. You're free to go . . . for now."

Winslow's sarcasm made me nervous, but I didn't let that slow me down. I turned around and walked away just as fast as I could.

The neighborhood was buzzing as I hurried away from the Chopper Shop. I'd been gone for at least an hour, and in that time people had arrived for work, noticed the unusual activity, and gathered on the corner to watch. I had to pass them, but I kept my head down and tried to avoid making eye contact with anyone. Finding Destiny and then talking to Detective Winslow had rattled me. I wasn't in the mood to talk about what had happened.

I heard my name but I pretended not to and successfully skirted the group of curious bystanders. As I was about to cross the street, I saw Ox coming down the sidewalk toward me. He looked worried, which was understandable considering the call I'd made earlier. When he saw me, he kicked up his pace and jogged across the intersection.

"What are you doing here?" I asked when he reached me.

He gave me a quick once-over and then turned to check out the Chopper Shop. "It's been an hour since you called. I came to make sure you're all right. You sounded pretty shaken up on the phone." Seeing the concern in his eyes made me feel like a jerk for being so short with him earlier.

"Well. Yeah. I guess I am," I said. Now that I was with a friend, my hands began to tremble and my legs felt weak. "It was awful."

"So she's really . . ." He glanced around to see if anyone was listening. "You know."

Nobody appeared to be paying attention to the two of us, but I kept my own voice low just in case. "Yeah. I found her inside."

Ox scowled so hard his forehead wrinkled. "How?"

"I don't know for sure, but I think she may have overdosed."

Ox stared down at his feet for a long moment. "How's Moose taking it?"

"I didn't get a chance to talk to him," I said. "The police kept us both busy with questions. I saw him from a distance, though, and he looked pretty rough."

"I can imagine." Ox rubbed the back of his neck with one hand. "I wish I could say that it's a shock, but it's not. Destiny's been messed up ever since I came here."

Maybe so, but I doubted that made the reality of her death any easier for Moose. "I feel just awful. I should have gone after her when she left Zydeco yesterday. She was in bad shape then. I knew it and I just let her go. I didn't try hard enough to find out where she'd gone."

"You're not seriously blaming yourself, are you? You couldn't have known this was going to happen."

"I guess not. But I can't help thinking I should have done something more. I don't know if Edie told you, but Destiny took some pills out of my office yesterday. One of the bottles was in her hand when she died. That means my prescription might have been the drugs that killed her."

Ox put a hand on my shoulder. "That still doesn't make this your fault, Rita. Maybe it was your prescription but you didn't force her to take the pills."

I gave him a shaky smile. "Tell that to the detective over there," I said, jerking my chin toward Detective Winslow. "He thinks I gave her the drugs."

Ox snorted a laugh that was loud enough to make a few people turn to look at us. "Oh, come on! Be serious."

"I *am*," I said in a harsh whisper. "He pretty much accused me of being her dealer."

"Obviously, the man's an idiot or he's just talking off the top of his head. He'll probably forget all about you in ten minutes."

I sure hoped he was right.

"Come on," Ox said, slinging his arm around my shoulder. "I'll walk back to Zydeco with you."

We turned to go and I realized that the crowd on the corner had almost doubled in size while we'd been talking. I caught a glimpse of Edgar Zappa at the edge of the crowd, watching the scene unfolding from behind a pair of sunglasses, and I felt a pang of sympathy for him. I didn't know for sure if he and Destiny had been having an affair, but what if they had been? I didn't want him to hear about her death through word on the street. That seemed cruel.

I tugged on Ox's sleeve. "There's Edgar. I want to talk to him for a minute before we go back to work."

"Edgar? Now? What's he got to do with all of this?"

"He and Destiny were friends," I said, downplaying the

relationship I suspected between them. "He has to be curious about what's going on."

"Everybody here is curious," Ox pointed out. "But okay. Let's talk to Edgar."

I'd have preferred to have the conversation without Ox, but I didn't know how to say so without making him wonder why. Nothing would be gained by starting rumors flying now, so I bit my tongue and made my way through the crowd with Ox behind me. Edgar stood on the curb, his blond hair tousled by the light morning breeze. I touched his elbow lightly to get his attention.

He whipped around to face me. "Oh. Rita. Ox. Looks like there's some excitement at the Chopper Shop this morning. Any idea what's going on over there?"

"Yeah," I said. "As a matter of fact, I do. Could I talk to you for a minute?"

He studied my face silently for a moment. At least, I think he did. All I could see was my reflection in his sunglasses. "Sure," he said. "What's up?"

"Not here," I said. "Too many people. Let's take a walk."

His mouth set in a firm line and he looked back at the Chopper Shop as if he was reluctant to leave. Finally, he shoved his hands into his pockets and gave a firm nod. "If you say so. Lead the way."

I waited to speak until we'd put the crowd behind us and I was pretty sure nobody could hear us. Even then it wasn't easy to find the right words. "There's no easy way to say this," I said. "And I might be crossing a line by saying anything at all, but I know that you and Destiny . . ." I trailed off, took a deep breath, and tried again. "The police are at the Chopper Shop because I found Destiny there this morning. She's gone."

"What do you mean gone?"

"I mean . . . I tried to help her, but it was too late."

Edgar's jaw tightened visibly as realization slowly dawned. He looked from me to Ox and back again. "Are you telling me she's dead?"

I nodded sadly. "I haven't said anything to anyone else.

I don't want word to get out before Moose can notify the rest of her family. But I know that the two of you were friends and I thought you should know."

Edgar pushed his sunglasses to the top of his head. His eyes were such a pale blue they were a little disconcerting. "But how? What happened?"

"The police think she may have overdosed," I said. "She had a bottle of pills in her hand."

"But that's impossible. She wasn't using."

"I'm afraid she was," I said. "She came to Zydeco yesterday to help with the collection of supplies for the neighborhood cleanup, but I had to send her away because she was obviously high on something."

Edgar shook his head firmly. "No. That's not possible. I talked to her yesterday morning. She was doing fine. She wouldn't have—" He cut himself off and rubbed his face with both hands. "She wouldn't have," he said again.

"But she did," I said. "I talked to her, Edgar. She could barely stand up straight and her words were slurred. She was on something, and she admitted to taking something for a headache."

"But she was so excited to help. She thought that would make certain people change their opinions about her. She wouldn't have risked messing that up."

Ox stepped into the conversation for the first time. "Hey. I know it's a shock. Maybe you didn't know her as well as you thought you did."

Way to be sensitive, Ox. I tried to dilute the sting of his comment with a reassuring smile. "What Ox means is that maybe something happened between the time you saw her yesterday and the time she came to help out. Maybe something upset her. If everything was okay between the two of you, maybe she had an issue with somebody else."

Edgar nodded almost absently. "Everything was fine with the two of us. We had breakfast yesterday. We were going to meet today for lunch. Things were finally looking up for her. She had no reason to start using again."

"Sometimes addiction is just too strong," Ox said. "Even if things are going well, a person just needs that fix."

Edgar shook his head. "It wasn't like that for her. Not this time." He paced the width of the sidewalk several times as he processed what we were telling him. His internal struggle was hard to watch. "This doesn't make sense," he said after several laps. "This doesn't make any sense at all. What was she even doing here this morning? She doesn't work this early. She's not a morning person."

"I wish I could tell you," I said. "All I know is that I got there a little before nine. All the lights were on and all the bays were open. She was in the back."

Edgar stopped pacing. "Where was Moose?"

"I didn't see him until after the police arrived," I said. "So Destiny didn't tell you that she was coming in early this morning?"

"No." He wiped his face with one hand and let out a heavy breath. "Last time I talked to her, she said she was going to her yoga class and then she was going to help you at Zydeco. She was excited about both things. The yoga was helping keep her centered and away from the drugs. Volunteering with the alliance was going to help change her image."

He clearly wanted to believe the best of her so desperately I didn't have the heart to tell him again how wrong he was. The truth was that she'd been high when I saw her yesterday. She'd stolen my pills. Ox was right. The addiction had been stronger than she was. But I didn't say anything more.

After a minute Edgar pulled his sunglasses from the top of his head and wiped the lenses with the hem of his shirt. "You think I'm being naïve."

"I think you're being a loyal friend."

He managed a thin smile. "Yeah. Maybe I just feel guilty. I just don't know how I could have missed that she was slipping."

"She probably didn't want you to know," Ox said. "She had plenty of practice hiding her addiction. Maybe she thought she could handle it. You know . . . keep it under control or something."

Edgar stopped polishing and looked up at the two of us. The sadness in his eyes was almost palpable. "Yeah. Maybe." He put his glasses back on. "I've got to go," he said suddenly. "Thanks for telling me about Destiny." And then he hurried off down the sidewalk, leaving Ox and me staring after him.

"That was tough," I said after a moment.

Ox nodded. "Yeah. He seems pretty torn up about it. Are you sure they were just friends?"

"I'm not sure of anything," I admitted. "But I don't want to make this all harder on Moose."

Ox nodded. "Gotcha. My lips are sealed."

I started walking toward Zydeco, ready to put the whole morning out of my mind. As if I could. But the more I thought about Edgar's reaction, the more it bothered me. Maybe he was lying. Maybe he felt responsible for her death because the two of them had had an argument yesterday and now he was racked with guilt.

Ox frowned down at me and said, "You're still thinking about Edgar. I can feel it."

"I can't help it. There's something wrong with this whole scenario."

"Yeah. A woman is dead. From an overdose."

"It's more than that," I said, batting his arm lightly. "Something doesn't add up."

"Not your problem."

"I know, but—"

Ox stopped walking and took me by the shoulders. "Not your problem, Rita. Leave it alone. Please. We have a lot of work on the schedule and I need you to be focused on Zydeco, not chasing down bad guys."

Way to ruin a moment. I made a face at him. "I am focused, okay? Don't worry about me."

And I was. Really.

At least, I would be.

Ten

I spent the rest of the morning pretending to take care of some paperwork in the office. By afternoon I felt normal enough to go back to work on the petunias. I piped the remaining blossoms and set them aside to dry, and I pretended not to be thinking about Edgar's reaction to Destiny's death. That wasn't easy since word had spread around Zydeco. Destiny, her drug habit, her stint in rehab, and the state of her marriage were the only things anyone wanted to talk about.

I was feeling edgy and raw, and I kept hoping the others would run out of steam and move on. But after a couple of hours I banned the subject for the rest of the day and told them to let the poor woman rest in peace. After that, they only spoke about it in whispers or when they thought I couldn't hear. And they moved on to my next least favorite topic—the near hit-and-run Monday night.

"Don't you think it's odd," Estelle asked as she sculpted a miniature golfer from gum paste, "that we've had two horrible tragedies in less than forty-eight hours? It's enough to make a person nervous."

Dwight was still working on carving the golf course,

but he shot Estelle a look from across the room. "Don't worry too much. It's not contagious."

Estelle rolled her eyes in exasperation. "Well, I know *that*. But they do say that bad things happen in threes. What's next? That's what makes me worry."

Ox laughed and shook his head. "Superstitious nonsense. There's nothing to it."

"But it's true!" Sparkle insisted. "It happens all the time. Like when my brother left home and my mom broke her arm, and then three goats from the commune died all in the same week."

Ox's expression sobered but his eyes danced with amusement. "I stand corrected. Never let it be said that I argued with dead goats."

"Very funny," Sparkle said with a frown. "I'm just saying that Estelle might be right. We should all be careful."

Isabeau frowned thoughtfully as she crossed the room for a mixing bowl. "Wouldn't it be weird if the two things were related somehow? Like, I don't know, like if somebody is trying to get rid of Moose and Destiny for some reason?"

Ox turned to give her a warning glare. "Do *not* go there."

"I'm just saying it would be weird," Isabeau countered. "Does anybody hate the two of them?"

Okay. I'll admit the question intrigued me. "Not that I know of. But as far as I know, nobody hates me either, yet several people have said the van looked like it was trying to hit me."

Estelle gave Ox and Dwight a stern look. "See?" As if my comment proved her point. "What if Isabeau is right? What if somebody has it in for Moose and Destiny? What if Moose is still in danger? Somebody ought to warn him."

"Somebody should keep her nose out of other people's business." Ox was speaking to Estelle, but he looked right at me. "It's none of our concern."

"How can you say that?" Isabeau demanded. "This whole

thing started when somebody tried to kill Rita. They could still be after her. I think that makes it our business."

Ox disagreed, and said so in no uncertain terms. But the conversation started me thinking. What if they were right? What if someone had tried to kill *me* with those prescriptions? What if Moose really was in danger? Even after the conversation moved on to safer topics, I was still chewing on the idea. I knew I was going to have to do something, but I couldn't just walk away from work. I finally finished my petunias for the Oakes baptism cake, and then spent the afternoon tinting fondant a pale shade of blue, rolling it out until it was barely an eighth-inch thick, and then cutting a hundred ovals with a cookie cutter. Tomorrow, I would attach the medallions to all three layers of the cake and add detailing to the petunias, and do some piping work, but overall I was pleased with my progress and glad that, in spite of everything, I'd managed to catch up. That would show Ox how focused I was!

At seven that evening, I locked up behind the rest of the staff, after looking up Moose's home address in the Magnolia Square Business Alliance directory. I was reluctant to intrude on their grief so soon, but I felt I owed Moose something for saving my life. I couldn't just let him walk around oblivious to the possibility of danger.

The Hazens lived in a small white frame house in a depressed neighborhood off Opelousas. Cars lined both sides of the street and yellowing lawns sat border to border with yards overgrown with weeds. I spotted their house easily, thanks to the two motorcycles in the driveway and a third on the lawn. This neighborhood was more similar to the one I'd grown up in than the one I lived in now, but my inherited Mercedes was out of place. I nosed it into an empty spot a block from the house and walked back.

My bruises had faded a bit and so had some of the stiffness and swelling, but that didn't mean I looked ready to go out in public. The surreptitious glances I got from two middle-aged women chatting at the end of a driveway made that abundantly clear.

Now that I was here, I started having second thoughts about my plan. Maybe I *should* keep my nose out of it. Maybe Winslow would warn Moose to be careful. Or maybe he'd warn him to be careful of me. I had a negative gut feeling about Winslow, and I'd learned to listen when my gut started talking.

Taking a deep breath for courage, I climbed the steps and rang the bell. I heard voices, and a few seconds later, Scotty Justus opened the door. His graying ponytail was lopsided and his yellow Hawaiian print shirt and khaki shorts seemed oddly cheerful for a man whose daughter had just died.

His looked me over with grief-glazed eyes. "Yeah?"

"I don't know if you remember me," I said. "I'm Rita Lucero. I run the cake shop just down the street from the Chopper Shop. I'm the one who . . ."

Scotty dipped his head slightly. "I know who you are. You found Destiny this morning. What do you want?"

All the openings I'd practiced on my way across town evaporated in the face of his anger and pain. "I—I just wanted to say how sorry I am for your loss. I know you must be devastated."

Scotty gave me an odd look. "Yeah, you could say that. Look, I'm sure you mean well but this isn't really a good time."

He was right. I shouldn't have come. I stammered an apology and turned to go as Zora swept up behind him and came to my rescue. I was surprised to see her there, especially after the way she'd talked about Destiny at the alliance meeting, but Scotty seemed comfortable with her, so who was I to judge?

She'd changed out of the blue tie-dye and now wore plain black slacks with a flower print shirt. Her hair was held back by a couple of mismatched barrettes. "Goodness, Scotty, don't keep Rita standing outside on the porch all evening." She nudged him out of the way and ushered me inside to a small kitchen. Moose sat at the table in front of a spiral pad filled with notes and numbers.

I couldn't read the notations, but I knew what they were. Death is not only emotionally devastating, it's also a lot of work. There are calls to make and people to notify. Travel plans to coordinate and a funeral to organize. The obituary to write and countless forms to fill out. I guess it's a good thing, in a strange way. Having something to do can keep grief from swallowing your mind whole.

Moose held his head in both hands, his pain palpable even from a distance. Zora motioned me toward a chair across from him. Scotty stalked to the fridge for a beer.

Zora sent Scotty a fond smile and put a hand on Moose's shoulder as she passed. "It was sweet of you to come by, Rita," she said. "Especially considering everything you've been through the past couple of days. How are you feeling?"

What could I say to that? I was alive. That just about said it all. "I'm fine," I said softly. "I just wanted to come by and offer my condolences."

Moose's eyes flickered up. Scotty uncapped his beer.

Zora smiled and said, "I'm sure they both appreciate that. I know I do. I was just about to make a pitcher of sweet tea. Can I interest you in a glass?"

I didn't want her to go to any trouble, but a glass of tea would give me something to do and a reason to stay until I could warn Moose. "That would be nice. Thank you."

"Not a problem." Zora set about putting a kettle on the stove and filling a pitcher with ice. "This has been the craziest few days, hasn't it? First the accident with you and Moose, and now Destiny. I don't know what's going on."

Scotty scratched at the label on his beer, peeling little strips of it and tossing them onto the table. "That makes two of us." He let out a heavy sigh and locked eyes with me. "I know one thing, though. You never should've given her those pills. If you hadn't, she might not have overdosed."

I blinked in surprise. "But I didn't give them to her! That prescription disappeared from my office Tuesday afternoon."

A deep frown creased Moose's face. "Are you accusing Destiny of stealing them?"

Well . . . yeah. But faced with their sorrow, I thought it best to keep my suspicions to myself. "I don't know who took them," I said. "Destiny came by to help with the collection, just like we talked about. She wasn't feeling well, so I told her to go home and promised her she could help with something else. After she left, I realized the pills were missing, but I didn't see her take them or anything. Have the police determined they're what killed her?"

Zora shook her head and again answered for Moose and Scotty. "We don't know what happened yet. There will be an autopsy, but all signs point to an overdose."

Moose grunted and slid down on his tailbone. "She didn't steal those pills, you know. She'd changed. Cleaned up. That last time in rehab—" His voice caught and he dropped his gaze again. "Those old issues were finally behind her."

I looked at Zora and Scotty for their reactions to that. Scotty's expression gave nothing away, but I suspected that Zora knew the truth. She shook her head almost imperceptibly, so I thought she must have seen my surprise. Even though I'd been vague about her addiction yesterday, I wasn't so sure that keeping the truth from Destiny's family would be a kindness. It would come out eventually. But Zora knew the men better than I did, so I deferred to her judgment.

"Look," Scotty said. "It's no secret Destiny used to have trouble with drugs and alcohol. She struggled with addiction for a long time, mostly because of how her mother raised her. In a way, I blame myself, too. I was never home when she was little. Wasn't welcome there, if you want to know the truth. I took the easy way out and avoided the hassle. I regret it now. Destiny wasn't one to leave old hurts behind. Maybe if I'd been around more . . . I don't know. Maybe I could have saved her."

Zora abandoned the pitcher of tea on the counter and came to sit beside Scotty. "You can't blame yourself," she said. "You did what you thought was best. And you were here for the last year of her life. You did what you could."

Scotty's lips curved in an attempt to seem grateful for the encouragement, but his eyes were wounded and sad, and guilt created dark shadows in their depths. "For all the good it did me. Or her. I could have done more. I *should* have done more. I never should have let her open the shop on her own yesterday."

"She didn't usually work in the morning?" I asked, finally spotting a chance to say what I'd come for.

"No," Zora said. "It was unusual."

Moose's face was so still, it could have been carved from stone. "A buddy of mine ordered the fight on pay-per-view last night. Scotty and I went to watch it and stayed out late. This morning Destiny knew we'd be hurting so she told us to sleep in." He caught back a sob and said, "God help us, we took her up on the offer."

I could have said a lot of things about living with regret after someone you love dies, but I didn't think Moose and Scotty wanted platitudes. They didn't help, and often they made the grieving person feel worse.

I tried to keep my voice soothing and asked, "Was she working alone this morning?"

Moose nodded. "We didn't have any repairs scheduled. I didn't expect it to be busy. I thought she could handle it, you know? Since she got out of rehab, she was trying hard to be more useful. Used to be she'd just show up whenever she felt like it and left the same way. I let her play around with the books some, but mostly she just spent the money." His sharp laugh turned into another choked sob. "I know how you disapproved of that, Zora, but she wanted to help so I let her. She loved shopping, so I let her do that too. I just loved to see her smile."

Zora got up and went back to making the tea. "Gracious, Moose, how you make it sound! I didn't disapprove. I just worried about you and Scotty. And about Destiny. I always thought she just needed a firm hand. It's a shame her mother never gave her one."

I wondered if Destiny's mother deserved so much of this blame, or if Scotty had been bad-mouthing her to Zora to alleviate his own feelings of guilt. "Is Destiny's mother still alive?"

Scotty nodded. "I called her this morning. She'll be here in a couple of days." He swiped his cheek with the back of his hand. "Destiny was such a sweet little thing when she was little. Even-tempered. Obedient. So full of life. I don't know all that happened, but she sure had to navigate some rough seas in her lifetime. Then she finally decided to get herself on the right course and this happened. I don't get it. Why her? Why now?"

"I wish I knew," I said. "Sometimes there are no answers." I knew it would hit hard when he learned the truth about her apparent relapse, but I decided to leave the subject of Destiny's drug use for now. "I don't want to pry, but doesn't it seem odd that someone tries to run me down one night, and Destiny dies of an overdose less than forty-eight hours later?"

Zora turned quickly, dropping a spoon into the sink. "Surely you don't think the two things are connected?"

"I don't know how they could be," I admitted, "but the timing makes me wonder. Can you think of anyone in the neighborhood with an axe to grind, maybe over the alliance?"

Moose lifted his eyes slowly. "You think whoever tried to hit you is connected to the alliance?"

"It's possible," I said. "It's really the only connection between Destiny and me."

Zora put one hand on her chest. "Do you think someone is after all of us?"

I didn't want to ignore a potential threat, but neither did I want to start a full-scale panic. "What if the driver of the van wasn't aiming at me on Monday night? What if the same person showed up this morning at the Chopper Shop expecting to find someone else?"

Moose stared at me without blinking. "Like me? You think somebody meant to hurt me?" The quiet man I'd come to expect disappeared right in front of my eyes. Moose shot up, knocking over his chair and slamming his massive fist on the table. "You think somebody killed Destiny because of me?"

"I didn't exactly say that—" Okay. Sure. That's what I'd been thinking, but his anger made me a little nervous.

"It was that asshat with the blown clutch," he said to Scotty. "What was his name? I'll kill him with my bare hands."

Scotty hooked an arm over the back of his chair. "John. Or Jack. Last name started with an S."

"Wait!" I said, raising my voice a notch. "It's just a theory. I might be completely off base." *Please don't run out and rip somebody in half.* I looked to Zora for help, but she was clearly shell-shocked.

"Or that other guy," Moose said. "The one I caught hitting on Destiny last week. Or that little pissant from Second Chances. Keon. That kid's nothing but trouble."

That got my attention. "Keon Fisher?"

Moose looked at me as if he'd forgotten I was in the room. "Yeah. That's him."

"You think he might have wanted to hurt you? Why?"

"It's a long story. But yeah."

Go ahead, I urged silently. *I have time.* He wasn't in the mood to share, and I could sense the natives growing restless, so I said, "Look, I'm not trying to stir things up. I just wanted to make you aware so you can be cautious until the police figure out what really happened."

"That shouldn't take long," Scotty growled. "All they have to do is arrest that idiot Felix Blackwater. Say what you want, Moose, I know he's the one who drove that van, and he's had it in for Destiny for months."

"Except that Felix was there when the van came at us," I reminded Moose. This wasn't going exactly the way I'd planned it. "I know that Felix tried to have Destiny removed from the alliance," I said. "But you know he wouldn't try to hit one of us. He's not the violent type."

"The man is an idiot. Certifiable. You know why he really wanted Destiny out of the way? He thought she was using again. Claimed that he saw her buying something on the streets a couple of nights before the meeting."

Uh-oh. "He told you that?"

Moose nodded. "He was waiting for me at the shop when I pulled in, said Destiny was a menace. A threat to polite society and all the kids around here. He said that if he ever saw her buying again, he'd call the police."

"But you didn't believe him."

"Hell no. She told me what she'd been doing, paying for some cookie dough she bought from a school fundraiser. Some menace, huh? Next thing you know, Felix will be wanting to put schoolkids in jail as drug dealers."

I admired his loyalty even if I did think it was misplaced. After all, I'd seen Destiny flying high as a kite. Still, I couldn't shake the feeling that something wasn't adding up. Could Moose really be *so* wrong about his wife?

Zora carried the pitcher to the table and went back for glasses. "I have to admit, Felix *is* a bit of a pill. Why, just last year he complained about the clothes women wear to my yoga classes. He said some of their outfits were too revealing." She pulled a lemon from the fridge and quartered it. "He wanted me to post notices requiring my clients to wear clothing he considered appropriate. Can you believe it?"

"The man's a freak," Scotty said with a sharp nod of his head. "Crazy as a loon. What did Destiny ever do to him, that's what I want to know."

I didn't know Felix well, but he'd never seemed like the vindictive type either. Though I couldn't deny that he'd been determined to remove Destiny from the alliance, if it was because she was using drugs again, why not say so? Why blow smoke in everyone's face by claiming it was about missing meetings?

"Felix wasn't the only person at the meeting who thought Destiny should lose her seat in the alliance," I reminded them.

Both Moose and Scotty frowned at that.

Zora poured tea into four glasses and then dropped heavily into a chair. "I think Aquanettia was behind it all."

Was she serious?

Moose scowled as he reached for his tea. "You could be right. I mean, the two of them weren't exactly friends, were they?"

Scotty ignored the glass Zora pushed toward him and took a long pull from his beer. "They fought over a bunch of silly shit. Aquanettia's stupid dog barks all the time. It drove Destiny nuts. She threatened to call the pound. Aquanettia told her she'd see her in hell first."

"I know you think it was nothing," Zora said, "but people can get violently angry over things that seem like nothing to somebody else. I read once about a guy who killed his friend over a game of Monopoly. And you can't deny that dog is annoying." She turned to me and explained, "He's a little bitty thing, named Gilbert. Yips all the time. And he didn't like Destiny at all—probably because Aquanettia didn't. Dogs pick up on that sort of thing."

Maybe so, but I couldn't imagine Aquanettia going off the deep end over a dog.

I tried to remember where Aquanettia had been when the van came around the corner. I was almost certain she'd still been upstairs, but I supposed she could have hurried down the back stairs, fired up the Second Chances van, and gone after Moose . . . but why? For marrying Destiny in the first place? Even if Destiny had been using again, nobody had any reason to hurt Moose. Maybe I was trying to make something out of nothing. None of it made any sense to me, and I felt silly for coming by in the first place. I finished my sweet tea, offered my condolences again, and beat an escape. It was time to take Ox's advice and leave well enough alone.

Eleven

I chewed over what I'd just learned as I walked back to my car. The nagging feeling that I'd missed something just wouldn't leave me alone. But for the life of me, I couldn't figure out what it was. I was so deep in thought, I didn't see the man leaning against my Mercedes until I was only a few feet away—too close to pretend I had somewhere else to go and walk the other way.

Winslow was just as rumpled as he'd been earlier. I'd bet everything I owned that he lived out of laundry baskets heaped with clean clothes he was too busy (read: lazy) to fold and put away. This evening his tie had some kind of stain on it and a toothpick dangled out of his mouth, adding to the middle-aged bachelor look he was trying to pull off.

He pushed off the car and grinned as I approached. "Well, well, well. I wish I could say that I was surprised to see you here, but I can't. Paying a visit to the boyfriend?"

I fought the urge to pay a visit to his face with the palm of my hand. However, knowing how the police feel about assault upon one of their own, I managed to control myself.

"No." I walked past him so I could get to the driver's side door. "I came to offer my condolences to the family."

"Really? Well, isn't that nice?" He came around the front of the car, beating me to the door and blocking it. He took a few minutes to get the toothpick in a new position. "I'm sure they all appreciate your concern. Do they know you were supplying Destiny with drugs?"

"Someone certainly tried to make them think I was," I said, remembering what Scotty had said earlier. *And for what must have been the twentieth time:* "For the record, I was not supplying her with anything. I barely even knew her. I found her body. I checked her for a pulse. I called 911. That's it." I waited impatiently for him to move out of my way.

He didn't budge, except to lean against the car again.

"Don't scratch it," I warned sullenly. "NOPD might not appreciate a bill for a new paint job."

"What I don't understand," he said, ignoring my warning, "is what you see in Moose Hazen. If I were a betting man, I'd put money on the notion that he's not your type."

That was the first thing Winslow had ever said I could agree with. "He's not, but he seems like a genuinely nice guy and he's grieving. I feel awful for him."

Winslow resituated the toothpick one more time. "Feeling guilty?"

"Of course not. Tell me, Detective, have you even considered the fact that someone tried to run me down on Monday night and then Destiny may have died after taking pills that were meant for me? If she hadn't stolen them, I might be lying in the morgue right now instead of her."

He rolled his eyes in my direction. "I'll keep that in mind. And who do you think tampered with the pills? Should I be dragging the pharmacist in for questioning?"

I thought about Sebastian with his big, open face and friendly smile and realized how foolish my idea sounded. "No, but Moose was there with me the night the van almost ran us down. He was the one who should have opened the shop instead of Destiny this morning. Maybe somebody's after *him*."

Winslow gave me the stink-eye, which wasn't all that

different from his usual expression. "Why would this fictitious somebody want to kill Moose? And why would this imaginary someone use thirty of your pain pills to do it?"

"That's how many there were?" I asked.

"Assuming you were telling the truth about not taking any yourself. I checked with the pharmacist this afternoon. So? Tell me . . . what do you imagine the motive to be for these attacks on Mr. Hazen?"

"There could be any number of reasons," I said. "Like a customer with a grudge. Or somebody who wanted Destiny for himself." Maybe I should have also mentioned Keon and Aquanettia, but I didn't. Aquanettia was a hard-working single mother doing her best to raise those boys on her own. I wanted to clear my own name, but I couldn't throw her or her sons under the bus without a good reason. Keon might be a troubled kid, but was he troubled enough to try killing a neighboring businessman? I'd need more than speculation to shatter Aquanettia's world.

Winslow didn't seem to notice that I was holding back. He just pushed off the car and pulled the toothpick from his mouth so he could point at me with it. "I don't know what you think you're doing, Ms. Lucero, but I'm warning you to stop. One of my confidential informants is dead, and I'm not happy about that. If you think I'm just going to write this off, you're sorely mistaken. And if I can gather enough evidence to prove it, I'll charge you in her death. This isn't a tea party, lady. I'm going to advise you to stop snooping around and attempting to influence witnesses. There's a name for that. It's called witness tampering."

Was he kidding? I looked into his eyes hoping to find a glimmer of amusement, but all I could see was steely determination and a pinch of disgust.

"I wasn't tampering with anything," I protested. I wanted to sound strong and confident but it came out sounding whiny and scared to death. "I came to pay my condolences. It's a social courtesy."

"Yeah? And that's important to you?"

His question made me nervous, but I nodded and tried

to put a little starch in my voice. "Yes it is. I was raised to have manners."

"I see. Then maybe you can tell me where sleeping with another woman's husband falls in the social courtesy arena."

He was really starting to annoy me. "I. Am. Not. Sleeping. With. Moose. Hazen." I spoke slowly and clearly, and I used small words that he could understand. "I am not, in fact, sleeping with anybody."

Oops. TMI. I could have held back that last part. But nothing gets me angry faster than being accused of something I haven't done. "Now would you please move out of the way?" I said. "I'm tired and I hurt all over, and I just want to go home."

Winslow moved, but he took his sweet time doing it. I wrenched open the car door and got inside, but he grabbed it before I could close it. Leaning both arms on the top of the window, he looked down at me with a smirk. "Be careful, Ms. Lucero. I'm watching you."

I sat there for a while after he walked away. My hands were shaking so badly I didn't dare drive. Was I seriously considered a suspect in Destiny's death, or was Winslow just jerking my chain? Did he seriously think I was dealing prescription drugs out of Zydeco? If I were, why would I use my own prescription to do it?

After a long time I finally calmed down enough to drive away and I made a solemn vow that the next time I had to talk to Aaron Winslow, I'd point out a few of the flaws in his theory. Beginning with the complete lack of logic.

I had a rib eye and a potato I'd intended to bake twice and fully load waiting for me at home, but I was already exhausted and the thought of cooking and waiting to eat held no appeal. I decided to pull into a fast-food drive-through instead. I ordered a portabella mushroom burger with fries and, in a moment of weakness, deep-fried cheese-cake bites with strawberry dipping sauce. And a Coke. Diet. To balance out the calories from the rest of the meal.

Two blocks from the drive-through, the smell of food began to get to me. I pulled into the parking lot of a supermarket and dug in. The burger was greasy but delicious, the fries perfectly crispy on the outside and soft on the inside. The cheesecake bites were a whole 'nother story. Not only had they spent too much time in the deep fryer, I would testify under oath that no actual strawberries were harmed in the making of that sauce.

Already regretting my decision to forgo the rib eye, I tossed my trash and pulled back onto the street. I was just wondering if the day could get any worse when my phone rang. I answered and found out that, yes, the day could indeed get worse.

"What did you say to Miss Frankie?!" Edie shrilled when she heard my voice.

"What do you mean, what did I say? What are you even talking about?"

"My baby shower? Does that ring any bells?"

Uh-oh. "Um . . . yeah. Listen. About that . . ."

"She just called here asking for my parents' address. My parents, Rita. You know we're not on speaking terms. And why is *she* planning my baby shower anyway?"

"Long story," I said. What with finding Destiny and all, the whole baby shower/Pearl Lee exchange had slipped right out of my mind. Now I also remembered that cousin Pearl would be showing up for work the next morning and I was nowhere near ready for her. But right now, I needed to calm Edie down so she wouldn't go into premature labor.

I had the feeling I'd need all my concentration for this conversation so I pulled off the road again. "I swear, I told Miss Frankie not to invite your family. I said it several times, but you know how she is. Once she gets an idea, she doesn't let go." Ever.

"You'd better convince her to let it go this time," Edie warned. "I am *not* going to let my mother ruin this for me."

"I'll talk to her," I promised. "I'll make it very clear that you don't want your mother and sister there."

Edie sighed heavily into the phone. "It's not that *I* don't want *them*," she said. "They don't want me, and they won't accept this baby. They've made that perfectly clear."

She sounded a little calmer, which I took as a good sign. "They're upset," I said. "Finding out about the baby was a shock."

"Don't you *dare* take their side," Edie warned. "I need *somebody* on mine."

"That's not what I meant," I said quickly. "Of course I'm on your side. I hope you know that."

"Maybe. All I know for sure is that you're weirded out about the pregnancy."

I wasn't sure what she was talking about. I'd tried so hard not to let any of the issues caused by my own failure to reproduce show around Edie, but she must have picked up on something. "I'm not weirded out," I said. I wanted to tuck what I was feeling into a hole and never look at it again, but I could hear the pain and fear beneath Edie's anger, so I decided to be honest with her. "I think I might be jealous."

I heard Edie's quick intake of breath, followed by, "Of what?"

"You. The baby. The pregnancy."

Edie actually laughed, and then she blew her nose. "Well, don't feel too bad about the pregnancy. So far, it's not as fun as people try to make it sound. You really don't want the morning sickness." She fell silent for a moment and then said, "Look, I'm sorry. I didn't mean to come down on you so hard, but getting that call from Miss Frankie really threw me for a loop."

"I should have warned you she was working on the baby shower," I said. "I should have known she'd do whatever she wanted."

Edie blew her nose again and hiccupped softly. "It's okay. It's just that this whole thing is such a mess. I know I screwed up. I'm thirty-five years old and pregnant, my mom isn't speaking to me, my dad just tells me to talk to my priest, and my sister won't even return my phone calls. I'm trying to make the best of a bad situation, and not doing a very good job of it."

Edie doesn't show vulnerability often, so being on the receiving end of her confidences made me squirm a little. I haven't had a close friend since high school and my girl talk skills are a little rusty. I asked myself what Aunt Yolanda would have said and then I tried that. "You didn't screw up. Maybe this isn't what you planned, but it doesn't have to ruin your life."

"Oh, yes it does. Just ask my mother. The only way I can make her happy is to marry the baby's father and become respectable. Can you imagine? She acts like it's 1950 or something. Well, that's not going to happen. Not in this lifetime."

Usually Edie avoided any mention of the baby's father, which, of course, made us all wildly curious. I wasn't convinced that Aunt Yolanda would go there, but in the interest of community spirit, I threw caution to the wind. "Have the two of you discussed marriage at all?"

"He doesn't even know about the baby. I haven't told him."

That surprised me. I said, "Oh," in what I hoped was a tone she couldn't read anything into.

"Don't you dare say that I need to tell him either. That's completely out of the question."

I couldn't help it. My mind jumped to a conclusion I didn't like. I blame Winslow for putting the whole idea of cheating into my head. "Why is that? Is he married or something?"

"No! At least, I don't think he is. But that's probably what my mother thinks."

I chose my next words carefully. "Well, even if he is, don't you think he'd want to know?"

Edie sniffed loudly. "He might. I don't know. But I can't tell him if I don't know where to find him."

"What does that mean? Did he run out on you?"

"Not exactly." She fell silent again and the only sound I could hear was the tap-tap of her feet as she walked the floor. "He didn't run out on me," she said after a long time. "He's in Afghanistan."

Okay. Wow. That put a whole new spin on things. "He's in the military?"

"No. He's a private contractor of some kind. The fact is, I don't even really know him. We met at the Dizzy Duke one night. The rest of you had gone home, and I was there by myself. And then, all of a sudden, there he was. He just sort of swept me off my feet."

It was hard to imagine Edie being swept anywhere, and I felt a *ping* of curiosity about the guy who had actually done it. "Really? You never said anything." At least not to me and, unless someone at Zydeco was lying, not to anyone else there.

"I'm not the one-night-stand type—you know that. But it was the night my sister got engaged and I was feeling pretty lousy. It's not that I'm not happy for her. I just always thought I'd find someone first. I'm thirty-five and single, and she's not even thirty yet and she's got this great guy . . . So *my* great guy bought me a drink, and we talked for a while. He was just so different and so kind, and he was heading off into enemy territory the next day . . . I never expected this to happen."

If he was that great, he really did deserve to know about the baby, I thought. "You don't even have an address where you can write to him?"

"I wish it was that simple. I don't even have a name."

I managed to get out another surprised, "Oh."

"Yeah. Right?" Edie stopped walking. "So there it is. My dirty little secret. I really don't want the others to know about this, okay? And my mother can *never* know the truth. Not speaking to me would be mild compared to what she'd do if she knew the father was a complete stranger. Can we just keep it between the two of us?"

"Absolutely," I said. But this changed things in a big way. Edie was more alone than I'd originally thought. She needed us far more than I'd realized. Under the circumstances, I had to make sure Miss Frankie minded her own business. And that wasn't going to be easy.

Twelve

After my encounter with Detective Winslow and my conversation with Edie, I had trouble settling down. I was too tired to talk to Miss Frankie and come out on top. And maybe I just needed a little TLC of my own. I changed into sweats and a tank top, rescued Cherry Garcia from the freezer, and settled down in front of the TV to watch that episode of *Castle*.

My mind kept drifting back to Destiny's murder and forward to babysitting cousin Pearl Lee so Miss Frankie could magically turn her into a functioning member of society. It sounded like that ought to be a piece of cake. My thoughts were so scattered, I grabbed a pen and paper and tried to organize a few of them. I couldn't put Pearl Lee to work on an actual cake, but there were dozens of small tasks I could assign her that would keep her busy and help the rest of the staff.

I made a long list of odd jobs, ranging from "put together cake boxes" to "help Edie with filing." Feeling pleased with myself for getting the Pearl Lee situation under control, I turned to a clean sheet of paper and started three new lists. I labeled one "People Who Might Have Supplied

Destiny with Drugs"; the second, "People Who Might Have Wanted to Hurt Moose"; and the third, "People Angry at Me."

I put Detective Winslow at the top of my list, just because I could. I figured turnabout was fair play. If he could suspect me for no good reason, I could do the same for him. Then I added him to Destiny's list, too. Maybe he was a dirty cop. Maybe he gave Destiny a fatal overdose to keep her from ratting him out.

Keon Fisher went on Moose's list. I had no idea whether he actually had a motive for trying to run Moose down, but I remembered Destiny telling me that she thought Keon was driving the van. If that was true, there must have been something going on that Moose had neglected to mention.

I put Felix Blackwater's name in Destiny's column followed by a question mark. There was no doubt in my mind that Destiny's loosey-goosey attitude about the alliance had annoyed him, and he'd been furious about her decision to run in the election, but I couldn't picture Felix as a drug dealer.

I added Moose and Scotty to Destiny's list as well. I didn't seriously think that either of them had a reason to want her out of the way. They'd both seemed grief-stricken. But I knew now that Moose had a temper. If he'd found out that Destiny was using again or that she was fooling around on him, he could have snapped. He could have easily doctored any pills he found in her possession.

Scotty was another story entirely. By his own account, his relationship with Destiny had been a troubled one. I got the feeling that Moose liked having Scotty around more than Destiny had. And there was no denying that Scotty been upset by the suggestion that her latest stint in rehab hadn't been successful. How many times had she gone for help? How many times had she failed? How many failed attempts to get it right could Scotty take? He and Moose had both known that Destiny would be at the Chopper Shop alone that morning.

I added Edgar Zappa to Destiny's column next. I didn't know what was going on between the two of them, but I thought there had been something. Were they having an affair? Had it gone bad? After some thought, I put him on Moose's list as well. Who had more motive to want Moose out of the way than a lover who wanted the woman they both loved all to himself? Even if they'd been just friends, he might have answers to questions Moose didn't.

Reluctantly, I added Aquanettia to Destiny's column and wrote "barking dog" and "election" next to her name. And then I put a big old question mark in case Destiny's dealer was someone else entirely.

I couldn't think of anyone else who might have wanted to hurt Destiny, and I still couldn't think of anyone nursing a grudge against me. But that feeling I'd had earlier kept bothering me. I was missing something important. I was almost certain of it.

Miss Frankie walked through the door to my office at ten on the dot Thursday morning, trailed by a voluptuous sixty-something brunette (surely not her natural color). The hair on both women had been teased and sprayed to withstand hurricane-force winds. Judging from the shiny texture of the second woman's complexion—visible even under layers of makeup—I suspected that from time to time she indulged in a little Botox. Or a lot. I wasn't sure her facial muscles could actually move.

Miss Frankie greeted me with a hug and a kiss on the cheek. "Good morning, sugar. Pearl Lee, this is Rita, Philippe's wife. Rita, my cousin, Pearl Lee Gates."

Was she joking? Pearly Gates?

Pearl Lee noticed my surprise and laughed. I was right. Nothing on her face other than her mouth moved. "It's a hideous name, isn't it? Trust me, it's not mine by choice. I only kept Bobby Lee's last name so I could cash the alimony checks. Getting your own name back after a divorce isn't easy. I know. I've done it four times already."

Both women sat across from my desk. Miss Frankie was wearing a sensible sea foam green pantsuit from circa 1974, and low-heeled sandals to match. Her makeup was subtle and understated, as usual. Pearl Lee wore an obviously expensive gray suit with a pink shell and pumps. Her makeup was more dramatic—smoky eyes and bright red lipstick. The cousins could not have been more different.

Pearl Lee looked around my office slowly, bored curiosity clouding her dark eyes. "So. This is it."

Miss Frankie swatted her knee. "Don't start, Pearl Lee." And to me, "She's been pouting about this all morning, so don't let her get to you."

Oh goody! Just what I needed, a surly sexagenarian. This week just kept getting better and better. "If Pearl Lee doesn't want to do this, maybe you shouldn't push her," I said, trying to strike a balance between pleasantly cooperative and "please don't leave this woman with me."

Miss Frankie gave me a stern look. "Don't *you* start now. I told you why Pearl Lee needs to work here. Everyone in the family agrees that the bailouts have to stop."

"I'm not a child," Pearl Lee mumbled.

"Of course not, dear, and this is your chance to prove it. And, Rita, you agreed to hire her."

"Well, yes, but . . ."

"So here she is." Miss Frankie stood and settled her handbag in the crook of her arm. She put a hand on Pearl Lee's shoulder and patted gently. "I'll be back to pick you up around five. This is for the best. You'll see."

Pearl Lee probably felt something about that, but her face didn't reveal what it was.

Realizing that Miss Frankie planned to leave, I smiled at Pearl Lee and said, "Would you mind waiting out in the reception area for a few minutes? I need to discuss something with Miss Frankie before she goes."

Pearl Lee uncrossed her legs and rose. "Of course not. I'll be right outside. Take your time."

I followed, and shut the door behind her. I wanted to ask Miss Frankie point-blank why she thought she could get away with inviting Edie's family to the shower after I specifically told her not to, but I knew I'd get more out of her if I used a little finesse.

Returning to my desk, I served up a friendly smile. "So . . . how are the shower preparations coming?"

Miss Frankie beamed and resumed her seat. "I'm having so much fun, sugar. I've been looking at decorations and invitations and themes, and I have so many ideas running through my head, I'm having trouble keeping them all straight."

"Good. I'm so glad to hear it." I sat back in my chair and tried to look nonchalant. "Have you set a date yet?"

"No, but I'm getting closer to nailing that down. I just need to clear up a couple of tiny details before I make the final decision."

"Oh? What details are those?"

Miss Frankie wagged a hand at me. "Now, Rita, don't you worry about that. You said you didn't want anything to do with planning the shower, so you just leave it all to me. I do need to get addresses from you, though. I'll be putting the guest list together over the weekend."

"Oh. Okay. What addresses do you need from me?"

"Home addresses for all the women who work here, and any other friends of Edie's she might want to invite. I could hand out the staff invitations here, but I think that would be a bit tacky, don't you?"

"I wouldn't worry about that," I said sweetly. "It can't be any worse than inviting people Edie has specifically said she doesn't want there."

Miss Frankie put her handbag on the floor. "I suppose you're talking about Edie's mother and sister."

I had her attention. She couldn't pretend not to hear me. The door was shut, slowing down any attempts at escape. "I suppose I am. You can't invite them, Miss Frankie. Edie doesn't want them there."

My mother-in-law's smile dulled ever so slightly. "Edie is being ruled by hormones right now. She doesn't really know what she wants."

I was so astonished I fell back in my seat as if someone had shoved me. "I think that's the most ridiculous thing I've ever heard you say. Of course she knows what she wants!"

"If that were the case, she'd be first in line to send her mother an invitation." Miss Frankie gave her shellacked auburn head a firm shake. "I don't know what the differences are between them, and I don't care. Family is family."

"With all due respect, Miss Frankie, it's not your decision. You can't force Edie and her mother to reconcile just because you think they should."

"This isn't about Edie or her mother." Miss Frankie's voice morphed from Southern syrup to solid steel. "This is about that baby. That child is going to need its parents and its grandparents. It's going to need aunts, uncles, and cousins. Edie and her mother are adults. They ought to be smart enough to put aside their differences and make things work."

"I don't disagree," I said. "I don't know what would have happened to me without my family after my parents died. But there are other considerations in play here and the fact remains that it's not your call in Edie's situation. We agreed that you would plan the shower, but that doesn't give you license to overrule Edie's decisions."

"She'll thank me later."

"That's what you said about Pearl Lee, but if you ask me, you'll be waiting for both thank-yous for a long, long time." The words slipped out before I could stop them and I regretted them immediately.

My mother-in-law's stony expression turned to ice right in front of my eyes. "What is that supposed to mean?"

I sighed, wishing I were better at sugarcoating things. "I'm sorry, Miss Frankie. I wouldn't hurt you for the world, but I think you're butting into things that aren't any of your business. I doubt Pearl Lee is feeling all that grateful for the job here, and I know Edie doesn't want help fixing her relationship with her mother. If she did, she'd ask you."

"Edie wants her baby to grow up estranged from its grandparents?" It was more of a challenge than a question.

"I'm sure she doesn't *want* that. But it's not up to you or me to take over and try to fix it. She was really upset when she called me last night. It took me nearly half an hour to calm her down."

To give Miss Frankie her due, I think she looked a little guilty for a second. I can't be sure, though. The expression was gone before I could really identify it.

"Just promise that you'll respect her wishes," I said.

Miss Frankie tweaked the collar of her pantsuit. "I think she's wrong."

"Duly noted."

"That baby needs its grandparents."

Since it would only have one set, I had to agree. "You'll get no argument from me. But again, not the issue."

She stared at me for a long time before she spoke again. "This thing can go both ways, you know. You have to promise me that you won't let Pearl Lee get away with anything. Keep her busy. She needs it. And for heaven's sake, don't let her anywhere near a man."

I laughed, hoping that meant that things were okay between us. "What am I supposed to do, keep her locked up in my office for eight hours a day?"

Miss Frankie gave me a pointed look. "If that's what it takes, then yes. I mean it, Rita. Keep an eye on her. She's a sneaky one."

Thirteen

For the twentieth time in an hour, I felt a sharp jab in my side followed by Pearl Lee's rapid-fire prattle as she nudged me, then made an off-color comment about the petunia parts I had her sorting for me. I spent most of the morning dusting the petunias I'd made earlier in the week with blue pearl dust so they'd be ready for the addition of stems and stamens. I say "dusting" but what I really mean is "*trying* to dust." I was failing miserably.

Doing anything with Pearl Lee underfoot turned out to be a job slightly more difficult than herding feral cats. No wonder Miss Frankie had handed her off to me. Pearl Lee's mind flitted from topic to topic without warning, usually landing on something involving men or sex. Or men *and* sex. She had a throaty laugh and probably would have had an infectious smile under all that dark red lipstick if not for the Botox. If I hadn't been responsible for her, I might even have found her amusing and eccentric. But I was responsible and she was, literally, a pain in the ribs.

I'd told the staff that Pearl Lee was here to learn some new skills, which was technically true. And any-way, it seemed kinder than telling the absolute truth. Not surprisingly, she bounced from task to task without finishing a single one as evidenced by the teetering stack of half-finished boxes, a roll of stickers with the Zydeco alligator and cake logo that had rolled under a table an hour ago and was still there, and a sink full of bowls that she claimed needed to soak. She'd interrupted me with so many questions I could barely form a thought, and I could tell that she was having the same effect on the rest of the staff. Isabeau had stopped chattering and plugged into a set of headphones so she could tune Pearl Lee out. Sparkle had disappeared with her cell phone twenty minutes earlier, and Estelle had scraped off the leaves she was piping onto the petunia cake three times already. Only Dwight seemed unaffected by Pearl Lee's constant interruptions.

We had far too much work to do to let her continue distracting us, so I gave up trying to finish the petunias and suggested that Pearl Lee help me pick up supplies. Ox gave my idea an enthusiastic thumbs-up and took over the petunias so I could leave with a clear conscience. Edie pulled together a list of items we needed, and a little after noon Pearl Lee and I set off on foot. Edie's list included items from both the market and the office supply store. Noting a few perishable items on the market list, I decided to stop there last.

The horrible humidity we'd experienced earlier in the week had faded a bit, so the summer heat was almost bearable. We strolled slowly along the sidewalk, partly because of the temperature and partly because Pearl Lee's shoes weren't actually made for walking. I took advantage of the pace to get her version of the events that had landed her in my shop. Maybe if I understood what made her tick, I'd have a better chance of making her time at Zydeco work for everyone.

I decided to start with the basics. "Is this your first visit to New Orleans?" I asked. "Or did you grow up here?"

Pearl Lee had linked her hands behind her back and walked with her face tilted toward the sky. She glanced at me from the corner of her eye and said, "I grew up here, just a hop, skip, and a jump from Frances Mae."

"Where was that, exactly? I know she grew up in the area, and I know her family owned a lot of land, but that's about it."

Pearl Lee tucked one hand under my arm and smiled—I think. It was hard to tell since her face didn't move. "Uncle Leroy and Aunt Caroline—that's Frances Mae's mama and daddy—lived in the old family place out in Vacherie. You ever been out that way?"

I shook my head in answer to her question. "I've only lived in New Orleans for a year and Zydeco keeps me pretty busy. I haven't done much looking around."

Her dark eyes flashed and I thought she must have been stunning when she was younger. She still would be if her face hadn't had that plastic quality. "Oh, baby, you should try to get out there. It's a lovely place. The best part of the whole week was going over to Aunt Caroline's to play. She had trunks of old clothes up in the attic, and us girls used to dress up and pretend we were belles of the ball."

Her eyes grew dreamy with memory. "Aunt Caroline Thibodeaux was Mama's older sister. She married well." Another facial tick that might have been a smile. "She married *real* well. The Thibodeauxes had scads more money than us Dumonds. Don't get me wrong. We had money. But Caroline certainly elevated herself."

Did I detect a note of bitterness? Envy? Miss Frankie was tight-lipped when it came to her family history. Pearl Lee seemed more willing to share, so why not let her? "Were Caroline and your mother close?"

"Close as sisters can be, I guess. They had their good moments and their bad ones, like any of us. When I was a girl—oh, maybe four or five—the two of them had a falling-out. Didn't speak for nearly ten years. They patched things up eventually, but it was rough going for a while."

I was so interested in her story I wasn't watching where I was going. I hit an uneven patch of sidewalk and nearly lost my balance, but I didn't let that distract me. "They didn't speak for ten years?"

"Didn't speak. Refused even to be in the same room."

Her eyes sparkled with amusement. "Of course, that meant that the rest of us had to tiptoe around to see each other, and Lord help us if Mama found out we'd talked to one of Caroline's brood. But we did it anyway." She slipped me a sly look. "The Dumonds are known for doing whatever they want."

"I've noticed," I said with a grin. I wondered if the rift between her mother and her aunt might explain why Miss Frankie was so concerned about Edie and her mother. "How old was Miss Frankie when they had their disagreement?"

"Well, let's see. She's ten years older than me, so she was probably fourteen or thereabouts."

"Do you know what came between them?"

Pearl Lee shook her head. "No, baby, my parents' generation didn't talk about things like that. None of us kids had the foggiest idea. It was something my mama did to upset Aunt Caroline, though. I do know that. The only communication they had in all those years was when Aunt Caroline sent a letter demanding an apology before some big family event. Mama never gave one, but that didn't stop Aunt Caroline from demanding it."

I was beginning to think my family was the exception to some rule I'd never heard of. Uncle Nestor and my cousins might fly off the handle from time to time, but if they were angry, they'd make sure you and everyone else around knew why. Sometimes the way they aired everything in front of anyone who wanted to listen filled me with resentment, but I think I'd rather have that than the silent treatment.

"What about your grandparents? Didn't they step in?"

"I'm sure they tried," Pearl Lee said. "But my mama was one stubborn woman. She never did listen to them, and Uncle Ellis—Mama and Aunt Caroline's big brother— just ignored the whole thing."

"Then what finally brought them back together?"

"Why, Frances Mae, of course. She was married and a Renier by then, but she came home one day and sat down with each of them. She must have had a real come to Jesus with them. To this day, none of us has any idea what she said, but whatever it was, it worked. Mama wrote a note of apology and everything went back to normal."

"Just like that?"

"Well, sure. Aunt Caroline had her apology. That's all she ever wanted."

I bit back a smile and tried to imagine anyone in my family letting go just like that. Well, no wonder Miss Frankie was so determined to work on Edie and her mother. She'd successfully conducted peace talks before, so why not do it again? But now I worried that the promise I thought I'd extracted from her a few hours earlier had been nothing more than lip service.

In spite of her flighty personality, I found myself enjoying Pearl Lee's company. Which may or may not have lulled me into a false sense of security.

To be honest, I'm not entirely sure what happened next. We were nearly at the office supply store when the door to Paolo's Pizza opened and four or five people poured out onto the street. I barely had time to register Edgar Zappa's sunlit blond hair among them when Pearl Lee impaled me with a razor-sharp elbow and whispered, "Who is that?"

I followed the direction of her gaze and was surprised to realize she wasn't staring at Edgar but at a man wearing khakis and a Hawaiian print shirt. His hairy legs ended in a worn pair of Birkenstocks, and a ponytail held by half a dozen bands trailed down his back. Going out for pizza the day after Destiny died? That seemed odd to me, but I guess to each his own. If he'd been a woman, his friends would have flooded the house with food and comfort. Maybe guys went for pizza when things got rough.

"That's Scotty Justus," I said. "His daughter died yesterday."

Pearl Lee blinked at me. "Seriously? What happened? Was she in an accident?"

"Actually, they think she died of an overdose."

Pearl Lee gasped and covered her mouth with one hand. "No!"

"Yeah. He's taking it all pretty hard." At least yesterday

I thought he was. Standing there on the curb with a cigar in one hand and a red plastic to-go cup in the other, he didn't give off the vibe I might have expected from a man who'd just lost his daughter.

"He's quite a looker, isn't he?" Pearl Lee whispered.

"I . . . suppose so," I said. "But I think he's taken. I'm pretty sure he's been seeing the woman who owns the yoga studio we just passed."

A calculating gleam danced in Pearl Lee's eyes. "Are they married?"

"No, but I think they're in a committed relationship." I might have been exaggerating that part. I really had no idea how committed Scotty and Zora were. I just knew that she'd seemed mighty comfortable at the house last night.

"Well, if they're not married, that means he's still on the market, doesn't it?"

"No," I said, scowling. "It means exactly the opposite."

Pearl Lee tried to make a pouty face. I think. "Oh, don't be such a stick in the mud, Rita. Life's too short. It won't hurt to say hello, will it?"

"It might. The man just lost his daughter," I reminded her. "I don't think he's interested in making new friends right now."

"But his loss is all the more reason to offer a hand of friendship. Come on. Introduce me." She grabbed my arm and started walking toward Scotty.

I sighed in frustration, but I went along. I knew I couldn't stop her, but maybe I could minimize the damage—or slip into the hardware store for some duct tape to put over her mouth. "Keep her busy," Miss Frankie had said. "Keep her away from men." So far, I'd failed on both counts.

When life hands you lemons, make lemonade. That's what Aunt Yolanda used to tell me. Pearl Lee's interest in Scotty was definitely a lemon, but after my initial reluctance passed, I saw an opportunity to chat with Edgar again. I wondered if he had any new thoughts about what happened to Destiny, or if he'd picked up on any talk going around. Considering my suspicions about the nature of his relationship with Destiny, I thought it strange that Moose hadn't mentioned Edgar as someone with an axe to grind. Destiny had told me that she was with Edgar when the van sped away, but what if she'd been covering for him?

Still holding my arm, Pearl Lee sashayed toward Scotty to strike up a conversation. Since I had reasons of my own to approach the group, I didn't try very hard to stop her.

I can't say Scotty looked pleased to see me, but he didn't look displeased so I took that as a good sign. Maybe Detective Winslow hadn't turned him against me after I left yesterday, though I'm sure it wasn't for lack of trying.

Pearl Lee fluttered her eyelashes at Scotty while I performed the introductions then she released my arm as a signal that I was free to go. I hesitated for an instant, but it was broad daylight and there were people around. And besides, Scotty was an adult fully capable of telling Pearl Lee "no." She might even listen to him.

Edgar had already moved away from the others and I wanted to catch him before he went back to work. I didn't have time to think of an excuse for chasing him down, so I had to just jump in with both feet. I set off after him, catching up a few feet from EZ Shipping. "Edgar?" I called before he could slip inside. "Do you have a minute?"

His pale blue eyes narrowed slightly. I figured he was surprised to see me standing there. "I guess so," he said. "What's up?"

"I've been wondering how you're holding up. Are you doing okay?"

He nodded uncertainly. "Sure. I mean . . . you know."

"Yeah. Um, I know this is probably a bad time, but the police don't seem to be making any progress finding the driver of the van that almost hit Moose and me the other night. Destiny told me that you were standing near the dollar store and you saw the van. Would you mind telling me what you saw?"

Edgar shrugged and brushed a lock of platinum blond

hair from his forehead. "I didn't see much. There wasn't much to see."

"Destiny said you recognized the van. Is that true? Any detail at all would help. I'm still trying to figure out why anyone would want to hurt me and I guess that I'm a little jumpy after what happened to Destiny."

Edgar cut a sharp look at me. "Well, you can relax. I don't think the van's driver was trying to hit you at all," he said. "I think he was after Destiny."

The air left my lungs in a *whoosh!* It was a full minute before I could speak again. "But she wasn't even there! She left the meeting earlier. She was with you, right?"

"That's not what I meant. I meant that you were standing there talking to Moose. In the dark it would be easy to mistake you for Destiny."

That shut me up for another long moment. I mean . . . *really*? I didn't know whether to feel relieved or insulted. "I don't think she and I look that much alike."

"Sure you do." He grimaced and said more softly, "Or you did. You're about the same height and size. Especially from behind, you look just like her."

Except for the part where I wore actual clothes. He probably meant it as a compliment, but the comparison left a sting anyway. Could he possibly be right? Had this all been about Destiny from the beginning? For the first time since that van had almost hit me, the accident made a sick kind of sense and her supposed overdose suddenly looked even more suspicious. But I wasn't ready to toss my other theories away just yet.

"Can I ask you a personal question? You and Destiny were friends. Was it more than that?"

"We were friends," he said. "Nothing more."

I held up both hands to show I meant no harm. "I'm not asking just to be nosy. I'm just wondering how close you were and if you know who might have wanted to hurt her."

Edgar arched a pale brown eyebrow. "Conducting your own investigation?"

"Mostly trying to get Detective Winslow off my back.

He's convinced that I had something against Destiny. He even thinks I supplied her with pills. Which, for the record, I didn't. I barely even knew her! But if the two of you were close, maybe you know if she had enemies." I paused, debating about how much to say. Finally, I blurted out, "What if the van incident and her death are related? What if you're right and she didn't take that overdose on her own?"

Edgar looked at me for a long time before he spoke again. "I don't know about enemies, but she ran with a tough crowd. Some of those people would kill their own mother for a hit."

"So she *was* using again?"

He slid a look toward Scotty, who was deep in conversation with Pearl Lee. I didn't think either of them was paying attention to us, but Edgar lowered his voice just in case. "I overreacted before when I said it wasn't possible. The truth is, she struggled with her addiction all the time. She was as determined to stay clean this time as I'd ever seen her, but I guess it's possible that she slipped up."

I'd seen the proof firsthand. "And Moose had no idea?"

"I don't think so. She wanted her family to think she'd finally kicked it for good. Scotty had already warned her that this was the last time he'd pay for rehab. That's why he moved in with them. He wanted to help keep an eye on her. And Moose told her that he'd file for divorce if she didn't get straight."

That surprised me. Neither Moose nor Scotty had given any indication that they'd reached the end of the line with Destiny. Neither had said anything about an ultimatum.

"Do you think Moose was serious? Do you think he would have filed for divorce if he'd known Destiny was on drugs again?"

Edgar nodded. "She was convinced of it. She'd run through a lot of their money, wasting it on anything she could shoot up or snort. They almost lost the shop six months ago, and they've been hanging on by a thread ever since. Maybe he wanted to stop her before he lost everything."

Interesting that Moose had neglected to mention that as well. I wondered if he'd bothered to tell the police. I'd seen his temper flare last night and I couldn't help but wonder what he might have done if he found out that Destiny was putting their livelihood in jeopardy again. Had he made up the story about watching the fight with friends? And what about that cookie dough she'd supposedly bought from a neighborhood kid? There had been two cups on the desk at the Chopper Shop. Maybe Destiny *hadn't* opened the shop alone. Maybe Moose had been with her.

I wasn't sure what to believe, but I didn't have time to think about it. From the corner of my eye, I saw Pearl Lee and Scotty wander off down the street arm in arm. I had more questions for Edgar, but they were going to have to wait. Pearl Lee was much more skilled in the art of seduction than I'd given her credit for, and apparently Scotty was more vulnerable than I'd thought.

I thanked Edgar and hurried after them, still trying to wrap my mind around what he had told me. Had the van driver mistaken me for Destiny? If so, had that same person killed her at the Chopper Shop? And if so, then who? Someone who felt threatened by her for some reason? That could have been her actual drug dealer afraid of exposure, her lover afraid of rejection, her husband afraid of losing everything, or even Aquanettia, afraid of losing the election. If Edgar was telling the truth, both Moose and Scotty had left out some crucial information. Not that they had to be forthcoming with me, but still . . .

And speaking of Scotty, just what was I trying to do as I chased him and Pearl Lee down the street? Which one of them was I trying to protect?

Fourteen

Luckily, Pearl Lee and Scotty only traveled a couple of blocks and I managed to keep them in sight the whole way. They ducked inside the Dizzy Duke, the Zydeco staff's favorite after-work hangout, which disturbed me since it was only eleven, which I thought was too early in the day to start drinking. I followed a few minutes later. By the time I got inside, they were sitting at a table near the front window. Except for a couple of good old boys talking guns at the far end of the bar, they were the only customers in the place.

I thought about hauling Pearl Lee out of there, but two things stopped me. On the one hand, I'd been raised to respect my elders. But on the other, she was acting like a hormonal teenager, and I figured the same rules probably applied; i.e., Pearl Lee was obviously drawn to the allure of forbidden love. Declaring Scotty off-limits would only make him more appealing.

As I hitched myself onto a barstool where I could keep an eye on the lovebirds, I noticed Gabriel doing some paperwork at a table tucked into a corner. Paperwork. Go figure. And here I'd thought he was just a pretty face. Seeing him was one positive in an otherwise not-so-good morning. At least I'd have someone to talk to while I decided what to do.

He grinned when he saw me and abandoned his work. My heart did a little flip-floppy thing, which isn't unusual when he's around. His smile faded, though, when he got a good look at my face. "Tell me the police have caught the sonofabitch who tried to run you down."

I shrugged. "Not that I know of. Nobody was seriously hurt, so I doubt they're putting in overtime or anything."

"I shouldn't have left the meeting before you," he said. "If I'd been there—"

His anger touched me, but really, what could he have done? I flashed a grin. "Unless you have some Spandex and a cape under your clothes, you'd probably just have ended up looking like this—or worse. I doubt Moose would have done the full body slam on you."

Gabriel snorted and fell silent for a moment, then sent me a slow sexy Cajun smile. "Well, no matter how banged up you are, it's good to see you. But you're drinking early. What's the matter? Having a rough day?"

"Having a rough week," I said, and cut my eyes toward Pearl Lee and Scotty. They sat knee to knee at the small round table and Pearl Lee was holding Scotty's hands in hers, patting gently as he talked. "I'm supposed to be keeping Miss Frankie's cousin busy at Zydeco and away from men. So far I'm batting oh for two."

With a laugh, Gabriel slid a coaster onto the bar in front of me. "I wouldn't worry too much. It all looks pretty innocent to me. You want a Coke or something stronger?"

"Coke. Diet. Technically, I'm at work. Plus, I should probably give chase if those two take off again. It's what Miss Frankie would want."

Gabriel put my ice-cold soda on the coaster before delivering a beer and a glass of white wine to Pearl Lee's table. He stayed there a minute making small talk. I sucked down half the soda and chased it with a handful of dry-roasted peanuts from a bowl on the bar.

After a while, Gabriel stopped chitchatting and came

back to the bar. He stood opposite me and said, "So that's Miss Frankie's cousin, is it? How did you end up with her?"

I answered with a rueful grin. "Long story. Let's just say I've learned my lesson about passing off jobs I'd rather not do. I do believe I got the short end of this particular stick."

"You went up against Miss Frankie," he said with a twinkle in his eye. "What did you expect?"

"You'd think I'd learn, wouldn't you?" I sighed and filled him in on the deal I'd made and Miss Frankie's plan to mend the rift between Edie and her mother. "Not only am I stuck trying to keep Pearl Lee under control, but now I have to keep an eye on Miss Frankie so she doesn't make Edie unhappy. Maybe I should have let that van hit me. It might have been easier to just get laid up in the hospital for a while."

At the mention of the van, Gabriel turned serious again. "Don't even joke about that. It's not funny. How are you feeling anyway?"

I shrugged. "I'm all right. A little sore, but getting better every day."

"That's good. So who's in charge of the case? Can whatshisname do anything?"

I reached for more peanuts. "I assume you're talking about Sullivan? He works homicide, which, thankfully, this is not. And anyway, he's out of town."

"Then what about the other guy? The one who was working with Destiny?"

I almost choked. "How do you know about him?"

"Bartender, remember? I hear things. Also, it helps to be a superhero with supersonic hearing."

I laughed. "Good to know. Unfortunately, Detective Winslow is not a member of the Rita Lucero Fan Club. I'm almost convinced that he was the one driving the van."

"Oh?"

"Yeah. Get this—he thinks I was Destiny's dealer. He probably even thinks I arranged a fatal overdose to keep her from turning me in. *And* he thinks I'm having a torrid affair with Moose."

Gabriel burst out laughing, which had every eye in the

building looking at us. "Sorry," he said as one by one they turned back to their conversations. "The van almost running you down and Destiny dying like that aren't funny. But the idea of you and Moose . . . It just . . ." He leaned close and whispered, "Should I be jealous?"

"Oh. Yeah. For sure. The man's built like a Mack truck and covered in colorful artwork. Plus, he's married. What's not to love?" I ate a few more peanuts and asked, "How well do you know him?"

"Moose?" Gabriel shook his head slowly. "We've both worked in the neighborhood for several years. We've talked in passing. He comes in for a drink now and then, but we're not exactly buddies. Why?"

"Do you know what their marriage was like?"

Gabriel glanced at Scotty and then back at me. "Why do you ask?"

I propped up my chin with one hand. "Edgar just told me that Moose threatened to divorce Destiny if he caught her using again, but Moose never said a word about that to me."

Gabriel held up one hand to stop me. "Hold up. When did you talk to Moose?"

"Last night. I thought I should offer my condolences, especially after the way he saved me."

"Yeah. And? The real reason you went?"

I tried to look outraged, but probably only succeeded in looking guilty. "I wanted to warn him to be careful in case the van driver was trying to hit him. I mean, think about it for a minute. That van comes at us one night and not even two days later his wife dies? I think he'd be smart to watch his back. And that's not the point anyway. The point is that Moose never said a word about threatening to divorce Destiny."

Gabriel didn't seem impressed by my deductive reasoning. "Do you know for a fact that she was using? Or is that idle gossip?"

I pretended to be shocked. "My aunt Yolanda would wash out your mouth with soap for asking that. Gossip is the devil's workshop."

"I thought that was idle hands."

I waved an idle hand in dismissal. "Whatever. All I know is that Destiny showed up at Zydeco the day before she died and I know she was high. What if Moose saw her like that?"

"Divorce is a little different from cold-blooded murder," Gabriel pointed out. "So Moose was fed up, huh? I can't say I'm surprised. But how did Edgar explain knowing about it?"

"He and Destiny were friends. She told him."

"Or so he says."

That was an interesting response. I shifted on my seat so I could see Gabriel better. Which meant I had to take my eyes off Pearl Lee, but I preferred the view in this direction anyway. "Meaning what? You don't believe it?"

"I don't know," Gabriel said with a shrug. "I'm just thinking out loud."

"Okay. What do you know?"

"Nothing, really. I'm just not sure I'd take what Edgar Zappa says at face value."

He definitely had my attention now. "Why not?"

"I don't think he's a fan of Moose's, that's all. They've butted heads in here a few times. Always when they've had too much to drink."

"Over what?"

Gabriel gave me a long look. "You're doing it again, *chérie*."

"Doing what again?"

"Getting involved in something you should leave alone."

I made a face at him. "You're the one who brought it up."

"I asked you about the van that nearly hit you. You went straight from there to Destiny's death and you're trying to turn it into a murder without even pausing to take a breath."

"Oh, come on," I joked. "I'm almost positive I've been breathing the whole time."

"It's not funny," he said, and to my surprise, he didn't even crack a smile. "Why don't you tell me what to expect, Rita. Will you be putting yourself in danger again?"

I like the guy. I really do. But sometimes he can be completely unreasonable. Like now. "I wouldn't have to do anything if Detective Winslow wasn't accusing me of selling drugs."

"And you just can't trust the police to get it right, can you?"

"Have you *met* Winslow?" I could feel the heat of anger rushing to my face. "On second thought, forget I asked. Because if you'd spent even thirty seconds in his company, you wouldn't have to wonder whether or not he'd get it right."

Everybody in the bar turned to look at us again—at least the good old boys did. I couldn't actually see Pearl Lee and Scotty.

Gabriel moved around behind the bar, putting some distance between us. "Why can't you just let the police do their jobs?"

"Why can't *you* understand that the police aren't interested in doing their jobs?" I snapped. I had one nerve left, and Gabriel was standing right on it. I pushed my glass out of my way and stood. "You know what, Gabriel? It's been a bad week and I don't have the energy to argue with you so why don't we just agree to disagree?" I dug out a five and slapped it on the counter. "Keep the change."

He shoved the bill back at me. "It's on the house."

He looked so smug, my last nerve snapped, and resentments I thought I'd buried bubbled to the surface. I tucked the money into my pocket. "Great. Thanks. It means so much more now that I know the Dizzy Duke actually *is* your house."

Gabriel groaned aloud. "Are you still upset about that?"

"Me? Upset? No! Why would I be upset about the fact that you lied to me for nine months?"

"I didn't lie," Gabriel growled. "How many times do I have to say that?"

I held up both hands in surrender. "So sorry. You're right. Let me rephrase that. Why would I be upset about the fact that you 'neglected to tell the truth' for nine whole months?"

He rubbed his face with one hand. "Fine. I'm sorry, okay? It just didn't seem like a big deal."

"Such a heartfelt apology," I said. "I feel so much better."

"At least I know how to apologize."

Okay. That did it. I had a pithy comeback on the tip of my tongue, but I swallowed it when I realized that I was looking at an empty table where Pearl Lee and Scotty used to be.

"What . . . where . . ." I searched the nearly empty bar to see if they'd moved to a different spot. They hadn't. "Where did they go?" I demanded.

Gabriel turned away and pretended a sudden interest in something on the counter behind him. "Who?"

"You know exactly who I'm talking about. Where are they?"

He looked over his shoulder and shrugged. "I don't know."

He looked innocent. Too innocent. Slowly, realization began to dawn on me. "You did that on purpose!"

"Did what?"

"You started an argument with me. You distracted me so they could sneak out. And don't even try to deny it. It's written all over your face."

Gabriel treated me to another of his sexy Cajun grins. "What can I say? I'm a sucker for romance."

"Romance? Please! Scotty's in mourning and they've known each other for all of five minutes!"

"And the lady wanted to talk with him alone. Was that too much to ask?"

"Yes!" I said, pointing an accusing finger at him. "Miss Frankie is going to kill you."

"Relax, *chérie*. It's not the end of the world."

"You'd better hope you're right," I said, slinging my purse over my shoulder and rushing toward the door. "Because if you're wrong, I'll kill you myself."

I was outside ten seconds later, but Scotty and Pearl Lee had already disappeared. I swore under my breath and tried to decide on my next move. Maybe I should just go back to Zydeco and let Pearl Lee surface when she was ready. Just because Miss Frankie wanted me to keep her under control didn't mean I had to break my neck doing it. Pearl Lee was an adult, fully capable of making her own decisions. Even if Miss Frankie didn't agree.

But this wasn't only about Pearl Lee. I also had to think about Scotty. He was vulnerable. Grieving. Not thinking clearly. Probably looking for comfort wherever he could find it, and Pearl Lee seemed only too ready to oblige.

I stood there battling indecision for a few minutes, then picked a direction and started walking. I didn't really think they'd gone to the Chopper Shop, but it was worth checking there to be sure. With Destiny's death so recent, Moose was probably at home attending to details. The empty building might give Juliet the privacy she wanted with her intended Romeo.

Halfway there, I called Ox on his cell phone. I gave him a rundown on Pearl Lee's disappearance and asked him to let me know if she showed up at Zydeco. He fussed a bit about all the work we had to do before the end of the business day. He was absolutely right, but I was in no mood for a lecture. I promised to be back in an hour and hung up before he could argue with me.

Thirty seconds later, my phone chimed Miss Frankie's ring tone. I contemplated answering for roughly two seconds, but quickly decided that ignoring the call would be the safest course of action. I could always return the call once I had Pearl Lee back.

To my surprise, I found half a dozen motorcycles in the parking lot when I reached the Chopper Shop, all three service bays open for business, and a Bob Seger song blaring from a set of loudspeakers. There was no sign of Scotty or Pearl Lee, but I could see Moose inside, perched on the corner of the desk and talking with a couple of long-haired biker dudes. I couldn't hear what they were talking about, and they all fell silent at once when they realized they weren't alone.

Moose blinked a couple of times, as if he was having trouble focusing enough to see me. "Hey, Rita," he said when he finally figured out who I was. He asked the other guys to give us a minute, and motioned me toward an old wooden chair when they were gone. "You're looking a little better today. How are you feeling?"

I gave my standard answer. "A little better every day. I'm surprised to see you here. I didn't expect you to be open."

His head dropped and he kicked the desk softly with the heel of his boot. "I had to do something besides make funeral plans. I was starting to go crazy just sitting home and staring at the walls."

"I understand that," I said. Grief is a strange thing and different for everyone. If he needed to keep busy, who was I to judge? "How's Scotty holding up?"

Moose wagged his massive head slowly. "As well as can be expected, I guess."

"I'm actually trying to find him," I said. "Have you seen him?"

"Not lately. He went out a while ago. Hasn't come back yet." He looked at me strangely. "I'd ask if I could help, but I'm guessing you're not here to get your bike serviced."

"And you'd be right. He . . . uh . . ." I hesitated, unsure how to explain my problem. "Do you have any idea who he was meeting?"

"Friends. I'm not sure who. He didn't say. Do you want me to have him call when he comes back?"

That might be too late. "The truth is, I last saw him with someone," I said. "A woman. She's the one I'm really trying to find."

Moose's leg stopped swinging. "A woman? Anyone I know?"

"I don't think so. She's a cousin of mine, I guess. In a roundabout way. Anyway, she just got to town and she's supposed to be working with me at Zydeco. We were out picking up a few things and we ran into Scotty. The two of them took off somewhere. I was hoping maybe they'd come here."

Moose glanced around the cluttered and greasy office. "Not many places for them to go unnoticed around here."

"Right. I realize it was a long shot, but I really do need to find her."

"Where were they last time you saw them?"

"At the Dizzy Duke. That was about fifteen minutes ago. They snuck out while I was distracted. Do you have any idea where Scotty might go if he wanted to . . . spend time with someone?"

Moose snorted a disbelieving laugh. "You've got to be kidding me, right? That's what you think they're doing? Well, I know damn well Scotty's old enough to make his own decisions, so unless this cousin of yours is underage—"

"Good grief, no!" I said before he could finish that thought. "She's definitely old enough. And if it was up to me, I'd just let them go and do their thing. But my mother-in-law—" How to explain Miss Frankie? I decided to skip that part. "And what about Zora?"

Moose's head snapped up and his brows formed a V over the bridge of his nose. "What's she got to do with it?"

"Well, you know, she and Scotty—" I broke off, figuring he could fill in the blanks on his own.

He just shook his head and looked confused. "What about 'em?"

"They're together, aren't they?"

"Scotty and Zora?" Moose actually laughed. "Um . . . no."

Now I was confused. "Oh, but I thought—that is, I assumed—she just seemed so—"

"She's a nice lady," Moose said. "She came over to help out after Destiny died. But that's all it was."

Wow. Talk about reading a situation wrong. My cheeks burned with embarrassment, but underneath that was a strong wave of relief. I felt better knowing that at least Pearl Lee wasn't currently wrecking Zora's home sweet home.

"Well, then," I said, eager to get out of there before I put my foot in my mouth again. "I'll just go back to work and wait for her to show up." I stood and turned toward the door.

"Hey, Rita?" Moose said before I could get away. "One question?"

I turned back and nodded. "Sure."

"You said that Destiny showed up at Zydeco to help collect supplies for the cleanup, right?"

I didn't want to talk about that, but I couldn't just dodge the question so I dipped my head and said, "Right."

"You said she wasn't feeling well."

"Right."

"What was wrong with her?"

I didn't want to answer that question either, but he deserved the truth. "I think she was on something," I said reluctantly. "She was having trouble walking and her words were slurred, and she was behaving strangely."

"Yeah, that's what I thought you were gonna say." He rubbed his face and let out a sigh that seemed to come from the bottoms of his feet. "She swore to me she was clean. She *swore* she wasn't using again."

"And you believed her," I said gently, "because she was your wife. Anybody would."

His eyes burned with sudden searing anger. "She lied to me. It wasn't the first time either. Every word that came out of her mouth was a lie." He stood and took a couple of steps away, then turned back and slammed his fist onto the desk. Everything on the desktop jumped and so did my heart. "She *lied* and I was such a damn fool I believed her."

I was in way over my head, and I didn't want to call attention to myself when he was smashing things, so I didn't say anything at all.

"Felix tried to warn me, you know. I told you that. He saw it."

"You loved her. You wanted to believe her," I said. "That's understandable."

"Yeah." He snorted softly and turned away again. "Yeah. I wanted to believe her. And the whole time she was robbing me blind and using the money to get high. What else did she do? Was she sleeping around? That's what Zora thinks, you know. I heard her telling Scotty last night. She thinks that Destiny was sleeping with Edgar."

Zora's not the only one, I thought, but I wasn't going to be the one to tell him.

"Was she?" he demanded.

Crap. He was staring at me, waiting for an answer. "Edgar denies it," I said. "He says they were just friends."

"Yeah, well, he would say that, wouldn't he?"

"It could be true," I pointed out.

"And it could be another lie."

He had a point. I'd taken Edgar's story at face value, but what if he *was* sleeping with Destiny? He'd seemed determined to convince me they were just friends. But were they? Or had their relationship been much more? And how far would he go to hide the truth?

"Did he know she was using?"

I nodded slowly. "He denied it at first, but then he said she was struggling to stay clean and that he was trying to help her."

Moose's face crumpled. "She told him and not me?" He dropped into a chair so hard it creaked in protest and buried his face in his hands.

I watched his shoulders shake and heard the heart-wrenching sounds of him sobbing. I stayed there, patting his massive shoulder and making "there-there" noises until he finally calmed down and I felt comfortable slipping away.

But as I crossed the parking lot, I wondered, who *was* this guy? Was he a tenderhearted teddy bear or a killer moose? I couldn't get a handle on him. I couldn't get a handle on any of them.

I just hoped I wouldn't end up paying for something one of them had done.

Fifteen

❧

I'd lost track of time while talking to Moose, but as I started past Second Chances on my way back to work, I realized that though I'd talked to Isaiah the other day, I still hadn't asked Aquanettia or Keon about the accident. I glanced at my watch, convinced myself that I had a few minutes to spare, and decided to take a chance on finding at least one of them at work.

I'm not a fan of the thrift store experience. After my parents died and I went to live with Uncle Nestor and Aunt Yolanda, money was tight. Adding another mouth to feed and body to clothe—a girl in a family of four boys—had taken a toll on a budget already stretched to the breaking point. Aunt Yolanda had been a genius at stretching a dollar, and I'd spent more weekends than I wanted to remember helping her look for clothes and household items amid the junk other people had no use for.

Losing my parents had turned me into a surly young woman determined to find fault with the world that had betrayed me. Wearing secondhand clothes had only added fuel to the flame. I'd vowed that when I grew up and ruled my own world, I'd never buy secondhand anything.

To psych myself up, I stopped in front of the gate and took a quick look around. I'd been here before, but only to attend alliance meetings. Going inside as a customer was a whole 'nother story. Like Zydeco, Second Chances occupied an old house that had been repurposed as a business. But while Zydeco's renovation was recent, Second Chances had undergone its change of life at least a decade earlier, and some of the improvements were already showing signs of age.

Five short steps led from the front walk to a long front porch, where two windows flanked the center entry. A well-tended hedge separated the shop from the street, and only a carved wooden sign discreetly wired to the front gate identified the old house as a business.

Inside the yard, however, the illusion of grandeur vanished. Old patio furniture and lawn ornaments lay all over the grass, and uneven stacks of terra-cotta pots lined the fence on one side. A long cracked driveway stretched along the other side, separating it from the Chopper Shop.

I opened the door and the familiar musty odor of old, used items assaulted me. I tried not to wrinkle my nose as I stepped inside, where a mishmash of items covered every imaginable surface. Aisles, narrow and mazelike, curved haphazardly through the mess.

I found Keon, a kid of about twenty with a bored expression, stocky build, and mocha skin sitting with his feet propped on a long glass counter and playing a handheld electronic game. He didn't even glance away from his game, acknowledging me only with an irritated, "Yeah?"

Killer work ethic, dude. Your mother must be so proud.

Keon didn't seem interested in small talk, so I tried to ease into the conversation with a little white lie. "I'm looking for a crib set for a friend. Do you know if you have one in good condition?"

Still not looking up, Keon gave a lazy shrug. "No idea."

Well. That was helpful. "Do you have an inventory list or something? I'm kind of in a hurry."

Keon punched a few game buttons with his thumbs. "Nope. You want to look around? Knock yourself out."

Okay then. Obviously I'd have to try another tack. "It's such a shame about Destiny from next door," I said. "Did you know her?"

Keon's eyes finally flickered up from the game. "Kind of. Not really." Now that he was actually looking at me, his eyes lingered on the bruises on my face. "You're the lady who almost got hit with our van."

I nodded. "Yeah. Rita Lucero. I work at Zydeco a couple of blocks down." I held out a hand.

He stared at it for a long time and then looked back at his game. "You ain't here for a crib, are you? What do you really want?"

I leaned against the counter and tried not to look annoyed by the snub. Maybe I wasn't as slick as I thought. "Okay. You got me. I'm trying to find out anything I can about the accident. Were you here on Monday night?"

Keon shook his head. "Not me. I heard about what happened when I got home."

"So you didn't see anyone outside near the van? You don't have any idea who might have stolen it?"

He curled his lip in what I thought might have been a smile. "I don't know nothing about that. Why are you asking anyway? Isn't that a job for the cops?"

I nodded. "It should be, but they're pretty busy lately. There's a lot of crime in the city. They don't have a lot of time to spare trying to figure out who tried to run me over."

"So why are you asking about Destiny? Other than the fact that you're the one who found her."

"Well, actually, the lead detective thinks *I* was her drug dealer. I'm just trying to prove him wrong."

Keon laughed, but as his smile faded, he gave me a long look and shook his head. "Guess that explains why that cop was in here yesterday asking all sorts of questions about you."

I think my heart stopped beating. "Like what?"

"Like did I ever see you and Moose together? Did I ever see you hanging around over there?"

My stomach dropped and my breath caught. Winslow must seriously think I'd been supplying Destiny's habit when I wasn't secretly rendezvousing with her husband. "Anything else?"

Keon shrugged. "I don't know. The usual, I guess. When did I see her last? Did I ever hear her and Moose fight? Shit like that. So did you get her drugs?"

"Of course not." I glanced out the window toward the Chopper Shop, but all I could see was the fence. "Did you see Destiny yesterday morning? Do you know what time she got to work?"

Keon laughed. "Work? Destiny didn't work. Do I know what time she opened the doors? Nope. Do I know who stole the van? Nope. Don't know. Don't care. All I know is it wasn't me." He went back to his game for a moment and then asked, "You sure guy who stole the van was trying to hit you?"

My spidey senses tingled. "No. Actually, I'm starting to think that someone was trying to hurt Moose or Destiny. Do you know anyone who might have wanted to hurt one of them?"

Keon's long fingers stilled on the game pad and his dark eyes glittered. I had the feeling he was about to say something important, but I didn't get the chance to find out. The back door flew open with a bang and his mother, Aquanettia, bustled inside, her arms loaded down with several bulging bags. A small ball of brown fur trotted in at her heels and circled her feet when she came to a stop. This must be the infamous Gilbert that Zora had mentioned.

"Keon, baby, I need you to go out back and get the rest of these T-shirts for me. And don't make plans for the rest of the day. We need to start handing them out so people have them before the cleanup."

Keon scuttled out the back door. Aquanettia put the bags on the counter, noticing me for the first time. "Oh! Rita!" she said. "I didn't see you there." She smoothed her hair and tugged down the hem of her shirt. Gilbert skittered across the hardwood floor toward me so he could sniff my feet. He must have ruled me out as a threat because he stood on his hind legs and pawed at me, begging for attention. I bent down to scratch behind his ears, which earned a smile from Aquanettia. Love me, love my dog.

"Are you here to do a little shopping?" she asked. "We got some nice clothes in on consignment the other day."

I shook my head quickly. "I was just talking to Keon about the accident on Monday night."

Aquanettia's smile faded. "Oh, goodness. What a close call you had. And to think it was my van they used." She shook her head and her expression sobered even more. "But what did you want to talk to Keon about? He wasn't even here."

"Are you sure? Someone told me they thought Keon was driving the van that night."

Aquanettia's eyes grew cold and hard. "That's a lie. Who told you that?"

I couldn't think of any reason to protect the dearly departed, so I told the truth. "It was Destiny."

"Well," Aquanettia said tersely, "she lied. But that was nothing new. Not to speak ill of the dead, but that woman wouldn't have recognized the truth if it had waltzed right up to her and introduced itself. Keon wasn't here that night."

"But why would Destiny lie about him?"

"She would have lied about anything," Aquanettia spat out. "That's why Felix tried to warn all of you about her." She opened one of the packages and shook out a T-shirt bearing a large blue magnolia tree on the front. "Her death was a tragedy, but at least we don't have to worry about her trying to worm her way onto the Board of Directors. Can you believe the way she tried to undo all the work we'd already done?"

Her attitude made me uneasy. "It's no secret the two of you weren't friends," I said. "But don't you think that's a bit cold? I mean yes, she was the competition—"

Aquanettia laughed harshly. "Oh, honey, that woman was never any actual competition. You can't think anyone would have actually voted for her."

"I don't know," I said. "I'm sure Moose would have, and Edgar seemed to support her."

Aquanettia gave an expressive roll of her big brown eyes. "Edgar. What a piece of work he is. He certainly surprised me. All Destiny had to do was twitch her hips and he'd do whatever she wanted."

"You think Edgar was interested in her? Romantically, I mean?"

"Are you kidding?" Aquanettia laughed and dropped into a chair behind the counter. "Honey, they were thicker than thieves."

I thought about Destiny's offer to let me have Moose the day she came to Zydeco, and shuddered. Had she been planning to dump Moose? Had he found out and slipped something into her coffee? "I can't say I saw them together before the meeting Monday evening, but they seemed pretty friendly that night."

Aquanettia glanced around to make sure we were alone and then leaned in conspiratorially. "I'm not one to talk bad about people, but 'friendly' doesn't even come close to describing it. I wouldn't say this to just anyone, but the truth is, that woman made poor Moose's life a living hell."

I wondered how much more forthcoming Aquanettia would be if she *weren't* being "discreet." "Do you think Moose suspected she was cheating on him?"

Aquanettia nodded. "Oh, he knew. They used to fight all the time about how often she went running off." She tapped her head just above the ear. "I guess they thought we couldn't hear them, but we heard just about every word. Moose told her just a few days before she died that he'd had enough. It wasn't the first time he drew a line in the sand, but maybe he meant it this time."

I didn't know how to respond to that, and thankfully I was spared having to come up with something to say. The bell over the door tinkled as a couple of young women pushing strollers came inside, and I beat a hasty retreat. I still had no proof that Destiny's death was anything but an accidental overdose, but the feeling in my gut was getting stronger all the time. Maybe the reason Moose didn't mention the ultimatum he'd given Destiny was that he'd never actually issued one. Or maybe he had, but instead of warning her off drugs, he'd told her to end the relationship with Edgar, or else.

I liked Moose when he wasn't angry, and I didn't want him to be guilty of murder. But I was starting to think that maybe he wasn't as surprised by Destiny's extracurricular activities as he pretended to be.

I quickly picked up the supplies on my list and hurried back to Zydeco, wolfing down a bag of chips for lunch. Ox and the others had finished the Oakes petunia cake while I was gone. Since the cake would be presented on a layered cake stand, he'd piped a mound of icing into the center of each tier, clustered the flowers, and added leaves before finishing with a piped bead border. All that remained was to deliver it by noon on Friday. The golf course cake was also due Saturday night, and we still had a lot of work left to finish it. I'd let distractions get in my way all week. It was time to redeem myself.

I got to work on the water hazard for the golf course cake, using Isomalt. Made from beet sugar, Isomalt has been around since the 1960s, and many professionals prefer using it to sugar for showpiece work since it's more resistant to crystallization, clouding, and the ravages of humidity. It's great for simulating water.

If it's prepared and stored right, it's also relatively easy to work with, but it's easy to mess up if you're not on top of the process. Determined to make up for having been gone most of the day, I carefully measured the Isomalt into a stainless steel pan and added a few ounces of distilled water. I put the pan on a burner in the kitchen and watched the flame to make sure it stayed centered on the bottom of the pot. When the mixture began to heat, I wiped down the sides of the pan with a nylon bristle brush, avoiding the natural bristles I usually prefer since those can turn the Isomalt an unsightly yellow color.

The mixture had just topped the 320-degree mark on my candy thermometer, a signal for me to watch closely so I could remove the pan from heat at 333 degrees and put it in water to stop the cooking process. And that's exactly what I would have done if Pearl Lee hadn't sashayed into the design room at that precise moment. And if she hadn't been beaming from ear to ear.

I forgot all about that hot pan full of Isomalt when I saw her. "Where in the hell have you been?"

Pearl Lee perched on one of the stools near my workstation. "Oh, don't be such a spoilsport. Scotty and I had a great time together."

"Terrific. Except you were supposed to be here, not off having a tryst."

"It was no such thing. I'll have you know that Scotty was a perfect gentleman. I tried to convince him to cut loose a little, but he wasn't in the mood, I guess."

"The man's in mourning," I reminded her. "His daughter just died. He might need a little more time before he's ready for a midafternoon roll in the hay."

Pearl Lee looked scandalized. "Why, Rita Renier, how you talk! It wasn't anything like that. The poor man just needed a shoulder to cry on."

"Lucero," I said when she paused to take a breath.

"What?"

"My name. It's Lucero, not Renier."

"Oh. Well, how very odd. But the point is, Scotty needed some breathing room. He wanted to get away from his son-in-law and the police and all the neighbors who think they know everything, and that old biddy who keeps hanging around his house all the time. So we ran off for a few hours. But it was all perfectly innocent."

"I sure hope you're telling the truth," I said. "But you know Miss Frankie will pitch a royal fit when she finds out."

Pearl Lee tilted her head. "Well now, baby, I don't see why Frances Mae has to find out anything about it. Can't you just tell her that I was here all afternoon just the way she said?"

"You want me to lie for you?"

"Don't think of it as a lie. Think of it as an investment in the future."

I laughed. "How would that be an investment?"

"Oh, honey, everybody needs a favor now and then. You do this one for me. I'll owe you one down the road."

"I don't think so," I said with another laugh. "I'm not doing anything that'll get me on Miss Frankie's bad side."

"What she doesn't know won't hurt her," Pearl Lee bargained.

I started to shake my head when the smell of burnt sugar caught my attention and I remembered the Isomalt. I swore under my breath and snatched the pan from the burner, but I was too late. The entire batch was ruined.

Apparently sensing that I was in no mood to negotiate, Pearl Lee hopped off the stool and headed back to the front of the house. I would have breathed a sigh of relief except she paused just before she walked through the door and waved one hand over her head. "Thanks, baby," she sang out. "I owe you one."

Sixteen

After Pearl Lee left, I threw myself into my work with a vengeance. Putting everything else out of my mind, I spent the next few hours molding palm trees from gum paste, and modeling a small set of golf clubs, four tires, and a few other details for the golf cart before turning my attention to making sand traps from crushed graham crackers. I sent Edie home around seven with strict instructions to eat well and get a good night's sleep. Around eleven, the rest of us packed it in after coming up with a game plan for finishing the cake the next day.

Just thinking about another day with Pearl Lee underfoot kicked up a craving for one of Gabriel's margaritas. Or two. He's a master at the craft. As I closed up at Zydeco, I briefly considered heading over to the Dizzy Duke. But I had to be up early and I'd need my wits about me. There was no way I could handle Pearl Lee and a foggy head at the same time. Besides, after the way Gabriel had covered for Scotty and Pearl Lee this afternoon, I wasn't in the mood to see him again so soon.

Dragging with exhaustion, I locked up and let myself out through the loading dock door. As I started toward my

Mercedes, I spotted Sparkle in the parking lot, standing between her car and mine. Actually, I spotted the gleam of light on the silver studs in her dog collar choker first. Her pitch-black hair and goth clothing blended into the shadows. She tossed a bag into the trunk of her Honda Civic and watched me closely as I walked toward her.

Her dark eyes roamed over the yellowing bruises on my face and the fading scratches on my arms. "You look awful. Are you sure you're okay?"

We'd been working together for hours, but she'd waited until now to ask. From anyone else, the delay might seem odd, but Sparkle likes to pretend that she's bored with the world and unconcerned about everyone in it. The fact that she had asked at all said a lot. She liked me! She really liked me! The realization touched me so deeply, I almost forgot how tired I was.

I grinned and nodded. "I'm fine. Feeling a little better every day."

"Do they know who was driving the van yet?"

"Not that they're telling me, but I'm sure they're working on it." Okay, I was being generous. I wasn't sure of anything, especially where Detective Winslow was concerned.

"Well, good." Sparkle fell silent for a moment, but made no move to leave.

Which made me think she had something else on her mind. I leaned against the trunk of the Mercedes and waited for her to let me know what it was.

"Estelle says you're planning a baby shower for Edie," she said after a few minutes.

Sparkle cared about the baby shower? That was a surprise. Maybe she was letting down her guard a little. "Actually, Miss Frankie is doing all the work," I said after glancing around to make sure Estelle wasn't hanging out in the shadows. Call me chicken but I didn't want Estelle to know that I'd passed off the job. "She's much better at planning parties than I am."

Sparkle nodded slowly, but a frown played across her

painted black lips. "Has Edie talked to you about the baby?"

Surprise number two. I was getting more curious about where Sparkle was going with her questions by the minute. "A little, but she's not saying much."

"That's the problem!" Sparkle cried, throwing up her hands in despair. I'd never seen her so animated before, and I wasn't sure how to react. "She's not talking to any of us, and some people are getting worried about her. They're starting to wonder if she's doing the right thing."

I took a cautious approach. "I'm not sure what you mean. Who wonders if Edie's doing the right thing about what?"

"The baby, of course." Sparkle seemed almost embarrassed to be talking about it, but she was obviously upset or she wouldn't have said anything at all. I had the feeling she wasn't just voicing the concerns of her coworkers either, but I played along. "You mean they wonder if she's doing the right thing to keep the baby?"

Sparkle shook her head. "That's not it. Edie wants the baby and I think she'll be a good mom." She sighed and leaned against the car, mirroring my posture. "But don't you think she ought to at least let the baby's dad be part of its life?"

She was wading into dangerous water now. Edie had already cut ties with her family because of their opinions. I was certain she wouldn't hesitate to do the same with Sparkle—or any of us, for that matter.

"I don't think it matters what you or I think," I said. "That's Edie's choice."

Sparkle rolled her eyes. "I know. I know. I'm just thinking about the baby. What kind of life is it going to have? Don't you think it deserves to know where it came from?"

I *so* didn't want to get in the middle of this, but I couldn't ignore the question. "I guess, if there's a great guy out there who would be a loving dad and who wants to know his kid. But what if he's not such a great guy? What if he doesn't care about the baby?" *Or what if Edie doesn't even know who he is?* "We don't know Edie's situation," I reminded Sparkle. "So speculating about what we think she should do is kind of pointless, don't you think?"

Sparkle did a maybe/maybe-not thing with her head and shoulders. "We'd know her situation if she wasn't being so secretive. She's only thinking about herself. She's not thinking about the baby at all. It's not easy growing up without a father. You know that."

"I do," I agreed. "But I was lucky. I lost my dad when I was twelve, but my Uncle Nestor was there to step in." I couldn't deny that Sparkle had a point, though. Even the most loving uncle hadn't been able to fill the void left by my father's death.

I wondered about Sparkle's past. I didn't know a lot about it except that she'd grown up in a commune and her parents were hippies. "Where is this concern for the baby coming from?" I asked. "I know you had an unusual childhood in some respects, but you grew up with both parents, didn't you?"

Sparkle looked down at her feet. "Well . . . sort of. I know that Liberty is my mom. She says she is anyway, and I'm pretty sure she's telling the truth. But I don't know where Bob fits into the picture. He's been hanging around for so long, I've just started calling him Dad. It's easier."

"Oh," I said brilliantly. I didn't know what else to say.

Sparkle lifted her head and laughed, and for a moment the smile on her face transformed her. "Yeah," she said. "I get that a lot. People really don't know how to react when they find out."

"So Bob isn't your dad?"

"He might be. He might not be. Liberty doesn't even know. She's all about doing what feels right in the moment but she's not big on keeping track of what she did and when she did it. That includes who she slept with. I have no idea who my real dad is or even if my brother River and I have the same one. Details like that just aren't important in my mother's world." A note of bitterness crept into her voice, and my heart went out to her. I'd had a rough time after my parents died, but I'd always been completely sure that they loved me. From the way Sparkle was talking, I didn't think she'd had the same assurance. I wondered how she would feel if she ever learned the truth about Edie's situation, and made a silent vow not to be the one who told her.

"I didn't even know you had a brother," I said when I found my voice again. "I guess I need to pay better attention."

Sparkle's smile faded and her familiar bored expression took its place. "I don't talk about him much," she admitted. "I haven't seen him in a while."

Interesting response. Apparently, River was a touchy subject as well. But she'd brought him up, so I went with it. "How long is a while?"

"This time? Five years. He got fed up with the whole commune thing and took off when he was seventeen. I was only twelve and I missed him like crazy. He came back once, right before I left, and he wrote to me a couple of years later. Bob forwarded the letter, so River and I kept up by mail for a while. Later we started e-mailing. I hear from him about twice a year."

"Sounds like you still miss him."

Sparkle shrugged. "I deal with it." Which, I was learning, meant "yes" in Sparkle-speak. "Look, I'm okay with my life so don't start feeling all sorry for me or anything. I just think Edie's kid deserves better, that's all. Would you help me talk sense into her?"

I laughed and shook my head. "I wouldn't try telling Edie what to do in this situation if my life depended on it. She's doing the best she can in a difficult situation. I think the best thing we can do is to just be supportive."

Sparkle had looked down at her boots again, but now her head whipped up and she stared at me with eyes wide as quarters. "You know who it is, don't you?"

Crap! What had I done to give her that idea? I shook my head quickly. "I don't know anything."

"Don't lie. You *know.* I can tell."

What was she? Psychic? "I don't know who the baby's

father is," I said firmly. "So you can stop asking. I couldn't tell you even if I wanted to." And that was the truth.

"But you know something."

I made a face at her and pulled out my keys. "What I know is that we both have a long day tomorrow. We should both go home."

"Now you're trying to distract me, but it's not going to work." Sparkle got between me and the car door. "You know something about the baby. What is it?"

"Forget it," I said. "If that's all you want, let's call it a night. I'm tired and I want to go to bed."

Sparkle stared at me, like she thought that if she glowered long and hard enough, I might cave. But I knew she didn't really want me to. Aunt Yolanda had taught me that a person who shares someone else's secrets with you can't be trusted with your own. If I blabbed to Sparkle now, she would never trust me again.

I stared back, holding her gaze with mine and refusing to blink. I'd played this game with my cousins a lot when we were younger and I'd gotten good at it. Only an earthworm down my back could make me blink first.

It took a while, but Sparkle finally broke. She sighed and reluctantly moved out of my way. "I'll find out sooner or later," she warned.

I tried not to gloat. After all, Aunt Yolanda had also taught me to be a gracious winner. So I flashed a smile as I slid behind the wheel. "I think it's great that you're concerned about the baby, but try not to worry. Edie's a responsible adult. She'll do the right thing."

"I hope so," Sparkle said. "For the baby's sake." I expected her to walk away now that we'd reached an impasse, but to my surprise, she wasn't finished with me. "Is everything okay with you? You seem kind of distracted."

"I guess I am," I said. "There's a vice cop who thinks I was supplying Destiny with drugs, and that's freaking me out a little."

Sparkle's mouth fell open. "No joke?"

"I'm afraid not. And something about Destiny's death feels off to me. I'm about seventy-five percent convinced she had help with the overdose that killed her."

"You think she was murdered?"

"Maybe. I can't prove it, though. And I'm not sure the police are even looking into it." Winslow seemed much more interesting in taking me down.

"So are you going to do the same thing with that as you're doing with the baby? Just sit back and hope for the best?"

The question stung. I put my key into the ignition and scowled. "I can't dictate to Edie what she should do with her life, and I can't prove Destiny was murdered just because I want to."

"But *you* didn't give her drugs," Sparkle said, as if that should matter to Detective Winslow. "And you're usually right about these kinds of things. You can't let somebody ruin Zydeco's reputation—and yours—just because he's a cop."

I appreciated her faith in me but it didn't change anything. "It's not that easy."

"Let's say she was murdered. Who do you think did it?"

"I have no idea."

"Oh, come on," she said. "You must have *some* idea."

I was relieved to leave the subject of Edie and the baby behind and touched by her faith in my innocence. Clearly, she needed to talk, so I motioned for her to get into the car and turned on the air conditioner so we'd be comfortable. "It could have been Edgar Zappa," I said. "I think he and Destiny were having an affair even though he claims they were just friends. Plus, he knew that Destiny was using drugs again. He says he was trying to help her, but I don't know. I think he's hiding something. How well do you know him?"

"Not well," Sparkle said. "I've used EZ Shipping to send packages home, but that's about it. Do you really think he and Destiny were sleeping together?"

"It's possible," I said. "Why? Don't you?"

She shook her head. "I don't see it. He's not really her type."

"Aquanettia seems to think that every man was her type. According to her, the two of them spent an awful lot of time together."

"Edgar's too quiet," Sparkle said. "Destiny would have tossed him like yesterday's trash after their first date unless he had something she wanted."

That was an intriguing thought. "Like what?"

"Money maybe? Or drugs?"

I tried to imagine tall, blond Edgar as a drug dealer. The image didn't fit, but I didn't dismiss the idea. "Maybe he found out she was using him," I said.

"And he snuck over to the Chopper Shop early one morning to kill her?"

"Maybe. Or maybe they met there for some reason and then he found out. Both Moose and Scotty were out late the night before. Destiny told them to stay home and sleep in. Maybe she arranged to meet Edgar when they could be alone. But even if that were the case, I'd never be able to prove it."

Sparkle chewed on one stubby black-polished nail. "If he was there, somebody could have seen him. What time are we talking about?"

"I found her around nine in the morning," I said. "If I could find someone who was in the area, and who saw Edgar, or even Moose or Scotty at the Chopper Shop, Detective Winslow would have to admit that something is fishy. Every one of them has denied being there."

"Then maybe you should find out if anyone saw one of them or somebody else at the Chopper Shop yesterday morning. Because if you're right and somebody did kill her, that means a murderer is walking around this neighborhood free and clear."

"And if I'm wrong?"

Sparkle shrugged. "Then you're wrong and you can let it go. But even if you're wrong about Destiny, somebody was driving the van that almost hit you."

She was right about that. "Edgar said that Moose was ready to divorce Destiny if she relapsed. According to Edgar, Destiny had spent so much money on drugs the Chopper Shop was in real trouble. Moose hasn't come right out and said that she put the shop in jeopardy, but he did admit that he let her do whatever she wanted for a long time. And I've seen his temper in action. It's not hard to imagine him snapping but he was standing beside me when the van came around the corner. So unless Destiny's murder was premeditated and Moose had an accomplice, I don't think he did it."

Sparkle thought that over and said, "Unless he saw an opportunity after the van almost ran you down and decided to kill her then."

I shook my head. "I might have believed that at first, but the longer this goes on, the less I think the van's driver was after me. Either he was trying to hit Destiny and went for me by mistake, or he was after Moose. If Moose did it and used an accomplice, who was it? Scotty? Destiny was a real piece of work, but do you really think her own father would be part of a plot to kill her?"

"Stranger things have happened. I know for a fact that Scotty and Destiny weren't getting along. Maybe he finally got fed up with her."

I shot a look across the seat at her. "How do you know they weren't getting along, and why are you just telling me about it now?"

Sparkle looked sheepish. "I forgot. It didn't seem like anything at the time, but I heard them arguing a few days before she died."

"Did you hear what they were arguing about?"

Sparkle shook her head. "Not really. They were in a booth at the Lotus Blossom. I was waiting for a take-out order. I didn't hear the whole conversation, but I know it had something to do with Aquanettia and the Magnolia Square Business Alliance. Destiny was planning to do something Scotty didn't agree with. He told her to step back and let it go but she just laughed and said she'd only be giving that bitch what she deserved."

"How did Scotty react to that?"

"That's what made me think about it," Sparkle said. "He got really quiet, but not in a good way. In the creepy way, you know? And he told her to back off or she'd be sorry."

My stomach turned over a couple of times as I considered the implications of that threat. But what could have made a father say something like that to his only daughter? Had I been wrong about Scotty? Had he and Moose planned Destiny's murder together? They each had motive. They both had the means, and together they had the opportunity to set it up.

But even if my suspicions about one of the men in Destiny's life were correct, it still wasn't enough. I had to find proof that someone else had killed Destiny in the first place or I might never get the target off my own back.

Seventeen

I didn't get a chance to think about drug dealers or possible murder plots on Friday. We were up to our necks in work, delivering the petunia cake for the Oakes baptism and trying to finish the golf course case. I put Pearl Lee to work double-checking client addresses on our mailing list, which she actually did when she wasn't filing her nails or learning to play Solitaire online. The fact that she'd done any work at all may have lulled me into a false sense of security.

I was at work bright and early Saturday morning, ready to do my bit for the neighborhood cleanup committee. And if I happened to find myself working alongside a neighbor—a neighbor who might have seen someone hanging around the Chopper Shop on Wednesday morning, for example—well, so be it. I'm not the type to look a gift horse in the mouth.

Aquanettia was already on-site when I pulled into the parking lot, barking orders to Isaiah and Keon, who were busy moving supplies into several stacks around the lot's perimeter. Each of her sons was wearing a stark white T-shirt with a blue magnolia tree on the chest, the shirts

Aquanettia had been unpacking when I stopped in at Second Chances.

Isaiah directed me to park in the far corner of the lot while Aquanettia shouted at Keon. "No, no, no! Don't put those there. I told you, we need each team to have the same supplies exactly! If you don't watch what you're doing, we'll end up with nothing but confusion."

Keon shot his mother an exasperated look and bent to pick up the box he'd just put down. Even though the sun had only been up a few minutes, sweat already glistened on his face and created a dark stain on his shirt. "It's no big deal, Ma. They're gonna be picking up garbage, not curing cancer."

Aquanettia sighed heavily at her son, but she smiled at me. "I'm glad you're here, Rita. We could use another hand."

I really wanted to slip inside for a cup of coffee, but I didn't want to seem uncooperative so I stirred up some community spirit and said, "Put me to work. I'm all yours."

"You're feeling strong enough? I don't want to make things worse if you're still feeling poorly."

"I'm good to go," I assured her. "Where do you want me?"

"I'm trying to get the supplies divided evenly into eight different groups. We'll split up into teams, each team taking a section of the neighborhood that I've marked on this map." She held out a clipboard and gave me a glimpse of a hand-drawn grid representing the Magnolia Square Business Alliance.

"Each group should have water, a selection of tools, garbage bags—" She broke off suddenly, scowling at my chest. "Where is your T-shirt? You're supposed to be wearing your T-shirt. Keon spent all day yesterday delivering those shirts and detailed instructions to every member of the alliance. You're supposed to be wearing yours for the cleanup today."

News to me. But that's why I wasn't running for Queen

of the World. Sometimes important details like that escape me.

"I haven't seen mine," I said. "Keon must have brought it by while I was out. Maybe I should go find it." And I'd begin my search at the coffeepot.

Aquanettia swiped a trickle of sweat from her forehead and waved me off. "Go. I don't know how we can expect to present a united front to the neighborhood if we can't even get that one little thing right."

I didn't get far before someone called my name. I turned back reluctantly and found Zora coming down the driveway carrying a couple of oversized tote bags. Her Magnolia Square T-shirt was stretched tight, revealing every bounce and jiggle as she walked. "I hope I'm not late," she said as she climbed the loading dock steps. "My neck has been giving me fits this morning." Sweeping a fringe of bangs out of her eyes, she turned to survey the work already under way. "It looks like you have everything under control as usual, Aquanettia."

Aquanettia smiled up from her clipboard. "So far, so good. I have you down to help Isaiah pass out supplies when the teams are assembled." She gestured toward a couple of dogwoods on the edge of the garden. "Your station will be right over there by those trees."

Zora squinted into the morning sunlight and then put one hand on the back of her neck. "I hope it's not going to be too strenuous. Do you have a chair I can use, Rita? I really won't last long at all if I have to stand."

I assured her that I did and tried again to get inside for coffee. I'd be no good to anyone unless I got a shot or two of caffeine under my belt. But as I reached for the door, Zora let out a heavy sigh and said, "I suppose you both know about the memorial service for Destiny?"

Maybe coffee could wait for a few more minutes. "I hadn't heard," I said. "When will it be?"

"Wednesday morning at eleven at the Falcon Brothers Mortuary. We don't know yet if the police will have finished the autopsy by then, but Moose and Scotty feel the need to do something. There will be a notice in the paper, of course. If you need the address or anything, just give me a call. I know it would mean a lot to both Moose and Scotty if some of the folks from the neighborhood were there."

I hate funerals and everything that goes with them, but I knew Zora was right. Besides, I felt an obligation to be there. Or maybe after finding Destiny's body I just needed closure. "Thanks for letting us know," I said, and made a mental note to talk to the staff about ordering flowers.

Aquanettia's broad mouth pursed tightly. "They've having it in the middle of the workday, meaning we'd have to close up shop? That's really not practical at all."

I was a little taken aback by her reaction. She was acting like they were purposely trying to inconvenience the rest of us. It wouldn't hurt to sacrifice one morning to pay our respects.

Zora's thoughts must have been running along the same lines because she said, "Well, you know how these things are. It will only be for an hour or so."

Aquanettia sniffed and flipped pages on her clipboard as she marched toward the stairs.

Zora looked at me with a roll of her eyes as Aquanettia walked away. "I suppose I shouldn't be surprised. She never did like Destiny."

"So you said before. Still, that seems like a harsh reaction to an argument over a barking dog."

Zora folded her arms across her chest and slid another look at me from the corners of her eyes. "Well, it wasn't just the dog, if the truth be told. There were other issues. I didn't say anything before because I didn't want to talk about it in front of her family."

She had my full attention now. "Oh?"

"Aquanettia accused Destiny of some . . . well, some disturbing behavior. Destiny denied everything, of course. Just as she did with everything else. I wanted to believe her, but I must admit, I sometimes had my doubts."

Curiosity was eating me alive, but I tried to act casual as I asked, "What kind of disturbing behavior?"

"Oh." Zora quickly looked down at her hands, as if she was flustered. "I probably shouldn't say. It was all so nasty—and it might not even be true."

She couldn't clam up *now*! I thought frantically, hoping to find a way to encourage her to keep talking. Strictly out of a sense of civic duty, of course. Sparkle had already admitted to being nervous and I'm sure she wasn't the only one. Didn't I have an obligation to my friends and coworkers to find out everything I could?

"I don't want to pry, but it might be important," I said. "Between you and me, I'm not convinced that Destiny took that overdose. I think she might have had help."

"What do you mean 'help'?" Zora looked confused.

"I think maybe someone slipped those pills to her somehow. Maybe in her coffee. There were two cups on the desk the morning I found her, so maybe she had company. If there was some big issue between her and Aquanettia, maybe you should tell the police about it."

Zora put one trembling hand on her chest. "You think Destiny was *murdered*?"

"I think it's possible," I said. "Whatever Aquanettia accused Destiny of doing, do you think it was serious enough for Aquanettia to want to hurt her?"

Zora took a couple of deep breaths, turned to look at Aquanettia again, and then slowly looked back at me. "It was about the boys. Isaiah and Keon. Destiny used to pull them away from their work at Second Chances, always asking one of them to lift this for her or move that. It was rough on Aquanettia because they'd just disappear right in the middle of a workday without so much as a word."

I didn't know whether to feel relieved or disappointed. Okay. Yeah. That would have been inconvenient, but it hardly seemed like a motive for murder. "I'm sure that upset Aquanettia," I said to humor Zora.

Her mouth thinned in her round face. "You don't understand. Aquanettia thought it was more than that. She thought Destiny was trying to—" She broke off and shook her head. "Those boys are good boys, but Aquanettia was afraid that Destiny didn't want them to stay that way—if you know what I mean."

I got an icky feeling in the pit of my stomach. Neither of the boys seemed to have liked Destiny, but maybe that hadn't mattered to her. "Are you saying that she tried to seduce them?"

Zora's mouth grew even thinner. "I don't know if it's true, but Aquanettia was convinced of it. She told Destiny to leave them alone, but Destiny thought it was funny. She loved to do things to annoy Aquanettia, so the more Aquanettia groused about it, the more Destiny played around with it."

"Do Moose and Scotty know?"

Zora nodded. "They know, but neither of them believes it. Aquanettia even talked to Scotty about it once, but he just called her a dried-up old busybody and ordered her off the property."

No wonder Aquanettia didn't seem interested in attending Destiny's memorial service. "What did Moose say about the accusation?"

The look in Zora's eyes grew soft and almost maternal. "Moose is such a sweetheart, he just didn't have it in him to think badly of the woman he married. It didn't matter what she did or how often she lied to him. But he didn't hold it against Aquanettia the way Destiny did. She thought Aquanettia was a joke."

"So that's why she decided to run against her in the election?"

"I'm sure it was," Zora said. "It's not as if she cared about trash pickup or the color of paint we all use. And she hated Felix almost as much as Aquanettia." She stopped suddenly and whispered, "Speak of the devil . . ."

I followed her gaze and saw Felix and Lorena walking down the driveway. Felix wore a baseball cap on his balding head and a smear of white sunscreen on his broad nose. Lorena carried a couple of small battery-operated fans and a bag of ice that was already dripping water as it melted. Aquanettia let out a cry of delight at seeing her second in command and immediately started issuing orders. Zora started away to join them, and my urgent need for coffee—and my T-shirt, of course—reasserted itself to first place on my priority list. I waved to the new arrivals and reached once more for the door.

At the top of the stairs, Zora turned back and said, "Please don't repeat what I just told you. I don't want to cause Moose and Scotty any more pain. You understand."

I smiled, but I didn't actually promise to keep her secret. I didn't know whether to think the worst of Destiny or give her the benefit of the doubt. But what I thought didn't mean a thing. It's what Aquanettia believed that mattered. If she thought that Destiny was trying to lead her sons astray, how far would she have gone to keep them safe?

By the time I got back outside, the troops had assembled. Even Moose was there, which surprised me. He'd told me he wanted to stay busy to keep from thinking about his wife's death, but I still hadn't expected him to show up this morning. I looked around for Scotty but I guess he didn't feel the same need. I couldn't see him anywhere. I had dutifully changed into my Aquanettia-sanctioned T-shirt and learned that Pearl Lee (who was also conspicuously absent) and I had been teamed with Sebastian from the pharmacy and Paolo from the pizza parlor. Our assigned work area was half a block along St. Georges Street.

It quickly became apparent that Sebastian needed to spend less time behind the pharmacy counter and more time working out. He put everything he had into tearing out a patch of wild grass and undergrowth behind Java the Hut, but it left him without enough oxygen to breathe and talk at the same time.

Paolo, a round man in his late twenties with hairy forearms and dark chest hair sprouting over the top of his T-shirt, used his spare energy to compare and contrast his property with everyone else's. Since I didn't want to waste time playing "Who Keeps the Cleanest Yard," I had plenty of time to think.

I briefly considered calling Miss Frankie's house to find out where Pearl Lee was, but if I did that, Miss Frankie might insist on bringing her down to help. I decided to thank my lucky stars instead.

I thought about Edie and the baby, and wondered how long it would take people to find out that Edie had no idea who her baby daddy was. When they did, which was inevitable, what would Edie say, and how would it affect morale at Zydeco?

It was nearly ten when I heard someone calling me. I looked up from shoveling weeds and dried brush into garbage bags to see Pearl Lee hurrying toward me in a pencil skirt that barely reached the tops of her knees and a white silk blouse unbuttoned to reveal a startling amount of cleavage. An expanse of long and surprisingly shapely legs ended in a pair of expensive-looking pumps. Call me cynical, but I was beginning to suspect that she had no intention of actually participating in the neighborhood cleanup effort.

I brushed a lock of hair from my forehead and felt gritty dirt smearing beneath my hand as I did. I looked like I'd been rolling in the mud. She looked ready for the catwalk. It wasn't easy to assume the upper hand under those circumstances, but I did my best.

"You're late," I pointed out as Pearl Lee gingerly sidestepped a pile of dirt on the sidewalk. "You were supposed to be here at eight."

She lifted her chin and looked down her nose. "That's an ungodly hour for anyone to be awake. I didn't think you were serious."

I leaned on the shovel handle and gave her a hard look. "I suppose you didn't think I was serious about helping with the work either."

Pearl Lee glanced around in horror. "Honey, this isn't work for a lady. This is the kind of thing a lady hires someone else to do for her. You ought to get out of those clothes, take a shower, and make yourself presentable."

I laughed and shook my head. "Not a chance. I'm committed. I gave my word, and I'm staying. You gave your word that you'd help out today. Or did you forget about that?" I turned back to the pile of weeds waiting for me to bag them up. "Obviously you're not here to lend a hand, so why don't you head back to Zydeco? I'll call Ox and have him find something for you to do."

Pearl Lee noticed a speck of dirt on the toe of her shoe and bent down to brush it away. "There's no need to do that. I have lunch plans with Scotty at noon. There's hardly enough time for me to get anything done."

"There's plenty of time," I said. "And since you're just getting to work now, you won't actually get a lunch break until after two."

Pearl Lee gaped at me for a moment before apparently remembering that a lady doesn't stare at someone with her mouth hanging open. She snapped it shut and lifted her nose so she could look down at me over it. "That's out of the question. I simply cannot change my plans on such short notice."

"Maybe you should make an exception," I said. "It's just as difficult for me to adjust the staff's schedule to accommodate your social life."

"Oh, please, Rita. Don't be silly. You don't need me there and none of those people would even notice if I never came back."

I refused to concede the point just because she was right. "Miss Frankie expects me to keep you busy," I reminded her, "and that's what I plan to do. If you won't look out for yourself, maybe the family is right to give someone else the job."

She looked up from her inspection of a fingernail. "What do you mean by that?"

"I mean that there's something weird going on around here. A young woman might have been murdered, and there could be a killer on the loose. It's hard to know who to trust, and I think you should be careful who you spend time with."

Pearl Lee flapped a hand at me, her eyes narrowed. "I can trust Scotty."

"How can you say that? You don't really know the first thing about him. I don't even know him all that well. I'm just saying that maybe you should be careful, that's all."

Pearl Lee adjusted the strap of her handbag on the crook of her arm. "That's the most ridiculous thing I've ever heard. Why, Scotty is the kindest, sweetest man there is. Gentle. Devoted. And he's just devastated about what happened to Destiny."

"You only met him a few days ago," I pointed out reasonably. "You might not know everything there is to know."

"And you don't know him at all. You just said so. I don't want to seem rude, baby, but at least I've spent some time with the man. And I *know* a good one when I see one."

According to Miss Frankie, Pearl Lee's less-than-stellar judgment in men was the cause of her current distress, but I didn't point that out. Frankly, I was tired of arguing. "Fine," I said. "Forget I said anything. Would you mind handing me one of those garbage bags from the sidewalk behind you?"

Pearl Lee glanced at the bags and shook her head. "I would, but I don't want to ruin my manicure."

Seriously? I did some rather pointed looking of my own, beginning with the dirt stains on my knees and moving up to the new hole in the thigh of my jeans. "I know this isn't the most appealing job around, but I really could use your help. I *am* paying you to work for me, you know."

"Oh, please. Let's not start lying to each other. You and I both know that Frances Mae is putting up the money to keep me tied up here. You don't want me here any more than I want to be here. So let's just call a thing a thing, shall we? I'll stop by and make an appearance every morning and I'll be back in the afternoon before Miss Frankie arrives to collect me. In the meantime, you do what you do, and I'll keep myself busy. What Frances Mae doesn't know won't hurt her."

It was a tempting offer. I'd known Pearl Lee just

seventy-two hours and already I wanted to pay for her return trip to Florida. But there was one major obstacle standing in my way. "It will never work," I said, grabbing the garbage bag for myself. "Miss Frankie will figure out what you're doing, and when she does, there'll be hell to pay."

"Has anyone ever told you that you worry too much? If Frances Mae figures out that I'm not spending my days as her paid lackey, I'll deal with her. *Really*, Rita. You need to lighten up." And with that, Pearl Lee pivoted on her three-inch heels and minced off down the street, leaving me, literally, holding the bag.

Eighteen

✣

I'd made the mistake of working all morning without sunscreen and I was already paying the price. My face and arms felt like they were on fire and I could feel a massive headache coming on. When Aquanettia came by just after noon to check on our team's progress and release us for lunch, I threw down my shovel without a second thought. I had planned to head over to Zydeco to make sure the staff was on schedule with the golf course cake, but all the physical labor, combined with the mouthwatering scents that had been coming from the smoker at Rubio's Ribs all morning, had worked up an appetite I couldn't ignore.

Rib lovers are split down the middle when it comes to the virtues of dry rub versus those of a good barbecue sauce. Rubio Santiago happens to be a dry rub man. I've been trying for months to tease the ingredients for his secret combination of spices out of him, but so far he's not telling. I can taste coriander, cayenne, and garlic, and I'd bet my Albuquerque roots that he uses chunks of mesquite to create flavor. Beyond that, I'm stumped.

I almost changed my mind about eating at Rubio's when I saw Aquanettia pacing back and forth in front of a very long line of hungry alliance members, all waiting for a plate of Rubio's magic. She checked her watch and sighed impatiently, as if the whole lunch experience was taking too long for her. Frankly, her hands-on approach to running the cleanup was starting to suffocate me.

Two things kept me from turning around on the spot. One, Felix Blackwater and the ever-faithful Lorena came inside a few minutes after me and I wanted to see what he could tell me about the accident and Destiny; and two, did I mention the aromas that had been taunting me all morning?

Felix was red-faced and sweating. Lorena's round cheeks were smudged with dirt and her short blond hair stood on end. Both of them looked ready to pass out. I hoped they weren't too exhausted to answer a few questions.

I wanted to talk with Felix and Lorena, but I didn't want to look like I was stalking them, so I stepped out of line and pulled out my cell phone, so I could let a few people move in front of me.

All around me voices rose and fell as members of the alliance discussed their lunch orders, talked about their morning's work, or complained about Aquanettia's leadership style. I smiled and nodded and responded appropriately whenever someone talked to me, but I kept one eye on Felix and Lorena the whole time and silently urged the line to move a little faster.

After what felt like forever, they caught up with me and I pretended to finish what I was doing with my phone. I slid back into line and we spent a few minutes exchanging greetings and chatting about the weather.

The conversation hadn't presented any chances for a smooth segue into the subject of murder, but I wanted to keep them talking, so I asked, "How did your morning go? Did you get a lot done?"

Felix, whose face was beginning to regain its natural color, wiped his brow with a sleeve. "Our group has done a great job. We've almost finished with the section Aquanettia assigned us. How'd y'all do?"

I made the mistake of brushing my sunburned arm

against the wall and regretted it immediately. "We only made it about halfway. We ran into a patch of grass that took a while to clear out."

Felix nodded knowingly. "I suppose we got lucky. We should be completely finished in an hour or two. I've been thinking that maybe I should lend Moose's group a hand when we're done so he can go home. Poor man shouldn't be out here chopping down weeds so soon after his wife's death."

"I was surprised that he showed up, myself," I agreed. "I thought he might skip today."

"You and me both," Lorena said with a tick of her tongue against her teeth. "Can you believe what's been going on around here lately? First, that van almost ran you over. And then Destiny dying like that. It's just too, too much."

"I guess Moose feels the need to keep busy," I said, "and who can blame him? I didn't see Scotty, though. I guess he's not helping out?" I knew he wasn't. He was meeting Pearl Lee for lunch, but it was a way to keep them talking so I could find out what they knew.

Lorena's face puckered. "No. He's got plans of some kind. Don't ask me what, though. I couldn't tell you." It wasn't what she said, but the way she said it. Disapproval dripped from every word.

I wasn't too happy about it either, but only because Pearl Lee wouldn't back off.

Felix gave the collar of his T-shirt a twitch and looked around to see if anyone had overheard us. "Now Lorena, let's not speak ill of our neighbors."

"I'm not speaking ill," Lorena said, scowling so deeply half a dozen chins formed under her round face. "I feel just awful for poor Moose, that's all. And now Scotty's turning out to be just as unreliable as she was. I guess the acorn really doesn't fall far from the tree."

"Lorena!"

"Oh, I'm sorry, but if you ask me, Destiny put Moose through quite enough over the past couple of years. Just when he thought she was finally getting her act together, this happens."

"Lorena, *please*," Felix hissed. "Somebody might hear you. You make it sound like she purposely got herself killed."

Lorena rolled her eyes, but she did drop her voice a few decibels when she spoke again. "I'm not saying that she died on purpose. I'm sure it was a horrible accident. But if you play with fire long enough, eventually you're going to get burned. I really only meant that she wasn't known for making the best choices. And that's not news. Everybody knows that."

Destiny's reputation wasn't what concerned me. The line inched forward and I tried to steer the conversation in a slightly different direction. "Moose told me that you were the one who told him Destiny was on drugs again," I said to Felix. "That must have been difficult for him to hear."

Felix gave me a look I couldn't read. "I suppose it was. He never has liked hearing the truth about her."

"Well, yeah, but who does like being confronted with an unwelcome truth? How did you find out she was using again?"

Felix tugged at his shirt again. "It was no big deal. It should have been obvious to anyone who was paying attention. She came into the market one day in a real mess. Her eyes were dilated and she could hardly form a complete sentence, just like she used to be before she went to rehab. Moose was working his ass off, holding down the fort, while she did whatever she felt like doing."

I had to believe him. I'd seen her in exactly the same condition. "So you felt sorry for Moose? That's why you told him?"

"Of course I did. Wouldn't you?"

The line moved again and we all moved with it. I caught sight of my red-hot face in the mirror and winced at how sunburned it was. "So was it just once that you saw her high?"

Lorena shook her head and answered for him. "If it had been, Felix wouldn't have said anything. We both saw her slipping back into that old life and we felt we had to speak up."

We were close enough to the dining room now to see

members of the wait staff walking by with plates of ribs, which made it difficult to stay completely focused on the conversation.

"I told Felix he had to tell Moose. It wouldn't be fair to just keep our mouths shut. Not when we saw the things she was doing."

I glanced back at her in surprise. "Like what?"

Felix put a hand on Lorena's arm. "I don't think we should speculate aloud. We don't *know* that anything was going on."

Lorena shook off his hand impatiently. "You might not want to believe it, but I sure do. A woman can always tell." She turned to me for backup. "Isn't that right, Rita?"

"That depends," I said. "What are we talking about?"

"Lorena!" Felix snapped. "Not here."

She gave her boss a resentful look and flicked her gaze toward Aquanettia. "Ask her."

I decided to go out on a limb and take a guess. "Does it have something to do with Isaiah and Keon? I know that Aquanettia had some issues with Destiny over them."

"Issues?" Lorena laughed through her nose. "I guess you could say that. Destiny was lucky those boys aren't any younger."

"Lorena, really." Felix wedged himself between us and glared at me. "You ought to be ashamed of yourself, Rita. Repeating gossip where anyone can hear you. Destiny might have been a bad seed, but Moose still has to do business in this neighborhood. He still has to work with the people here. That's why I told him about the drugs. She was ruining the shop's reputation, and if *that* story gets out, it will ruin more than that."

Felix seemed genuinely concerned about Moose, but since Lorena was in a chatty mood, I pushed a little harder. "Did you actually see her doing anything inappropriate?"

"Everything she did was inappropriate," Felix said. "Now let the matter drop."

"Is that why you tried to have Destiny removed from the alliance? To protect Moose?"

"I tried to have her removed for the reasons I stated at the meeting. She never even bothered to come to any of the meetings. You know that. Everybody knows it."

"But Edgar said she was ill," I reminded him.

"Edgar," Lorena said with another soft snort of derision. "The man of a thousand excuses. Sick? Yes. By her own choice. Nobody forced her to pollute her body that way."

"She had no business voting on matters that would affect the rest of us," Felix said. "We're talking about my livelihood—and yours. Did you really want someone like her having a say? Running for office?"

I looked around at that restaurant full of neighbors and wondered if I'd been on the wrong track all this time. Had one of these laughing, sweating, and chattering people killed Destiny to permanently remove her name from the ballot? None of them looked like a cold-blooded killer, but everybody knows that looks can be deceiving.

We'd finally reached the head of the line and I turned my attention to the all-important selection of side dishes. Rubio allowed three sides with each entrée, but with a dozen to choose from, the decision wasn't always easy. Corn on the cob (fresh, not frozen) and hush puppies (deep-fried nuggets of cornbread so named because Confederate soldiers used to toss them to the dogs to keep them quiet) made the cut almost immediately. Choosing between Rubio's macaroni salad (a tangy mayo dressing over macaroni cooked al dente, cubes of sharp cheddar, and fresh peas) and collard greens (cooked in butter and pork fat) proved to be tougher.

Before I could make my final pick, the door flew open so hard it hit the wall and bounced off again. Windows rattled and every conversation in the line behind us ground to a screeching halt. Scotty Justus loomed in the doorway, his chest heaving, his eyes wild. He glanced around, but it only took a moment to find who he was looking for.

"You!" he shouted, pointing at someone behind me. "Just what in the hell do you think you're doing?"

Everyone swiveled to look, including me. That's when

I realized that he wasn't aiming that finger at someone else. I put a hand on my chest and squeaked, "Me?" just to be sure.

"I want to talk to you. Outside. Now."

Right that minute it wasn't hard to picture him trying to run down his own daughter in a murderous rage. The last thing I wanted to do was go anywhere with him, especially alone. But I was also determined to figure out what really happened to Destiny. If Scotty was going to open up to me, he probably wouldn't do it in public. And since the police weren't likely to even try getting information from him, I had to take a risk.

Still, I was reluctant to leave the relative safety of Rubio's as I followed Scotty out the door. For a laid-back beer-guzzling Parrothead, he sure had a head of steam worked up. Even his ponytail looked angry.

The minute we hit the sidewalk, I decided to go on the offensive. I didn't want him to think he could just waltz into a room and call me out, expecting me to come running. Which, of course, I had. But I thought it was important to establish ground rules going forward.

"What's this all about?" I demanded. "And how dare you shout at me like that?"

Scotty put both hands on his hips and leaned in close. "You're lucky I didn't drag you out of there. You told Pearl Lee that I killed Destiny? Are you insane?"

Wait a minute! What? "I never said you killed her," I assured him. "I said it's possible that *someone* killed her. Because it seems a little too convenient that somebody tried to hit her with a van and then she died of an overdose not even two days later."

His eyes narrowed but he looked more confused than angry now. "What are you talking about? Destiny was nowhere near that van."

"I don't think the driver knew that. I think that whoever it was mistook me for her."

"That's insane."

"Is it? What if I'm right? She was going to rat out her

dealer . . . probably. What if someone killed her to keep her quiet? Because I think there was someone with her at the Chopper Shop on Wednesday morning. Someone she knew. Someone she'd sit and have coffee with."

Scotty swiped at his forehead with the back of his hand. I could tell that my arguments were getting to him. "The police said it was probably an accidental overdose."

"I know. But what if they're wrong? Detective Winslow won't even listen to me, but he might listen to you."

Scotty stared at me for what felt like forever. "Look, I'm sure you mean well, but I think you're imagining things. Moose doesn't need this, and neither do I. Losing Destiny has been hard enough on him. She was my kid, but she was messed up, okay? That's all it was."

I couldn't believe my ears. "That's it? You're just going to shrug it off? Destiny was messed up, so forget it?"

"This is none of your business. Stay out of it."

"Why? Because you don't want me to discover the truth?"

His confusion evaporated in a blink. "You really are insane, aren't you? She was my *daughter*."

"And no father has ever killed his daughter in the history of the world? Sorry. I wish that meant more than it actually does."

Scotty swore long and loud.

I waited patiently for him to calm down, and by patiently I mean that I held my breath and prayed he wouldn't kill me. I thought about Gabriel asking me if I was going to put myself in danger and felt a little guilty about doing it again. But Winslow had me in his crosshairs, and his threat to charge me somehow in Destiny's death had scared me. Sometimes a woman's gotta do what a woman's gotta do.

"As far as I know," I said when Scotty's colorful vocabulary finally wound down, "you don't have an alibi for the time of the murder. There's only your word and Moose's that you were both at home sleeping. The fact is, either one of you could have snuck out without the other one knowing. Do you know for sure that Moose never left the house?"

He looked as if he wanted to throttle me, but he kept his hands on his hips and clenched his jaw a few times instead. "Somebody ought to lock you up."

The fact that he was able to show some restraint gave me a bit more courage. "If I can't figure out who really killed your daughter, you might just get that wish. Detective Winslow would like nothing more than to put me in a cell and throw away the key."

"And your solution is to warn Pearl Lee about *me*?"

"I didn't accuse you," I said. "I suggested that Pearl Lee show a little restraint. You just lost your daughter. I didn't want Pearl Lee making a nuisance of herself. She can be a bit enthusiastic."

"Well, she's also been a source of comfort. We're both adults. We can make our own decisions, so back off. Because if you keep going, you just might end up regretting it."

I know I should have been frightened, but I was too angry to think clearly. "Or what?" I challenged. "You brought me outside to threaten me? Okay. Message received. Is there anything else? Because if not, I'm going back inside."

Scotty stared at me with eyes as cold as death and again I expected him to try hitting me, but he stuffed both hands into the pockets of his shorts and strode away.

I let out a sigh of relief and my knees turned to rubber. Somehow, I managed to turn around and reach for the door handle, but when I spotted a man in a rumpled suit leaning against the wall just a few feet away, a cold chill crept up my spine. It was clear from the expression on his face that Detective Winslow had overheard the whole conversation.

Nineteen

The conversation with Scotty and then spotting Winslow stalking me took some of the joy out of the ribfest. Having to start over at the back of the line didn't help. Neither did the covert way the other diners slid glances at me when they thought I wouldn't notice. By the time the host finally sat me at a table—a tiny little thing stuck in the corner near the kitchen—I was in a foul mood.

I ate quickly, keeping my head down to avoid conversation. I made the mistake of looking up once and thought I saw Gabriel sitting near the window. But since I wasn't in the mood for another lecture from him, I scooted into the corner and prayed he wouldn't notice me.

After lunch, I trotted over to Zydeco so I could check in with Ox and found that they'd encountered a few problems of their own. Abe, our baker, had accidentally knocked over an entire tray of gum paste pine trees, and the fondant on the golf cart had cracked, putting the whole cake behind schedule. I promised to come back to help as soon as I finished with the cleanup, but Ox didn't look happy as I walked out the door. I couldn't blame him. I'd have felt the same way if I'd been in his shoes.

On my way back to the cleanup, I stopped by the drugstore for sunscreen, but I had a feeling that even slathering it over every inch of exposed skin wasn't going to help. It was too little, too late.

By four that afternoon, I was dragging. Sebastian, Paolo, and I had finally finished our assigned section of the neighborhood. We'd bagged all the garbage and arranged it on the curb, where a local trash company would pick it up on Monday. We carried the tools back to Zydeco and put them into the storage shed, after which the guys went off to get a beer and I hobbled across the loading dock to begin my workday.

As I reached for the door, I spotted Detective Winslow in the front seat of a dark-colored Crown Vic that was nudged up against a tree. Was he *kidding* me? My temper flared, but I was too tired and sore for a confrontation. I owed whatever energy I had left to Zydeco.

After washing up and covering my dirty clothes with a chef's jacket, I threw myself into the effort. Okay, maybe *threw* is the wrong word. The heat and sun had sapped my energy and finding focus wasn't easy, so I kind of crawled up to my workstation. But I did my best under the circumstances, adding detail to the buttercream grass "rough" in between yawns.

Pearl Lee sashayed into the design area a whole five minutes before Miss Frankie came through the door, and somehow managed to make herself look like she'd been there all afternoon. I was furious with her for ratting me out to Scotty, but way too tired to talk with her about it. Had she even considered the possibility that she was putting me in danger by telling him what I'd said? Did she care?

I threw myself into my work, doing what little I could to help Ox and Dwight load up the golf course cake—which was a masterpiece, by the way.

And then I packed up and headed for home. To my dismay, Winslow was still there when I hit the parking lot. I tossed my bag into the Mercedes, gave him a little salute as I drove past, and pulled out onto the street. But the more I thought about the day I'd had, the angrier I got.

For the past two days Pearl Lee had ignored every word I said and refused to take direction. She'd thrown me under the bus with Scotty, who had called me out in front of half the neighborhood. She'd even enlisted Gabriel in her schemes, and he was supposed to be on my side.

I was tired of fighting. Tired of the struggle. Tired of feeling like I was always climbing uphill. I knew I couldn't just flip a switch and change everything that was wrong, but I could put an end to one of the battles.

Telling myself that I had to set some firm boundaries before I had to work with Pearl Lee again—and I use the term *work* loosely—I turned the car around. The best way to get Pearl Lee's cooperation would be to talk to her while Miss Frankie was around. So we could avoid any further misunderstandings.

My mother-in-law lives in a rich old neighborhood full of classic old houses and rolling green lawns. At dusk, just before the sun slips below the horizon, I swear you can see money dripping from the trees. By contrast, I grew up on the wrong side of the tracks in a poor Hispanic neighborhood in Albuquerque. Driving into this neighborhood used to intimidate me in a big way. After living in Miss Frankie's world for the past year, I'm gradually getting used to having upscale connections but I still don't feel like I belong.

When I pulled up in front of that big white house and saw that it was dark, I realized that Miss Frankie and Pearl Lee weren't home, but I didn't want to leave and risk losing my nerve and my opportunity, so I parked in front of the house and settled down to wait.

Sometime later, I woke up with a start to the sound of someone tapping on the window by my head. It took me a few seconds to gather my wits and figure out where I was. Another heartbeat or two to realize that I was looking at Detective Winslow's ugly mug.

Groaning aloud, I leaned my head back on the seat. "Go away!"

"Would you roll down your window, ma'am?"

I did as he asked, but I made sure he knew I wasn't happy about it. "What?"

"Would you mind telling me what you're doing here?"

"I'm waiting for my mother-in-law to get home. I need to talk with her about something."

"Is that right?" Winslow took a step back. He ran a glance over my car before looking up the driveway at the house. "This is her place?"

"Yeah." I tried to stretch my legs, but I'd been sitting in one position too long. They wouldn't move. "I suppose you're going to tell me it's against the law to sit here."

Winslow returned his eyes to me. "The good folks who live in this neighborhood don't take kindly to folks loitering."

"I'm not loitering," I said as I used both hands to straighten one leg. "I'm waiting. There's a difference. What are you doing here anyway?"

Winslow lifted both hefty shoulders. "Working on my case."

I arranged the other leg in a more natural position and nearly wept at the needle-sharp pricks that meant the blood was flowing again. "By following me?"

"If need be."

My legs burned. My muscles ached. My face was on fire and my head was pounding. As if all that weren't bad enough, my stomach was painfully empty. "I didn't sell drugs to Destiny Hazen," I said, shoving open the car door. "How many times do I have to tell you that?"

"You can tell me as many times as you want. I'm gonna keep following the evidence."

"None of which leads to me," I said. I pulled myself out of the car and put both hands on my back, arching gently to stretch the muscles. "But knock yourself out. You won't find anything. I barely even knew her."

Winslow sucked something from a tooth. "You knew her well enough to share your prescription painkillers."

"She stole those out of my office. I've told you that."

"Yes, you have," Detective Winslow admitted as he hitched up his pants with his elbows.

"You don't have any real evidence against me, and you won't find any."

"So you say."

"Because it's true." I slammed the car door and scowled at him. "Isn't there some kind of law against the police harassing citizens?"

He gave me a smarmy smile. "Ah, but I'm not harassing you. I saw you in the car, unmoving. In light of current events, I was concerned. I came to check on you and make sure you hadn't taken too many pain pills yourself."

How sweet. "I couldn't even if I wanted to. Destiny stole mine. I suppose you just happened to be in the neighborhood."

"As a matter of fact, I was. Lucky for you."

"Yeah. I sure *feel* lucky. But as you can see, I'm perfectly all right. Thank you for your concern." That last bit nearly choked me.

"I'm sure glad to see it," he said. "I also happened to notice you having a small disagreement with Scotty Justus this afternoon. Would you mind telling me what that was about?"

I worked up some phony dismay. "Don't tell me you didn't get close enough to hear? What a shame."

"Would you answer my question, ma'am?"

"It was nothing."

"Looked kind of like something from where I was standing."

"Oh? And why were you standing there in the first place?"

"Working my case," he repeated with another shrug.

I felt a primal scream stirring deep inside me, but before it rose to the surface, Miss Frankie's car rounded the corner. I forced down the scream and walked away. I didn't let myself look back, but I could feel Winslow boring holes in my back with his eyes the whole way. And I told myself that I had to find some way to get Detective Winslow off my back soon. Otherwise, I might just give him a reason to lock me up.

Twenty

✦

Winslow slithered back to his car just as Miss Frankie and Pearl Lee pulled into the driveway. Pearl Lee bounded out of the car first, waggling her fingers at me as she tottered past. Miss Frankie got out a little slower, but she hugged me with her usual enthusiasm. "What a pleasant surprise, sugar. I'm *so* glad you're here. I swear, you must have read my mind. I have a few things I need to go over with you."

After the day I'd had, her hug felt like soft fleece. I wanted to wrap myself in it and stay there for hours. "Oh? Something concerning Zydeco?"

Miss Frankie released me, then looked down. "Rita, sweetheart, what *have* you been doing?"

I took a look at my clothes and grimaced at what I saw. "Pulling weeds and hauling trash. I didn't realize until we started working today just how badly the neighborhood needed to be spruced up."

"Well, you're a sight," she said, completely failing to notice that my "helper" was *not* grunged out to match. "You just run on up to the shower. There's a robe in Philippe's old room and we can throw your things into the washer while we eat." She started walking toward the back door. "I wanted to talk to you about Edie's baby shower. I'd like your opinions on the location and the menu. I've narrowed both down quite a bit, but you know Edie better than I do. You'll probably have a better idea about what she'd like." She didn't pause for a response from me and I wasn't fast enough to slide one in before she changed the subject. "You look exhausted, but luckily supper's all ready to heat up. I'll pop it into the oven."

The thought of a hot meal and a shower nearly made my knees buckle. Miss Frankie is a terrific cook and I was starving. "It sounds wonderful," I said as we entered the kitchen. "But I'm not planning to stay that long."

Pearl Lee had paused at the table and was digging around in her purse. She glanced up when I spoke, and she wagged a finger at me. "Don't be silly. You look exhausted. Let us take care of you."

I somehow managed not to laugh at that. Apparently she mistook my admirable restraint for unspoken agreement. "Now really," she said, taking my arm and tugging me toward the front of the house. "You can't sit down for a meal looking like that." It seemed as if everyone I'd run into that day had been pushing and pulling me around. Having Pearl Lee pass judgment on me was too much. Maybe a shower and some clean clothes would help me feel better. It sure couldn't hurt.

As gently as I could at that moment, I jerked my arm from her grasp. "I know where the bathroom is. I can get there on my own."

Pearl Lee's eyes rounded in shock and she shot a "Did you see that?" look at her cousin.

Miss Frankie gave me the raised eyebrows that meant I'd just committed a serious social faux pas. "Are you all right, sugar?"

"I'm fine," I said, barely resisting the urge to rat out Pearl Lee right then and there. But I knew how my mother-in-law would react if I went on the attack so I put a little honey into my smile and tried to handle the problem Southern style. "It's just been a long day."

"I'm worried about you," Miss Frankie said, coming around the island for a closer look at me. "You haven't slowed down a bit since that van almost hit you the other night."

"I haven't had a chance to slow down," I said, struggling to keep my smile in place. "We have a couple of large orders this week, and of course, there's everything that comes with being part of the Magnolia Square Business Alliance." *Which was your idea, by the way.*

Pearl Lee turned her Botox-injected face back in my direction. "I admire you for getting your hands dirty. I really do. My mama would turn over in her grave if I'd done what you did today."

If I'd said what I was thinking right then, my mother-in-law would never again consider me refined enough to run Zydeco. I already felt like I was walking a razor-thin line. "Yes. Well. It comes with the job, I guess."

Miss Frankie took my chin in her hand and checked my face thoroughly. "When I suggested that Zydeco become part of the alliance, I didn't realize it would mean putting you to work like that. Couldn't you have sent someone else to do the actual physical labor?"

"If I had done that," I said, "Zydeco would have been the only member business without its management there. I know you're concerned about appearances but that would have made us look worse than digging in and getting a bit dirty."

"If you say so." Miss Frankie's frown deepened a little further. "I suppose you know best. But it might have been nice if one of the others had been able to help you. Obviously, all that work took a lot out of you."

I slid a look at Pearl Lee, who had suddenly developed a deep fascination with Miss Frankie's china cupboard. "I was supposed to have help," I said. "Edie is our other alliance member, but since she's in the middle of a high-risk pregnancy, her doctor said absolutely no to helping. I thought I had someone else lined up but it didn't work out."

"Oh, that sweet thing," Pearl Lee simpered. "So brave."

I ignored Pearl Lee partly because I wanted to smack her, and partly because I'd just remembered what Miss Frankie said out on the driveway. "Did you say you wanted to talk to me about the baby shower?"

She shooed me toward the door. "Yes, but we can do that while we eat. Run upstairs. We have about thirty minutes before supper is ready. Pearl Lee, why don't you tear the romaine for a Caesar salad?"

Pearl Lee kicked off her shoes and practically skipped across the room, eager to show Miss Frankie what a willing helper she was.

I climbed the stairs slowly, then grabbed a towel from the linen closet and the robe from its hook in Philippe's childhood room. I was in and out in less than a minute, too tired and emotional to risk a meaningful encounter with his things. We'd been on the verge of divorce when he died, but losing him had made me realize that divorce and separation don't always kill love. Sometimes they just alter its appearance for a little while. I had loved Philippe completely once, and I was coming to terms with the fact that part of me always would.

In the bathroom, I turned on the shower and stepped under the spray. I'm not sure anything has ever felt any better than that hot water melting away the stiffness in my joints and the soreness in my muscles as it carried off the dirt I hadn't been able to clean off at Zydeco. By the time I returned to the kitchen, Miss Frankie and Pearl Lee were sitting at the table surrounded by mouthwatering aromas and glasses of sweet tea, laughing together at something.

Miss Frankie hopped up and poured a glass for me. "Just in time," she said as she put it on the table in front of me. "Pearl Lee and I were just talking about the time our uncle Ellis shot himself in the leg, trying to keep my daddy from finding his secret hunting spot. You never heard a man make such a fuss."

I smiled tiredly and asked, "Which one? Uncle Ellis or your dad?"

Miss Frankie sat again and folded her hands on the

table. "Uncle Ellis. Bless his heart, he was a real piece of work, that man. He thought the sun rose and set on his grandnephew Philippe, though."

Pearl Lee dashed a tear from the corner of her eye and sighed. "Lord, but I hate change. I wish things could just stay the same forever." Catching back a sob, she stumbled to her feet and went in search of a tissue.

Miss Frankie let out a shaky sigh and got up to pull dinner from the oven. "Change is hard," she agreed. And then she shook off the mood and was back to her old self. "Speaking of change, Rita, we really need to nail down a date and time for the baby shower. We need to get moving in case Edie goes into labor early, but I can't settle any of the other details until we've talked."

I looked over to see what she'd made for dinner, but all I could see was a covered casserole dish. "What does Edie say? Have you asked her?"

"Well, of course not. I'm working on surprising her."

I laughed and reached for my glass. "Good luck with that. You already asked her for addresses. She knows about the shower."

"She knows there *is* a shower in the works," Miss Frankie corrected me. "She doesn't know where or when or—" She cut herself off suddenly and cut a sharp glance at me. "Or any of the other details."

That fleeting look made me uneasy. "What details?"

Miss Frankie pulled a pan from the stovetop and removed the lid. Steam drifted up around her head. "Oh, you know," she said with a casual wave of the lid. "Decorations, food, flowers . . ."

"The guest list?"

Miss Frankie transferred something creamy and rich into a serving dish. "I do want to get your opinion on the venue."

The pleasant glow from my own shower evaporated and I sat up a little straighter. "Venue? What venue? I thought we'd just have the shower at Zydeco some evening after work."

Miss Frankie gave me some big, wide amber-colored eyes. "Oh, Rita. Really." She laughed and sprinkled parsley over the dish. "You can't have it at Zydeco. That's hardly an appropriate setting to celebrate that sweet little baby, and there's certainly not enough room."

A warning buzz skittered across the back of my neck. "There's plenty of room," I said. "We're having a small shower, remember? It's just for the Zydeco family, and maybe a few other friends if Edie has anyone else she wants to invite."

"I'll work out those details," Miss Frankie said without looking at me. "You're not to worry about the guest list. But I would like you to look at the menu I've discussed with the caterer."

I stood so I could look her in the eye. "We don't need a caterer. I thought we agreed on that."

Miss Frankie smiled sweetly and pulled another serving dish from a cupboard. "I know what you think, and I know how Edie feels, but I simply cannot put together a skimpy little party for that baby." She held up a hand to stop me from interrupting. "Don't argue with me, Rita. I've been a mother and I know a thing or two about stubborn pride and regrets. And besides, we made a deal. I'll take over the shower. You give Pearl Lee a job."

"Well, yes, but—"

"You've done your part, and you've done it beautifully. I couldn't be more pleased. Pearl Lee certainly seems happy with y'all at the bakery. She was telling me all about the golf course cake and how beautiful it's going to be. I couldn't resist sneaking a peek at it while I was there. She seems happier than I've ever seen her, and I'm sure it's because she's contributing something of value."

Or because she'd been chasing after Scotty for three days. But how could I admit failure after *that*? My brain was too sluggish to keep our conversation straight. And then Pearl Lee came back into the room and gave me an almost maternal kiss on the top of my head, adding to the confusion I felt. "But the thing is," I said around a yawn,

"Edie has been very clear about what she wants and what she doesn't want."

"Yes, of course. She wants a happy, healthy baby. That's the most important thing of all." Miss Frankie carried the salad to the table and the scent of garlic made my stomach rumble. "Now no more talk about the shower or about Zydeco until after we eat," she said firmly. "I can show you the menu later, if you're not too tired." Her smile stretched her mouth wide, and her expression seemed as sweet as it could possibly have been—but the glint of steel in her eye made me suspect that I'd been outmaneuvered once again.

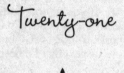

Twenty-one

Three hours later, I rounded the corner onto my street for the third time and began the search for a parking space. I'd circled the block twice, on the lookout for Detective Winslow. I wouldn't have put it past him to camp out and wait for me on my home turf, and I was way too tired and frustrated to want another encounter with him. For the first time in days, luck was on my side. I didn't see him anywhere.

The restaurant next door was doing a brisk business, so I parked at the far end of the block and walked back. It took me a while to get out of the car and walk home, but that gave me plenty of time to think about dinner at Miss Frankie's. We'd indulged in a lot of polite small talk while we ate, all pretending not to notice the big old elephant sitting in the middle of the table. I'd bided my time, waiting for a chance to talk to Pearl Lee, but just as we were finishing the meal, she developed a debilitating headache and escaped.

Maybe she was telling the truth; maybe all that Botox had finally caught up with her. Whether Pearl Lee was actually in pain or not, she'd dodged another bullet. All I could do was help Miss Frankie wash up and then head home. Not only had I failed to solve a single problem on my list, but Miss Frankie's talk about venues and catering for the baby shower had added a couple. She'd pushed a folder into my hands as I left and asked me to get back to her with my thoughts. I'd given them to her right then and there: No special venue. No caterer. She was to plan a nice, little shower for Edie and a few friends. But I knew that wasn't the end of it. The folder still in my hands was proof of that.

What little positive energy I had left drained away when I realized that my house was completely dark. I hadn't expected to be out so late, so I hadn't left the porch light on. It wasn't a huge thing, but right that minute it felt almost overwhelming. I tripped over an uneven piece of sidewalk on my way across the lawn and battled tears of frustration as I struggled to get the key in the lock.

"Rita?"

The voice came out of the darkness and startled me. I whipped around, holding my keys in front of me like a weapon. "Who's there?"

A shadow stirred near the fence and Gabriel stepped into the moonlight. He held his arms high in surrender and a slow sexy Cajun smile curved his lips. He swaggered toward me wearing a tight pair of jeans and a dark T-shirt that made it clear to anyone with eyes what terrific shape he was in. "Hey, hey, hey! Calm down, *chérie*. It's just me."

I let out a sigh of relief and lowered the keys to my side. "You scared me half to death. What are you doing here?"

He reached the bottom step and stopped there. "Waiting for you."

"Why?"

"Why not? I had some time and it's a nice night. I didn't expect to wait so long, but I'm not complaining. I discovered that the little shop on the corner has great coffee and the Thai restaurant next door keeps their restrooms clean. The owner of that knitting shop on the other side, though"— he jerked his head at the shop in question—"is an extremely unpleasant woman."

I laughed and moved to one side so he could join me

on the porch. "Awww, what happened? You couldn't win her over with your charm and good looks?"

Gabriel climbed the steps and stood close enough for me to catch the faded scent of his cologne. A delicious shiver tickled my spine, but I tried to ignore it. My porch isn't big so I couldn't move far, but I did take a step back and put a little distance between us.

"She thought I was up to no good," he said. "She threatened to call the police."

I hadn't forgotten how he'd distracted me so Pearl Lee could slip away with Scotty, and I still wasn't happy about it, but it was nice to see a friendly face. "If I could get the key in the lock, I'd invite you in. You might even be able to talk me into making coffee."

With a gentleness that almost made me cry, Gabriel took the keys out of my hand and unlocked the door on the first try. "Sounds great to me," he said, handing the keys back to me. "I heard what happened with Scotty this afternoon. I came to make sure you're hanging in there."

I tossed my keys and my bag onto the small table just inside the entryway and kicked off my shoes. "I'm fine. It was a little disconcerting, but he didn't actually *do* anything."

Now that we were in the light, Gabriel ran his dark eyes over me, taking stock.

"Don't say it," I warned. "I know I look like yesterday's trash."

"You look fine," he said. "Just sunburned and exhausted. You want to talk about it?"

"More than almost anything," I admitted. He'd never been to my house before, so I nodded toward the back and said, "Kitchen's this way. I'll make some coffee and see if I have some cookies or something. Will that do?"

He smiled and followed me down the hall. "You don't need to feed me."

"The cookies are for me," I said with a grin. "But you're welcome to share." Once in the kitchen, I focused on making coffee. "What are you doing off work so early?"

Gabriel took a chair at the table, angling it so he could

watch me work. "I wanted to see you so I talked Brandon into working overtime."

That was odd. I slid a glance at him and tried to read his expression. "Just because you heard about Scotty?"

Gabriel shrugged. "Edgar said Scotty looked madder than a three-legged gator. What was it all about?"

I pulled a dozen pecan balls from the cookie jar, tasted one to make sure they were fresh, and arranged them on a plate covered with a lacy paper doily. "I suggested to Pearl Lee that she might want to be careful around Scotty. Apparently, she shared my concerns with him. He took offense."

Gabriel frowned. "You think she should be careful because . . ."

"Because she's only known him for five minutes, and she's moving too fast. Plus, I'm supposed to be keeping her away from men. That stunt you pulled at the Duke put me in a bad spot. Miss Frankie thinks I'm doing this super job of keeping Pearl Lee busy, yet she's out doing who knows what with Scotty. This can only end badly."

Gabriel leaned back in his chair. "Not necessarily. Maybe they'll fall madly in love and live happily ever after."

I laughed and carried the plate to the table. "I wouldn't get my hopes up. And more seriously, the police still don't know how Destiny actually died. What if Scotty killed her?"

Gabriel reached for a pecan ball, but his eyes clouded. "You really think he could've killed his own daughter?"

"It's a possibility," I said. "He doesn't *really* have an alibi. Moose vouched for him, but what if Moose is lying? He was ready to divorce Destiny if she started using again—which she had. I told you what Edgar said, didn't I? That she'd spent so much money before she went to rehab, the Chopper Shop was in serious trouble?"

"Do you know that for a fact?"

I went back to the kitchen and grabbed a handful of napkins. "Moose admitted that he let her spend whatever she wanted. If she spent him into a deep hole he couldn't get out of, that might give him a pretty strong motive for wanting her out of the way, especially if there's insurance involved."

"Assuming she didn't actually die of an accidental overdose."

"I know she didn't." I tapped my chest over my heart. "In here."

"Rita—"

"Just hear me out," I said. "She really wanted to turn her life around. She had a deal with the district attorney to reduce the charges, or maybe drop them completely, if she gave them the name of her dealer. You heard what she said at the meeting. I'm sure she planned to do it."

"She was using again," Gabriel pointed out. "Maybe she wanted to change, but addiction is a hard thing to beat."

"I know that, but somebody almost hit me with that van right after she hinted about that deal. I was talking to Moose at the time. The driver could have thought I was Destiny. Or maybe he knew I wasn't Destiny and planned the attack as a diversion."

"Because he was planning to kill her on Wednesday morning." Gabriel sounded skeptical.

"When he knew she'd be at the shop early—and alone. Think about it, Gabriel. We only have Moose's word, and Scotty's, that she told them to sleep in that morning. What if she didn't? What if they made that up so it would sound like a last-minute decision?"

Gabriel chewed for a moment. "But why would either of them do that?"

"I don't think Scotty and Destiny were that close," I said, putting the napkins on the table next to the cookies. "He said himself that he wasn't around much when she was growing up. And he told me she wasn't all that happy to have him around. The only reason he moved in with them was to make sure she didn't start using again. Maybe he was fed up with the drugs and the screwing around. From what I hear, Destiny wasn't all that particular about who she slept with. Maybe Scotty was tired of her ruining the family name."

Gabriel shook his head slowly and patted the chair beside his. "Sit down, Rita."

"Why? So you can tell me I'm getting involved where I shouldn't? So you can warn me I'm going to get myself hurt?"

"No, so you can rest. You look like you could fall over any second. And I want to look at your face while I'm talking to you. It's hard to carry on a conversation when the other person is moving all over the place. So you sit. I'll get the coffee when it's ready." I didn't move. He grabbed my hand and pulled me over to the chair. "I mean it, Rita. Sit." When I did, he took both of my hands in his. "You want to know the other reason I came over tonight?"

I nodded uncertainly. "Sure . . . I think."

"You know how I feel about you getting into dangerous situations." I started to argue with him, but he put two fingers on my lips and kept talking. "I don't know what it is about police investigations that revs your engine, but they do. Until tonight, I figured this one was like the others and I was all set to tell you to back off and butt out. But that cop—Winslow—was in the Duke tonight, talking to people. About you."

My heart dropped into my stomach and they both crashed to the floor. I didn't know whether to cry or throw up. "What did he want?"

"He was trying to find somebody who'd tell him you and Moose are sleeping together."

Crying was off the table as an option. I was definitely going to be sick to my stomach. It didn't matter whether it was true or not—give some people enough alcohol and they'll say anything. "And did he? Find someone?"

Gabriel shook his head. "Not that I know of. I vouched for you and so did Old Dog Leg." Old Dog Leg was a friend of mine, an old blind jazz musician who occasionally sat in with the house band at the Dizzy Duke.

I appreciated Dog Leg's loyalty, but I didn't expect Detective Winslow to put much stock in the word of a blind man. He'd probably use Dog Leg's physical limitations to challenge any testimony the old man gave.

"I don't know what Winslow has against you," Gabriel

said. "But it's obvious the guy's trying to pin something on you. So I'm here to warn you, and also to offer my help."

Had I heard that right? My heart was beating so loudly, I couldn't be sure. "Your help?"

"Hey," he said, giving my hands another gentle squeeze. "Don't sound so surprised. You know we make a good team. I know you didn't give Destiny drugs, and if you need help proving that to Detective Wingnut, I'm your man. So tell me what you need from me. I'm at your service. Other than Scotty and Moose, who else is on the suspect list?"

I could only blink at him. *Blink. Blink.* "Aquanettia," I said when the cogs in my brain were running in sync again. "There were some real issues between them. I've heard from more than one person that Destiny made a play for her sons, Isaiah and Keon."

Gabriel nodded slowly. "I've heard the same rumors— usually about Keon. Isaiah keeps his nose clean, but Keon's had his own issues with drugs, and he has connections. I'm sure Destiny used those whenever she could—*how*ever she could."

Blink. Blink. "Keon's an addict?"

"Recovering. He seems to be doing well, but I'm sure that if Aquanettia thought Destiny was trying to pull her baby boy back into the life, she'd have come out swinging."

Aquanettia's name took a giant step to the top of my mental suspects list. "Why hasn't anyone else mentioned that?"

"Circling the wagons, I'd guess. Aquanettia and the boys have lived here forever. You're . . . new. People around here don't air their dirty laundry in front of strangers."

My breath caught and that old feeling of not belonging made my stomach lurch again. I shouldn't have been surprised. After all, getting me involved with the community was the excuse Miss Frankie used for signing me up for the alliance in the first place. "But a woman is dead," I reasoned. "And Keon's past might have a direct bearing on how she died. And the police are trying to pin the responsibility for her death on *me*." A new thought occurred to me and I gasped aloud. "Do the others think I'm guilty?"

Gabriel shook his head, which might have made me feel better if he hadn't also answered my question. "I'm sure they don't. Really. The thing is, nobody really knows you."

I'm pretty sure my heart stopped beating completely. "But I've been here a year—"

Gabriel touched my cheek with the backs of his fingers. "Baby, you could live here twenty years and you'd still be the new girl in town. But we'll get this straightened out. I promise you that."

I held on to that promise with both hands. I had to. It was the only lifeline I had. "So Aquanettia had a good reason to want Destiny out of the way, and if Keon is really trying to stay away from drugs, maybe he was trying to get Destiny to back off."

"Or maybe Isaiah was protecting his little brother," Gabriel agreed. "Anyone else?"

"Edgar had some kind of relationship with her," I said. "And Felix sure wanted her removed from the alliance. He knew that she was using drugs again. Maybe he *really* wanted to protect the neighborhood from her. And half the alliance was on his side before we took the vote," I reminded him. "It could be almost anyone."

"So where do we go from here?" Gabriel asked. "Do we check alibis? Look for witnesses? Go over the crime scene searching for evidence? Do we need gloves? Baggies? Give me a job and I'll do it."

His offer was just about the nicest thing anyone had ever given me. I leaned up and kissed his cheek. "We keep our eyes and our ears open," I said. "If you get a chance to talk to someone who might have information, take it. But don't let Detective Winslow catch you. I don't want him to decide you were an accomplice or something."

The coffeemaker beeped to let me know it was finished brewing and Gabriel got up to gather everything we'd need. I hated knowing that Detective Winslow was still hot on my trail, and I had no idea whether Gabriel and I could clear my name. But knowing that he was on my side made me feel better than I'd felt in days.

Twenty-two

❧

I slept fitfully until sunrise Sunday morning, and then finally gave up trying. I had too much on my mind to rest. Gabriel's late-night visit had left me hurt, confused, and grateful for his friendship. I just didn't know which one was strongest.

I went downstairs and caught a glimpse of overcast sky and a few drops of rain spattering against the window as I put on a fresh pot of coffee and stirred together a batch of blueberry muffins. Zydeco is closed on Sundays and I didn't want to be around people anyway, so I spent the morning taking care of a few chores. I'd ignored the house for too long.

By the time I started a load of laundry, the sky had darkened and the storm had gathered strength. I turned on the television and listened with half an ear while I dusted, ran the vacuum, and wiped down the bathroom sinks and counters. While the laundry dried, I tried my hand at a crossword puzzle, unloaded the dishwasher, and arranged my spices in alphabetical order. And the whole time I worked, I thought. A lot. Right up until the local news anchor started talking about the murder of local business-woman Destiny Hazen.

Shaking like a leaf, I sat down in front of the TV just in time to catch the anchor's interview with Detective Winslow. He'd actually cleaned up for his fifteen minutes of fame. His hair was brushed, his suit clean and unwrinkled. In fact, he looked almost trustworthy as he explained that the police had determined that Destiny's overdose had been accompanied by some suspicious bruising and a few other unnamed pieces of evidence. Those led them to conclude that she had been murdered.

My stomach rolled over when I thought about him making this announcement on a Sunday morning. They must have been working on it all weekend. Not good.

Based on forensic evidence, the police placed the time of death somewhere between midnight and seven in the morning. I found her around nine, so she'd been dead at least a couple of hours before I got there. I didn't know whether to high-five myself for calling it first, or bury my head in my hands and cry. Meanwhile, Detective Winslow was assuring the good citizens of New Orleans that an arrest in the Destiny Hazen murder case was imminent.

Maybe the general population of the city felt better hearing that. I suddenly felt a whole lot worse.

I turned off the TV and puttered around the house for a little while longer, but the interview had rattled me. I needed to get outside. I wasn't going to find Destiny's killer in my kitchen. I couldn't clear my name from the laundry room. And I couldn't think about anything else.

I decided to go in to work for a few hours. I was seriously behind on paperwork, and I had a blog entry to write, bills to pay, and a staff meeting Monday morning I wasn't fully prepared for, all of which gave me a better than average chance of keeping my mind occupied.

Battling wind and rain, I drove across town and was all set to park on the street in front of Zydeco when I saw Scotty and Pearl Lee walking under a huge, family-sized umbrella. Scotty wore a red Hawaiian print shirt, shorts, and sandals. Pearl Lee wore a red suit and matching pumps, which she carefully protected from puddles.

What was she *doing* here, with Scotty, on a Sunday? Was she completely oblivious, or had she heard that the police had just announced his daughter had been murdered? I hadn't forgotten Scotty's warning and he still made me nervous. But Miss Frankie would never forgive me if I let Pearl Lee get herself hurt or killed.

I decided to follow them, though it wasn't easy to do in the rain—especially since I couldn't exactly pretend to be out for a casual stroll. Luckily, they were too engrossed in their conversation to care what was going on around them. After about half a block, Pearl Lee let go of Scotty's hand and leaned up to kiss his cheek. He dropped his head and stood there, letting the rain hit him on the back. He didn't seem to notice, or maybe he just didn't care.

After a minute, they walked on, and when they reached the corner market, they slipped inside out of the storm. I arrived a few minutes later—it took me a while to figure out that my umbrella had rolled under the front seat—to find them standing in front of the beer cooler, Pearl Lee leaning into Scotty and giving him an unobstructed view of her various charms.

I groaned out loud and at the same time heard a sharp intake of breath coming from behind me. I turned and found Zora staring at the two of them with wide, hurt eyes. Her pale hair hung in limp wet strands to her chin and her plain face seemed even rounder and wider than usual. She saw me looking at her and turned away quickly but she looked so wounded I couldn't just let her go.

"Zora? Wait!" I hurried after her, slipping a little on the wet floor.

She kept going, remarkably surefooted in her rubber-soled orthopedics. She pushed through the door and out into the parking lot. I hesitated for a heartbeat and then raced outside after her. Call me crazy, but I was guessing her feelings for Scotty went a little deeper than friendship after all.

For a woman her size, she sure moved fast! By the time I got outside, she was already half a block away.

Using my umbrella as a shield against the rain, I ducked my head and jogged after her. "Zora! Wait! Please! I need to talk to you for a minute."

Cars passing on the street splashed water onto the sidewalk, and the sound of the rain hitting the pavement made it hard to hear. So when Zora looked over her shoulder and wiped a lock of rain-soaked hair out of her eyes, I was surprised. I was even more surprised that she actually stopped and waited for me to catch up to her.

She put her hands on her full hips and stared me down. "What?"

"I just—I—" I stepped over a dried palm frond on the sidewalk and tried to catch my breath. "Look, I'm sorry about Pearl Lee. She's a bit out of control."

Zora squinted at me in confusion. "What are you talking about?"

"The woman with Scotty. She's been working with me at Zydeco. I know she's a bit over the top. I just wanted to say that I'm sorry if she upset you."

"Oh. That." She barked a laugh and shook rain from her collar. "You don't really think I care about *her*?"

"Well . . . yes. I mean, you seemed surprised to see them together. I thought you looked hurt."

"Hurt?" Zora smirked and started walking again. "Oh, honey, Scotty's a friend, that's all. He's free to see whoever he wants and so am I."

Then why had she just stormed out of the market? "So the two of you aren't a couple?"

"Of course not."

"Why did I think you were?"

She raked an impatient look across my face and stepped under an awning. "I'm sure I don't know."

"You seemed so comfortable the day I came by to offer

my condolences about Destiny. Almost like you were one of the family."

Her lips curved, but the smile didn't even come close to her eyes. "I felt sorry for those two men, that's all. They seemed so lost when Destiny died. So that's what you wanted to talk to me about? That's what was so important you had to chase me down in the middle of a rainstorm?"

"I told you, I was concerned about you. I'm glad you're okay."

"Oh. Well . . ." She looked a little sheepish. "Thank you."

"I guess you've heard the news about Destiny?"

"What news is that?"

I told her about the news story I'd just seen and watched her recoil in shock. "I'm sorry. I thought you knew."

She shook her head slowly. "No, I haven't had the TV on today."

"You knew Destiny pretty well, didn't you?"

"Me? No."

"Oh. I thought you did from the way you were talking at the alliance meeting."

"You must have gotten the wrong impression," she said. "I barely knew her at all."

"But you said things about her relationship with Moose—about how he let her get away with murder."

Zora laughed, but it sounded more like she was clearing her throat. "Goodness, Rita. Everyone in the neighborhood knew how Destiny was. Everyone knows that she put Moose through the wringer."

"It wasn't my imagination, Zora. I sat right there and heard you say those things."

"But you're imagining some kind of 'special relation-ship' that just doesn't exist." She used both hands to put air quotes around the phrase. "I'm friendly with Moose and with Scotty, but no friendlier than anyone else in the neighborhood. What is it to you anyway?"

If Zora didn't know that Detective Winslow had me on his short list of suspects, I saw no reason to tell her. "The police haven't solved Destiny's murder," I said. "And I was nearly hit by someone who stole a van from Second Chances just before she died. The more I think about it, the more convinced I am that the driver was someone who saw the opportunity to hurt Moose or Destiny but hurt me instead. I'm sure you can understand why I'm concerned."

A gust of wind showered us both with rain and Zora moved a little closer to the building. "You said the other day that you thought the two incidents might be related, but surely you're wrong."

"I don't think so. Someone stole the van at the end of our meeting. Why would a random stranger choose a time like that to steal a vehicle from a business surrounded by people? I think that the driver was someone who was at that meeting."

Zora glanced nervously up and down the street as if she wanted to remind herself who to watch out for. "You think it was one of *us*?"

"Yeah, I do. Did you see anyone slipping around to the back of the building that night?"

"Of course not! If I had, I would have told the police."

"Did you happen to pass the Chopper Shop that morning?"

"I may have passed by. I had a dozen errands to run. Do you think the killer was there?"

I tried to set her mind at ease. "He was probably long gone before you showed up. I'm just trying to find someone who was around that morning. I keep thinking that some-body must have seen something."

Zora sighed heavily. "I'm sorry, but this is all just too much. I wish I could help. I really do. But don't you think it's naïve to believe Aquanettia about the van? I mean, we only have her say-so that it was stolen. If you want my opinion, I think she knows who was driving the van that night—and it might have been her. You saw how Aquanet-tia reacted to the idea of Destiny running against her in the board elections."

"Well, yes," I said uncertainly. "But do you really think Aquanettia snapped?"

"I think the Fishers had more opportunity to sneak through the fence and kill Destiny than anyone else in the neighborhood. And nobody would have been any the wiser." Zora looked up at the sky and pulled her collar up around her neck. "If you'll excuse me, I really need to get back to work."

I nodded and tried to decide how I felt about what she'd just said. "Of course. If you think of anything else, would you let me know?"

"Don't you think that's information I should share with the police? If I *do* happen to remember anything, I mean."

With Detective Winslow? Not in a million years. But I couldn't say that, so I smiled an innocent-as-a-newborn-baby smile and chirped, "Yes. Of course. That's what I meant."

She gave me a "sure it was" look. I didn't know her well enough to guess whether she'd mention our conversation to Detective Winslow, but I hoped she wouldn't. The last thing I needed was another warning from him.

She glanced behind her a couple of times, and I realized that I'd frightened her. Maybe I should be a little more careful in the future. I didn't want the whole neighborhood to freak out. She rounded a corner and I tried to decide what to do next. But it was a no-brainer, really. The paper-work at Zydeco could wait awhile longer. What I really needed to do was go shopping.

Twenty-three

I adjusted my umbrella and walked quickly through the rain, reaching Second Chances just as the wind picked up again. Leaving my umbrella on the porch, I found Isaiah at the register, an open book on the glass counter in front of him.

He looked up as I entered and offered a friendly smile. "Hey, Miss Rita. What are you doing out in this weather?"

My jeans were wet to below my knees and my shoes were soaked through. I wanted to rush home and change into clean, dry clothes, but I didn't want to just start asking questions, especially if Gabriel was right about Isaiah trying to protect his brother. "I'm looking for a baby shower present," I said, using the same excuse I'd used last time I was here. "I'd like to get my friend a crib and maybe a changing table. Do you know if you have anything like that here?"

Isaiah tilted his head while he thought. "Crib? Yeah. Maybe." He stood and stretched his arms high over his head. "You want me to go check?"

"Why don't I go with you?" I suggested, thinking that would save us both time. "You can show me where to look."

A clap of thunder shook the building, and Isaiah's eyes rolled toward the ceiling. "Yeah. Sure. Whatever you want." He came out from behind the counter and motioned for me to follow him.

I did, and tried to start a conversation while we maneuvered through the narrow aisles filled with junk. Aunt Yolanda would have loved shopping here. Me? Not so much.

"You're in school, right?" I asked as we passed a stack of mismatched towels.

"Yes ma'am. I'm going to Delgado."

"Do you like it?"

He shrugged and glanced back at me. "Yeah, I guess. It's better than nothing."

I grinned at his ringing endorsement. "What are you studying?"

He started up a narrow set of stairs to the second floor. "I'm going into cybersecurity. That's my plan anyway. We'll see what happens. I'm taking a course on hacking right now. It's pretty interesting stuff."

I climbed the stairs behind him and stepped onto the second floor landing behind him. "I'll bet it is. Are they teaching you how to hack or just teaching you how to combat it?"

"A little bit of both. Gotta know how to do it if you want to stop it." He gestured toward the first of three former bedrooms that overlooked the backyard. "I think there's a crib in there, but Mama may have moved it." He turned to go. "If you need anything, just yell."

I assured him I would. I glanced out the nearest window and spotted a few motorcycles scattered around an otherwise empty yard, a Dumpster filled with trash, and a door leading into the back of a building. "Is that the Chopper Shop?" I asked, even though the answer was obvious.

Isaiah craned to see what I was looking at and nodded. "Yeah, that's it. I heard that Destiny was murdered. That's messed up."

"Yeah, it is. You've got a good view. It's too bad you

weren't here that morning. You probably could have seen who did it."

A frown tugged at Isaiah's lips. "Yeah. Maybe. Or maybe I'd have been killed right along with her."

That was a possibility, too. "What time did you get here that morning?"

"I don't know. Around ten, I guess. The police were over there when we drove up. I don't even know what Destiny was doing here at that time of the morning."

"Moose told me that he and Scotty were out late the night before. She offered to open the shop so they could sleep in," I said.

"You're the one who found her, right? What were *you* doing there so early?"

I hadn't expected him to turn the tables on me. I didn't want to admit that I'd come by to confront Destiny over the theft of my pills, so I went with an answer I hoped wouldn't make me look guilty. "I stopped by to thank Moose for pushing me out of the way of the van. But of course, he wasn't there. I got there a little around nine. She could have been dead a couple of hours before I found her. It's disconcerting to think that someone who works around here might be the one who killed her."

Isaiah nodded slowly. "Yes ma'am, it is. You think the police are ever going to find who did it?"

I tried to get a good look at his face without appearing to look at him at all. Was he asking because he was worried about himself or someone he loved? Or was he just curious? Unfortunately, he'd turned his back and was walking toward the stairs.

"I don't know," I said. "I'm not sure they're really looking." And then, because the possibility that I might take the fall for Destiny's murder made me a little sick, I changed the subject. "Did you ever find out who stole your van?"

Isaiah paused at the top of the stairs, one hand on the railing. "Not yet. But that's not surprising. I don't think the police are really looking for the thief either." He looked around at the jumble of merchandise surrounding us. "I should get back downstairs. Are you sure you're all right to look around up here on your own?"

I wasn't ready for our conversation to be over, but I couldn't think of a way to prolong it. "I'll be fine," I assured him. "Don't worry about me."

He hurried down the stairs, and as his footsteps receded, I got busy pretending to shop for a crib. I moved slowly through the rooms, passing racks of children's clothing and tripping over the handle of a wagon that held a wide assortment of old baby dolls. I briefly considered a video baby monitor system until I realized it was missing one of its electrical plugs.

Tiny puffs of cool air reached me now and then from a slow-moving ceiling fan, but the August heat and the humidity from the storm made sweat pool under my arms and trickle down my back even while I shivered from the chill of the wet clothes. I heard the door open and close downstairs a few times, and the low murmur of voices reached me. I couldn't make out what they were saying, but I could tell that someone else—a woman—had come into the store.

Lightning flashed every few minutes, and the overhead lights flickered. I dashed away perspiration from my forehead with my sleeve and moved across the hall into the second bedroom. At that exact moment, the lights blinked out and a cry of alarm from downstairs brought me around on my toes.

My heart jumped into my throat, and I was tempted to cry out myself. It was so dark on the second floor of that old house I just knew I wouldn't have been able to see my hand in front of my face. Not that I checked. I was far more concerned about getting out of that crowded room without breaking my neck.

Raindrops hit the side of the house and beat a rapid rhythm on the windows. I could hear voices coming from downstairs, which made me feel a little better. At least I wasn't alone. Boards creaked as the old house took another hit from the wind. And then I heard a sound that made my blood freeze in my veins.

Footsteps, low, steady, and ominous, moved toward the stairs. I waited for somebody to say something, reasoning that if I'd been coming to help, I would have called out reassurance of some kind. But nothing broke the eerie silence except the scuff of shoes on the floor. When the sound shifted as someone began to climb the steps, fear dried my mouth so completely I couldn't even make a sound.

I was alone and defenseless just a few feet from where Destiny had been killed. I might be alone and in the dark with the person who had killed her. Until this moment, Isaiah had been at the bottom of my suspect list, but had I been too trusting?

Suddenly frantic, I felt around for someplace to hide, but in the dark, I only succeeded in knocking over a display of some kind. I listened in dismay as the footsteps paused and readjusted, realizing that I'd just revealed my location.

Lightning lit up the sky again, and I saw a shadow move in front of the open door. It stopped moving and turned slowly toward me. By some miracle, I found my voice and let out a bloodcurdling scream.

A beam of light hit my face and I recognized Isaiah at the other end of the flashlight. He looked worried, not homicidal. And instead of the diabolical laugh of a homicidal maniac I heard him say, "Miss Rita? Are you all right? I came to get you."

A wave of relief hit me, followed immediately by embarrassment. "I'm fine," I said, suddenly grateful for the dark so he couldn't see the humiliation on my face. "Thanks. You startled me."

"Yeah." He looked at the pile of old board games I'd knocked over. "I guess so. You want me to help you to the door?"

"No. Thanks," I said, waving away the offer. "I can make it. Just don't move the light." And as I picked my way over the mess and through the secondhand merchandise, I realized that maybe I'd gone a little overboard. It had been nearly a week since I looked up and spotted those headlights coming at me, and I was no closer to figuring out who'd been driving the van than I was that very first night. I'd been trying for days to clear my name with Detective Winslow, but I still had no idea who'd killed Destiny and left me to take the blame. In fact, the only thing I'd succeeded at all week was working myself into an irrational panic.

Much as I hated to admit it, maybe it was time to take a step back. Maybe it was time to get back to normal.

Twenty-four

I spent all day Monday trying to concentrate on work and doing a pretty good job of it. I conducted the staff meeting in the morning and put together a schedule that I thought made the best of everyone's talents. That afternoon, I crumb-coated a four-tier wedding cake, created a dozen gum paste calla lilies in assorted sizes, and ran interference between Edie and Sparkle a handful of times. I'd even managed to keep Pearl Lee on task putting labels on boxes for two whole hours—which I'm pretty sure was a world record.

I was proud of myself, not just for what I'd accomplished, but because I'd refused to let thoughts of the murder investigation distract me. Much. But as I heard another argument between Sparkle and Edie begin to escalate on the other side of the design room, I started to think maybe "normal" was overrated.

"You told the Beekmans *what*?" Sparkle said in a loud voice. "Are you insane?"

"Yes," Edie shot back sarcastically. "Yes, I am. Thanks for asking." She sighed so heavily I could hear it from where I stood. "Come on, Sparkle. It's a tiny little change. What's the big deal?"

I looked up from piping the fifth of ten buttercream leaves for the wedding cake and groaned aloud at the sight of my two employees squaring off again. Six arguments in as many hours, and all over things neither one of them would consider an issue if they hadn't already been irritated with each other.

I was learning that there's a fine line to walk between being too hands-on as a manager and not being involved enough. Unfortunately, that line wasn't always easy to spot. I looked on, waiting to see if they would work it out or take it to the next level. I wasn't their mother, and I refused to get in the middle of every little squabble—but I also didn't want their disagreements to have a negative impact on the rest of the staff.

"It's no big deal to you," Sparkle said with a sneer. "You're not the one who has to repaint half a cake."

"It's not half," Edie said. "It's one tiny part. The customers changed their minds." She tossed the invoice onto Sparkle's table. "What did you want me to tell them? 'Sorry, no can do. Sparkle will blow a gasket'?"

Sparkle brushed the invoice aside roughly. "Do you *mind*? I'm working here." Her voice dropped, making it hard for me to hear what she said next.

Edie had no trouble at all. She shoved her face into Sparkle's personal space. "What's *that* supposed to mean?"

Sparkle turned to reach for something, saw me watching, and checked herself. "Nothing. It doesn't mean a thing."

That was probably as close to an apology as Edie was likely to get, but she didn't see it that way. "Like I believe *that*. You just won't let it go, will you? You think you're so much smarter than me? You think you have the right to tell me what to do—"

"I offered you one piece of advice," Sparkle said with a wave of a hand. "And it was a good one, too. But you don't care. Forget about what the baby needs. Don't worry about what kind of life it's going to have. Let's just make sure we don't inconvenience Edie."

"This is *my* baby," she said. "How I decide to raise it is none of your business."

"It's a baby, not a possession," Sparkle growled. "You don't own it."

"I never said I thought I owned it," Edie said through clenched teeth.

Sparkle was having a little more trouble remaining unemotional. "Then give the poor thing a chance, why don't you? Give the baby's dad a chance. Do you even know how it feels to wonder where you came from?"

Edie threw up both hands and turned away. "I give up. You're certifiable. You really are. Just stay away from me from now on, okay? If you feel the need to fix something, and obviously you do, take care of your own damn life. Leave mine alone."

I put down the piping bag and wiped my hands on a towel. Things had gone too far, and I had to intervene. "Hey, you two," I said in what I hoped was a friendly but firm tone. "That's enough. Leave each other alone."

Sparkle looked like a panther ready to spring. "I wish I *could* leave her alone, but I have to work with her. We all do. And lately everybody knows that's not so easy."

"We *work* together," Edie said. "That doesn't make it okay for any of you to offer opinions about my private life."

Sparkle threw up her hands and gave us all a wide-eyed look, made all the more dramatic considering how heavily she caked on the black eyeliner. "I'm just trying to help."

"I don't want your help," Edie shot back. "Why can't you understand that?"

I took a few steps toward them. "Look, this is getting out of hand. You do need to work together, so put aside your personal differences and focus on the job."

Sparkle gave me a mutinous look and turned at the same moment Edie took a step away. She ran straight into Sparkle, who lost her balance and brushed against a tray of buttercream roses Isabeau had finished only minutes earlier.

The tray teetered precariously and would have fallen if Sparkle hadn't caught it. "Watch what you're doing, would ya?"

Fire sparked in Edie's eyes. "Oh! So now *that* was my fault, *too*?"

Sparkle held up both hands and looked around at the rest of us. "I didn't see anybody else trying to push me over."

"Sparkle," I said, raising my voice to make sure she heard me, "I need to see you now, please."

Edie shot her a triumphant smile and headed back toward the front of the house. Sparkle put her hands into the pockets of her black hoodie and slouched toward me. Everyone else suddenly got real busy pretending to work.

"I know what you're going to say," Sparkle said with a resentful look at Edie as she disappeared through the door. "You don't have to actually say it."

I sat on a stool and motioned for her to do the same. "Good, because I don't really want to." I grinned and waited until she curled one corner of her lip in response. "Look, I understand this whole baby thing is a big deal to you," I said. "I even understand *why* it's such a big deal. But it's starting to affect what we do around here. The two of you almost ruined a whole day of Isabeau's work."

"Almost," Sparkle clarified with a sharp glance. "I caught the tray before it fell."

I sighed and lowered my voice to make sure the others couldn't overhear us. "Yeah. Thank goodness. But what's next? Seriously, Sparkle. It really is getting out of hand."

She looked like she wanted to argue with me, but I held up a hand to stop her.

"I can't tell you what to do away from work. If you really want to bug Edie about her choices on your own time, I can't stop you. But you're not making any headway, so what's the point? In fact, you're probably just making her more determined to do it her way."

Sparkle chewed the corner of her lip and kicked the heel of her black leather lace-up boot against the stool. "She's not thinking about the baby."

"Of course she is. She's just not thinking the way you want her to, and she never will if you keep pushing. You know how Edie is."

Sparkle didn't say anything for a full minute, and I thought she might have actually heard me. But she's as hardheaded and stubborn as Edie is, which is why we were having these issues in the first place. And her next words made it clear she wasn't backing down at all. "If Edie won't listen to me, she might listen to the baby's father. You should go talk to him and tell him what she's doing."

I let out a brittle laugh. "Even if I knew who he was," I said, "my answer would be no."

"He has the right to know."

"But it's not my place to tell him. I'm *not* getting involved. Period. End of story."

"So you're just going to sit back and let Edie screw the kid up?" Sparkle's voice echoed off the walls of the design room and I think everyone in the room stopped working again and looked over at us.

I lowered my own voice even further. "You don't know that's what she's doing. I know you have issues about the way your mother raised you, but you can't just assume that Edie's situation will work out the same way."

Sparkle rolled her eyes and stood. "You can't assume that it won't."

"You're completely missing the point," I said. I may have added an eye roll of my own. "It's *none of our business*. It doesn't matter if you're right or wrong. It's not your call. Or mine. Just let Edie figure it out, okay? You worry about your own stuff, I'll worry about mine, let Edie worry about hers. Everybody will be happy." Yeah, right. But as fantasies go, I thought it was a pretty good one.

Sparkle suddenly became fascinated with the sleeves of her hoodie. "I heard from my brother a couple of days ago," she said after she pushed one sleeve up and adjusted it until she was satisfied. Her voice sounded kind of dreamy and faraway, as if she was thinking something through as she spoke. "I wrote to him after you and I talked. I wanted to see if River remembered it all differently, you know? I thought maybe I was off base. But I'm not, Rita. He wrote back and he agrees with me."

"Even so . . ." I said.

She tilted her head and looked at me from the corner of her eye. "He's coming here next week. It's his birthday, and he's going to see Liberty and Bob. Don't ask me why. Anyway, he's going to stop and see me for a couple of days. Maybe I'll ask him to talk to Edie."

"I don't think that's a good idea," I said. "No. Wait. I know it's not."

"But he's a guy. He knows how they think."

"That's not exactly a compelling argument." I cast about for a new way to tell her to back off—one that wouldn't send her off into a creative funk—but nothing came to mind.

And maybe I could have figured out a way to get through to her, but a loud scream tore through the air and got everyone in the design room racing toward Edie's desk. Ox made it through the door first, with Dwight right behind him. Estelle and I hit the door at the same time and engaged in a brief skirmish over which one of us would get through next.

She won by a hip.

Isabeau and Sparkle raced in behind me, and Pearl Lee brought up the rear. I barely heard Edie over the chaos. She said something about a crash, or maybe it was broken glass, in the employee break room. In any event, we were off again with the whole herd thundering toward that room.

This time I managed to skim through the door a hair in front of Estelle, which may not have been the smartest move. I felt a *whoosh* of hot air coming in through the broken window a second before Estelle plowed into my back.

I stumbled a little, almost fell over one of the tables,

and grabbed the back of a chair to hold myself upright. "What happened?"

Ox gestured toward something on the floor, the crowd parted, and I saw a large rock surrounded by shards of glass. "What? How did that—"

"Somebody chucked that rock through the window," Dwight said. "Probably kids."

"But why would anybody do that?" Isabeau asked, pushing past Sparkle and Estelle to stand beside me.

"I'll bet whoever it is, is still out there," Edie cried, shaking a finger in the general direction of the front door. "I'll bet we could catch them if somebody moves fast enough."

Ox accepted the challenge and the rest of us followed like lemmings. Dwight and Ox seemed prepared to kick some ass. I was busy calculating how much it would take to repair the window and what a claim for damages might do to our insurance premium. I rushed out onto the front porch just as Dwight and Ox took off after a group of laughing teenagers wearing baggy pants and sweatshirts at the other end of the block.

"Don't hurt anybody," I shouted after them.

Isabeau put a hand on my shoulder and tried to reassure me. "It's okay. Ox knows what he's doing."

"I hope they catch the little creeps," Estelle mumbled, and turned toward the door. "I'm going back inside. It's too hot out here."

Edie followed her and Sparkle trailed them slowly. I was all set to go with them until I saw someone else hurrying away from Zydeco. He was wearing a bright yellow Hawaiian print shirt and khaki shorts, and he cast a furtive look over his shoulder before slipping into a building about a block away. Suddenly I had the uneasy feeling that Dwight and Ox were chasing the wrong culprits.

"Don't hurt anybody," I shouted again and raced down the stairs to follow them. I just hoped that I could catch up with them before they did something stupid.

Twenty-five

Thankfully, the teenage boys had disappeared before Ox and Dwight could find them. Ox and Dwight seemed disappointed but I was relieved. Maybe those kids were the rock tossers, but I was reluctant to accuse anyone without proof.

If only Detective Winslow felt the same way.

Back at Zydeco, the guys dug through hurricane supplies in the storage shed, looking for the piece of plywood cut to cover that particular window, while I placed a call to our insurance carrier. An hour later, they had the broken window covered, I had a claim in process, and we were all back at work.

Not surprisingly, though, it was hard to stay focused. I kept wondering if Scotty really had thrown that rock through the window. My "evidence" against him was circumstantial at best, and it seemed like an odd way for him to threaten me, but it was effective. I couldn't deny that seeing him right after the window broke had spooked me.

I wasn't the only one who had trouble staying on task either. We all stayed late, but we spent more time talking about who threw the rock and why than we did actually working. Needless to say, we didn't get much done for the rest of Monday.

We were all back bright and early the next morning, though, trying to make up for lost time. The rest of the staff was anyway—I spent all morning looking for someone to repair the window, and talking to a handful of people at the insurance company. Thankfully, Edie and Sparkle spent most of the day ignoring each other, which meant that when I finally joined the others to work on the wedding cake, I actually got a few hours of uninterrupted work time.

We locked up on time that evening and everyone walked to the Dizzy Duke for a drink, except Edie, who went home to put her feet up and look through baby books.

I was hoping Gabriel had found time to do a little sleuthing and that he'd have information for me, but he wasn't behind the bar when I arrived. I found out later that he had the night off. I was disappointed, but reminded myself he'd call or stop by if he had anything to report.

After ordering a margarita, I spent a while chatting with the rest of the staff. We talked about everything but work, starting with our current favorite TV shows and recent movies and music before moving on to meatier topics.

Everyone had something to vent about. Ox told us that his father had received a diagnosis of high blood pressure and shared a few stories about the older man's struggle to change his lifestyle. Isabeau confided that her parents were separating after thirty years of marriage, and had a few choice words about her father's new girlfriend. Estelle confessed that the police had picked up her niece for shoplifting and told us about her sister's struggle to cope.

As the evening progressed and liquor flowed, the conversation turned into a game of one-upmanship, something we frequently "played" over drinks. Even Sparkle got into the game, telling the others about her childhood, the questions about just who her parents were, and how she wasn't even sure where her brother was at the moment. I noticed she didn't mention his impending visit, but I kept my mouth shut.

I wasn't in the mood to play "Who's Got it Worst?" and

Dwight, whose relationship battles with his older sister were the stuff of epic legend, was uncharacteristically silent as well. He ran his fingers through his shaggy hair repeatedly as he listened to the others, and he seemed distracted or maybe worried.

After about an hour, I started making noises about leaving. To my surprise, Dwight stood when I did and offered to walk back to Zydeco with me. I urged him to stay with the others, but he insisted that he was ready to go home, so we said our good-byes and stepped outside into a night thick with fog that had rolled in off the river.

We walked in companionable silence for about half a block, which was when curiosity got the best of me. "You seem quiet tonight," I said. "Do you have something on your mind?"

Dwight glanced at me and shrugged one bony shoulder. "Yeah. I guess."

"Is it anything you want to talk about?"

"Yeah. Maybe." He kicked at a pebble on the sidewalk and watched it skitter away before he spoke again. "What's going on with Sparkle and Edie lately?"

The question surprised me. I'd been imagining a bunch of different possibilities ranging from money trouble, to a sick family member, to a possible new girlfriend. I hadn't expected him to be worried about his coworkers. "It's just stuff," I said. "Sparkle thinks Edie's making a mistake, not telling the father about the baby. Edie doesn't appreciate Sparkle's opinion. They'll work it out." I smiled as I said the last part, but I wasn't sure which one of us I was trying hardest to convince.

Dwight scratched the stubble on his chin. "Sparkle thinks Edie should tell the baby's father."

I cut a glance at him. "Yeah." I got a squidgy feeling in my stomach and hoped Dwight wasn't about to admit to being the guy. I just *knew* that would make everything at Zydeco worse. But if that was it, then Edie had lied to me about her one-night stand and I didn't want to think she'd done that. Deciding I'd rather know now than be blindsided later, I jumped in with both feet. "It's not you, is it?"

Dwight jerked backward and brayed a laugh. "Me? No! What made you ask that?"

I grinned at the stunned look on his face. "Just making sure. Apparently, you already know what's up with the two of them. So what's really on your mind?"

He spent some time raking his hair and rubbing his chin and then finally asked, "Do you think Edie's going to stay after the baby is born?"

Squidge. "I do," I said. "Why? Don't you?"

"Yeah. Probably, I guess. It's just that everything's going to change when the kid comes. You know it will. Have you thought about what you'll do if she wants to leave?"

Squidge-squidge. "Of course I have, but I really don't think that's going to happen. She'll need her job more than ever once she's a single mother."

Dwight slowed and I adjusted my pace to match his. "I've been wondering if we should start looking for someone else. Just in case, you know?"

I gasped in shock. "You think I should be looking for Edie's replacement? But she hasn't given me any indication she wants to leave." Not since the night she told me she was pregnant anyway, and I tried hard to forget about that. "I know there were a few things she thought of as problems in the beginning, but we've worked them out." A new thought occurred to me. I stopped walking entirely and grabbed his arm. "Or do you know something I don't know?"

He shook his head quickly. "She hasn't said anything to me. I just know how my sister was after my oldest niece was born. One day she was all set to go back to her job, the next day she didn't want to leave the baby, even for five minutes. It made my brother-in-law nuts. But what if Edie has some"—he waved a hand around, searching for the right word—"some epiphany? What if she and her mother work things out and she decides to move home?"

That question hit me like a fist in the stomach. That was a possibility I really hadn't considered. Feeling agitated because of Dwight's train of thought, I started walking again. "Do you really think that could happen?"

"Of course it could. Family's family. She's pissed at her mother now, but that could change with one phone call. My sister stops speaking to me at least once a year. I call and tell her what I jerk I was. She forgives me, and we're good until the next time I make her angry. That's how family works."

Maybe some, but not the one I'd grown up in. But Dwight could be right. If Miss Frankie had her way, Edie and her mother would make up before the baby came. Of course I wanted that, too, but would Edie bail on us if she had her family's support? I didn't want to think so, but what I knew about being a mother could fit on the head of a pin. Ditto for what I knew about being a daughter.

We'd reached Zydeco's driveway and turned down it together. I could see my Mercedes in its usual spot and Dwight's battered Jeep a few spots over. The Mercedes looked a little off balance, but I chalked that up to the fog and the odd shadowy shapes it and the moon created together.

"Well, you might be right," I told Dwight. "But I'm not going to start interviewing Edie's replacement yet. Even if she *wants* to stay home with the baby, she's far too practical to do something rash. I'm pretty sure she'd go nuts in a week if she and her mother tried to live under the same roof."

"Flat."

I did a double take over his odd response and laughed. "Yeah. A week flat."

Dwight shook his head and pointed at the Mercedes. "No, I mean I think you have a flat tire."

I looked again at the Mercedes and saw that he was right. The front tire on the driver's side was flat as a pancake. I swore under my breath and threw my hands up in the air. Angry tears burned my eyes and a giant lump of self-pity filled my throat. "Are you *kidding* me?" I squawked. "Enough is enough already. What am I supposed to do *now*?"

"I can change it for you," Dwight offered. "It's no big deal. You have a spare, right?"

"I don't know," I admitted. "It was Philippe's car. Whatever he had is what I have." I like to think of myself as strong, competent, and independent, but cars are outside my area of expertise. When I was a kid, Uncle Nestor took care of all the car stuff. If he was too busy, one of my (male) cousins would do it. Aunt Yolanda and I barely had to worry about putting in gas and turning the key. Once I got married, Philippe took over, and I'd gone back to Uncle Nestor's when we separated. I barely remembered where to find a jack, much less how to put it together. And looking at that tire after the week I'd had just about did me in.

Dwight must have sensed my confusion. I don't know what gave it away—maybe the rush of tears streaming down my face? Anyway, he held out his hand and wiggled his fingers. I handed over my keys and tried to shut off the waterworks.

While Dwight ducked into my trunk, I sat on the bumper of his Jeep to wait for the verdict.

"Bad news," he said a few minutes later. "There's no spare in here."

"Of course there isn't," I grumbled, diving deeper into my pity party. "That would be too easy. I guess I need a tow truck or something?"

Dwight pulled his head out of the trunk and joined me on the Jeep's bumper. "I'll give you a ride home," he said. "And I'll pick you up again in the morning. Tomorrow we'll call a friend of mine who owns his own shop not far from here. He's a great guy and honest. And he has good prices. He'll get that tire patched up in no time."

I wiped my eyes and worked up a tremulous smile. "Thanks."

"Not a problem," he said. "That's what friends are for."

That brought on a fresh round of tears. I gave a loud and, I'm sure, unattractive sniff. Dwight got up, reached into his glove box, and handed me a wad of napkins. They looked clean enough, so I wiped my eyes and blew my nose, trying to pull myself together. "I'm sorry," I said, hiccupping softly. "It's been a rough week."

"Yeah. So I gathered." Dwight sat beside me again and nudged me gently with a shoulder. "For what it's worth, we're all on your side. Everybody here knows you're not a drug dealer and we know you didn't have anything to do with that woman Destiny's death. We all know it's just a matter of time before the police figure it out, too."

I think I always knew they believed in me, but hearing him say it aloud was truly music to my ears.

"I hope you're right," I sniffed. "But with Detective Winslow on the case, I'm not so sure."

"He's a jerk," Dwight agreed. "What did you do to get on his bad side?"

"I wish I knew. Treating me like his number one suspect makes no sense. There's no real evidence against me, and the only motive is something he made up. But nothing I do or say seems to make any difference."

Dwight shrugged as if none of that mattered. "Sullivan's got your back, though, right?"

I shook my head. "He's out of town. He doesn't even know what's going on. I felt another *squidge*, this one a little closer to my heart. Logically, I knew Sullivan wasn't ignoring me in my time of trouble, but logic doesn't belong at a sobfest.

Dwight just sat there while I pulled myself together and then asked, "Feeling better?"

"Not really," I said, although the tears had acted as a release valve and my stress level actually did feel a bit lower. I gave him a scathing look. "You think I'm feeling bad because Sullivan isn't riding in on his white horse to save me?"

"You're not?"

I ignored him. "You can give me that ride home now. It's late and the window guy is coming early in the morning. And it's Destiny's memorial service at eleven. It's going to be a busy day."

Dwight nodded. "What time are we leaving for that?"

We? I hadn't really expected him to go with me, but I wasn't going to turn him down. "We should probably get out of here in time to pay our respects before the service starts."

"Okay. I'll tell the others." I was not going to cry again,

but my heart melted a little hearing that the whole staff planned to be there.

"What time should I pick you up for work tomorrow?"

I did some quick calculations and said, "Is seven too early?"

"I'll be there on the dot. Don't want to let my boss down." I smacked his arm, but there was no heat in it. Neither of us spoke again until we were in the Jeep with our seat belts fastened.

"Thanks," I said as he turned the key in the ignition. "You're a good friend."

He flicked a glance over my face as he shifted into reverse and gave me a little chin jerk to acknowledge what I'd said. It wasn't much, but it didn't have to be.

The Mercedes was missing one flat tire by the time Dwight and I got to work the next morning. The car sat up on an industrial-strength jack steadied by a couple of cinder blocks while it waited for Dwight's "guy" to come back with the tire. Seeing that he was already at work on a fix made me feel downright optimistic. Well, that and the fact that I'd told Pearl Lee to stay home today. I didn't want her tagging along to the memorial service.

I headed straight to the break room for a cup of coffee, and carried it to my office so I could catch up on some paperwork. I found a note from Sparkle asking for Monday off so she could spend time with her brother. I made a note on my calendar so I wouldn't forget and picked up the next item on my desk. I'd just opened an envelope containing the annual report Zydeco had to file with the state of Louisiana when the phone on my desk rang.

Edie appeared in my doorway at the same time. "Sorry," she said with a nod toward the phone. "I know you're busy, but it's Dwight's mechanic friend. I figured you'd want to talk to him."

"You're right. Thanks." I snagged the phone from its cradle and answered with a chipper, "This is Rita."

"You're the woman that owns the Mercedes, right?"

"That's right. And you are—"

"Ken. I'm a friend of Dwight's. He asked me to take a look at that tire of yours."

"Mmm-hmm," I said as I sipped my coffee. "And? How soon will you able to patch it?"

"Well, that's the thing, see? I'm not going to be able to patch it. You're going to have to get yourself a whole new tire."

I choked a little on the coffee so I put the mug down. "I'm sorry. What?"

"I can't fix that tire, ma'am. You're going to have to get a new one."

"You can't patch it? But I thought—that is, Dwight said—"

"Yeah. Under normal circumstances, I could put a patch on it and you'd be good for the life of the tire. But the thing is, that tire of yours doesn't have any life left. That's what I'm trying to tell you. It wasn't just a nail in the tire. That thing's got a gash in it probably six inches long."

Something skittered across the back of my neck. All along my back and arms, my nerves twitched. But I didn't want to jump to conclusions, especially not the wrong one. So I asked him, "What could have caused something like that?"

Ken sighed heavily and then said the words I dreaded most: "Only one thing I know. It didn't happen by accident, that's for sure. Somebody slashed that tire."

All the air left my lungs in a *whoosh!* I swallowed my fear and let anger take its place. I had a pretty good idea who had slashed that tire. It was the same person who had tossed that rock through the window. And I was determined to put an end to it now—before somebody else got hurt.

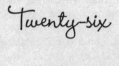

Twenty-six

Much as I wanted to confront Scotty the very next time I laid eyes on him, I didn't actually do it. Aunt Yolanda always says there is a time and a place for everything. I was furious about the slashed tire and the broken window, but rational enough to know that Destiny's memorial service was neither the time nor the place for a showdown.

We locked up the shop shortly after ten, packed ourselves into a couple of cars, and drove to the mortuary. I rode with Ox, Isabeau, and Dwight in Ox's truck. The rest of the crew rode in Estelle's car. Ox and Dwight sat in the front and talked softly about inconsequential things. I didn't feel like talking at all, which worked out just fine since Isabeau was uncharacteristically subdued as well.

Even though I thought we'd left Zydeco in plenty of time, we hit some traffic and arrived just a few minutes before eleven. Several cars were in the parking lot, but it wasn't full by any means, which made my mood droop even lower. I thought someone as young as Destiny should have a huge funeral, filled with family and friends who mourned her passing.

We joined up with the rest of the staff and filed inside

together. The overpowering scent of funeral flowers—
probably my least favorite smell in the entire world—hit
me the instant I stepped through the door, and soft organ
music floated down from speakers that I suspected were
hidden in the ceiling. The funeral director handed each of
us a small printed program and pointed us toward a room
at the end of a short hallway, where Destiny's casket was
surrounded by several framed pictures of her at various
stages of her life. Among them I noticed what looked like
a wedding picture, and a young Destiny with a woman I
guessed was her mother.

I spotted Felix and Lorena talking with Sebastian in
one corner of the room. Scotty and Moose, both of whom
looked uncomfortable in dark suits, were standing near a
middle-aged woman who sobbed into a handkerchief. She
bore a resemblance to the woman in the picture, so I pre-
sumed she was Destiny's mother. Zora sat beside Edgar
near the front of the room, and Isaiah and Keon had
claimed a couple of seats near the back. Not too surprisingly, I didn't see Aquanettia anywhere and I wondered if
she knew her sons were here. I noticed a few other familiar
faces from the alliance and a handful of women about
Destiny's age sitting together and chatting quietly, but that
was the extent of the crowd.

At least I thought it was—until I spotted Detective Winslow hovering between two large flower arrangements at
the back of the room. He nodded at me and I nodded back.
I wondered why he was there if the case was now a homicide, but I wasn't curious enough to ask him.

I'd been planning to say something to Destiny's family,
but after finding out about my slashed tire, I was too angry
to talk to Scotty and I didn't want Detective Winslow to
start speculating again just because I offered condolences
to Moose, so I followed Isabeau to an empty row of seats
and sat down. Estelle sat next to me and Sparkle sat next
to her. Edie walked all the way around the bank of chairs
so she could sit next to Ox, putting several of us between
her and Sparkle, which was probably a good idea.

Once she was settled, Isabeau glanced around the room and leaned over to whisper to me. "Did you see that detective in the back of the room?"

"Yeah. I did."

"He's probably here to see if he can figure out who killed Destiny, don't you think?"

I nodded. "Probably."

Estelle looked over her shoulder to see Winslow for herself. "Do you think the killer is here?" she asked in a stage whisper that I'm sure everyone in the building could hear.

I put my finger to my lips and whispered back, "I'd almost bet on it."

Isabeau craned her neck to get a better look at everyone. "Who do you think it is?"

Oh, good. That wasn't obvious at all. "I don't know," I said. "But do me a favor and stop trying to figure it out while Detective Winslow is watching. I don't need any more trouble from him."

Estelle checked behind us again, I guess to make sure Winslow hadn't missed the fact that we were talking about him. "You're right," she said out of the corner of her mouth. "He's watching you like a hawk."

"I figured he was." I tried not to sound exasperated. Really, I did. "But please don't look at him again, okay? Just sit here and look at the flowers or something."

"Right," Estelle said with a wink. "You want us to be inconspicuous."

I glanced up and down the row at our group. Pregnant Edie was munching on M&M's while we waited for the service to start. Dwight wore a suit so wrinkled he could have taken it from Detective Winslow's laundry basket. Ox cleaned up nicely but still looked like Mr. Clean, and Isabeau, for once, didn't look like a cheerleader. She'd pulled her hair into a messy bun and held it in place with something that sparkled in the light every time she moved her head. Estelle wore a shapeless navy dress with bright pink flats and carried an oversize yellow purse that clinked

when she walked, and Sparkle wore her usual black clothing, lips, and nails. Her only ornamentation was a heavy
silver cross on a chain around her neck.

Yeah, I thought, holding back a grin. Inconspicuous.

A few minutes later, just as the funeral director asked
everyone to be seated, the doors opened and Pearl Lee
teetered inside a step ahead of Miss Frankie. I barely held
back a groan of dismay. I should have known Pearl Lee
would find a way to come. I held my breath, expecting her
to do something inappropriate like rush to Scotty's side
and fling her arms around his neck. To my surprise, she
followed Miss Frankie to the row in front of us and sat
with her hands folded in her lap. Both cousins gave me a
quick smile.

The memorial service was brief—a couple of hymns,
a couple of prayers, remarks from a clergyman whose
address was so impersonal I could only conclude that he'd
never actually met Destiny, and a musical number by one
of the women I'd noticed earlier who turned out to be a
friend of Destiny's from high school. The whole thing was
punctuated occasionally by soft crying, most of which
came from the front row, where Destiny's mother sat
between Moose, who tried hard to keep his emotions under
control but failed, and Scotty, who kept his head down
most of the time. I kept an eye on Edgar, too, but though
he knuckled away a few tears, he certainly didn't act like
a grieving lover. Felix wore a solemn expression that never
wavered, and Lorena, who looked almost bored, fanned
herself with her program through the whole service.

When the last notes of the final hymn died away, the
pallbearers moved into place and the family followed the
casket outside to the hearse. The rest of us remained
respectfully silent until they disappeared, and then began
gathering our things to leave. I felt strangely disappointed,
not only by the service, but because if anyone there was
guilty of drug dealing and murder, I sure hadn't spotted
any sign of it. I wondered if Detective Winslow had seen

something I'd missed, but when I looked at the spot where he'd been standing, he'd already disappeared.

While Miss Frankie and Pearl Lee lined up to compliment the clergyman on the service, the others from our group moved away, talking softly among themselves. Ox came to stand beside me and asked, "So, what's the plan? Do you want to go to the cemetery?"

An involuntary shudder skittered up my back. If there's anything I hate worse than a funeral, it's a cemetery. "I'd rather not, but if you want to, that's fine."

He shook his head and his mouth twitched slightly. "Naw. I'm good. What do you say we all grab some lunch on our way back to work?"

I gave that idea an enthusiastic thumbs-up. Zydeco was closed and we were all here together, and I wasn't the only one of us who'd had a tough week. "Sounds perfect. We'll let Zydeco pick up the tab. What do you have in mind?"

He shrugged as we started toward the door. "Anything's fine with me. Do you have a preference?"

I was paying attention to our conversation, so I didn't notice Zora talking to Keon in the doorway until it was too late. I plowed into Keon's back before I could stop myself. He swore and tried to keep his balance, but he stepped on my foot in the process. A sharp pain shot up my leg and I accidentally elbowed Zora in the side as I tried to keep from falling. She jerked backward and dropped her purse. She made a grab for it, but she must have twisted her head the wrong way because she let out a howl and clutched her neck. Ox jumped in to help steady her, but I knew she'd had trouble with her neck since her accident, and I felt horrible about causing her more pain.

"I'm so sorry," I said, bending to pick up her bag myself. "I didn't see you there."

Keon took a couple of steps backward and shoved his hands into his pockets. "It's all good. No harm done. You're all right, aren't you, Miss Zora?"

She closed her eyes briefly. After a moment she tried

to smile but her mouth was pinched and tiny white lines radiated out from her lips. "Yes. Yes. I'm fine. At least, I will be."

She didn't *look* fine. "Did you drive here today?" I asked.

She gave a little nod.

"If you're in a lot of pain, maybe you shouldn't drive home," I said. "Is there someone who can drive you?"

"I'd offer, but we were just heading out to lunch with the staff," Ox said. "Keon? Are you going back that way? Maybe you could drive Miss Zora home."

Keon hunched his shoulders and shook his head quickly. "I can't," he said, taking another few steps backward. "I got stuff I've gotta do. In fact, Isaiah's probably tired of waiting for me already. Y'all take care." Before we could say another word, he loped off down the hall as if he couldn't get away from us fast enough.

Ox and I exchanged a stunned glance. "What was that about?" he asked.

"I have no idea." I handed Zora her purse and she excused herself to go to the ladies' room. As she walked away, I realized that one of us would have to drive her back to her place. It really wasn't how I wanted to spend the next hour or so, but she was hurt because I hadn't been paying attention, so I stepped up and took responsibility. "You go on to lunch with the others," I said. "I'll drive Zora home and join you as soon as I can."

"It's no big deal," Ox said. "I can take her."

I waved him off. "No. Go. I'm the one who ran into her. I'll do it. Just text me and let me know where to find you. Do you have the company credit card on you?"

"Always."

"Good. Use it to pay for lunch if the check gets there before I do."

He grinned and walked away. I tried not to slip into a funk, but it wasn't easy. Technically, I know that an after-funeral lunch with friends shouldn't be fun, but I still hated missing out. And since this week was turning out to be almost as bad as last week, I could have used a break.

Maybe I shouldn't be so pessimistic. I could probably take Zora home and still make it to lunch. After all, how much trouble could the woman possibly be?

"Hey! Rita! A little help?"

I heard Ox calling me, but I'd been back at work for two hours already and I was still fuming. How much trouble could Zora be? Turns out the answer to that was "a lot." It had taken me nearly twenty minutes just to find her after Ox left and another ten to get her outside and settled in her car—a Prius, of all things. Which meant another fifteen minutes for instructions on how to drive a hybrid and forty minutes for the drive to her house, which, I swear, was way over on the Mississippi border.

She'd fallen asleep after just five minutes on the road, so I had to pull over and dig around for her registration to find her address. And let's not even get into how much time it took to wake her up and get her to the door once we got there. After which she shut the door in my face without even letting me inside. Then there was the wait on her front porch for a taxi and the ride back to Zydeco.

"Hey! Rita! Help!"

I finally glanced up and saw Ox trying to balance on top of a stepladder while holding the top tier of the wedding cake in both hands. The ladder swayed unsteadily beneath his feet, but Dwight was doing his best to steady the bottom tiers of cake, so he couldn't give Ox another hand. The look on both their faces told me they were in trouble. It was just the three of us in the design room. Isabeau, Sparkle, and Estelle had gone on break a few minutes earlier.

I tossed aside the piping bag I'd been using and raced toward them, slipping between workstations and shoving stools out of my way. I got there as the top tier of the cake began to slide out of Ox's hands toward the floor.

With my heart in my throat, I threw myself under the cake and caught it just before it hit the ground. Unfortunately, it wasn't a clean catch. My hand smooshed a large section of painted buttercream and I could feel cake on my fingers.

My instinct was to jerk my hand away to avoid further damaging the cake, but I knew that would be the worst thing I could do. I waited until Dwight balanced the bottom of the cake, steadied the ladder, and then finally turned to help me with the tier I was holding. I felt the weight shift and gently pulled my hand away so I could get a good look at what I'd done.

Sparkle had spent hours painting a beach scene on the cake, and now half of it was just a big smear of blue, aqua, and tan. Rows of tiny beading designed to mimic a sash on the bride's dress, so intricate it had kept Isabeau working through lunch for two days in a row, were gone.

I felt a little sick as I assessed the damage. Ox, it seemed, felt even worse.

He dropped onto a stool and put his head in his hands. "This is bad," he groaned. "I don't know how it happened, but I screwed the whole thing up. There's no way we can deliver this cake to the client in the morning."

Dwight put the mangled top tier on a nearby table and handed me a towel. "We'll figure it out," he said. "We've fixed worse than this."

At least, that's what I think he said. His last words were cut off by the sound of running feet and a high-pitched screech as Isabeau burst into the tight circle we'd made around the cake.

Her blond ponytail swished from side to side and she clapped both hands over her mouth. She stared at the cake with wide blue eyes and let out a little moan as she slowly pulled her hands away. "What *happened*?"

Ox put an arm around her shoulders and squeezed gently. "I'm sorry, babe. I lost control of the cake. The ladder . . ." He was still at a loss to explain, and I hadn't been paying attention so I was no help at all. "Rita and Dwight tried to save it," he said, and broke off with an elaborate shrug, letting the cake speak for itself.

I felt like a complete jerk and gave myself a mental kick for letting my mind wander. What if I had been paying attention? Could I have saved the cake? I really needed to get my head in the game. My inattention might have just cost everyone hours of unnecessary work.

Tears shimmered in Isabeau's eyes, but she took a deep breath and blinked a few times to clear them away. "So we have to do all that again."

"I'm afraid so," I said. "I'm sorry."

"It's not your fault," Dwight assured me.

I gave him a grateful smile, but he was being far too kind.

"We have to redo that whole thing by eight in the morning?" Sparkle had returned, too, and now she moved into the circle we made. "There's no way we can do that. Do you know how many hours it took to paint it the first time?"

"Nobody feels worse about this than I do," Ox said, "but I'm afraid it's going to be an all-nighter. We can't just fail to show up because we had some bad luck. There's a couple getting married in the morning and they're expecting a cake."

"He's right," I said. "It's a pain, and I'm sorry, but we don't have any choice. It won't be so bad if we all stay to help. Dwight, can you stack another tier? Estelle can crumb-coat it and then get started mixing the buttercream."

Dwight had already removed his hair and face nets sometime while I wasn't paying attention. He nodded gamely and started putting them back on. "Do we have three more lemon mist cakes in the cooler?"

"I sure hope so," Ox said. "But if we don't, we'll just have to substitute with whatever we do have and knock something off the price to compensate."

I hated the compromise, but I knew he was right. The clients wouldn't be happy with a substitution, but they'd be even more upset with no cake at all.

Ox turned toward the kitchen. "I'll see what I can find and I'll let you know."

Still trying to dodge barbs of guilt, I looked at the rest of my staff, who were watching me with expressions ranging from mild irritation at the inconvenience to heartbreak over their lost work. I would have given anything for a chance to undo the damage, or send them all home and fix it myself, but both options were impossible.

So I did the next best thing. "I know this puts a kink in everyone's plans, but I'll bring in dinner for everyone who stays. It's not much, but it's the least I can do. What sounds good? Let's make it something local so I don't waste time driving across town."

My question didn't exactly earn a rousing response, but Ox tossed out a few suggestions and everyone else did the same. After agreeing on Chinese from the Golden Dragon and phoning in our order, Edie and I set off together to pick up the food. We walked slowly because we had to for Edie's sake. Her doctor encouraged her to get a little mild exercise, but the pace she set had me chomping at the bit, wanting to hurry so I could get back and do my share of the work.

Dwight's questions from the night before rolled through my mind as we walked. I knew Edie was feeling edgy thanks to Sparkle's well-meaning interference, but what if Dwight was right? What if she decided to bail on us when the baby came? Didn't I deserve a heads-up? Didn't the rest of the staff deserve an easy transition?

I eased into the subject by asking about her most recent doctor's appointment, the day before.

"Nothing's changed," she said with a frown. "But I feel fine. I don't know why Dr. Simpson insists on treating me as if I'm about to break."

"She just doesn't want you to take any chances with the baby," I said. "But in your case, no news is good news, right? You're no closer to going into premature labor or whatever?"

Edie shook her head, but she put her hands on her back and arched her spine slightly.

I shot a concerned look at her. "Are you okay?"

"I'm fine," she said impatiently. "I'm pregnant, not sick. I wish everyone would stop treating me like I'm fragile."

"Okay," I said with a sheepish grin. "Sorry. I don't mean to hover. Have you decided whether to stay in your apartment or get a bigger one?" *Like, say, a few rooms in your parents' house?*

She shook her head. "I haven't decided yet, but I've got time. I'll probably keep the baby in my room at first anyway, so there's no rush."

I nodded and fell silent while trying to figure out how to ask what I really wanted to know.

Edie kept sliding glances at me as if she had something to say. She spoke up first. "You have to do something about Sparkle," she said eventually. "She's driving me absolutely nuts."

I knew I had to tread cautiously. "I know it doesn't feel like it to you, but she really is just trying to be helpful."

"She's being a pain in the butt. You've seen what she's like. She's been just plain weird lately."

We stopped at a corner and waited for a car blasting a heavy bass beat to pass before I spoke again. "Has she told you why this is such a big deal to her?"

Edie looked up at me, her almond-shaped eyes narrowed in suspicion. "Something about her childhood. Her mother. No father. Blah, blah, blah. Look, I know that sounds awful, but I've had to start tuning her out so I won't go crazy. I'm sorry for her. I really am. But her family junk doesn't give her the right to tell me what to do with my baby."

I didn't want to take sides in this argument. They both had valid points. But I had to say something, so I asked, "What exactly is Sparkle saying to you?"

Edie waved a hand in front of her. "Oh, you know. The same kinds of things my mother says. That I should get married. That I should at least make the baby's father part of our lives. I should, I should, I *should*. I can't stand the way everyone thinks they know what I *should* do. They don't have a clue what I'm going through."

I took another very cautious step. "Maybe if they did have a clue, they'd be more understanding."

"What do you mean?"

"Only that if they don't know the circumstances, how can they understand the choices you're making?"

"The circumstances are nobody's business but mine. But you'd never know that to hear Sparkle talk. She actually asked me for the father's name so *she* could talk to him."

I let out a disappointed sigh. *Bad idea, Sparkle. Really bad idea.* "What did you tell her?"

"Nothing. What could I tell her?" Edie gave me a suspicious look. "What did you want me to tell her?"

"Nothing. But . . . Look, I'm not saying you need to broadcast your situation to the whole world, but your friends might be more supportive than you think. I had no idea what you were going through until you told me."

"And apparently that was a mistake."

"No!" I put a hand on her arm. "I haven't said a word to anyone, and I won't. But if Sparkle understood the situation, I'm sure she'd back off. A little information can make a big difference. That's all I'm trying to say."

Edie stared at me for one long and thoroughly awful moment. "So until I told you, you agreed with her and my mother? You thought I should find the baby's father and drag him into the middle of all this?"

"That's not what I said."

Edie stopped walking abruptly right in front of a dark alley that stretched from one end of the block to the other. One dim light burned at the far end of the alley and a bulb glowed over the back entrance to the Chopper Shop. Everything else seemed deserted. I suppressed a shiver of apprehension and tried not to get caught up in thoughts of Destiny's murder and the recent strange happenings at Zydeco.

"So . . . what? You think I can't do this on my own? You think I need a man around to help me?"

Now she was purposely misunderstanding me. Out of

respect for her raging hormones, I tried to stay calm but it wasn't easy. "I didn't say that either."

"Well, here's a news flash for you, and Sparkle, *and* my parents: I don't need help. I'm doing just fine on my own. You can all just *back off*." She turned back in the direction we'd come and walked away.

"Edie, that's not what I said!"

She waved a hand over her head and kept going. I stood there for a minute, debating whether to go after her or give her some space so she could cool off. It wasn't a difficult choice. She'd made it clear that she wasn't interested in excuses or explanations, and I wasn't in the mood to beg her to be reasonable. She wasn't the only one going through a tough time.

With a sigh of frustration, I turned toward the Golden Dragon. I was going to have to carry food for the whole staff back to Zydeco on my own, and I wasn't happy about it. As I started walking, I heard the scuff of a shoe on pavement in the alley and for a split second thought maybe Edie had changed her mind and come back.

But instead, as I turned to look, something hit me from behind. Pain shot up my shoulder and across my neck. My knees buckled and I let out a cry of pain. A second blow landed on my shoulder, knocking me off balance. I stumbled forward, trying desperately to keep myself upright even as I saw the pavement rushing toward my face. I heard something metal hitting the pavement somewhere near my head, and then for the second time in a week, everything went black.

I don't know how long I was out, but I woke up to the soft touch of a hand on my cheek and a worried voice calling my name. I tried to open my eyes, but pain seared my head and I couldn't manage more than a slit before the light made the pain worse.

"Oh! Thank God!" I heard the voice say. "I was afraid

you were dead." The warm touch left my cheek and I felt someone take my hand. "Squeeze if you can hear me."

I did my best, but it hurt like hell.

"Good. That's good. I've called for help, so just lie there until someone comes, okay? I don't dare try to move you. I don't think I'm strong enough."

Very slowly, I focused on the face swimming in front of me. It seemed to take forever for Edie's face, her waterfall of dark hair, and her worried expression to take shape.

"What happened?" I croaked.

"I don't know. I was on my way back to apologize. I found you lying here."

"Somebody hit me," I said on a groan. "I don't suppose you saw who it was?"

Edie shook her head and gently brushed hair away from my eyes. "I didn't see anything or anybody. Can you see me okay? How many fingers am I holding up?"

I squinted until I could see her hand in the dim light. "Two."

"Now?"

"Still two. Seriously, Edie, that's making me feel worse. Can we just not talk for a minute?"

"But I'm supposed to keep you awake, aren't I?"

"I don't know."

"I think I am. I think I read that with a head injury you have to make sure the injured person doesn't fall asleep. Can you remember your name?"

"Rita Lucero. Now please stop worrying so much."

"I can't. Are you really okay?"

I would have nodded, but I thought it might make my head fall off. "As okay as I can be." Slowly, details about the attack began to return. My head was pounding, but my shoulder and back had taken the brunt of the impact—lucky for me.

I inched up onto my elbow and looked around into the shadows. "Do you see a pipe or something metal anywhere? I think that's what he used. Maybe the police will be able to get some fingerprints from it."

Edie got to her feet and made a circle around me. "There's nothing like that here. Are you sure that's what he used?"

"I think so." I managed to sit, but I cradled my head in my hands as if that might stop the splitting headache. "I heard something metal hit the ground. I'm sure of that."

Wasn't I? I groaned and closed my eyes again. Yep. This was, without a doubt, a very bad week. I couldn't wait for someone to figure out what was going on so this whole nightmare would be over.

But I was also very aware that I was lucky to be alive. And I wondered if I'd be so lucky next time.

Twenty-seven

✦

Edie stayed with me until the paramedics loaded me into the ambulance for what was turning into my weekly ride to the emergency room, but I wouldn't let her accompany me to the hospital. The staff still had a cake to fix—without me—and they still needed dinner. Dwight came to drive Edie to the Golden Dragon and I went to the hospital alone. I didn't even want to think about what this was going to cost, but when I wasn't feeling sorry for myself or trying to remember something about the attack, money was all I could think about. I'd managed to find group coverage for Zydeco's small staff, and I was paying through the nose to include maternity coverage for Edie. Individual policies, like mine, had a high deductible and distressingly low payout ceiling. I had no idea how many acts of violence the policy would cover. I'd never thought to ask.

For the next three hours, I answered questions for hospital staff and then for a couple of uniformed police officers before submitting to examinations by nurses and other support personnel. After another lengthy wait, a doctor looked me over and assured me I would live. She sent someone in to bandage my shoulder, asked me a few questions about the prescriptions I'd been given just a few days earlier, and finally wrote me a couple of new prescriptions before telling me I could leave.

As the doctor was leaving the examination room, I overheard one of the uniformed officers telling her that Detective Winslow was on his way. Apparently he wanted "a few words" with me and had asked that the emergency room staff keep me there until he arrived.

I didn't know if they could legally detain me, but regardless, it wasn't going to happen. I was *so* not in the mood for a conversation with Winslow. I wouldn't put it past him to accuse me of attacking myself.

Determined to get out of Dodge and avoid what I knew would end up as an inevitable charge of assault on a police officer, I shut the door and tried to undo the ties on my hospital gown. Pain tore through my shoulder and raced down my back when I reached behind me. My knees buckled and I cried out, but I grabbed the railing on the bed and managed to stay on my feet. I took a couple of deep breaths and waited for the worst of the pain to subside. Then, fighting back tears, I worked first one arm and then the other out of the sleeves and slowly inched the gown around so the ties were in the front.

I'd just managed to untie the bottom bow when I heard loud voices and rapid footsteps outside my room. I froze and stared at the door like a deer in headlights. A moment later the door flew open and Miss Frankie burst inside. Pearl Lee surged inside right behind her.

I was weak with relief to see them instead of Detective Winslow, but I was also irritated by the invasion of privacy. I clutched the edges of the robe together. "Do you mind? I'm getting dressed! How did you get in here anyway?"

Pearl Lee closed the door behind her quickly. Miss Frankie took one look at the bandage on my shoulder and clapped her hands over her mouth. Tears welled up in her eyes and a sob caught in her throat. I hated seeing her so worried, and as my initial irritation faded a little, it occurred to me that their arrival could be a blessing in disguise. With their help, I might be able to get dressed and slip out before Detective Winslow showed up.

"Stay there," I ordered Pearl Lee as I picked up my jeans from the chair. "Don't let anyone in."

"Oh, sugar, just *look* at you," Miss Frankie said, automatically stepping forward to help me. "I didn't believe Ox when he called. I thought he was playing some kind of joke."

Even with another pair of hands, it took forever to get into my pants and fasten them. "When did Ox call you?" I asked as we worked. I'd been in the ER for hours, after all.

She looked around the room, spotted my shirt, and reached for it. "It's been a while," she said. "They kept us waiting in there forever and nobody will tell me anything. How on earth did you get hurt?"

"Edie and I were going to pick up dinner for the staff," I said. "Somebody hit me. That's about all I remember until Edie woke me up and called for help." Okay, so I left out a few things. I didn't want to burden Miss Frankie with the gory details about our argument.

Pearl Lee had been studying her manicure, but as I spoke, she glanced up with a horrified look in her dark eyes. "My goodness! Where did it happen?"

"We were on our way to the Golden Dragon. It happened at the end of that alley that runs behind Second Chances and the Chopper Shop."

Miss Frankie scowled as she worked my shirt over one arm and then the other. "That certainly seems to be a dangerous area. Did you see who attacked you?"

"No. I heard footsteps and I started to turn around. That's the last thing I remember."

"But Edie saw, right?" Pearl Lee asked. She gasped before I could answer and asked, "Is *she* all right? Was she attacked, too? What about the baby?"

"She and the baby are fine," I assured them both. "Can we talk about this later? I'd really like to get out of here."

Looking confused, Miss Frankie stopped working entirely. "Edie was there?"

"Not exactly," I said. "She was on her way back to Zydeco when I was attacked."

"But you said she woke you up," Pearl Lee said helpfully.

"She did." I checked the clock on the wall and realized that twenty minutes had passed since I'd found out that Winslow was on his way. "It's complicated. I'll explain everything later. I just need my shoes and my bag."

Miss Frankie bent to pull my shoes from beneath the chair. "So you don't know who hit you."

"No, but I can guess who it was." I met Pearl Lee's wide-eyed gaze, hoping to see a flash of guilt or even just the realization that she was at least partially responsible for my current condition. "Scotty Justus got all up in my face yesterday at lunch. Tonight, somebody attacked me just a few feet from the Chopper Shop. It doesn't take much to connect the dots."

Miss Frankie looked shocked. "You think Scotty Justus attacked you?"

Pearl Lee's wide eyes narrowed, and the concern in them turned to ice. So much for sympathy. "That's a very serious accusation," she said. "Did you actually *see* him?"

I rolled my eyes. They were the only part of my body that didn't hurt. "I didn't see him or anyone else," I said again, and I tried to get my shoes from Miss Frankie without moving my shoulder. "But that doesn't mean he didn't do it."

Miss Frankie handed over my shoes one at a time. Slowly. "But *why* would he?"

"It's complicated," I said again. "Would you mind grabbing my bag?"

Miss Frankie nodded absently. "I'm sure you know best, sugar." She looked over at Pearl Lee and explained, "Rita's very good at figuring out things like this. If she says it was Scotty, it probably was."

I could see Pearl Lee wanting to argue, but if she did that, Miss Frankie would probably guess what she'd been doing with her time. Frankly, I thought their relationship could benefit from a little honesty. "Well, I'm almost positive it was Scotty," I said. "Unless he has an alibi. What do you think, Pearl Lee? Does he have one?"

Pearl Lee laughed. "Oh, Rita, how would I know that? I'm not even sure I know who you're talking about," she said, while boring a hole through my skull with her eyes. "But then, I've met so many new people since I arrived, it's impossible to remember them all."

Miss Frankie gave me an odd look. "Are you sure you're all right, Rita? You're behaving strangely. How could Pearl Lee possibly know whether or not this Scotty person has an alibi for the time of your attack?"

I planned to answer that question . . . later. "Let's finish this conversation in the car," I said. "I'm tired and more than ready to get out of here. Would you mind giving me a ride back to my place? My car is still at Zydeco."

Miss Frankie put a gentle hand on my back and steered me toward the door. "I won't close my eyes for a second if you're alone. You're coming home with me." I started to protest, but she cut me off before I could get a word out. "Don't even think about arguing with me, Rita. You're staying with me for the next few days and that's final. Someone needs to keep an eye on you."

I wanted to curl up in my own bed in my own house, but my head was swimming, and getting dressed had left me with a thick shaft of pain pulsing through my shoulder. Maybe she was right, I conceded reluctantly.

"If you insist," I said. "I have my prescriptions, so there's nothing keeping me here. Let's go."

In an actual effort to be helpful, Pearl Lee opened the door with a flourish. I poked my head out into the hall and did some reconnaissance. I spotted a couple of women in scrubs behind a desk at the end of the corridor, but other than that, the hall was empty.

Miss Frankie came up behind me. "Why don't you wait here for someone to bring you out in a wheelchair? I'll bring the car around."

In the interest of getting out of there quickly, I refrained from arguing. "That's a great idea," I said, even though I had no intention of sticking around. I did, however, like the idea of a getaway car waiting for me at the front door.

Miss Frankie hurried off, leaving me alone with Pearl Lee. As soon as Miss Frankie turned the corner, I started after her. Pearl Lee fussed a little, but I guess she could tell that I meant business. She finally settled down and offered me a shoulder to lean on, putting an arm around my waist to help steady me.

"He didn't do this to you, you know. Scotty's not a violent person."

"Oh, so *now* you know who he is?" I laughed bitterly. "Are you for real?"

Pearl Lee merely shrugged. "Don't judge me. You can't possibly understand the life I've lived."

"You're right about that," I said. "I don't know why you insist on defending him. You didn't see his face when he barged into Rubio's."

"He was upset. Surely you can understand that."

I twisted to look at her and barely suppressed a cry at the pain that caused. The pain and frustration brought me to the end of my rope with cousin Pearl Lee. I checked up and down the hall to make sure Detective Winslow wasn't coming toward us and then unloaded on her.

"Okay, Pearl Lee, I want you to listen to me and listen good. I've been putting up with your crap for almost a week and I've had enough. I understand now why your family decided to put you on a short leash."

Her mouth fell open and anger bubbled up into her eyes but I didn't care.

"I'm no good at having conversations like this, Southern belle style," I said. "So we're going to do this the Mexican way. No more mincing words. No more dropping pretty hints and hoping you'll understand me. I'm going to say exactly what I mean, and you need to know that I mean what I say. You are through lying to Miss Frankie as of right now. Either you tell her the truth about what you've been doing since you got here, or I will. Is that clear?"

Tears shimmered in Pearl Lee's eyes. "Rita, I don't know what I've done to upset you—"

I cut her off before she could finish. "Save it. You know exactly what you've done. But it ends now. Tonight. As for Scotty: You go right ahead and think that he's Mr. Wonderful. I reserve the right to disagree. I think the man is a psychopath."

"Well, you couldn't be more wrong."

"Whatever. If he did this to me, if he killed Destiny, I'm going to do everything I can to put him in prison for the rest of his life."

Pearl Lee did her best to give me a pouty face in spite of all the Botox. "You're going to feel mighty foolish when the truth comes out."

"I'm sure one of us will," I said. "I just hope we're both alive to figure out which one." And then I limped away from her with as much dignity as I could muster.

She stood there until I was about halfway to the other end of the hall and then slowly came after me. I didn't know what she'd do with my ultimatum, but I'd drawn the line in the sand and I had every intention of following through with my threats. If she didn't come clean with Miss Frankie, I'd do it for her. Let the chips fall where they may.

As for Scotty, putting him behind bars might be a bit more difficult, but I sure meant to try.

Twenty-eight

⚜

I awoke the next morning to the pleasant aromas of coffee and bacon, two scents that I'm pretty sure could raise me from the grave if the need ever arose. Miss Frankie had settled me in Philippe's room and I'd fallen asleep the minute my head hit the pillow. I thought I'd heard raised voices once, but I wasn't sure if they'd been real or part of a dream.

Desperate for caffeine and food, I slipped a robe over the pajamas Miss Frankie had loaned me and limped downstairs. I knew she'd object to me showing up for breakfast without dressing first, but I wasn't sure I could manage alone and I hoped she'd be in a forgiving mood since I was injured and all.

It took forever to get to the bottom of the stairs. I was so focused on getting one foot in front of the other without falling, I didn't notice the suitcases stacked up by the front door until I was standing in the foyer.

Well, now . . . that was interesting. Were they Pearl Lee's? Did that mean she'd actually told Miss Frankie the truth? Maybe those raised voices last night had been real.

I didn't want to be responsible for a driving a wedge

between family members, but I wasn't the one who'd been lying to Miss Frankie. I wasn't the one who'd been sneaking around and hiding what I was doing. If Pearl Lee's shenanigans had finally caught up with her, she only had herself to blame.

Feeling lighter than I had in several days, I turned toward the kitchen and sniffed appreciatively. I pushed a lock of bed hair out of my eyes and opened the door. "Miss Frankie, you sure do know how to give a girl incentive—"

I focused on the scene in front of me and the words froze in my throat. Miss Frankie stood in front of the range. Pearl Lee was pouring coffee into Miss Frankie's best china cups, and a couple of strangers stared at me from chairs at the table. A middle-aged woman with a porcelain doll face and almond-shaped eyes looked horrified by my appearance. Her companion, a large man of about the same age with graying hair and wide blue eyes, kept his head down and darted sidelong looks at me every few seconds.

That lock of messy hair fell back into my eyes and I clutched the robe tightly in front of me. "I'm sorry. I didn't realize you had guests."

Miss Frankie wagged a spatula in my direction. "Don't worry about it, sugar. You run back upstairs and dress. We'll wait for you."

I turned around obediently, and it wasn't until I was halfway up the stairs that reality broke through the medication-induced haze in my brain. Oh. My. God. I stopped in my tracks and turned around again. *Oh. My. God!* I wanted someone to tell me I'd imagined those two people in the kitchen. I wanted someone to convince me that they weren't who I thought they were. But even if someone had tried, I wouldn't have believed them.

Edie was going to freak out. She'd probably blame me and want to finish the job Scotty had started last night. And to tell the absolute truth, I wouldn't have blamed her.

Dumbfounded and unable to think clearly, I took a couple of steps back down the stairs, then changed my mind and climbed up to the second floor. I had no idea what I was going to do about this, but I'd have a much better chance of holding my own against Miss Frankie if I was dressed. Whatever "my own" was in this situation.

To my dismay, my jeans and T-shirt had disappeared from Philippe's old bedroom while I slept and a fluorescent pink jogging suit hung in their place. A clean pair of granny panties and some tube socks sat on the chair by the window along with a bra that wouldn't even dream of containing "the girls."

Was she *kidding* me?

I dug around in Philippe's childhood dresser, hoping I'd find some of his adult clothes. I found a couple pairs of clean boxers and a stack of white undershirts that I could have worn if I'd had the full use of both arms, but everything else had probably been here since his junior high school days. There was no way I could squeeze my thighs into any of his jeans. No way to pull a T-shirt over my head. So the jogging suit it was.

I dressed as quickly as I could, rolling the waist of the jogging pants a couple of times to make them look less like "mom" pants and also to take up the slack in the length since my legs were about half as long as Miss Frankie's. After zipping the jacket to hide my braless state. I shoved my hair around gently, but there was really no hope for it. After that, I went back to the kitchen, where everyone but me seemed to be in a fantastic mood. They were so busy chatting, nobody even noticed me until I cleared my throat to get their attention.

Miss Frankie hopped up when she saw me and grabbed both of my hands to tug me toward the table. "Rita, how *are* you feeling?"

"Fine," I lied. "What's going on here?"

"Come. Sit down. We have guests."

"I can see that." Determined to take control of the situation myself, I extricated my hands from her tight grasp and offered one to Edie's father. "I'm Rita Lucero," I said. "You must be Mr. Bryce."

He stood to shake my hand. "Call me Charlie. And this is my wife, Lin." He waited for me to sit before he resumed his own seat. "You're Edie's boss at the bakery, right? I take it you didn't know we were coming."

I was pretty tired of Miss Frankie's shenanigans, too. I shot a harsh look at her, which she managed to ignore, and then gave the Bryces my best smile. "No. I didn't realize you'd be here. This is quite a surprise. When did you arrive?"

"Just this morning. Miss Frankie told us about your accident. I hope you're feeling better."

I waggled a hand in a so-so gesture and spoke to my meddling ex-mother-in-law. "I can't imagine why you didn't tell me they were coming. Does Edie know?"

"We thought it best not to tell her," Mrs. Bryce said in a softly accented voice.

"Are you sure that's wise?"

Lin Bryce picked up her coffee cup in both hands and brought it almost to her lips. "Yes, I am. Edie is being completely unreasonable. Telling her would have only made things worse. I do hope you're not encouraging her in this . . . thing."

And by *thing*, she meant her soon-to-be grandchild? I hid my curled lip behind my own cup and tried to figure out how to respond without making everything worse. "I'm supporting her," I said after I got a bit of caffeine into my system. "She's a friend."

Pearl Lee appeared at my side with the coffeepot. "They have a very tight-knit group at Zydeco. Edie is in good hands." I appreciated the vote of confidence as much as I hated that she was using the moment to suck up.

Mrs. Bryce's mouth pinched tight with disapproval. "Considering the choices she has been making lately, I doubt that very much. We did not raise our daughter to behave this way. Something is influencing her, and not in a positive way."

Ouch! My smile froze and I glanced at Charlie for his reaction. He put a big bear hand on his wife's shoulder.

"Now, Lin, let's not start off on the wrong foot." He smiled an apology all around the room. "My wife is understandably upset by what's going on. I'm sure you can understand."

I was raised to have manners. Really, I was. But I'd had a rough couple of weeks and I was in no mood for their holier-than-thou attitudes. "Yeah, well, Edie's upset, too, and she's the one who's pregnant and alone."

Lin gave me another pinched look. "And whose fault is that?"

"She wasn't raised to be fast and loose," Charlie said, as if that explained everything.

"Edie isn't fast and loose," I said. "She's anything but that."

"And yet she's pregnant with a child out of wedlock." Lin put her cup down on the saucer with a *clink*. "I think that proves otherwise."

"Edie doesn't make a habit of sleeping around," I said. I tried to remain calm and rational, but my voice rose a little with every word and I was practically shouting by the time I finished.

Miss Frankie appeared at my side and put a hand on my shoulder. "Rita, the Bryces are my guests. I invited them here, and I insist that you treat them with respect while you're in my house. I think we should arrange to meet Edie for dinner tomorrow. You talk to her in the morning and we can all get together tomorrow night—if you think you'll feel up to it, that is."

My face burned from the sting of her rebuke, but the way she just kept pushing made my blood boil. "I'm not going to sit down for dinner with Edie and her parents," I snapped. "You weren't even supposed to invite them. Edie doesn't want them here. I can't even count the number of times I told you to stay out of it."

Miss Frankie's eyes flashed but she kept that smile on her face. "I don't think this is the time or place for this conversation."

"I can't talk to you privately," I shouted. "You just ignore me and do what you want anyway. Now Edie's parents are here and they're acting like Edie sold state secrets or burned the flag or something, and you expect me to set up a dinner as if there's no problem? I can't even tell you how wrong that is. They have a grandchild on the way who is going to need its family, but all they can think about is what a bad person Edie is. No wonder she didn't want them here."

Charlie got to his feet and Lin's face turned to stone.

Miss Frankie straightened her shoulders and looked down her nose at me. "We all know that you're not yourself, sugar. You'll apologize to the Bryces, of course. They're here to straighten this mess out, that's all."

Anger buzzed around in my head, and every word Miss Frankie spoke only made it louder. "I doubt very much they want to reconcile with Edie. They're here to shame her, and because you just couldn't keep from meddling. This is none of our business, Miss Frankie. You should have kept out of it and let them work it out on their own. I can't *believe* you put me in the middle of this."

She pulled her hand away as if the heat of my anger had burned her. "It was the right thing to do."

"No," I said. "It wasn't." I put my cup on the table and stood. "I'm not getting involved in this, Miss Frankie. Don't expect me to smooth the way for you. You're on your own. But you should know that if Edie leaves Zydeco over this, it's going to take a long time for me to forgive you."

I wanted to pick up my keys and purse and make a dramatic exit, but everything I'd brought with me was upstairs in Philippe's old bedroom so I had no choice but to limp upstairs again. By the time I got there, I was so exhausted all I could do was collapse on the bed. I lay there for a long time, staring at the ceiling and wondering how Edie was going to react when she found out that her parents were in town.

Miss Frankie isn't one to leave bad feelings unresolved, so I expected her to come after me and insist that we talk. When an hour passed, and there was no sign of her, it was clear she wasn't going to come, and that spoke more strongly about how she felt than anything else could have. Well, so what if she was angry with me—I was angry with her, too, so I guess we were even. Maybe I owed her an apology for flying off the handle, but I still couldn't believe she'd had the nerve to bring Edie's parents to town.

Eventually, I called a cab to take me home. I expected Miss Frankie to stop me from leaving, but she didn't even make an appearance as I limped back down the stairs and out the door. I knew the ball was in my court now, both in my relationship with Miss Frankie and the battle over Edie's right to live her own life. The trouble was, I didn't know which play to make, or how to run it once I made up my mind. I only knew I didn't have much time to waste.

Twenty-nine

❧

First things first. The moment the cab driver dropped me at home, I took off that dreadful pink jogging suit and changed into a pair of sweatpants, a strapless bra with a front closure that I could actually fasten without hurting my shoulder too much, and a soft cotton shirt that buttoned down the front. Getting dressed was a chore but I felt more human once I was wearing my own clothes. That led me to try brushing my hair, which proved to be more problematic. I gave up after a few minutes, secured the tangled mess with a clip, and called it good enough.

I still didn't know what I was going to do about Miss Frankie, but I couldn't just sit back and let Edie get blindsided by her parents. I had to tell her they were in town, but I didn't know how to do that without making her angry. I decided I could use some advice, so I turned to the wisest person I know—my aunt Yolanda. To my dismay, the call went straight to voice mail. I left a message and hung up but by that time all the exertion had wiped me out. I put the phone on the nightstand so I could hear it if it rang, and lay back on the bed. It was only noon, so I figured Edie would still be at work for at least five more hours—I thought Miss Frankie would wait for me to apologize before contacting Edie herself, which meant that I could close my eyes for a few minutes and still have plenty of time to talk with Edie today. I just needed five minutes. Maybe ten. Then I'd go to Zydeco and start cleaning up the mess Miss Frankie had created.

I woke up sometime later to the sound of someone banging on my door. Late afternoon shadows bathed my bedroom, which meant I'd been asleep for hours. I was so groggy, I completely forgot about my shoulder until I sat up. When I did, I remembered my injury in a hurry. Cradling my arm to keep my shoulder from moving again, I began the laborious process of making my way down the stairs.

The banging sounded so insistent, I figured Detective Winslow must have tracked me down. I just knew there would be hell to pay for leaving the hospital before he got there.

Bang, bang, bang! "Rita? Are you in there?"

I recognized Edie's voice and I was both relieved and worried at the same time. Relieved because it wasn't Winslow—yet. Worried because this had to mean I was too late. Miss Frankie had gotten to her first, and now she was here to . . . to do what?

Quit?

Probably.

I rubbed my face and tried to clear my head. Maybe I could talk her out of doing something rash, but if I hoped to do that, I'd need to think. My brain felt as if it was misfiring badly.

Bang, bang, bang! "Rita! Come on. Open the door!"

I pulled in a calming breath and took the last four steps as quickly as I dared. I flipped the locks and opened the door to Edie. She stood on the porch, her eyes wild and her face so pinched with emotion the resemblance to her mother hit me between the eyes.

"Sorry," I said. "What's going on?"

Edie brushed past me into the house, looked around for

something, and then lunged for the switch on the wall. The lights came on and she turned to get a good look at me. "I've been worried sick. We've been calling you for hours. Why didn't you answer your phone?"

I was still muddled, so I had trouble following her. "You . . . Wait. *What?*"

"I was up half the night waiting to hear something from the hospital," she said. "Nobody there would tell me anything. And then this morning, Ox said Miss Frankie had taken you to her house." She put a large baking dish covered with foil on the coffee table and then shooed me toward the couch, talking a mile a minute while she helped me sit and put my feet up. "We figured everything was okay, but when Ox called Miss Frankie's to talk to you, she said you weren't there. What the hell are you doing here by yourself?"

Edie was concerned about me? That must mean she didn't know about her parents . . . but was that good or bad? At least she wasn't angry—yet. But now *I* had to tell her, and that wasn't going to be easy.

My heart started beating faster and my throat grew tight and dry. "You're here to check up on me?"

"Of course." She plumped a pillow and wedged it carefully behind my shoulder. "How's that? Does that feel all right?"

I nodded. "I'm really okay," I said. "I should have called. I'm sorry."

"Yeah, you should have." She picked up the baking dish and turned toward the kitchen. "Don't move. I brought dinner. And just so you know, I'm staying the night." My confusion must have been evident because she waved toward the front door and explained, "My bag is out in the car. I'll get it after we eat."

"You don't have to stay with me," I said automatically.

She gave me her mother's face again. "You are *not* staying alone. It's either me or Ox and Isabeau. Or Sparkle. They all offered to come over—if you don't want me, I'll call one of them."

I held up both hands as far as I could without wincing. "Okay, okay. I give. There's no need to call anyone else."

She gave me a satisfied smile and disappeared into the kitchen, leaving behind a whiff of something from inside that dish that I couldn't identify. I thought about following her into the kitchen, but two things stopped me. One, I was surprisingly comfortable where I was, and two, a few minutes alone would buy me time to think.

Edie rattled around in the kitchen for a while and then reappeared with a plate containing a lump of overcooked meat, a mound of greens, and another of rice riddled with flecks of green onion. "It's not much," she said as she handed me the plate. "But it's what I had on hand."

"You cooked?"

She gave me a stern look. "Don't laugh. I'm trying to eat healthy for the baby."

And this was how she did it? Interesting. She went back to the kitchen and I got busy trying to figure out what she was serving me. Edie and I met at pastry school, but baking was not her forte. Apparently, cooking wasn't either. I picked at the meat and decided it must be pork, extremely well done. The fried rice was easy to figure out, but the greens gave me a bit more trouble. The leaves were flat and dull, so I ruled out kale. I took a sniff and crossed spinach and beet greens off the list. That left collard or mustard greens as possibilities.

I'm not a big fan of bitter greens, even when they're prepared well, but I can eat them if they're done up right like they are at Rubio's. These were not. I just knew I'd have trouble choking down the limp pile of dull leaves on my plate, but I didn't want to offend Edie before I told her about her parents. I'd just have to take one for the team.

While I was giving myself a pep talk, Edie came back from the kitchen with her plate so I did my best to look enthusiastic about the meal in front of me. "This is really nice of you," I said, forking up a bite of the meat. "How did things go at work today?"

"Everything went fine," Edie said as she settled into a chair facing the couch. "What did the doctor tell you?"

"A few bruises," I said. "Nothing serious. I'll be back to normal in a couple of days." I chewed. And chewed. And chewed that dry, tasteless piece of pork. If Edie was still speaking to me after tonight, maybe I'd offer to give her some cooking lessons—for the baby's sake.

"I didn't get a chance to ask you last night. Did you notice anybody in the alley when you came back?"

Edie looked at me strangely as she ate some rice. "But you did ask. You don't remember?"

"It's kind of a blur," I admitted. "What was your answer?"

"I've thought and thought about it, but I didn't see anybody at all. You don't have any idea who did this to you?"

"Oh, I have an idea," I said. "I just don't have any proof. I'm pretty sure it was Scotty Justus."

Edie stopped chewing. "Why would he hit you?"

"I think he killed Destiny. He knows I suspect him and he's trying to shut me up."

"Why would he kill his own daughter?"

"I haven't worked out all the details yet," I admitted. "I know that he was fed up with her drug use and I know their relationship was strained." But even I had to admit that as motives go, those were weak. "Maybe he didn't want her to turn in her drug dealer," I said. And then a new thought occurred to me. "Maybe he was supplying her with drugs. He was a shrimper for a long time. Maybe that was just a cover for drug running. Anyway, tomorrow I want to talk to everybody I can. Someone *must* have seen Scotty last night."

"Well, I'm sure someone did," Edie said. "He's there every day. What you need is to find somebody who saw him coming after you with a weapon." She put her fork on her plate and shook her head slowly. "What you really need is to step back and let the police do their job. I mean, it's obvious that you're making someone nervous. If you keep digging, they'll strike again and you might not be able to walk away next time."

She wasn't saying anything I hadn't thought of myself, but hearing it still sent a shiver of apprehension up my spine. "I'd be happy to step back if the police would actually do their jobs," I said. "Detective Winslow is apparently trying to pin Destiny's murder on me. If I want to keep myself out of prison, I can't wait for someone else to look into it."

Edie rolled her eyes. "You won't go to prison, and you can't undo dead."

"You don't know I won't be arrested," I said. "You haven't seen how Detective Winslow acts. I don't have an alibi, and I can't prove that I didn't wig out and kill Destiny."

"He can't prove you did," Edie reasoned. "Please don't keep putting yourself in danger. It's freaky enough just knowing that someone dangerous is on the loose."

"I'll be as careful as I can," I promised, "but I can't just sit around and wait. What time did the attack happen anyway? I'm a little fuzzy on some of the details."

She let out a resigned sigh. "We left Zydeco at around seven, so if you factor in the time it took us to walk there and our . . . conversation, I'd say maybe seven fifteen."

"Who was still at work then? Second Chances would have been open, right? And the Chopper Shop."

"The drugstore and EZ Shipping are both open until nine," Edie said. "And I saw lights at the Feathered Peacock. Zora must have had a late class going on." She pulled a small notebook from her bag and started making a list. "To give to the police," she said.

Over the next few minutes, we came up with half a dozen other possible witnesses, including Felix and Lorena from the market on the corner, anyone working at Paolo's Pizza, and the crew at Rubio's Ribs. It would take weeks to work through the list in my spare time. I'd just have to focus on the likeliest witnesses first.

I'd toyed with my food while we talked, but once the list was complete, I had a hard time hiding my lack of enthusiasm. Luckily, I wasn't the only one.

Edie ate another bite of rice and made a face. "This is horrible, isn't it?"

I laughed. "It's a valiant effort."

"My poor baby is doomed," she said, setting her plate on the coffee table. "I've been reading all this literature about what to feed it, what I'm supposed to eat while I'm pregnant, and what I'm supposed to avoid. No caffeine, limit the fish, watch out for mercury. No deli meats, no soft cheeses, no smoked seafood . . . And that's just for now. After the baby's born, there are a million things to remember, and I can't even cook one edible dinner. I can't feed the baby *cake* for every meal." She buried her face in her hands and wailed, "What am I doing, Rita? Am I making a mistake?"

This was so unlike the Edie I'd known since pastry school, I didn't know what to think. Even if I'd been able to think clearly, I was in way over my head. I wasn't qualified to give the kind of advice she wanted, so I decided to start with what I knew. "Cooking isn't that hard," I said. "It's definitely something we can work on."

She picked up a lump of green with her fork and shook it at me. "This was supposed to be simple, and I ruined it."

"It just takes practice," I told her. "Relax. You don't have to be a superwoman. There's no rule that says you have to make everything your baby eats from scratch."

"Oh, yes there is," she cried. "There are rules about everything! About breastfeeding and what kind of diapers to use and what kind of wipes are bad for the baby. Then there are bottles and car seats, and pacifiers, and . . . Really, Rita, what *am* I doing?"

"Right now, I'd say you're panicking, but try not to do that," I said gently. "You still have almost four months to go. There's time. And you're going to be a good mother, Edie. I'm sure there's a lot to figure out, but you'll get there. If anybody can wade through all the rules and make sense of them, you can."

She sighed heavily and sank down in the chair, kicking her feet out in front of her and staring at the small mound of her stomach. "Thanks, but what if I go into labor early? Sure, I'm usually good with rules and things, but in this case I'm not so sure I agree with you. I'm really starting to wonder if I can do this on my own."

I sat forward a little too quickly and pain tore up my shoulder again. I did my best to ignore it. I didn't want Edie to start worrying about me again. She had troubles enough of her own. "Are you really having second thoughts about the baby, or are you just having a bad day?"

She shook her head slowly. Maybe even a little uncertainly. "I don't think so. I want the baby, but I'm scared out of my mind. What if I screw it up? What if I . . . I don't know. What if I do something wrong?"

"Is that what you're worried about? That you might make a mistake?"

"*A* mistake? No. A million of them? Yes." She sighed again and looked up at the ceiling. "I mean, it's not like I'm bringing home a houseplant. We're talking about a human being here. I could ruin its life."

Clearly, she was freaking out. Maybe I was just being a coward, but I couldn't justify adding another problem to her list right then. I scratched "Tell Edie about her parents" off my mental list of things to do and rescheduled it for later. Like tomorrow morning.

"Well," I said. "I guess you could ruin the baby's life, but I don't think you will."

She looked at me from the corner of her eye. "Oh. Okay. That makes me feel so much better."

"Hey, I'm doing my best here," I said with a laugh. "Remember, this is all new to me, too." I put my plate on the coffee table and said, "You'll feel better if you eat—but not this. Let's order in. I'll buy. What sounds good?"

Edie rolled her head across the back of her chair. "I don't know. What can I eat that won't stunt the baby's growth? Ooh! I know! Pizza!" She produced an industrial-sized bottle of antacid tablets from her bag. "I would kill for a slice of extra cheese, pineapple, and green olives."

"Weird. You can get that combination on your half. I'll have pepperoni." I felt around for my phone and realized

I'd left it upstairs. "Do you have your cell handy? Mine's in my bedroom."

She nodded and pulled her phone out of her pocket, but she checked the screen before she handed it over, and that tight, bitter expression she'd inherited from her mother was back. "You have *got* to be kidding me. My mother hasn't spoken to me in three months. Now she's calling every hour on the hour. She called half a dozen times this afternoon and here's *another* missed call from her. What is she up to?"

Uh-oh. The warm fuzzies evaporated and I sat up a little straighter. "Um . . . Edie?"

She looked up from the phone and I saw anger suddenly morph into worry. "You don't think there's some kind of emergency, do you? Like maybe something's happened to my dad or my sister?"

"I—no." I stumbled over my words, stopped, and tried to pull myself together. "Tell Edie about her parents" zipped right back to the top of my list. "I don't think there's anything wrong. As a matter of fact, I think she's calling about something else entirely."

Confusion clouded her eyes. "Like what?"

"They, uh . . . Well the thing is, they're here." I held up a hand to stop the tirade I knew was coming. "Miss Frankie invited them. When I woke up this morning, they were already at her house. I had no idea."

"They're here? In New Orleans?"

"Yes, but don't be angry. I mean, of course you're angry. You have every right to be angry. I told Miss Frankie a million times not to get involved, but you know how she is."

"So they're *here*?"

I nodded miserably. "They want to have dinner with you tomorrow night. Miss Frankie asked me to set it up, but I refused to get in the middle."

Edie blinked a couple of times and then dashed a tear away with a fingertip. "They came? Are you serious?"

I was about to say something else, but her reaction stunned me into silence. All I could do was nod.

"You saw them?"

"I did."

Edie stood and walked in a tight circle, tucking a lock of her straight, dark hair behind one ear in a nervous gesture I knew only too well. "How did they seem?"

"I don't know. Fine, I guess."

She stopped walking and gave me a "Duh!" look. "Mad? Sad? Ready to apologize? What did they say?"

I desperately wanted to sugarcoat my answer, but I knew she'd find out the truth soon enough, and then she'd never trust me again. "It wasn't pretty," I admitted.

Edie threw up her hands in disgust. "Of course it wasn't. Why am I even surprised? Okay. Let's have it."

I tried, but I just couldn't make myself repeat the things her parents had said that morning. "Well, you know them better than I do. You know how they feel. They haven't changed their minds."

"So they still expect me to get married."

"Actually, the subject of marriage never came up. And if it makes you feel any better, they don't blame you for the situation, but they're awfully upset with me."

She gaped at me. "With *you*? Why?"

"Well, apparently you know better than to get pregnant and I'm a bad influence." As soon as the words left my mouth, I wished I could call them back.

Edie's face burned and her voice rose to a pitch only dogs should have been able to hear. I don't know what she said, but I'm pretty sure she hadn't learned any of those Chinese words from her mother. Lin would have washed out Edie's mouth with soap and then blamed me for that, too.

I let her go on until she started running out of steam, and then tried to inject a note of reason. "I know you're angry," I said gently. "But try to calm down—for the baby. I'll order the pizza. We'll can eat and talk this over."

"What is there to talk about?" Edie shouted. "I can't believe those two!" She flopped down in her chair and looked up at me through her bangs. "And Miss Frankie!" She shook her head in disbelief. "How dare she?"

"I know. I know. I'm angry with her, too. She's gone too far."

"Way too far," Edie agreed. "She had no right. What about my sister? Was she there?"

"I didn't see her."

"Of course not. Why would she come?" Edie sighed again and closed her eyes, making a visible effort to calm down. "I guess I only have one more question," she said after a minute.

"What's that?"

"What time is dinner tomorrow and where do we meet them?"

My mouth fell open. "You want to go?"

She cut a glance at me. "No! I don't *want* to. But if I don't, my mother will think I'm admitting I'm wrong and she'll decide I'm too ashamed to look her in the eye. I can't let her think that."

"So you're going."

She stood again and looked down at me. "No. *We're* going. There's no way I'm doing this alone." And with that she picked up our plates and carried them into kitchen.

Thirty

❧

Shortly after ten the next morning I waved Edie off to work and carried my new set of prescriptions into Magnolia Street Drug. I'd promised on my honor to take the day off work so I could heal, and I'd agreed to go with her to the dinner from hell if I could get Miss Frankie to speak to me long enough to give me the details. I wasn't the only one who'd made concessions. Edie had reluctantly agreed not to argue with me about trying to find someone who could put Scotty in the alley when I was attacked—as long as I kept my cell phone in my pocket and checked in frequently.

Inside, Sebastian was working behind the counter, his curly hair slightly mussed and a pair of dark-rimmed glasses perched on the end of his nose. He gave the prescriptions a quick once-over and entered them into the computer, then turned a raised eyebrow on me.

"I heard what happened the other night. The whole neighborhood is buzzing about it."

That didn't surprise me but it did make me uncomfortable. I've never liked being talked about. I gave a half-hearted shrug. "Wrong place, wrong time, I guess."

"Seems like you do that a lot. You really ought to be home in bed. Somebody could have come in to get these filled for you."

"I'm all right," I lied. "I have things to do and I'm not going to let some crazy person frighten me into hiding."

"Well, I hope you'll be careful," Sebastian said with a worried scowl. "You've obviously gotten on the wrong side of somebody very dangerous."

"Thanks. I'll do my best. Before you start filling those, can I ask you a question?"

Sebastian looked up with a shrug. "Sure."

"Were you working here night before last?"

He looked confused but nodded. "Yeah, until around nine."

"So you were here between seven fifteen and seven thirty?"

His shoulders tensed and he laughed uneasily. "Why do you want to know? Don't tell me you're checking my alibi."

"Not at all," I said with a little wave of my hand. "I'm looking for someone who might've seen what happened. Can you see the alley from here?"

Sebastian glanced toward the window and then back at me. "A little, but the pharmacy counter closes at seven. I stayed in the back to do the monthly inventory."

"You closed up right at seven?"

Sebastian nodded solemnly. "On the dot, if not a minute or two early. It was a quiet night."

"I guess it was too much to hope that you saw someone running away holding a lead pipe and muttering something about 'that meddlesome baker.'"

Sebastian's shoulders relaxed and he slid a weak smile in my direction. "Hey, I wish I *could* help. I don't like what's going on around here at all. First you and Moose almost got hit by that van, then Destiny was killed! And now you've been attacked again. This is scary stuff. Believe me, if I knew anything, I'd tell you."

I wanted to believe him, but I couldn't forget what Gabriel

had said about how the locals closed ranks against newcomers. Would Sebastian truly be honest with me if it meant hanging Scotty out to dry? I'd just have to take a chance. "Do you remember seeing Scotty Justus around that time?"

"Scotty?" The smile slid from Sebastian's face. "Not that I recall. Why?"

"I think he might be the one who attacked me."

Sebastian looked horrified. "Scotty? No!"

"And I think he threw a rock through the window at Zydeco and slashed my tire. How well do you know him?"

"Well enough, I guess. Like I know most people around here. I just can't believe he'd do something like that."

I wasn't going to waste energy trying to convince him. "Was anyone else working last night? Maybe one of them saw something."

Sebastian thought for a moment and then gave me the names of two high school students who'd been working the registers and the manager of the night shift. "But I doubt they'll be able to tell you anything. I don't think any of them were outside when you were being attacked."

"What about customers?" I asked. "Was anyone here around that time? Maybe one of them could help me?"

Sebastian pulled off his glasses and cleaned them with the hem of his lab coat. "I really didn't pay much attention to anyone out there shopping," he said with a nod toward the front of the store. "But like I said, it was slow. And I couldn't tell you about pharmacy customers even if I wanted to. It's against the law."

Of course it was. "Well, it was worth a shot," I said. "I'll quit bothering you and let you work. How long will it take to fill those prescriptions? I'll wait if it's not going to be too long."

"It should only take a few minutes." He put his glasses on and started to turn away again, then turned back and wagged the prescriptions at me thoughtfully. "You know who might have seen something? Edgar. I just remembered, he stopped in a few minutes after seven. I'd just closed up the pharmacy when he came in."

My heart jumped and I leaned forward eagerly. "Edgar Zappa? I wonder if he saw anything when he left here."

Sebastian shrugged. "You never know . . . I guess it won't hurt to ask."

I hoped he was right. Because asking the wrong person about what happened last night might hurt very much indeed.

I let him get to work on filling my prescriptions, then bought a Diet Pepsi and slugged down one of the pain pills before tucking the rest into a secure pouch in my purse and heading off to talk to Edgar. His place, EZ Shipping, is a small store in the middle of a run-down strip mall about half a block west of the drugstore. The direct route there would take me right past the alley where I was attacked the night before. I set off confidently, but after about thirty yards everything inside me grew cold and tight. My feet refused to keep walking down that street, and my heart slammed so hard against my chest I thought I might have to go back to the emergency room for a panic attack.

It took twice as long to walk around the block and I felt silly avoiding the alley, but even in the middle of the morning I couldn't make myself go near the place. I felt exposed and unprotected. If Scotty wanted me dead, he might not let a little thing like broad daylight stop him.

It was almost eleven when I walked into Edgar's shop. He was behind the counter helping an elderly woman with a couple of boxes she wanted to ship to her grandson who was serving in the military. This was his fourth deployment in six years, and . . . I tuned out when I began to suspect that she was going to share her entire family history before those boxes went anywhere.

I was meandering up and down the aisles when my cell beeped with a new text message from Edie, reminding me to call Miss Frankie for the particulars about tonight's dinner. I wasn't sure which part of that conversation I dreaded most: the part where Miss Frankie chided me about the way I'd acted yesterday, or the part where she made sure I knew that she'd been right all along about bringing Edie's parents to town. But avoiding the inevitable wouldn't change anything.

Since Edgar was tied up for the foreseeable future, I went outside to make the call before I could talk myself out of it. The phone rang half a dozen times before Pearl Lee picked up. I guess after my meltdown yesterday she'd decided not to go back to Zydeco, which was fine with me. She told me that Miss Frankie had gone next door to visit with her friend Bernice. I was pretty relieved not to actually reach Miss Frankie. I could use a little more time to decide what I was going to say to her. I asked her to have Miss Frankie call with details for dinner.

By the time I went back inside, the customer was finally counting out her money. I could see impatience dancing in Edgar's pale blue eyes as she slowly put her wallet back into her purse and verified a few details, but I don't think she was aware of his frustration. When the door closed behind her, he grinned at me and ran his fingers through his hair. "Sorry about the wait, but I guess it gave you plenty of time to look around. Did you find anything you'd like?"

"Actually, I just came by to ask you a few questions if you don't mind."

His smile faded slowly. "Sure. What's up? It must be important for you to come here in the middle of a workday."

"I think it's important," I said with a smile designed to get him talking. "I was talking to Sebastian a few minutes ago, and he said that you were in the drugstore Wednesday night around seven."

"Was I?" Edgar's gaze flicked toward the ceiling, as if he was trying to remember. "If he says so, I guess I was."

"You don't recall? The night before last? The night of the memorial service?"

Edgar straightened a stack of papers next to the register. "Yeah. I nipped in for a minute. I needed a couple of things. What's this about anyway?"

"Somebody attacked me about that same time," I said. "I'm trying to find witnesses. Did you see anyone while you were out, or notice anything unusual?"

Edgar looked at me with wide eyes. "You were attacked?"

"You didn't know?"

He shook his head quickly. "No. How would I?"

I shrugged. "Word gets around."

"Not this time. I haven't heard a thing. What happened?"

He looked genuinely confused, but I wondered if that was true. According to Sebastian, the neighborhood was buzzing with the news. How had Edgar missed hearing about it?

"I wish I knew," I said. "Somebody hit me from behind."

"You weren't seriously hurt, I hope?"

"Not seriously," I agreed. "It happened by the alley that runs behind the Chopper Shop. Did you pass that way to get to the drugstore?"

Edgar nodded. "It's the quickest way to get there from here."

"And did you notice anyone else hanging around near the alley?"

"Not that I remember," he said. "But I was in a hurry. I was working alone, realized I was out of toilet paper, and ran over there to pick some up. I was in and out in a minute and I wasn't really paying attention to anything around me. I didn't see anybody until I got back here."

"You had a customer waiting?"

"No, but Zora was here. She'll vouch for me. She was in tears, just sitting on the bench on the curb," he said with a nod toward the window. "I asked her what was wrong, and she said that she'd just had a nasty argument with Scotty."

Bingo! Scotty had been in the neighborhood. My heart did a little tap dance of joy. "Did you see Scotty yourself?"

"Me? No."

"Did Zora mention where she and Scotty were when they had their argument?"

Edgar shook his head. "Not exactly. I assumed they were at the Chopper Shop, though. She told me that she went to see him. I figured that's where she went."

So she'd argued with Scotty and they were both riled up when they parted company. She'd run back to the Feathered Peacock, while Scotty had taken out his anger on me. It made perfect sense, but it was circumstantial "evidence" at best, and I was convinced that Detective Winslow wouldn't take it seriously unless someone else came forward with the information. I bumped Zora to the top of my possible witness list.

"Did she say what they argued about?"

Edgar shook his head. "No, but I can guess. Poor guy. She will *not* leave him alone."

That was an odd comment considering Zora's claim that she and Scotty were just friends. "But it's not as if they were a couple," I said. "She's not even interested in him."

Edgar gave me an odd look. "Who told you that?"

"Well . . . Moose for one. And Zora herself told me that there was nothing going on between her and Scotty."

Edgar flicked another glance at the window and chewed a lip. "Zora was probably trying to save face after Scotty dumped her," Edgar said. "You know how that goes. You're head over heels in love with somebody and they choose someone else. It hurts. It's embarrassing." His gaze flickered to the floor and then to something at his side, and I wondered if we were still talking about Zora and Scotty or if he was thinking about someone else. Like Destiny.

"You and Destiny were close," I said gently. "You must miss her."

His head snapped up and his jaw tightened. "I don't know what you're implying."

"But I'm sure you can understand why some people speculated about the two of you."

"We weren't sleeping together," Edgar growled.

"I never said you were. But those aren't the only rumors I've heard. Maybe Scotty got upset with her over some of those things. Did Destiny and Scotty get along well?"

"He was her dad."

"Yeah, but that doesn't mean they never argued."

Edgar put both hands on the counter and glared down at me. "What does that have to do with anything?"

"Maybe nothing. I'm just thinking that whoever killed her is probably the same person who has been after me. I was under the impression Scotty didn't like some of the things Destiny was up to when she was alive, that's all."

Edgar slammed his fist on the counter with such force I jumped. "Destiny wasn't like that," he said. "She loved her dad. So the two of them weren't close. They were working on it. But things were complicated."

"Meaning what?"

"Meaning nothing." He seemed to realize that he'd said more than he intended.

"She was your friend," I said. "Who do *you* think killed her?"

He was silent for a long time before he finally answered. "Only one person it could have been, isn't there? It had to have been Moose."

"But Moose was standing next to me when that van came around the corner," I reminded him. "He saved my life."

"I don't know how he did it but my money's on him. He didn't understand that her addiction was an illness. None of them did. Destiny needed help."

"Moose and Scotty didn't want to help her?"

Edgar looked so miserable, I felt sorry for him. "Nobody did but me. Oh, Zora tried, but Moose was always on about the money and Scotty kept saying it wasn't that bad." His voice caught and tears shimmered in his eyes. "We weren't lovers, Rita. I was her sponsor."

Whoa! I let that trickle into my brain for a moment. "You mean like with Alcoholics Anonymous?"

"Yeah, but it's Narcotics Anonymous. I didn't tell you before because it's 'anonymous' for a reason."

Boy, had I been wrong about that! "So that's how you knew about the deal the district attorney offered her?"

He nodded. "She came to me for advice. She wanted to know what I thought and I told her to go for it." He didn't say it, but I knew he was feeling guilty for encouraging Destiny to take the deal.

"Do you know who her dealer was?"

"She never would tell me. Probably because she knew I'd blow the whistle myself. Anyway, that's all I know. Now if you don't mind, I have work to do."

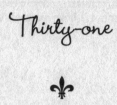

Thirty-one

Edgar refused to say anything more to me, so I left EZ Shipping and headed over to Zora's yoga studio. But the Feathered Peacock was shut up tight when I got there, the blinds drawn and the door locked. The sign in the window said "Closed." Apparently, Zora didn't have any classes this morning but her schedule left me at loose ends.

I desperately wanted to find someone who could put Scotty in that alley at the time of the attack, but the trip across town to the drugstore, the walk around the block to EZ Shipping, and the stroll to the Feathered Peacock had worn me out. In addition to feeling as if I could curl up in a ball and sleep for hours, the pain pill I'd swallowed earlier was making me light-headed.

Reluctantly, I admitted that I'd never make it through the dinner with Miss Frankie and the Bryces unless I got some downtime. Once again leaving the Mercedes at Zydeco, I called another cab and went home, where I found a message from Miss Frankie on my land line telling me to meet them for dinner that evening at Rubio's. Her choice surprised me; I love Rubio's but it's a BBQ joint and I'd expected her to pick a more upscale restaurant. According to her message, the Bryces also wanted a tour of Zydeco after we ate. Whatever.

It was unusual for Miss Frankie to call my home number instead of my cell. I could only guess that she was no more eager to talk to me than I had been to call her.

I texted Edie the details and promised to meet her at Zydeco before dinner, then put everything and everyone else out of my mind and fell asleep. I work up at four, stiff, sore, and hungry from having missed lunch. I stood under a hot shower for a while, hoping that would ease some of my aches and pains, scrounged a power bar from the pantry, and wolfed that down while I dressed. I was in a cab and on my way back to Zydeco a little after six.

Edie was edgy and pacing nervously when I walked through the front door. She'd chosen a simple black calf-length maternity dress that didn't hide the baby bump but didn't accentuate it either. She'd obviously taken pains with her hair, and her makeup was flawless and understated. I thought her parents would approve, but what did I know?

She raked a look over my outfit and sighed with relief at what she saw. In honor of her crazy parents, I'd chosen a conservative outfit: black pants, a silk tunic with three-quarter sleeves, and a pair of low-heeled black pumps I could walk in.

"You look great," Edie said, and then held out her arms to invite my opinion. "What do you think? Is the dress too short?"

I laughed at the sarcasm. "You look great. Relax, okay?"

"Relax? How am I supposed to do that? You've met my mother. You know how she is."

Yes. Well. There was no tactful response to that, so I changed the subject as we set out toward the restaurant. As we walked, I told her about my conversations with Sebastian and Edgar earlier that morning. "Obviously, Scotty was hanging around here in the neighborhood that night," I said after I'd told her what I'd learned. "All I need to do now is talk to Zora to prove it."

"Talk to her?" Edie cried as she stepped over a raised

piece of sidewalk. "Are you crazy, Rita? What if Scotty finds out you're still asking around about him? He's already determined to keep you from figuring out what he did."

"To keep from proving it, you mean. I've already figured it out."

Edie let out a frustrated sigh. "You're going to get yourself killed if you're not careful."

"I'll wind up in prison if I don't find the evidence I need to prove that Scotty's behind all the violence." Edie still looked skeptical, so I tried to reassure her. "I'm just going to talk to the woman, that's all. If she can tell me that Scotty was at the Chopper Shop around the time he attacked me, I'll try to convince her to talk to the police."

"And then you'll leave it alone? No matter what she tells you? Promise?"

"I can't promise that," I said with a laugh as we crossed the street toward Rubio's. "What if she won't admit to seeing Scotty that night?"

"Rita!"

"What? The two of them are friends. They had an argument, but that doesn't mean she'll throw him under the bus just because I ask her about it."

Edie slowed her step and stopped walking in front of the restaurant. "It's a sad state of affairs when I'd rather talk to you about murder than have dinner with my own parents. Do you think they're already here?"

I checked my watch and nodded. "I'd almost bet on it. Miss Frankie doesn't believe in being late." Edie looked so nervous I couldn't help but feel sorry for her. "Are you okay? Ready to go in and face the music?"

"I guess we might as well get it over with," she said, but she held back, unmoving, her eyes clouded with nervous energy.

I put an arm around her shoulders. "Let's go in. I promise I won't let them beat you up."

She laughed and we walked inside together. Unlike the other day at lunch, there was no line of customers waiting for a table, which made it easy to spot Miss Frankie and

Edie's parents. They were already at a table for six near a window that looked out onto the street, which meant they'd seen us arrive.

"Come on," I muttered to Edie under my breath. "Don't let them see you sweat." And then I pasted a big old smile on my face and walked through the dining room toward them.

Miss Frankie greeted me with a smile and a hug that probably looked warm and friendly from the outside. I knew her well enough to feel the coolness of her welcome, which meant things between us weren't okay. Not by a long shot. But my mother-in-law would rather chew nails than appear discourteous in public, so she put on a good face and I pretended not to notice.

Taking their cue from Miss Frankie, the Bryces greeted us with smiles and Charlie even stood and gave Edie an awkward embrace. Lin couldn't make herself go that far, but she did manage to say her daughter's name without choking, which was probably quite a concession on her part.

Edie and I sat on one side of the table facing her parents. Miss Frankie held court at the table's head and presided over the meal with a watchful eye. We made polite conversation about the weather as we ate, and the history of the neighborhood. After a while we segued into a discussion of a few items in the local news—carefully avoiding any talk about the rash of violence and the ongoing murder investigation.

Finally, the meal was over and the time for avoidance was past. Our server whisked away our dirty dishes and Miss Frankie linked her hands together on the table in front of her. "I'm so glad you could all make it tonight," she said with a pleased smile. "We have a few details to work out regarding the baby shower while we're together so I thought we could do that now."

Everyone mumbled their agreement and Miss Frankie smiled approvingly. "Edie, your parents will be staying until Monday, so that means we need to have the shower before they leave. I think Sunday afternoon sounds like a good time, don't you?"

"Sunday?" I said, surprised. "As in two days from now?"

Miss Frankie's smile didn't waver, but I saw a flash of something in her eyes. "Is that a problem for you, Rita?"

"For me? No. It just seems so sudden. It would be nice to give the guests a little more notice."

"Under normal circumstances, I'd agree with you, but we're just talking about a few friends and family. It won't take long to pull it all together." Miss Frankie reached out to Edie, who was staring at her, shell-shocked. "Are you quite all right, dear? You haven't said a word."

"Yes, I'm—I'm—" She shifted in her seat and darted a glance at her mother. "Is this it? My parents haven't spoken to me in months and now we're just going to pretend like everything's all right?"

Lin Bryce gave her daughter a sharp-eyed look. "Your father and I would like to know our grandchild. Someone needs to watch out for the baby and make sure it's raised properly."

Edie threw her napkin onto the table. "That's *my* job. And if that's all you want, don't bother."

Charlie scowled at her. "Now, Edie, don't speak to your mother that way." He switched to a hearty smile and said, "And we were doing so well, too."

Lin started in again and I winced inwardly, fully expecting the evening to disintegrate right before my eyes, but Miss Frankie cleared her throat pointedly and Edie's mother immediately fell silent. It was a thing of beauty—and maybe a little disturbing.

"Your parents and I have been talking," Miss Frankie said to Edie. "They understand that you're an adult, fully capable of making your own decisions. They aren't happy with the situation you're in, but they are pleased that you've decided to keep the baby when there are other options you could have chosen. They love you and they don't want to lose out on having a relationship with their first grandchild."

Edie looked first at her father, who gave an encouraging nod, and then at her mother, who sat staring straight ahead. No one spoke, so Miss Frankie went on. "Everyone here has a choice. You can either hang on to your anger or put it behind you and move on. Your parents would like to move forward. So now, let's talk about the menu for the shower. Are there any dietary restrictions I should be aware of?"

Edie shot an uncertain look at me. I sympathized with her. I'd come up against Miss Frankie's force of will more than once and I'd never come out the winner. But maybe this time Miss Frankie was right. Letting go of anger wasn't easy, but clinging to it wouldn't accomplish anything.

"I can't have sushi," Edie said. "Or caffeine." She took a shaky breath, then pulled herself together and rattled off a list of verboten items. Miss Frankie skillfully segued into discussing what Edie *did* want to eat, and Lin spoke up a couple of times with suggestions of old family favorites. By the time we were ready to pay the bill, the mood had lightened a bit. Dinner hadn't provided a magical fix, but at least Edie and her parents were talking again, providing a ray of hope that they might restore their relationships in time.

We moved from the restaurant to the sidewalk, where Charlie partnered with Edie, Miss Frankie and Lin walked together, and I brought up the rear. That was fine with me. As soon as we got this visit to Zydeco over with, I was more than ready to make my excuses and go home. I noticed lights on at the Feathered Peacock as we passed by, however, and thought that maybe I'd swing by and see Zora for a minute before I went home.

It didn't take long to reach Zydeco, but by that time I was so deep in thought that when Miss Frankie and Lin stopped abruptly in front of me, I plowed right into Lin's back—which earned me another death stare. *Sheesh!* I really needed to pay more attention to where I was going.

I started to offer an apology, but Miss Frankie cut me off, wagging a finger at Zydeco's broad front porch. "The *door*, Rita. Look at the door."

I had to move out around them to see, but when I did, every nerve in my body tingled. Under the gleam of the porch light, I could see bright red paint splashed on the steps and a dripping from a word streaked across the bakery's pristine white doors.

Jezebel.

Charlie let out a low whistle. Edie gasped and clasped her hands over her belly, and the blood drained from Miss Frankie's face.

"We might have to forget the tour tonight," I said.

Lin pursed her lips in disapproval and delivered another death stare in my direction, saying, "This is where you have my daughter working? What kind of neighborhood is this?"

"It's usually a very fine neighborhood," I said, and prayed that nobody would contradict me.

Miss Frankie looked at me from beneath a set of perfectly arched eyebrows. "Rita? What is this?"

"Apparently, a case of vandalism," I said, stating the obvious.

Lin said something I couldn't understand and Charlie put a protective arm around his daughter and spoke quietly to his wife. "I'm sure it's not about Edie. Let's not jump to conclusions, all right?"

Just then, I heard a familiar laugh behind me and turned as Pearl Lee and Scotty came up the sidewalk together. My heart started racing and my fight-or-flight instinct kicked in—heavy on the flight option. Scotty was the last person I wanted to see right then, but I told myself he probably wouldn't try to kill me in front of half a dozen witnesses.

Pearl Lee was decked out in a rhinestone-encrusted dress with spaghetti straps and a pair of black pumps. Scotty had put on a pair of long khaki pants with a pale blue Hawaiian print shirt. A strap of leather held his hair at the back of his neck, and his sandals looked almost new. They must have had quite a night planned for him to dress up.

The two of them stopped walking when they saw us all standing there. Pearl Lee shifted around uncomfortably when she saw Miss Frankie. Luckily for her, Miss Frankie seemed more concerned about the paint on the door than Pearl Lee's companion or my obvious failure to keep her away from men.

Scotty took one look at the paint splattered door and his smile vanished. "What's this?"

"That's what we all want to know," Miss Frankie said, and then she seemed to realize that Pearl Lee was with a male companion. She gave me a hard stare. "What's going on here, Rita?"

"Ask Pearl Lee," I said. "She was supposed to tell you all about it yesterday."

Back to Pearl Lee. "Where have you been?"

Pearl Lee lifted her chin defiantly. "We've been at dinner."

"For how long?" I asked.

"We had reservations at seven," Scotty said. "Why?"

"Have you been together the whole time?"

"Every minute," Pearl Lee answered for him. "So if you think Scotty did this, you're wrong."

I could see Edie shaking her head, trying to warn me to stop talking. Charlie very nearly blew a gasket. "You did this?" He patted his pockets and got frustrated. "Where's my cell phone? Somebody call the police."

Scotty just looked outraged and maybe a bit confused. "Why would *I* do this?"

It was a good question. I could figure him slashing my tire and breaking the window, but although I really wanted to catch him red-handed, I couldn't imagine him doing this, especially if he'd been with Pearl Lee all evening.

"Maybe you should take the Bryces home," I said to Miss Frankie. "Try to convince them that Edie's not in any real danger."

Miss Frankie gave a businesslike nod and began herding all three of the Bryces down the walk toward her car. While

I was distracted, Pearl Lee click-clacked on her heels toward Zydeco's front porch.

"No!" I called after her. "Don't touch anything."

Scotty slouched up the stairs behind her.

"Don't touch anything," I said again. "It's a crime scene."

Pearl Lee put her hands up and backed off a step or two. Scotty bent down and picked something up. He held it up to get a better look and it sparkled in the light.

Pearl Lee leaned in closer to get a look. "What is that?"

"This?" Scotty came down the stairs and dropped it into my hand. "It's an earring."

I stared down at the old-fashioned clip in the shape of a heart studded with something sparkly. Diamonds? "Where did it come from?"

Scotty put his hands in his pockets again and rocked back on his heels. "My guess is that your vandal lost it while she was working. You want to know who that belongs to?"

I lowered my hand slowly. "You know whose it is?"

"I should. I bought the pair of them last Christmas."

Okay. That surprised me. I just didn't know what it meant. "Whose is it?"

He shrugged. "They belong to Zora now."

Pearl Lee gave a shriek and lunged between us. "Zora? You? Gave that? To *Zora*?" She leaned in closer and tried to snatch the earring out of my hand. "Are those diamonds? Are they real?"

I moved the earring out of her way and shoved it into my pocket. Scotty sputtered something that sounded like a denial, but it didn't make a dent in Pearl Lee's anger.

"You said you weren't a couple," she said, shaking an accusing finger in his face. "*You* said you didn't care for her."

"I didn't," Scotty protested. "We weren't. I told you the truth, babe."

Pearl Lee turned from him in a huff so he tried explaining to me. "They were a Christmas present for Destiny. We found them when we were going through some things for the police. Moose gave them to Zora because she was so helpful in those first few days. I told him I didn't mind. He didn't want them and what was I going to do with them? She got the idea that because I bought them, they meant something special. Something about . . . us. But that was all her. I had nothing to do with it."

I didn't want to believe him, but dammit, I did. "So you're saying you think Zora did this?"

"She must have, unless she gave the earrings to somebody else."

"She's a menace," Pearl Lee said with a sniff of disdain. "And she's obsessed with you, whether you want to admit it or not. I've had enough of her."

"She's lonely," Scotty insisted. "And she misread a few signals. That doesn't make her obsessed. But this doesn't make sense. She has a beading class on Friday evenings. She never misses it."

I had a feeling she'd missed it tonight. "Tell me, what did you and Zora argue about two nights ago?"

Scotty frowned thoughtfully. "We didn't. What gave you that idea?"

"Edgar said he found her sitting on a bench, crying, and she told him that you'd been in an argument."

Scotty shook his head slowly. "It's not true. Why would Edgar lie about that?"

My spidey senses were on high alert. "I don't think Edgar was lying," I said. "I think that's what she told him. I think *Zora* was the one who lied. I hate to say it, but I think Pearl Lee might be right." I glanced at her, but she wasn't where she'd been only a minute or two before. "Pearl Lee?" I checked all around us, but I couldn't see her anywhere. "Where in the hell did she go?"

Scotty hopped over a hedge and hurried to the sidewalk, then turned back to me and shook his head. "I can't see her, but I have a bad feeling about this. I think she's gone after Zora."

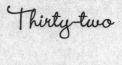

Thirty-two

We devised a plan in two-point-three seconds, but it took a little longer than that to put it into action. Neither of us knew what Pearl Lee had in mind, but both of us were worried. Scotty knew where Zora's beading class was, so he offered to go there to make sure she was all right. I said I'd go to the Feathered Peacock and make sure Pearl Lee didn't do something stupid. We exchanged cell numbers and went our separate ways.

My brain was spinning as I walked back to Zora's yoga studio. I'd done too much. Every step hurt, but I went as fast as I could. If Zora was the one who'd vandalized Zydeco tonight, did that mean she'd thrown the rock through the window? Slashed my tire? *Zora?* She'd seemed so matronly. So nurturing. So caring.

It was hard to believe she'd been responsible for all the vandalism, but even harder to argue with the evidence. After the way Scotty had reacted tonight, I was also having a hard time believing that he'd attacked me twice and killed his own daughter. I was beginning to think that maybe I wasn't a very good judge of character.

Lights gleamed from the Feathered Peacock when I

arrived, making it look warm and inviting. I said a little prayer that Zora wasn't there, and I tried the door. It opened right up, emitting the pungent aromas of sandalwood and citrus and the sound of voices.

I let myself inside and followed those voices through a room filled with hardwood floors and shining mirrors. Soft lighting made the wood gleam, and candles burning along a low shelf were reflected in the wall of mirrors. A handful of yoga mats were rolled up and stacked in the corner, but the room was otherwise empty.

The voices were louder now, so I moved to the end of the hall and peeked into an open door. Pearl Lee sat at a small round table with a half-empty cup of tea in front of her. It must have taken me even longer to get here than I thought. Zora stood in front of a small counter, slicing a lemon. Beside her sat another cup, and a teakettle steamed on the nearby stove as the water cooled.

After the way Pearl Lee had run off, it was difficult for me to understand why she was calmly drinking tea with her arch-nemesis. Maybe it was a Southern belle thing. Zora spotted me in the doorway and smiled as if we were old friends. "Rita! What a lovely surprise. Come in. Join us. There's still plenty of hot water. Would you care for some tea?"

Not especially, but I couldn't just walk out the door and leave Pearl Lee to fend for herself, even if they were being oddly civilized. Miss Frankie would never forgive me if something happened to her. I moved into the room and tried not to look suspicious of Zora, which was really hard to do when I could plainly see flecks of red paint on her sensible walking shoes.

"Do you have a preference?" she asked. "I have several varieties to choose from."

I shook my head. "Whatever the two of you are having is okay with me." I sat, choosing a seat that would let me keep an eye on Zora and tried to look nonchalant as I nestled a tea bag in my cup. "Pearl Lee, why did you run off? I was worried about you."

Pearl Lee waved a hand in front of her. "It's fine, Rita. Zora and I are just having a friendly chat."

Zora carried the kettle to the table and filled the cup with hot water. "Well, I don't know how friendly it is," she said, standing over me with that kettle of boiling hot water in her hands. "But we are having a chat."

"Oh? Well, catch me up. What are the two of you talking about?"

"About Scotty, of course." Pearl Lee took a delicate sip of her tea. "I'm just explaining to Zora that Scotty and I are together now."

Zora put the kettle back on the burner, and I swallowed a sigh of relief. "I'm trying to explain to Pearl Lee that I don't care about Scotty," she said, cutting another slice of lemon with a *thwack* of the knife on the cutting board. "Really, dear, how many times do I need to tell you that?"

Pearl Lee sipped again and smiled at Zora over the rim of her cup. "We found your earring at Zydeco, along with the message I assume you left for me. That's hardly the work of someone who doesn't care about a man."

"Whoa!" I said with an uneasy laugh. "Let's not go there. We don't know that Zora did anything." I tried to send Pearl Lee a warning with my eyes.

It missed and went right over her head. "Scotty ishn't intreshted in you, Zhora. You might ash well accept it." Pearl Lee sounded so odd I took my eyes off Zora for a split second. Pearl Lee gave her head a wobbly shake, as if she was trying to wake herself up. Then she giggled softly and drank some more tea. "Thish ish good," she said, still slurring, "but it's a touch bitter."

Zora slowly put the knife on the cutting board. "Is it? I was hoping you wouldn't notice."

I had a bad feeling about this. I pushed my cup as far away from me as I could get it and that's when I spotted the syringe on the counter beside the sink. "What's wrong with her?"

"With her?" Zora tilted her head toward Pearl Lee. "I'm afraid she's just taken a massive overdose."

Everything inside me turned to ice as pieces of information slid into the previously empty blanks in my head. *Zora* had killed Destiny. *Zora* had almost hit me with the van. *Zora* had, no doubt, hit me in the alley and then run off to establish an alibi using Edgar to do it. I shot to my feet and skirted the table, trying to reach Pearl Lee. "What did you give her?"

In a flash, Zora picked up the knife and held it to my throat. "Just some sleeping pills. Back away and leave her alone."

I fumbled for my phone and managed to pull it out of my pocket, but Zora was too fast for me. She slashed downward with the knife, slicing the side of my hand with the blade. I tried to hang on to the phone, but the pain was too severe. I dropped it onto the floor and watched it skitter under the table, out of my reach. Pearl Lee made a sound that might have been a word and sagged to the floor like a rag doll.

"Please!" I said. "Let me help her."

Zora looked at me as if I were the crazy one in the room. "I don't think so. She's just getting what she deserves."

"Why? Because Scotty preferred her to you?"

"Because she turned his head." She sneered down at Pearl Lee and her glittery outfit. "Look at her. What man can resist a woman who dresses like that? I tried to tell him what she was like. I tried to warn him, but he just wouldn't listen." She wiped her brow with the back of her hand. "He *never* listens."

I had a feeling she was talking about Destiny now, and my stomach lurched. I didn't want to hear what crazy thoughts were inside her head, but I had to keep her talking. If she hurt me any more, I'd be down for the count and I wouldn't be able to help Pearl Lee at all.

"You tried to help him with Destiny," I said as I looked around for something to staunch the flow of blood from my hand. "I'm guessing he didn't appreciate that either?"

Zora sneered at me. "I'm guessing that you're trying to get me to confess to murder. Do I look stupid to you?"

I wouldn't have used the word *stupid*, but I thought she was definitely in need of mood-altering drugs. Aloud I said, "But you did kill Destiny, didn't you? Why?"

Zora wiped her forehead again with one hand and gestured with the knife toward the door behind me. "I'm sorry, dear, I just don't have time for chitchat. I'm a little busy trying to decide what to do with you."

I wiped blood on my slacks and grabbed a tea towel from the table. "It's too late," I said as I clumsily wrapped my hand. "Scotty has already figured it out. Even if you kill me, he's calling the police right now. He'll tell them that you've been dealing prescription drugs in the neighborhood."

Her round face twisted with anger. "I am *not* a drug dealer."

"How do you do it?" I inched a little closer to Pearl Lee and checked to make sure she was still breathing. "Where do you get the drugs from? Who is your supplier?"

"You make it sound so sordid. You're as bad as Destiny turned out to be. You have no idea what it's like to live in constant pain. You have no idea how difficult it is to work through the medical system."

"So you sell drugs because the system is messed up?" *How noble.*

"Some people have pills they don't need, and some people have money and no pills. I am a facilitator, not a dealer. Now stop talking. Let's walk out front and make sure the door is locked."

I couldn't let her do that. I was still holding out hope that when Scotty realized Zora wasn't happily beading a few blocks away, he'd come to the yoga studio and find us. But if I was going to get the upper hand, I'd have to find some kind of weapon and then try to catch her by surprise. The most important thing was to get her away from Pearl Lee so Zora wouldn't use that knife on her while she was down.

Feigning resignation, I turned around and moved back into the hallway. I searched frantically for something I could use to defend myself but Zora hadn't left so much as a speck of dust on the floor. I could feel her behind me, breathing heavily, the knife just inches from my shoulder blades. Whatever I did, I'd have to move quickly. I couldn't afford to hesitate.

Mentally moving ahead, I tried to remember what I'd seen in the room with the hardwood floors. Yoga mats in the corner. Candles burning on a low shelf. They weren't much, but the mats might work as a shield and the candles would at least give me some kind of weapon.

The hallway stretched out endlessly in front of me. It seemed to take forever to get to the door at the other end. I tried to steady my breathing so I wouldn't give Zora any clues about what I was planning.

Three feet. Two.

Even in my injured state, I was younger and in better shape than Zora. My injuries would slow me down and make me less pliable than normal, but I had to at least try to save myself. I waited until I was halfway across the room and then ducked and lunged for the stack of yoga mats.

Zora cried out in rage and threw herself after me. I grabbed a mat with one hand and held it in front of me. I felt the knife hit the mat, but thankfully the rolls of padding absorbed the blade. Using all my strength, I shoved it at Zora and used it as a battering ram.

She lost her balance and hit the floor. I tried to pull the knife out of the padding, but it was in too deep so I tossed the mat with the knife still embedded in it as far away as I could and threw myself on top of her. Zora was stronger than she looked. She bucked me off and I landed on my injured shoulder. Hard. Searing pain tore through my back and up my neck. Tears burned my eyes, but I fought them back. She'd caused me enough pain already. I wasn't going to let her beat me now.

We scrambled across the floor together, both of us trying to get to the knife first. I lost the tea towel in the process, but I didn't care. I grabbed one thick ankle and tried to slow her progress. She elbowed me in the chest and knocked me back a few inches.

I saw her hand, inches away from the yoga mat and the knife, and decided to go with plan B. I dove for the row of candles, grabbed one, and heaved it at her with all my might. Hot wax flew everywhere and Zora let out a yelp, but it didn't slow her down at all. Before I could pick up another candle, she jerked the knife out of the mat and came at me with a roar.

I ducked, tucked, and rolled, grabbing another candle in the process. Every inch of my body screamed in pain, but I couldn't give up now. Zora had already killed once, and she'd left Pearl Lee for dead in the other room. I knew she wouldn't hesitate to kill me.

I tossed the second candle and the knife hit the floor. I scrambled toward the reception area, hoping to get outside before she could lock me in. I had to call for help. It was the only way to save us.

When I'd put a foot or two between us, I got to my feet, wincing as pain radiated from my shoulder into every extremity. My heart was pounding, my ears roaring with fear and panic. I could hear Zora coming after me, her footsteps heavy and determined.

I raced past the reception desk and reached for the front door just as Zora grabbed me around the waist and jerked me backward. I kicked and screamed, flailed with my arms, and fought to see where she had the knife. I tried to remember anything I knew about self-defense, but my mind was completely blank.

By some miracle, one foot connected with Zora's leg with a satisfying *chunk*. She stumbled a little, and I knew this was my chance. I kicked again and locked both hands together to use as a club. The cut on my hand burned and dripped blood, but I couldn't let that stop me. Twisting toward her, I brought my hands down on her throat as hard as I could. She staggered again and her grip on my waist loosened enough for me to slip away.

She was between me and the door now, cutting off my

escape route. I looked around frantically for something in this room I could use to protect myself and spotted a letter opener on the reception desk. I closed my fist around it just as she grabbed me again. My strength was ebbing fast, but I drew on every last drop I could find within myself and plunged the letter opener into her shoulder.

She screamed in pain and staggered backward, grabbing at the shaft and trying to pull it out of her shoulder. That was all I needed to reach the door and tear it open. I raced out onto the porch, shouting as loud as I could for help. I was aware of someone racing toward me, of a familiar voice taking up my cry for help, and the sound of a police siren nearby. Red and blue lights streaked through the night, but I didn't have time to wonder how they'd arrived so quickly. I felt arms slide tenderly around me and looked up into Gabriel's worried brown eyes. I don't think anything has ever looked so good to me. At that moment, he really did look like a superhero.

Thirty-three

❧

Sometime later, I took a sip of weak hospital coffee, grimaced, and put the cup on the table in front of me. My hand throbbed beneath the bandage the paramedics had applied at the Feathered Peacock, but I was feeling lucky that I was alive to feel the pain.

Pearl Lee had been rushed to the hospital, still alive but not by much. I was sitting in a tiny waiting room with Gabriel, who hadn't left my side for a minute. That was great, except for how he'd also badgered me into letting the paramedics bring me in. I understood his concern, but I'd had enough of this place. I didn't mind waiting here for word about Pearl Lee, but I refused to come back as a patient—at least not for a few months.

The police had found Zora trying to slip out the back door. She'd put up a fight, but she'd also lost a lot of blood from that wound in her shoulder. It hadn't taken long for them to subdue her and haul her off to jail. I was still having trouble believing how completely she'd fooled me.

Moose and Scotty sat across the room from us, which felt a little awkward given that I'd been convinced that at least one of them was a cold-blooded killer for the past ten days. They'd come running up to the Feathered Peacock a few minutes after the police arrived, ready to slay dragons or do whatever it took to save Pearl Lee and me. Which was actually really sweet. I thought Scotty had looked a little disappointed that it was all over before he got there. I know he was genuinely concerned about Pearl Lee.

Over the past few hours I'd picked up enough of the story to know that when Scotty had realized Zora wasn't happily beading, he'd also realized that something was seriously wrong. Since the beading class was held just two doors away from the Dizzy Duke, Scotty had gone to the bar looking for Moose, who was there drowning his sorrows in Jack Daniels. And that's how Gabriel found out that I was in trouble. He'd told Scotty to call the police and then he'd torn out of the Duke and come to my rescue.

Now we all sat together while somewhere a team of medical professionals tried to save Pearl Lee's life. Too agitated to sit still, I stood and paced until the sound of rapid footsteps in the corridor drew me to the door hoping that one of the doctors was coming with good news. Instead I saw Miss Frankie clutching the hand of her best friend and neighbor, Bernice, and talking to someone at the nurses' station. I had called Bernice while Gabriel and I were en route, explaining the situation and asking her to go next door so Miss Frankie wouldn't be alone when I told her about Pearl Lee. Bernice, a sweet little lady with a poof of white hair and an accent as smooth as Southern Comfort, is a real trooper and tougher than she looks. Even though she'd been ready for bed when I called, she'd offered to drive Miss Frankie to the hospital and meet us here.

Miss Frankie glanced in my direction, saw me in the doorway, and hurried down the hall toward me. We still had issues between us, but this probably wasn't the time to talk about them. Putting all the awkwardness out of my mind, I hugged both her and Bernice, who had trailed her down the hall.

"How is she?" Miss Frankie asked. "Have you heard anything? What do the doctors say?"

"We don't know anything yet," I said. "They're working on her now."

"Where is she? Here in the emergency room?"

"Probably. I really don't know. They're not saying much. Would you like to sit down? We may be waiting for a while."

Miss Frankie's amber-colored eyes were dark with worry and her lips quivered. "I just can't believe this is happening. Sugar, I need you to tell me everything. How on earth did she end up with that horrible woman?"

"I'll tell you the whole story," I promised. I put an arm around her and gave her a gentle squeeze. She leaned against me as she had more than once in the past year, and I changed my mind about that apology. Maybe this was the perfect time for it.

I asked Bernice to give us a minute. She disappeared into the waiting room and I led Miss Frankie a few feet away from the door. "I'm so sorry this happened," I said. "I failed you. Not only did I *not* keep Pearl Lee busy at Zydeco and away from men, I let her get seriously hurt." That was a major understatement, but I didn't want to make the situation appear too bleak. Pearl Lee had to be okay. She just *had* to.

Miss Frankie looked astonished by what I'd said. "Oh, Rita, nobody can contain Pearl Lee. She's always been that way. We give it a gallant try, though. I suppose it helps a little. The truth is, I never should have asked you to take her on. It was sheer selfishness on my part."

"Well, so was my handing Edie's baby shower over to you," I admitted. "I thought anything would be better than having to plan that shower. Turns out, I was wrong." I paused, took a deep breath, and then let out the rest in a rush. "About the other day—I shouldn't have shouted at you the way I did, especially not in front of the Bryces. It was horribly rude. I just hope you can forgive me."

Miss Frankie put her fingers on my cheek. Her hand was cool and soft, her touch gentle. "Rita, you know how much I love you. You're family and that means there's no problem too big for us to get around. So don't you worry for a minute. We'll work it all out, okay?"

Tears stung my eyes and I was way too tired to fight them. I sniffed and nodded and hugged her tightly, especially since she didn't even point out that she'd been right to bring Edie's family to town. "I love you too, Miss Frankie."

"I know you do, sugar."

We stood that way for a minute, crying a little and hugging a lot and leaning on each other until Miss Frankie gently pressed me away. She reached for my hand and scowled down at the bandage that she seemed to notice for the first time. "Goodness, Rita, I think you're the one who needs someone to watch out for her. I'm going to want to hear all about this, too. But right now let's find out where they've taken Pearl Lee. I insist that someone tell me what they're doing to her every minute."

I waved to Gabriel as Miss Frankie dragged me past the waiting room and tried to signal that I'd be back later. It took us three full hours and a whole lot of gentle persuasion, but we finally got the answers we were looking for. Pearl Lee was weak but she was alive, and the doctor assured us that she'd be back to normal in no time. I drew on Miss Frankie's earlier example and decided not to tell him that Pearl Lee hadn't exactly been "normal" to begin with. There are some things that just don't need to be said out loud.

The baby shower decorations were beautiful—vintage canisters filled with pale roses sat in the middle of half a dozen round tables; lengths of cloth in delicate pastels streamed out from a cluster of blue and pink balloons to form a canopy in the middle of the ceiling. Fairy lights twinkled all around us, giving Zydeco's conference room a magical appearance.

"I think it looks lovely, sugar. Don't you?"

I nodded at my mother-in-law and returned her smile. Keeping the shower small-ish wasn't the only concession she'd made. She'd given up the search for a "perfect" venue and agreed to hold the shower here. I wanted her to know that I appreciated her efforts. "It's perfect," I said. "Thank you for doing this."

She slid a sidelong glance at the bandage on my hand. "I guess it's a good thing you asked me to do it after all. I can't imagine what we'd be doing today if you hadn't turned the planning over to me."

"Plastic tablecloths and crepe paper streamers," I said with a grin. "I can almost guarantee it."

She looked out over the room again. "I'm awfully glad you're here today, Rita. I don't know what I would have done if that woman had succeeded in killing you."

"Well, she didn't," I said gently. "And Pearl Lee's recovering nicely. We'll both be around to argue with you awhile longer."

"Yes. Well." Her lips curved again ever so slightly. "Don't make a habit of *that*. Pearl Lee's already up to her old tricks. By the way, she has requested that we bring a piece of cake to the hospital for her."

"That's easy enough."

"You did invite that nice young man who came to your rescue, didn't you?"

"Which one?" I teased. "Gabriel or Scotty?"

Miss Frankie gave my arm a pat. "You know I'm talking about Gabriel, sugar. Edie specifically requested that I add him to the guest list."

"Well, don't be surprised if he doesn't show up. I don't think baby showers are his thing."

"You never can tell, can you? Take Scotty, for instance. Pearl Lee seems genuinely interested in him, and he actually seems to care for her. Maybe it's not such a bad match this time. I guess time will tell."

We were interrupted then by the sounds of voices and footsteps, and a moment later everyone on the reduced guest list burst into the room. Almost everyone, that is. Sparkle had gone to the airport to pick up her brother, but she and Edie had patched things up, and she promised she'd be back for the party.

Edie looked happy and healthy. Charlie beamed like

the proud grandpa-to-be he was, and Lin accidentally smiled at me once. After delivering a stern warning for me to relax and stay where I was, Miss Frankie rose and assumed her duties as hostess.

To my complete surprise, Gabriel, looking all sexy-Cajun-ish in jeans and a tight-fitting black T-shirt, wandered in a few seconds later. He stopped off to pick up a beer and a glass of wine, then sauntered over to me. He bent to kiss my cheek, grazing the side of my mouth slightly in the process. A delicious shiver filled my body with warmth as he sat next to me. "You look like a crash test dummy, *chérie*. You really need to stop letting yourself be used as a punching bag."

I made a face at him. "Oh. Good idea. I'll see what I can do."

He grinned and held out the wineglass. "For you."

I looked at it longingly and then shook my head. "Thanks, but I shouldn't mix alcohol with the pain pills the doctors gave me." My third set in two weeks. I think I'd set some kind of record. This prescription was stronger than either of the other two and made it hard to think clearly. But with my hand out of commission while the knife cut healed, I'd be benched from decorating for a while anyway.

"Thanks again for coming to my rescue the other night," I said. "I don't know what would have happened to Pearl Lee and me if you hadn't shown up when you did."

Gabriel leaned forward, resting his elbows on his knees and holding the glass in his hands. "You don't have to thank me every time you see me, you know."

"I know. I'll stop in a month or two, I'm sure. But you really ought to milk my gratitude for all it's worth while you've got it."

He treated me to a lopsided grin that had a stronger feel-good effect on me than any pain medication. "If I thought you were up to it, I most definitely would." He ran an assessing look over my fading bruises and bandages. "How long do I have to take advantage of that offer?"

I laughed and gave him a little bump with my undam-aged shoulder. "Seriously. Thank you."

"For nothing," he said. "I'd do it again if I had to, but I really hope you won't do anything like that again."

"I couldn't just sit back and let Zora kill Pearl Lee."

"You could have called the police."

"And say what? I think this nice old lady just vandalized my business? As far as I knew, I was going to stop a catfight."

Gabriel gave me a skeptical look. "Are you saying that you hadn't figured out she killed Destiny by then?"

"Would you believe me if I told you I knew it all along?"

"Not for a minute. By the way, your friend Detective Winslow came by last night."

"Oh? I've been expecting him to show up here with an apology."

"You might be waiting for a while. He really isn't a member of the Rita Lucero Fan Club but it's his loss." Gabriel turned toward me, his gaze darkly intense. I could tell he was going to say something important and I leaned forward in anticipation. But just as he started to open his mouth, Sparkle appeared in the doorway with a tall young man. They were clearly related, though his hair was lighter than her dyed black locks, and he sported a dark tan—the exact opposite of his sister. He had an open, friendly face and a curious look in his eye. I liked him immediately.

I stood up to welcome him, and that was when all hell broke loose.

Edie shot to her feet so fast her chair tipped over behind her. "Sparkle? What are you *doing*?"

Her brother looked surprised. "Hey," he said to Edie. "Is this your party?"

Sparkle's black-rimmed eyes widened a lot. "I asked Miss Frankie. She said it was all right."

The commotion had claimed everyone's attention. But really, after everything we'd been through the past couple of weeks, was it such a big deal? Apparently, Edie was more emotionally fragile than I'd thought. It was her baby shower, after all, but I was a little embarrassed that she'd pick a fight with Sparkle and make a scene now over an extra party guest.

I started toward them, determined to intervene before

this argument could get out of hand. "It's okay," I told Edie as I came up behind her and led her a little bit away. "Sparkle's brother is in town for a few days, and I didn't think one more guest would throw everything completely off."

Edie whipped around to face me and lowered her voice. "That's Sparkle's brother? Are you kidding me?"

I shook my head uncertainly. "No?"

She leaned in close and whispered something, but she was speaking so softly I couldn't hear her.

"What?" I whispered back.

She darted a quick glance over her shoulder. Everybody was watching us. They weren't even pretending not to. "That's *him*."

"Him who?"

She rolled her eyes in exasperation since obviously I wasn't picking up what she was laying down. She came right up to me, so close our noses almost touched. "*Him*. The guy from the bar."

I knew I was missing something, and I knew it was huge, but the haze of the medication along with her whispered and obviously angry hints slowed me down. "Him?"

"Oh, for God's sake, Rita. It's the guy. My one-night stand. The guy I slept with. The baby's father. And you're telling me he's Sparkle's *brother*?"

I heard a gasp. Edie spun around and I looked up to find Sparkle standing right behind us. Emotions flashed across her face too quickly for me to read them. I think both Edie and I were expecting an explosion.

"For future reference," I muttered, "his name is River."

Edie took a step back and put her hands over her belly. I stepped forward to put myself in harm's way one more time. If Sparkle was going to hit anybody, well, I was already drugged up so I figured it wouldn't hurt too badly. River moved a few steps closer, still looking pleased to be there—and still not seeming to realize what sort of party it was that he'd crashed. "It's really good to see you again," he said to Edie. "I can't believe we ran into each other like this. It must be fate or something."

"What's going on?" Miss Frankie called out. "Is there a problem?"

"No. No. Everything's fine," I said. "Everybody . . . do something fun."

Edie scowled at River. "I thought you were going to Afghanistan."

"I did. Just got off the plane a couple of hours ago," he said. "This is a kick, huh?"

I didn't take my eyes off Sparkle. I still didn't know what she was going to do. Then, without warning, she launched herself at Edie, catching me in the process of what turned out to be a group hug. Sparkle was beaming, an honest-to-goodness full-on smile. I'd never seen such a thing on her face before. Her dark eyes sparkled with delight, and for the first time since I met her, I understood why Sparkle's parents chose her name.

She released the two of us and turned on her brother, throwing her arms around his neck. I glanced at Edie, a little worried about her reaction. To my surprise, tears brimmed in her eyes. "She's happy," Edie whispered. "She's really happy."

River looked as confused as the rest of us, but he hugged Sparkle back and laughed softly. "I haven't seen you look like this since you were a kid. What's going on?"

She took a step back, leaving both hands on his shoulders. "The baby," she said softly. "It's yours."

He didn't move a muscle. "What baby?"

"Uh," Edie said nervously, "mine."

"I think it's time the two of you were properly introduced," I said, putting a hand on each of their shoulders. "Why don't we slip out for a few minutes. The two of you can chat in my office."

Edie nodded and River managed to get one foot in front of the other. Sparkle skipped along beside him, grinning from ear to ear. "It's what we've always wanted," she said as we left the party behind. "We're finally going to have a family."

Recipes

Sugar Plum Spice Cake

½ cup shortening
2 ½ cups sifted cake flour
2 teaspoons baking powder
1 ½ teaspoons baking soda
¾ teaspoon salt
¾ teaspoon cinnamon
¾ teaspoon ground cloves
1 cup granulated sugar
⅔ cup packed brown sugar
1 ¼ cups buttermilk
2 eggs

Preheat oven to 375°F. Grease two 9-by-1½-inch pans and set aside. In a large bowl, stir the shortening to soften. Add the dry ingredients. Add 1 cup buttermilk and stir until the mix is dampened, then beat with a mixer on low speed for 2 minutes. Add the eggs and remaining buttermilk and beat 1 minute.

Pour into prepared pans and bake in preheated oven for 25 minutes. Cool on racks about 5 minutes before removing from pans.

Ice with Fluffy Boiled Frosting when cool.

* * *

Fluffy Boiled Frosting

Great with the Sugar Plum Spice Cake.

> 1 ¼ cups sugar
> ⅛ teaspoon cream of tartar
> ⅛ teaspoon salt
> 6 tablespoon water
> 3 egg whites
> 1 teaspoon vanilla extract

In a small (1-quart) saucepan, heat the sugar, cream of tartar, salt, and water over medium heat until boiling. Set a candy thermometer in place and boil until the temperature reaches 260°F or until a little mixture dropped into cold water forms a hard ball. Remove from heat.

In a small mixing bowl with a mixer on high speed, beat the egg whites until soft peaks form.

Pour the syrup in a thin stream into the egg whites, beating constantly; add the vanilla and continue beating until the mixture forms stiff peaks.

Optional: Add 1 cup cooked prunes, cut into ½-inch pieces, well drained. Spread between the layers and on the top and sides of the cake.

* * *

Rubio's Famous Smoked Pork Ribs

Serves 6 to 12

6 racks pork ribs (this will be 4 to 5 pounds if using
baby back ribs or 6 to 8 pounds if using spareribs)*
Rubio's Dry Rub Seasoning (see recipe below), or
you can use your favorite barbecue sauce or
other dry rub.
* Note: Baby back ribs are cut from the lower back rib
section of a pig's loin. Each rack usually contains
10 to 13 ribs and weighs roughly 2 pounds. Baby
back ribs are meatier and leaner than spare ribs,
which come from the pig's belly section.

Preheat your smoker to 200°F to 225°F. Pork ribs can be
smoked with about any kind of smoking wood. Oak and
hickory are the most popular, and Rubio prefers hickory.

Prepare Rubio's Dry Rub Seasoning or use your favorite
recipe.

* * *

Rubio's Dry Rub Seasoning

You can find many dry jerk seasonings widely available
to buy in any grocery store, but here's Rubio's favorite
recipe that you can make at home:

3 tablespoons firmly packed dark brown sugar
2 tablespoons coarse salt
2 tablespoons coarsely ground black pepper
2 tablespoons ground coriander
2 teaspoons garlic powder
2 teaspoons onion powder
2 teaspoons dried thyme

> 2 teaspoons ground allspice
> 1 teaspoon ground cinnamon
> 2 to 3 teaspoons cayenne pepper or chili powder (This
>   is an approximate measure. Use an amount that will
>   please your personal taste and your family's.)

Combine the ingredients in a small jar with a tight-fitting lid. Shake until the ingredients are well blended. Store the mixture in an airtight container in a cool, dark place until ready to use.

Rinse the ribs in cold water and pat dry.

Remove the membrane. This is the thin, paper-like skin you find on the back of each rack of ribs. Some people swear by removing the membrane. Some leave it on. Rubio takes it off because the membrane prevents the meat from taking in the smoke, so it creates a barrier to the seasoning.

To remove the membrane, lay the ribs on a flat surface meat side down. Using a sharp knife, begin peeling the membrane at one corner of the rack near the bone and work across to the other end. You'll probably want to trim and toss any excess fat, but don't remove it all, because the fat gives your meat flavor.

Rinse the ribs again and pat dry.

Generously rub the ribs with the seasoning of your choice. Use your hands and rub it in thoroughly. Cover the ribs in plastic wrap and place in the refrigerator for several hours (or overnight) to let the dry rub work into the meat. Remember that the longer it sits, the spicier the meat will be.

Remove the ribs from the refrigerator approximately 1 hour before cooking.

Cook low and slow: Like traditional barbecue, smoked ribs should be cooked on a low heat for a long time. Maintain your temperature at 200°F to 225°F for maximum flavor.

Plan on 1 hour of smoking per pound of ribs. You can smoke each full rack for around 4 hours, or even more. Don't try to rush the results by raising the temperature to speed up the cooking time. Cooking your pork on a higher temperature will result in tough, chewy meat.

During the last 30 minutes of cooking, you can begin to brush the ribs with a glaze or sauce—but Rubio doesn't know why you'd want to.

Your ribs are done when you can easily pull the meat from the bones. The internal temperature should register at least 165°F. Remove the meat from the smoker and let the ribs rest as you would any meat. Wait at least 10 to 15 minutes before cutting in.

To serve: Cut down the middle of each strip of meat between each rib bone. Serve the smoked ribs plain (delicious) or with your choice of sauce.

*   *   *

Rita's Blueberry Muffins

This recipe produces 8 deli-sized muffins topped with a cinnamon-sugar crumb topping. Fill the muffins cups to the top edge for the oversized muffins. You can change it up by adding extra blueberries if you're a real blueberry fan.

MUFFINS

> 1 ½ cups all-purpose flour
> ¾ cup sugar
> ½ teaspoon salt
> 2 teaspoons baking powder
> ⅓ cup vegetable oil
> 1 egg
> ⅓ cup milk
> 1 cup fresh blueberries

TOPPING

> ½ cup white sugar
> ⅓ cup all-purpose flour
> ¼ cup butter, cubed
> 1 ½ teaspoons ground cinnamon

Preheat oven to 400°F. Grease muffin cups or line with muffin liners.

Make the muffin batter by combining flour, sugar, salt, and baking powder. Measure the ⅓ cup vegetable oil in a 1-cup measure. Add the egg and enough milk to fill the cup. Mix the liquid ingredients with the flour mixture and then gently fold in the blueberries.

To make the topping, combine all the topping ingredients and mix with a fork. Fill muffin cups right to the top, and sprinkle evenly with the crumb topping mixture before baking. Bake for 20 to 25 minutes, or until done.

* * *

Pecan Balls

Makes about 4 dozen cookies

They'll go fast, so you may want to double the recipe.

> ½ pound butter (As always, use real butter instead of
>   margarine for the best flavor.)
> 4 tablespoons sugar
> 2 cups flour
> ½ teaspoon salt
> 1 cup chopped pecans
> 2 teaspoons vanilla extract (Real vanilla has a much
>   better flavor than vanilla flavoring.)
> powdered sugar for dusting

Preheat oven to 350°F.

Cream together all the ingredients except the powdered sugar. Roll into small balls about the size of a walnut and place on an ungreased cookie sheet. Bake for 20 minutes.

Remove from the oven and let cool slightly. While still warm (not hot), roll in the powdered sugar. Roll again when the cookies are completely cooled.

> "[McKinlay] continues to deliver well-crafted
> mysteries full of fun and plot twists."
> —*Booklist*

FROM *NEW YORK TIMES* BESTSELLING AUTHOR

Jenn McKinlay

Going, Going, Ganache

A Cupcake Bakery Mystery

After a cupcake-flinging fiasco at a photo shoot for a local magazine, Melanie Cooper and Angie DeLaura agree to make amends by hosting a weeklong corporate boot camp at Fairy Tale Cupcakes. The idea is the brainchild of Ian Hannigan, new owner of *Southwest Style,* a lifestyle magazine that chronicles the lives of Scottsdale's rich and famous. He's assigned his staff to a team-building week of making cupcakes for charity.

It's clear that the staff would rather be doing just about anything other than frosting baked goods. But when the magazine's features director is found murdered outside the bakery, Mel and Angie have a new team-building exercise—find the killer before their business goes AWOL.

INCLUDES SCRUMPTIOUS RECIPES

jennmckinlay.com
facebook.com/jennmckinlay
facebook.com/TheCrimeSceneBooks
penguin.com